The GUNS Alexander B. Rossino
OF SEPTEMBER

A novel of McClellan's Army in Maryland, 1862

Alexander B. ...
10/08/24

SB
Savas Beatie
California

Library of Congress Number (LCCN): 2019946415

First edition, first printing
ISBN: 978-1-61121-476-5

Savas Publishing Digital Edition
ISBN: 978-1-94066-994-6

SB
Savas Beatie
989 Governor Drive, Suite 102
El Dorado Hills, CA 95762
916-941-6896
sales@savasbeatie.com
www.savasbeatie.com

Savas Beatie titles are available at special discounts for bulk purchases
in the United States. Email or call us for details.

Cover images: Library of Congress

Maps by Gene Thorp

Proudly published, printed, and warehoused in the United States of America.

Dedicated to the late Ted Alexander.
You are not forgotten.

Table of Contents

Dramatis Personae

Joseph J. Bartlett: Colonel, Commander of the Second Brigade, First Division, Sixth Corps, Army of the Potomac. Instigator of Slocum's attack on the right at Crampton's Gap, September 14, 1862.

Ambrose Everett Burnside: Major General, Commander of the 'Right Wing,' Army of the Potomac, until September 15, 1862. Nickname: "Old Burn."

Samuel Carey: Private, Twenty-Third Ohio, First Brigade, Kanawha Division, Ninth Corps.

James M. Comly: Major, Commander of the 23rd Ohio, First Brigade, Kanawha Division, Ninth Corps, Army of the Potomac. Promoted after the wounding of Rutherford B. Hayes.

Jacob D. Cox: Brigadier General, Commander of the Kanawha Division, Ninth Corps, Army of the Potomac. Promoted to commander of the Ninth Corps on September 15, 1862.

George Crook: Colonel, Commander of the Second Brigade, Kanawha Division, Ninth Corps, Army of the Potomac. Promoted after the capture of Colonel Augustus Moor in Frederick on September 12, 1862.

George A. Custer: Captain, Aide-de-Camp for General McClellan.

Abner Doubleday: Brigadier General, Second Brigade, First Division, First Corps, Army of the Potomac. Promoted to command of the First Division on September 15, 1862.

James C. Duane: Captain, engineering battalion, and aide-de-camp to General McClellan, Army of the Potomac.

Hugh Ewing: Colonel, Commander of the First Brigade, Kanawha Division, Ninth Corps, Army of the Potomac. Promoted to brigade command after promotion of Scammon to division command.

William B. Franklin: Major General, Commander of the Sixth Corps and the 'Left Wing,' Army of the Potomac, until September 15, 1862.

John Gibbon: Brigadier General, Fourth Brigade, First Corps, Army of the Potomac.

George H. Gordon: Brigadier General, Commander of the Third Brigade, First Division, Twelfth Corps, Army of the Potomac.

George S. Greene: Brigadier General, Commander of the Second Division, Twelfth Corps, Army of the Potomac.

Rutherford B. Hayes: Colonel, Commander of the 23rd Ohio, First Brigade, Kanawha Division, Ninth Corps, Army of the Potomac. Wounded in action September 14, 1862.

Jacob Higgins: Colonel, Commander of the One Hundred and Twenty-Fifth Pennsylvania Volunteers, First Division, Twelfth Corps.

Joseph Hooker: Major General, Commander of the First Corps, Army of the Potomac. Nickname: "Fighting Joe."

Thomas J. Kelly (fictional): Private, Twenty-Third Ohio, First Brigade, Kanawha Division, Ninth Corps.

Henry W. Kingsbury: Colonel, Commander of the 11th Connecticut, Third Division, Ninth Corps, Army of the Potomac. Killed September 17, 1862.

George Love: Private, Twenty-Third Ohio, First Brigade, Kanawha Division, Ninth Corps.

Joseph K. F. Mansfield: Major General, Commander of Twelfth Corps, Army of the Potomac. Mortally wounded September 17, 1862.

George G. Meade: Brigadier General, Commander of the Third Division, First Corps, Army of the Potomac, after transfer of John Reynolds to Pennsylvania.

George B. McClellan: Major General, Commander, Army of the Potomac. Nickname: "Little Mac."

William H. Medill: Major, Commander of the 8th Illinois Cavalry, First Brigade, Cavalry Division, Army of the Potomac.

Dixon S. Miles: Colonel, Commander of Federal garrison at Harpers Ferry.

David Parker (fictional): Private, Twenty-Third Ohio, First Brigade, Kanawha Division, Ninth Corps.

Alfred Pleasonton: Brigadier General, Commander of the Cavalry Division, Army of the Potomac.

Fitz John Porter: Major General, Commander of the Fifth Corps, Army of the Potomac.

Jesse L. Reno: Major General, Commander of the Ninth Corps, Army of the Potomac. Mortally wounded September 14, 1862.

John F. Reynolds: Brigadier General, Commander of the Third Division, First Corps. Assigned to command of Pennsylvania Militia and transferred to Harrisburg.

Israel B. Richardson: Major General, Commander of the First Division, Second Corps. Mortally wounded September 17, 1862.

James B. Ricketts: Brigadier General, Commander of the Second Division, First Corps, Army of the Potomac.

Isaac P. Rodman: Brigadier General, Commander of the Third Division, Ninth Corps, Army of the Potomac. Killed September 17, 1862.

Delos B. Sackett: Colonel, Aide-de-Camp for General McClellan.

Eliakim P. Scammon: Brigadier General, Commander of the Kanawha Division, Ninth Corps, Army of the Potomac. Promoted from colonel after Jacob Cox took over command of the Ninth Corps from Jesse Reno. Nickname: "Old Granny."

John Sedgwick: Brigadier General, Commander of the Second Division, Second Corps, Army of the Potomac.

Lucy Settle (fictional): Women's rights advocate, spinster, resident of Middletown, Maryland.

Simon Sutherland (fictional): Slave, friend of Lucy Settle, resident of Middletown, Maryland.

Truman Seymour: Brigadier General, Commander of the First Brigade, Third Division, First Corps, Army of Potomac.

Henry W. Slocum: Major General, Commander of the First Division, Sixth Corps, Army of the Potomac. Nickname: "Old Slow-Come."

Samuel D. Sturgis: Commander of the Second Division, Ninth Corps, Army of the Potomac.

Edwin V. Sumner: Major General, Commander of the 'Center Wing," Army of the Potomac, until September 15, 1862. Nickname: "Bull."

George Sykes: Brigadier General, Commander of the Second Division, Fifth Corps, Army of the Potomac.

Jacob Szink: Lieutenant Colonel, Lieutenant commander of the One Hundred and Twenty-Fifth Pennsylvania Volunteers, First Division, Twelfth Corps. Wounded September 17, 1862.

Orlando B. Willcox: Brigadier General, Commander of the First Division, Ninth Corps, Army of the Potomac.

Alpheus S. Williams: Brigadier General, Commander of Twelfth Corps, Army of the Potomac until September 15, 1862. Resumed command September 17, 1862, after the wounding of General Mansfield.

Emma Wilson (fictional): Widow, former member of U.S. Sanitary Commission, resident of Frederick, Maryland.

Prologue

Late summer, 1862.

Major General George Brinton McClellan's 87,000-man Army of the Potomac is sprawled across the hills and valleys of west-central Maryland.

Robert E. Lee's Army of Northern Virginia crossed north of the Potomac River eight days earlier in the hope of rallying Marylanders against the national government in Washington, D.C. When no such uprising occurs, Lee shifted his operations west to the region between Hagerstown, Boonsboro, and Harpers Ferry. He divided his army to capture the 14,000-man Federal garrison at the ferry, and planned to reassemble his force for a battle with McClellan that he hopes will end the war. Lee is awaiting the outcome of the operation.

Miles to the east, "Little Mac," as his troops fondly call McClellan, knows the Southern army is operating in western Maryland. He does not know the enemy's ultimate objective, nor has he discerned Lee's purpose for advancing north of the Potomac. He is certain, however, that the Harpers Ferry garrison is in grave danger and that his army is the only hope for its salvation.

He therefore pushes his army west toward Frederick and the inevitable clash with Lee that he knows must come.

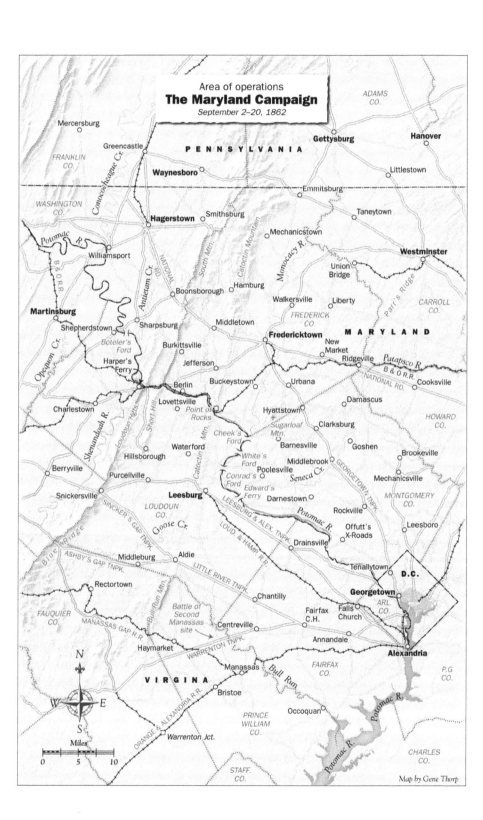

Area of operations
The Maryland Campaign
September 2–20, 1862

ADAMS CO.

Mercersburg

FRANKLIN CO.

Greencastle

PENNSYLVANIA

Gettysburg

Hanover

Waynesboro

Littlestown

Emmitsburg

WASHINGTON CO.

Conococheague Cr.

Hagerstown   Smithsburg

Mechanicstown

Taneytown

Potomac R.

Williamsport

B & O R.R.

NATIONAL RD.

Antietam Cr.

South Mtn.

Catoctin Mountain

Momocacy R.

Union Bridge

Westminster

Parr's Ridge

CARROLL CO.

Boonsborough   Hamburg

Martinsburg

Shepherdstown   Sharpsburg

Boteler's Ford

Harper's Ferry

Opequon Cr.

Middletown

Walkersville   Liberty

FREDERICK CO.

Fredericktown

MARYLAND

New Market

Ridgeville

Patapsco R.

B & O R.R.

NATIONAL RD.

Cooksville

Burkittsville

Jefferson

Berlin

Buckeystown

Urbana

Damascus

HOWARD CO.

Charlestown

Shenandoah R.

Loudoun Hgts.

Short Hill

Lovettsville

Point of Rocks

Hyattstown

Sugarloaf Mtn.

Clarksburg

Waterford

Cheek's Ford

Barnesville

Goshen

Brookeville

Hillsborough

Catoctin Mtn.

White's Ford

Poolesville

Middlebrook

Mechanicsville

GEORGETOWN TNPK.

MONTGOMERY CO.

Berryville   Purcellville

Conrad's Ford

Seneca Cr.

Snickersville

Leesburg

LOUDOUN CO.

Edward's Ferry   Darnestown

Rockville

LEESBURG & ALEX. TNPK.

Potomac R.

Offutt's X-Roads

Leesboro

SNICKER'S GAP TNPK.

Goose Cr.

LOUD. & HAMP. R.R.

Drainsville

Middleburg   Aldie

ASHBY'S GAP TNPK.

LITTLE RIVER TNPK.

Tenallytown

D.C.

Rectortown

Chantilly

Georgetown

ARL. CO.

BLUE RIDGE

Bull Run Mtn.

Battle of Second Manassas site

Centreville

Fairfax C.H.

Falls Church

FAUQUIER CO.

MANASSAS GAP R.R.

Haymarket

WARRENTON TNPK.

Annandale

Alexandria

Manassas

Bull Run

FAIRFAX CO.

P.G CO.

VIRGINIA

Bristoe

N
W   E
S

ORANGE & ALEXANDRIA R.R.

Occoquan

PRINCE WILLIAM CO.

Potomac R.

Miles

Warrenton Jct.

0   5   10

STAFF. CO.

Potomac R.

CHARLES CO.

Map by Gene Thorp

1

Friday, September 12, 1862
(Near Sundown)
Headquarters of the Army of the Potomac
One mile southeast of Urbana, Maryland

in the ankle-high grass outside of his tent, General George McClellan unbuttoned his dark blue coat and stared into the orange-tinted sky. To the southwest, located out of sight beyond the mountains, lay Harpers Ferry, Virginia, its garrison threatened with capture by Thomas "Stonewall" Jackson. All that day, news had come in hinting at the Confederate noose tightening around the Ferry, yet McClellan remained powerless to stop it.

Time, he imagined, was slipping away from him like grains of sand in an hourglass, each minute bringing Colonel Dixon Miles and his men closer to their fate. Digging into his vest pocket, the general drew out a round gold watch and studied its face: a quarter past six. Time to rescue the Ferry that day had run out. Would tomorrow bring another opportunity?

A drop of perspiration trickled down McClellan's temple, and he lifted his kepi to wipe it away. "Marcy, that parlous fool, Halleck, has doomed those men," he muttered to the balding older man standing over his shoulder.

General Marcy scratched at his blonde mutton chops, remaining silent out of professional courtesy. McClellan often spoke acidly of the general-in-chief of the army. While Marcy, McClellan's chief of staff and the father of Little Mac's wife, Ellen, remained loyal to his son-in-law, it made him uncomfortable to discuss Halleck in so negative a tone.

McClellan slapped his kepi against his thigh as he warmed to his subject. "Just today, Halleck gave me command over Miles's garrison at the Ferry. Just today, Marcy! More than a week ago, I pleaded with the man, and with the president, for that matter, to order Miles to evacuate the trap in which they've left him. Halleck denied me, claiming I need not worry as everything was in order. Rubbish! Old Brains indeed," spat the general. "The man couldn't think his way out of a blind alley. Lee commands an army of more than one hundred thousand men. Miles is but a morsel waiting to be gobbled up. Now, I am supposed to rescue him? How might that be accomplished, I ask? How?"

"I'm sure you will think of something, general. You always do," observed Marcy, hoping the simple platitude would steer McClellan away from the disagreeable topic.

The general pulled the kepi back onto his head and turned toward his canvas tent in the day's failing light. His gaze did not meet Marcy's as he called for his orderly to light the oil lamp on the table. Ducking under the flap, Little Mac nodded his thanks and sent the man to find him something to eat, pulled off his coat and hat, and draped them over the back of a chair. He then fell heavily into the seat, while rubbing his eyes and leaned over the table to ponder the latest intelligence. General Marcy entered to stand beside him.

A newly arrived message from Lincoln confirmed information from other sources that Rebels had been seen crossing back into Virginia at Williamsport. *Probably the whole Rebel army will be withdrawn from Maryland*, Lincoln had written.

Perhaps. Other sources placed strong Rebel forces around Hagerstown, just miles from the Pennsylvania state line. "What are you after, Bobby Lee?" Little Mac whispered, his brown eyes drifting to the area between Pennsylvania and Virginia encompassed by Washington County, Maryland.

"General, may I enter?" McClellan looked up to see Colonel Thomas Key, his judge advocate, and confidant, standing just outside.

"Yes, yes, Key, by all means, come in," waved McClellan.

Tall and thin with a dark mustache, pince-nez glasses, and a goatee, Key stepped into the yellow light beside Marcy. Ordinarily, McClellan shared little with his subordinate's concerning strategy, but Key was an exception. The general admired his expertise in law, literature, and mathematics, so he kept the clear-thinking Key close. If one man could be another man's shadow, mused Marcy gazing upon the two, Key acted the part of McClellan's flawlessly.

"If I may say so, general, you appear . . . vexed," observed Key.

"I've been placed in a difficult position thanks to the feeble brain trust at the War Department," confirmed McClellan. "They have given me command over the garrison at Harpers Ferry, but I fear it may be too late to save Colonel Miles and his men."

"Is there nothing that can be done?" asked Key in a quiet tone the general found soothing.

Rising to his feet, Little Mac pointed to a line on the map depicting the road from Frederick City to Harpers Ferry. "I sent instructions to General Pleasonton this morning to have his cavalry explore the approaches to the Ferry and open a route, if he is able. Pleasonton, however, remains in Frederick proper and I have heard no firing from the direction of the river."

"What does this tell you?" inquired Key.

"It tells me that at least some Rebel troops remain between Pleasonton and Miles's garrison. It also tells me that the main Rebel force is still in Maryland. Just this morning, I learned that Lee's army departed Frederick in two columns. One moved southwest toward the Ferry. The second moved northwest toward Hagerstown. This afternoon, news arrived of Rebel troops crossing south into Virginia from Williamsport. I am almost certain that Harpers Ferry is Lee's objective, and that he sent a column to accomplish its capture. What his overriding goal might be beyond that remains a mystery."

"I see," nodded Key thoughtfully. "Governor Curtin thinks General Lee may wish to invade Pennsylvania. This was your opinion also, until recently, I think?"

A scowl brought together McClellan's thick eyebrows as he peered at the Mason-Dixon Line on his map. "I no longer think that, Key. Governor Curtin is edgier than a cat on hot bricks. He cries continually that his state is the Rebel goal, but I have yet to see evidence of it. Lee could move north, but at present I am rather sure he will not. After all, my objective this entire campaign has been to reduce Lee's options for maneuver."

Key moved around the map, contemplating McClellan's observations while rubbing the hair on his chin. Some aspects of military science still evaded him, although he always appreciated its reliance on geometry. Opposing forces jockeyed for position by leveraging angles of approach and lines of march. Lee's army rested within a large triangle, with Harpers Ferry forming one corner to the south, Hagerstown a second to the north, and an as yet indistinct third point to the east. McClellan sought to understand how the triangle might change shape so he could shift his army to meet the Rebels.

"You moved General Burnside's right-wing of the army north from Washington to cut Lee off from Baltimore, didn't you, sir?" he asked.

"Yes, and then Lee moved northwest," replied Little Mac as he tapped a point on the map. "This leaves only the northern and southern routes open to him, practically speaking. General Reynolds and the Pennsylvania militia guard the northern path. Should Lee move in that direction, Reynolds could delay him long enough that we might come up and take the Rebel army from the rear. I did not agree when Washington ordered Reynolds away days ago, but I have since come around to the advantage of having him at Harrisburg. If anyone can put backbone into raw militia, it is John Reynolds. South is the path Lee is most likely to take. Supplies in the Shenandoah lie that way, as does Miles's command at the Ferry. Lee can take it, strike a blow for his cause, and seize the arms and supplies there without meeting us in battle. It's what I would do, were I in his place."

"Sounds reasonable," agreed Key.

Marcy nodded as well, asking, "But what can you do to frustrate him?"

"This is the question, isn't it? My fear is that Secesh will skedaddle too quickly for me to catch him." McClellan took up a pencil, placed it on the map, and slid it point-first toward the north. "If Lee moves this way, I will order this army to Hagerstown to cut the Rebel line of supply from Virginia. That will force him to turn and fight. If he moves south, which he presently appears to be doing, we will punch a hole at Harpers Ferry and overtake him near Winchester."

McClellan pulled the pencil back to Urbana, their present position, and slid it southwest to Winchester for emphasis. "The difficulty will be pushing through at Harpers Ferry," he added, waving the pencil as he did so. "The way there is very narrow and can be easily defended."

"Hence the importance of holding it," volunteered Marcy.

"Precisely!" exclaimed McClellan, tossing the pencil onto the table.

Key watched the instrument roll to the edge and fall out of sight. "Knowing this, general, what will you do?" he asked.

Little Mac rubbed the underside of his nose to wipe away a knot of mucus. "I—blast this hay fever! Pardon me, colonel," he replied, drawing a handkerchief from his pocket. "I intend to wait for more information before deciding on a final course. General Burnside's command is moving on Fredrick City. I will go there tomorrow to confer with him and plan our next move. Sooner or later, we must march to the rescue of the Ferry, but I must hear from Pleasonton before deciding how we should proceed."

Key stared down at the map, thinking he might have an idea worth voicing. "Respectfully, general, could you not open a direct route to the Miles through Knoxville on the Potomac?"

"No, Key! Have you not heard a word of what I've said?" McClellan shot back. "Do you recall the ancient Battle of Thermopylae?"

Embarrassment reddened the colonel's face. "No, sir. Military history is not my strong suit."

"Ah, no matter, Key. I am here to tell you," skylarked McClellan. "At Thermopylae, a small force of Greeks led by the Spartan general Leonidas delayed the advance of a much larger Persian army under King Xerxes by occupying a defensive position in a narrow pass between the sea and the mountains. The geography of Knoxville is similar. The path there between the river and the mountain is so narrow the enemy could stop an entire corps with a single brigade. If Lee covered the road there with artillery posted on the heights across the river, it would be flat suicide to send troops through that passage. We cannot go that way. We must instead force the pass at Crampton's Gap and open a path into Pleasant Valley."

McClellan thrust an outstretched finger at a pass on the map near a village named Burkittsville several miles north of the Potomac. "In the meantime, we must clear a path for General Pleasonton to approach the Ferry. I'll order him and Burnside to have General Reno's Ninth Corps seize the pass where the National Road crosses Catoctin Mountain west of Frederick City."

Marcy nodded in agreement. "Clearing that range will let Pleasonton enter the valley and determine the strength of any Rebel command there."

"It will," continued Little Mac. "General Franklin's Sixth Corps will move to Buckeystown, just south of Frederick, where it can wait to advance on the outcome of tomorrow's operations. General Sumner will move his Second Corps closer to Frederick at Monocacy Junction. If Pleasonton can open the route to the Ferry, I will send Franklin in that direction and use Sumner to support Burnside. Either way, I will drive the Rebels back across the Potomac and rescue our cause."

"And raise your reputation, general," suggested his judge advocate.

McClellan cocked an eye at Key. "Not this again, colonel. We will consider the issue of what to do about my enemies in Washington after we have secured the country."

"But general, the issues are one and the same, are they not? A victory vindicates your leadership in the eyes of the people. The radicals in Congress seek to make this war about the abolition of slavery. The administration now also leans this way. In doing so, they reject our policy of conciliation toward the South, guaranteeing the war will continue and grow even bloodier and more bitter than it is now," explained the passionate Key. "If we can only show—"

"If we can only show that further armed resistance is futile," interrupted McClellan, "and that the national government seeks to restore the Constitution as it existed *before* the outbreak of war, the people of the South might be reconciled to our reunion." The general sighed heavily and shook his head. "I know well the issues at stake, Key, and there may come a time when, for the good of the country, we need to turn our attention from the Rebels to my enemies in Washington. Now is not that time. Let us win first and then seek to restore peace."

"Of course, sir," demurred the colonel, slipping his hands into his coat pockets.

The small gathering fell silent when an orderly appeared carrying a tin plate. Waving for the man to enter, McClellan dismissed Key and Marcy. He chewed a crust of bread and looked over a letter he had begun writing to his wife a few hours earlier:

My dearest, I have been interrupted here by news that we have Frederick. Burnside and Pleasonton are both there. The next trouble is to save the garrison of Harpers Ferry, which is, I fear, in danger of being captured by the Rebels. If they are not taken by this time, I think I can save them; at all events, nothing in my power shall be left undone to accomplish this result. I feel sure of one thing now, and that is that my men will fight well. The moment I hear that Harpers Ferry is safe I shall feel quite sure of the result. The people here cheer the troops as they pass.

McClellan sat back to muse on his last sentence. Union sentiment in Maryland was stronger than he had expected. Slavery, after all, remained common in the state, and only one year earlier, a mob had attacked government troops in the streets of Baltimore. Fighting in the company of a friendly populace made an important difference to the ranks, and McClellan could sense the improvement of morale in his men. Everything seemed to be coming together, even though the Army of the Potomac he now led had been cobbled together from pieces of its previous incarnation and from those of John Pope's short-lived Army of Virginia.

Pope. A repulsive individual, thought McClellan. *What Lincoln and Halleck saw in him is beyond me.*

The general tore off another piece of bread and popped it into his mouth as his thoughts flitted to accusations in the press that he had dallied in reinforcing Pope, allowing Lee to whip the Army of Virginia on the old battlefield near Bull Run. Congress had even launched an investigation of the matter and relieved Fitz John Porter from corps command just when the army needed the man most.

"The fools!" he muttered. "I am beholden to a squawking gaggle of imbeciles and half-wits in Washington." Perhaps Key's advice made sense. With the army once again firmly in his hands, he could turn it back on Washington and force the national government to sue for peace.

Would America laud me as the man who brought an end to the war, or would they call me a latter-day Julius Caesar? McClellan cast a furtive glance about the tent to ensure that he was alone. Using the army against the administration amounted to treason. No one could hear him considering it.

McClellan listened to Marcy giving orders outside. *I am fortunate to have Marcy with me,* he thought. *Reliable friends are few and far between.*

The twilight passed into night, and the hum of activity around McClellan's tent subsided. Inside, the general brooded in solitude amid a hush pregnant with hope for the following day.

2

Friday, September 12, 1862

Mid-Afternoon

Vanguard of the Ninth Corps, Twenty-Third Ohio Volunteer Infantry Regiment,

Kanawha Division

Monocacy River, near Frederick, Maryland

The shriek of a rifled artillery shell startled Thomas James Kelly awake. Bleary-eyed after marching along the National Road since sunrise, the private had long since succumbed to the stupor that overtakes men on the move; hour after tramping hour of seeing only the stain of perspiration spreading down the back of the man directly ahead of him. Now the vanguard of Brigadier General Jacob Cox's Kanawha Division had come under fire, bringing the ranks to a fitful halt.

"Can you see the gun?" asked David Parker, Kelly's closest friend in the veteran Twenty-Third Ohio Volunteers. One of three regiments in the division's First Brigade, the all-Buckeye Twenty-Third served alongside volunteers with the Twelfth and Thirtieth Ohio. A battery of six guns, also manned by Ohio crews, completed the roster.

Standing on the outside of the column, Kelly struggled to catch a glimpse of the action above the rows of indigo caps lined up ahead of him. Unable to see, he stepped out of the ranks to get a better look. "Give me a minute, laddie, and I'll tell ye," he replied to Parker in a Gaelic lilt.

Craning his neck, Kelly spied water sparkling off to the left. A tall stone bridge over the river stood at the base of the valley in front of them, the gravel turnpike beyond the bridge continuing straight up a sloping ridge between fields of wheat, corn, and clover. Past the farms, on the valley's far side, Kelly made out the steeples of Frederick City, their division's objective for the day.

A puff of smoke appeared in the distance. "I see the gun!" he yelped. "It's in the road ahead of us!" A second projectile slammed into the hillside off to their right. Dirt and rocks pattered down as the men clutched their caps.

"One piece? That's it?" marveled Parker.

"That's it, boyo. Tis all I—wait!" The Irishman paused a moment. "There are two more off to the left about two hundred yards away, along with ... well, it could be a Reb skirmish line." Iron rounds carved a deep "whoosh" as they sliced through the still air before crashing into the ground well behind them.

Kelly's gaze settled on Lieutenant Colonel Rutherford B. Hayes, the regiment's commander, who had wheeled his mount from the front of the column and was trotting back down the ranks.

"Colonel's a coming, Davey."

"Twenty-Third Ohio, step to the right of the road, if you please!" shouted Hayes.

Captain John Skiles paced out from the ranks and drew his saber. "Alright, boys, you heard the order. C Company, right face!" he pointed with the blade before taking a moment to shove the curious Irishman back into the column. Kelly, Parker, and their comrades took firm hold of their Springfield rifled muskets and shifted eyes right. "Front rank! Take down that fence!" The order sent men scurrying up the embankment toward the sturdy rail fence crowning the top.

Working the posts to and fro, the Ohioans tore the rails from their seating as another Rebel shell landed near the First Brigade. An unintelligible order from the front of the column redeployed part of the brigade to advance to the bridge at the double-quick behind a squadron of cavalry already sprinting toward the span. Cries rang out as the rows of musket-carrying men lunged ahead.

"C Company, forward march!" bellowed Skiles, sending the Buckeyes up the embankment.

Once in the grassy field beside the road, the regiment stopped to reorganize into columns. Then it trotted off after the Thirtieth Ohio, which was already advancing on the right. The enemy guns continued booming as Colonel Augustus Moor's Second Brigade slowly closed the distance on the far side of the bridge. The Federal batteries rolled onto the crest of the ridge near the Twenty-Third as the men of C Company descended the long grade toward the river. Arriving at the steep bank, the head of the tidy column dissolved into a tangled mass as the men wearing flat-soled brogans slipped awkwardly into the water. Kelly's turn soon arrived, and he plunged with both feet into the Monocacy beside Davey Parker and several others. Someone behind them cursed at the uneven footing.

After getting across, Kelly, Parker, and the rest of the regiment scaled the embankment and moved into a field of clover, where they paused to suck in gulps of air. The Irishman peered over his shoulder at the guns deployed on the ridge they had just traversed. It never ceased to amaze him how loud artillery was or how the gunners could ever stand it. The shells screamed above Moor's brigade, which had formed a battle line astride the National Road off to the left. A bugle call focused everyone's attention back on Lieutenant Colonel Hayes.

"Captains, form up your men!" called Hayes from atop his horse.

Kelly and his well-drilled comrades shifted to the spot where Captain Skiles directed them, and each man straightened the line by reaching out his left hand to touch the man beside him. Off to the right, Kelly spied the ranks of the Twelfth and Thirtieth doing the same. "Davey look—it's the whole damned division!"

Parker took in the sight for a few long seconds. "All this for a few mangy Secesh? Our regiment alone could have cleared them out."

"Better safe than sorry," Kelly shrugged. "We can't see what's on the far side of that ridge, lad."

Shots cracked from the guns of Rebel skirmishers positioned along the road, the minié balls sizzling past above the Buckeyes' heads. "Sure, they're shootin' high! Bully for you, ye grayback bastards!" cried Kelly, his voice joined by the hoots of other men shaking their caps to egg on the enemy.

Regimental buglers blew the call to advance, and Moor's brigade stepped off. The colonel, followed by several riders, thundered toward the enemy gun position on the ridge now just a few hundred yards in front of them. The southern troopers, though, knew their craft. In less than a minute, the gunners had limbered their pieces and lashed their horses westward over the crest.

"Twenty-Third, on at the quick step!" cried Hayes, prompting a guttural cheer from his boys.

The men of the Old Northwest surged forward, skirting homes, and leaping fences until the outbuildings of Frederick hove into view. Smoke rose from the streets, and the blast of an artillery piece rang out among the houses. As quickly as they had moved to attack, Hayes bellowed the order to halt, and the blue tide rolled to a stop in a field outside the city.

"Rest arms," shouted Hayes as he spurred his horse in the direction of General Cox. The Kanawha Division's commander sat atop his mount next to Eliakim Scammon, the chin-bearded sporting general in command of the Second Brigade.

"Ho, that was good craic!" gasped Kelly to his friend.

"What?" puzzled Parker.

"Fun," Kelly wheezed back.

"Well … it was easier than Carnifex Ferry . . . for sure," Parked replied, referencing a fight in western Virginia one year earlier when the Twenty-Third had attacked a line of Confederate works. "Just skirmishers, though," he continued, still catching his breath. "Driving the next line might not be so easy."

When Captain Skiles ordered the men to fall out, Kelly, Parker, and the rest eased their packs off their backs and slumped to the ground. Pulling off his blue kepi, Kelly wiped the perspiration from his brow and smoothed his greasy black hair.

"Davey, have ye been here before?" he asked.

Parker removed his cap and shook his head, letting the late summer air cool his wet, sand-colored curls. "Nope. Never ventured east of the Ohio River before the war. You?"

"Aye, I have," nodded Kelly as he stared off at the spires of Frederick. The sight of church steeples warmed his heart. Without thinking, his hand moved to a strand of rosary beads inside his tunic pocket. Collecting the beads in his palm, Kelly worked them one-by-one between his fingers out of firm Catholic habit. "Didn't stay long. Our wagon train passed here back in fifty-two, just after I came to this country."

"I remember now. You entered at Baltimore City, didn't you?"

"I did. Full of Paddies the city was then, all of us fleeing the old sod for a new start. The hunger, ye know?"

Parker watched Kelly's gaze grow misty, as it always did when he spoke of his home country or coming to this one. He and his people had suffered in ways Parker could never imagine.

Kelly let his mind drift to the tidy front of a whitewashed cottage with a thatched roof, his lips forming a slow smile as the scent of heather and cut grass filled his nostrils. Just then, a light breeze washed over them, tousling the raven strands on Kelly's head. His imagination soared at the feeling, taking him far away on a touch of the North Atlantic wind.

HOME!

The word boomed in Kelly's thoughts, filling him with such a deep longing that his bones ached. A stout woman in a humble linen dress, her head covered with a hand-woven shawl, exited the cottage. She peered about calling his name, which brought Kelly, not yet a teenager, scrambling to her down a rocky lane. His mother held open her arms, and Kelly threw himself into her embrace, his head nestling against her bosom and nostrils taking in the scent of lye soap. The memories filled Kelly's thoughts, quickening the pace of his fingers over the rosary. He felt his mother's arms around him, cradling him, loving him, infusing him with a tenderness and contentment that he had nearly forgotten. The seconds ticked by as he willed himself to remain in the past, holding on desperately to what once had been.

"Thomas James Kelly, you're the light of me life," she said, her eyes sparkling. "I thank the good Lord above for sending ye. Tell me you'll never leave, for if ye do I'll be miserable the rest of me days."

"I promise, Ma, I'll never leave. So, help me God," Kelly vowed, gripping his mother all the tighter. Her question and his loving reply never changed. Neither did the painful memory of his kindly, quiet father, taken too soon by malnutrition. Or his sister, who had never possessed a strong constitution, a few months later.

The vision began to fade, elbowed out of his mind by the sound of men arguing, talking, laughing, and singing around them. The cottage and the cool ocean breeze fell away, leaving Kelly with the emptiness he had felt since he left. All that remained before him was the face of his dear mother, who had lived long enough to apologize with her dying breath for being the one to leave him alone in the world.

A loud shout close at hand jarred Kelly fully back to the present. His eyes shot open, and he squinted when the sunlight proved too bright. Captain Skiles was yelling at someone as he passed by. When his vision cleared again a few seconds later, Kelly found Parker staring at him.

"You alright? Where'd you go just now?"

"A place I ain't been in donkey's years."

Parker frowned. "Donkey's years?"

"A long while, boyo."

Kelly felt a tear running down one of his cheeks, and he quickly wiped it away. "For Christ's sake, Davey, keep this quiet, will ye?" he hissed. "The lads'll give me no end o'trouble."

A mischievous grin spread across Parker's face. "Sure, old friend, I'll keep still … at least 'til you cross me next. Then the whole world'll hear about it. I promise."

Kelly grimaced as Parker poked the sore spot in his soul. "Some mate you are, Davey Parker." Then Kelly paused. "Look sharp! Captain's coming back."

Skiles strode past as the two friends sat up in the grass. "Into column now, boys," he hollered. "We've got orders to move."

Hefting his Springfield, Kelly rose beside Parker while the regiment gathered around them. The other regiments lined up in the surrounding fields until General Cox, brown-bearded and seated atop a muscled charger, emerged from the city with orders for the division to move. The men of the Twenty-Third stepped across the field to enter the road near the outskirts of town. The road there forked left, and they entered the town proper.

"Why, Davey, would you look at that!" Kelly laughed. "They've decorated the place for us."

Parker's lips parted into a grin as he took in the red, white, and blue bunting hanging from the open windows. Joyous townspeople flooded the streets waving star-spangled flags and hats. Some even held up their babies, who fussed and cried in fear of the strange noises. Ladies laughed and called to them from the street sides. One blew a kiss in Kelly's direction, and with a wink he reached out to catch it.

"This here's a different kind of war!" he exclaimed. "Never seen a city come out to cheer."

"It's a damned sight better than western Virginia!" marveled Parker.

Images of that place flitted through Parker's mind. For nearly a year, the Twenty-Third Ohio had fought Rebel guerrillas in a dismal wilderness. The western part of the Old Dominion remained Union loyal, but the local populace rarely greeted Yankees with the enthusiasm of Frederick's inhabitants. The war there had disintegrated into a bitter cycle of ambushes and manhunts through the forest, leaving many of Parker and Kelly's friends dead or gravely wounded. "The only good bushwhacker is a dead one," thought Parker, but he refused to let cloudy thoughts dampen his spirits on this glorious September day and he dismissed them from his mind.

The crowd grew into a deep throng yelling deafening cheers. A young woman, overcome with joy, rushed from the side of the street to throw her arms around the man in front of Parker. She kissed his cheek with eyes sparkling and then grabbed Parker by the collar of his jacket to plant her lips on his sweat-slickened face. Parker giggled like a schoolboy as the woman pulled at him. "Thank God you've come!" she cried. "You heroes have saved our poor town from those filthy Rebels!"

"You're welcome!" he shouted back at her, tipping his hat.

Then a toothless man with a scraggly white beard and open shirt scuttled up carrying a half-empty bottle. "You boys want a slug?"

"Aye!" Kelly called to him, his mouth salivating for a taste of the cure.

The besotted stranger lurched to Kelly's side. "It's rye whiskey, of course." He belched before handing over the bottle. "This country's famous for it."

Kelly poured a long hot stream of rye into his mouth and gulped it down. "Ah, that's grand!" he declared. "Davey this is good whiskey! Not exactly in the style of the old country, but I'll not be turning it down! Have a swallow."

Parker grabbed the bottle from his friend and tilted it back for a long drink. The rye coursed down his gullet like a torch, his eyes watering as he gasped with approval.

The stranger snatched back the bottle, showing his gums in a wide toothless grin before taking a swig and staggering drunkenly toward the crowd. Looking back along his regiment, Lieutenant Colonel Hayes spotted the souse and wheeled his horse into him, knocking the drunk hard to the ground.

"Aieee! What do you mean by this?" cried the man as his bottle skidded off into the street.

"By God, I'll not have you plying my men with spirits," growled Hayes. "Off with you!" Taking a moment to find his feet, the old sot shot a hateful stare at Hayes and disappeared.

"Oy, the colonel needn't have done that," groused Kelly, sucking the taint of rye from his mustache. Warmed by the whiskey, Parker threw a playful elbow at his friend and tried to look serious when Hayes trotted past staring hard at them.

The column marched through the town center and up a low slope beyond the city, where a large meadow beckoned. Orders came for the regiment to fall out, and Captain Skiles sent men to pull down the roadside fence. Kelly and Parker participated in the work before finding a comfortable resting spot on the sprawling clover.

Scanning the growth, Kelly looked unsuccessfully for one with four leaves before turning his thoughts to food. "Jesus, Davey, I'm so hungry I'd eat the balls off a skunk," he grumbled, easing himself down onto his knapsack.

Parker cocked an eye at his friend. "Good grief, that's wretched, Tom. I'll never understand half of the things that come out of your mouth."

"That may well be, but I'll never understand your Protestant ways either! A miserly, tight-arsed lot ye are."

Parker ignored the taunt and rose to collect firewood from a stand of trees across the turnpike. With luck, the commissary wagons would be up soon, and they could procure something more to eat than hardtack crackers. The division's other regiments flooded into the fields around them, and in the gathering gloom, Parker watched as men sought out rocks to pile into fire rings and others hauled fence rails to burn. Sergeant Bill Lyon organized a detachment to do the same for C Company, and before long, they had several healthy blazes crackling inside fieldstone circles. A few men produced potatoes they had dug during the march and commenced slicing them up. Others gathered empty canteens and left to fetch water. One of the men emerged from the twilight with a whole roasted chicken in his hands.

"Christ almighty!" gasped Kelly, his mouth watering at the sight of it. "Where on God's green earth did ye get that?"

"In Frederick City," the man beamed. "The ladies was handing out all manner of eatables. Didn't you get any?"

Parker and Kelly gaped at one another and shook their heads. "A swallow of whiskey is all we got. Is there more food to be had?" asked Parker.

"Sure is," declared Sam Carey, another comrade from C Company. Carey walked into the firelight gripping a small sack in his hand. "I got some salt pork, a wedge of hard cheese, raspberry jam, half a loaf of bread, and a newspaper. All from one family!"

"Golly, Sam, that's a haul!" declared Parker. "Care to share?"

"Of course. Here," he offered, extending the bread. "Cut this up and pass it around." Carey handed over the loaf and Parker tore into it with his pocketknife.

The hoped-for commissary wagons never arrived, but the men shared what they had, and thirty minutes later, they rested easy in the clover. While Parker removed his boots and rubbed his aching feet, Kelly adjusted his seating position and reached into a small leather pouch to draw out a large pinch of finely cut tobacco. He studied it for a moment before stuffing it carefully into his white clay pipe, tamping it softly with his little finger as if it was a lost art. Once satisfied, he lifted a long stick he had set into the edge of the fire and used the flaming end to ignite the dried leaves, puffing clouds of smoke from the sides of his mouth as he did so. George Love, sitting next to Sam Carey, produced what Kelly had silently longed for the most—a bottle of the famed local rye he had tasted earlier in Frederick. Eagerly taking the bottle from Love, he gulped down a mouthful. Then he passed the bottle to Parker with a long "ahhhhhh." The liquor made its way around the circle, the men doing their best to keep it out of sight lest some officer came by and took it from them.

At length, Carey pulled out his newspaper and held it up in the flickering light.

"The *New York Tribune!*" grumbled Parker sitting up from his repose. "That's an abolitionist rag of the worst sort, Sam. Couldn't you find anything more agreeable to read?"

Carey shrugged. "I didn't have much of a choice. The man who gave me all the food pushed this paper onto me, too. I'm hoping to learn something about what's going on elsewhere. This one's a bit dated, being from August, but all news is new to them who ain't read it before," he declared. "Mind, I ain't in sympathy with abolition, though. That's a nest of vipers, I say."

Kelly plucked the pipe from between his lips and spat into the grass. "Well said, Sam. I'll wager not a man here joined the army to free the nigger, did he?" No one within hearing distance disagreed.

"Well now, here's Old Abe Lincoln saying the same thing," remarked Carey as he angled the paper to get better light. "Says here he wrote a letter to Horace Greeley."

Hisses sang out around the fire.

"Someone ought to do the world a kindness and hang that man," grumbled Parker, his thoughts tainted dark by the rye. "Without his kind, we'd have never taken up arms. I don't care much for darkies, mind, but I sure as shootin' won't stand by while the Johnny Rebs ruin our nation through armed rebellion. That's treason, as sure as I'm sitting here! Men like Greeley pushed them to it."

Heads nodded in the flickering firelight.

"What's Uncle Abe have to say?" asked Kelly, scratching an itch under his light blue trousers.

Carey cleared his throat. "Says here, 'dear sir . . . I have just read yours of the nineteenth addressed to myself through the *New York Tribune*,' and so forth. 'I would save it the shortest way under the Constitution,' et cetera and so on ... ah, here we go. 'My paramount object in this struggle is to save the Union and is not either to save or to destroy slavery. If I could save the Union without freeing any slave, I would do it, and if I could save it by freeing all the slaves, I would do it; and if I could save it by freeing some and leaving others alone, I would also do that. What I do about slavery, and the colored race, I do because I believe it helps to save the Union; and what I forbear, I forbear because I do not believe it would help to save the Union.'"

Carey looked up at his comrades. "About says it all, don't it? Old Abe says the Union is what we're fighting for, not the darkies."

"It didn't sound all that clear cut to me," grumbled Parker. "Sounded more like a bunch of 'I'da done this if not for that' politician chatter. Guess a man's gotta 'spect double talk out of that sort."

"Did say saving the Union is utmost, though," contributed Carey.

Parker shrugged. "Good enough for me, I guess."

"It's one reason I signed up to fights with ye boys—in addition to the healthy bounty," winked Kelly as he exhaled a pungent puff of smoke. "You don't know how good it is here. Where I'm from, the English treat us common folk no better'n dogs. We can't own land. We can't hold public office. Heck, our churches can't even have steeples, or display the cross."

"That's because you're Papists," shot back George Love. "If I didn't already know you and where your loyalties lie, Tom Kelly, I'd reckon you can't be trusted, either. Papists swear allegiance to Rome, not to their home country."

The words lifted Kelly into an upright position as if invisible hands had yanked him off of his knapsack. He pulled the pipe from his lips and gripped it tightly between his fingers. "'Tis a good thing I know *you*, George Love, because if I didn't, I'd come over there and make ye eat those hateful nativist words. I joined this man's army to prove me loyalty to the flag of me new homeland. Don't ever question me motives, or so help me God, I'll put ye on yer backside."

"Alright, that's enough!" declared a tipsy Sergeant Lyon. "Every man here knows Tom Kelly's a loyal man and a good fighter to boot. Why, he even saved your life once, George, when that filthy gang of bushwhackers came at us by the Gauley River. Remember? Old Tom here shot one of 'em down just as he took a bead on you. The man had you dead to rights, too." Several men who had witnessed the event murmured in agreement. "Kelly's a Papist, sure, but he's not the kind of Papist you're yapping about. He's loyal to the colors and hates rebellion as much as any man here."

Exasperated, Love slapped his knee. "I ain't questioning anyone's loyalty; leastways yours, Tom, and I'm sorry I said it. All I meant by it is that Papists take orders from the Pope. Everyone knows it. Why, I reckon even old Tom here would admit the importance of Rome to his church. But I've served with you boys for more than a year now, and I can say without hesitation that I trust and respect all of you to a man, Tom Kelly included. That acceptable to you, Tom?"

Sucking contentedly on his pipe, Kelly reclined on his knapsack. "It is," he replied, discharging a stream of bluish smoke. "It is, indeed."

"Good, then that's settled," confirmed Sergeant Lyon. "We'd best bed down now. Today we took Frederick, but the Rebs ain't far off. I 'spect we'll find 'em again tomorrow. Until then, rest up. Today was a good day. Tomorrow we might not be so lucky."

Impressed by the sergeant's good sense, Kelly pulled out his woolen blanket and tapped the ashes from his pipe. After all was squared away, he took the rosary out of his pocket and prayed silently for God to watch over them that night. By the time he had finished, several men around him were already snoring. Looking up at the cloudless sky, Kelly sighed deeply, closed his eyes, and dropped off into a deep and dreamless sleep.

3

Saturday, September 13, 1862
Sunrise
Encampment of the Eighth Illinois Cavalry Regiment
West of Frederick, Maryland

cavalry trooper bearing a steaming cup of coffee picked his way through the firelight toward an officer lying curled up in the grass. Lowering himself to a crouch, the trooper carefully placed the cup on the ground and paused to study the sleeping figure.

The man's head lay propped on his saddle, partially hidden under a broad black hat that had seen better days. He had pulled a thin woolen army blanket tightly around his shoulders, stretching the stamped letters "U.S." across his back above light-blue trousers that ran down to dusty black leather boots. Ringlets of strawberry blonde glistened under the brim of the man's hat, their length well beyond anything allowed by army regulations. Even more peculiar were the curious blonde mutton chops that encircled his face. Gathering in fullness on his cheeks before meeting in a yellow tuft beneath his long nose, even the extravagant whiskers of General Burnside could not compare to them. Never had the kneeling trooper seen such a display of hirsute grandeur.

Several days earlier, Major Medill had informed the headquarters staff that General McClellan treated this captain with unusual largesse, so they were to do the same. Granting him the freedom to observe the goings-on in General Pleasonton's command, the man roamed as he pleased. Even with the captain's privileges, the crouching trooper still wondered how in God's name, he kept his Samsonian locks. Major Medill would have had any other man in the outfit court-martialed for it, or at least held down and sheared like a sheep.

Shaking his head, the trooper laid aside the questions in his mind and poked the sleeping man's shoulder. "Sir, it's time to rise and shine. The major says we're to be off soon."

George Armstrong Custer slowly lifted the hat from his face, his icy-blue eyes cracking open to regard the shadowy figure hovering over him. "Mm, thank you, Gus," he mumbled. "I didn't hear the bugle."

Shivering in the cold morning air, Custer propped himself up.

"The bugle hasn't sounded yet, sir. Here, I thought you could use this." Lifting the cup, Gus handed it to Custer.

"You're a good man," said Custer, gently sipping the hot black liquid. "Ah, that's got bite! Just how I like it."

"The Eighth is happy to oblige," grinned Gus with satisfaction. A Commissary Sergeant mustered into the army in September 1861, Gustavus A. Stanley attended to the needs of Major William H. Medill and his staff. His duties included keeping an eye on men like Custer, whom General Pleasonton had attached to their regiment.

The first notes of reveille blared out, bringing Gus to his feet. Looking east, he watched tendrils of wood smoke swirl skyward from banked campfires in the fields around Frederick City. Thousands of dark figures gathering around them stretched themselves awake as the rising sun threw the town's steeples into a black profile.

Setting his wide-brimmed hat atop his head, Custer lifted himself stiffly off the ground and shook his right leg to get feeling back into it. "Say, Gus," he yawned, smacking his lips. "Where is the general?"

"In town, I gather." The sergeant jerked his thumb toward the city. "He spent the night with friends."

"Sleeping in a nice warm bed, no doubt!" Custer frowned before bending to gather his blanket and saddlebags. "Have we anything to eat?"

"Sure do. Old Shipman is firing up bacon and biscuits for us, thanks to the generous folks in these parts. He's a fine cook if you don't mind things on the well-done side," volunteered Gus with a wink. "Finish your coffee and come over."

"I'll do that," nodded Custer as Gus strode off. Kneeling to pull a photograph from his saddlebag, Custer peered at it in the sunlight. "Good morning, mother," he smiled, gently touching the photo before tucking it back away. Buckling on his pistol and the fine saber of Toledo steel he had acquired during a raid the previous summer; Custer hoisted his saddle from the dewy ground and carried it to his horse. The animal stood tied to a picket line where Custer had secured it the night before.

Snickering as he approached, the horse tossed its head when Custer lofted the saddle onto its back. "And a good day to you, too, Wellington! Did the orderly take care of you last night?" The soot-colored Morgan let out a snort before lowering its head to crop a clover patch.

"Ah, I see!" said Custer. "Well, if fodder cannot be found, you must make do with what's at hand. It's the same with me, I tell you. In the field, every one of us must catch as one can."

Stooping low, Custer tightened his saddle's belly strap before setting Wellington's bit and adjusting the reins. Once he had secured his saddlebags, he gave the horse a final loving pat.

"Custer, come on quick if you want to eat!" hollered Gus, urging the captain to break his fast while he still could.

Custer sipped coffee among the other members of Major Medill's staff when a darkly bearded officer on a dappled gray clomped into the encampment with several aides in tow. The sun peeked through the clouds behind the general, bathing his worn uniform in a wash of yellow light. General Pleasonton nodded his greetings and called for Medill to get his regiment moving. Then he peered down at Custer, who had just tossed the grainy dregs of his cup into the dirt. "Well, captain, I expect we'll meet with the Rebels today," he declared.

"That's fine with me, sir. This hide and seek we've been playing is tiresome."

Letting out a laugh, Pleasonton leaned forward in his saddle. He had grown to like the eccentric captain in the short time they had served together. "Bully for you, Custer!" he called out. "I'm sure you'll find your way into the thick of the fight despite your orders to stay back. Remember that General McClellan needs your eyes and ears more than your pistol and saber."

"Hmpf," snorted Custer through his bushy mustache. "This is war, general. Fortune favors the bold." Chuckling at the man's pluck, Pleasonton held his tongue. "Sir, may I ask where we're headed today?" inquired Custer.

"You may, captain. The commanding general wants us to seize the pass atop Catoctin Mountain." Pleasonton gestured to the ridge west of where they stood. "He wants us to proceed into the valley beyond and find the main body of the enemy. General McClellan believes that at least a portion of Bobby Lee's army marched through here only two days ago, and by all accounts I've heard, he is correct. Another column is said to have marched toward Jefferson, and maybe the Potomac River. The general wants us to confirm if the column ahead of us continued on to Hagerstown or stopped at Middletown."

"And if we find the enemy, are we to give battle?" asked Custer with a curious glint in his eyes.

"We may bring on an engagement," Pleasonton nodded, tightening his reins as his horse stepped in a tight half-circle, "but I expect General Burnside's men will do the heavy fighting should any be required. His command will follow us just in case. I tell you, Custer, we're hot on their tail."

"And if the Rebels went north?"

Pleasonton tugged thoughtfully at the tip of his short beard. "It's possible, I think. General McClellan warned of enemy cavalry in that direction, so I've sent Colonel McReynolds's brigade and a section of artillery down the Emmittsburg Road to find out.

We will proceed with the Third Indiana in front, followed by the Eighth Illinois, and then the First Massachusetts."

Pleasonton turned away at the sound of thumping hooves. "Speaking of Illinois boys, here is Major Medill now," he said, acknowledging the officer who pulled up alongside him. A tough Midwesterner by birth, Medill sported a black goatee that hung to his breast. Well-combed and scrubbed, Medill did not look like a man who had spent the last week in the field. "Sir, the men are ready to move," he reported, touching the black brim of his kepi.

"Alright then, Captain Custer, you mount up, too, and let's be off," said Pleasonton, and cinching up his reins, he spurred his horse toward the National Road and the summit of Catoctin Mountain beyond.

The Hoosier cavalry of Major George H. Chapman closed in behind Pleasonton, obscuring him from Custer's view. Medill's troopers fell into a column behind them and Custer, after hurrying to his horse, wheeled Wellington in pursuit of the rumbling mass. Up the dusty turnpike they thundered, the countryside rolling higher in a series of sunny foothills. A hard turn to the left bore them further along the macadamized road, and Custer eased Wellington ahead alongside the main column. He had just managed to catch up with Major Medill when the unmistakable crack of small arms fire caught his ear. A rider sprinting from the front reined in close to Medill. "Sir, the general reports Rebel pickets ahead!" the man shouted. "You are to hold here for further orders."

Pop! Gunfire rang out. *Pop, crack, crack.*

Medill brought the column to a halt and a cloud of dust raised by hundreds of hooves settled around them like a mist. "Corporal, what's ahead of us?" asked Medill.

"Sir, a Rebel skirmish line is on this side of the hill, just below the crest."

"Any idea how far back their main line is?"

"No, sir."

"How strong is it?" asked Custer out of turn, drawing an irritated glance from Medill.

"Looks to be several dozen in position on the left of the road," replied the courier, his brown mare dancing restlessly beneath him. "Some are behind a low stone wall. Others are spaced out among the trees and rocks. They command the road and the fields to their front.

Pop! Pop! More rounds cracked out ahead of them.

Scowling, Medill pulled out his binoculars to study the mountainside. Light whiffs of smoke wafted in the fields bordering a steep ravine and heavy tree cover obscured the sharper ascent on the right. Pleasonton had ordered the Hoosiers in front to dismount and lead their horses into the fields on the left. Medill considered doing the same, but ordered his men to remain in the saddle while he walked his mount in search of a route up the hillside.

Realizing what Medill was after, Custer spurred Wellington to his side. "Major, let me go and see what's happening before you send men up there," he pleaded.

Pleasonton had ordered him to keep Custer out of action, but Medill warmed to the idea nonetheless. "Alright, Custer," he responded. "You made your reputation as a scout, so I'll count on you to keep your head and stay safe. Take Private Heaton here with you." Tilting his head at the trooper behind him, Medill added, "it wouldn't do to have you injured and unable to return."

"No, sir, it wouldn't! Not at all," shouted Custer, and snapping a salute, he waved for the carbine-toting trooper to follow him. The two men spurred toward the summit as Frank Clendenin, Major Medill's Chief Bugler, blew the call to dismount. Within a few minutes, the bark of rifled-musket fire grew louder, and Rebel minié balls whistled above Custer's head. He coaxed Wellington into a stand of trees, dismounted, and tied off the horse. Waving for Heaton to do the same, Custer pulled his Colt Model 1860 pistol from its holster and walked slowly into the thicket ahead, straining his eyes for any sign of movement.

Not a Rebel in sight. Custer motioned for Heaton to follow, and together the two men crept up a steep incline covered with brush and lichen-covered scree. The skirmish fire grew heavier now, and a bugler blew a few notes well off to their left before falling silent. Distracted, Custer failed to catch the order. A voice near them shouted, dropping Custer behind a bush. They had come up on the enemy, but still had not seen a single man in the rugged terrain.

"Sir, should we go any farther?" whispered Heaton.

"Look over there," said Custer, pointing to a line of dismounted Union troopers in skirmish order about one hundred yards to their left. Counting two dozen men, Custer and Heaton watched them crawl uphill on their bellies or stalk behind landscape features that offered cover. Every so often, a man would rise to fire at some unseen enemy before ducking back out of sight. Beyond the skirmishers, another small body of men worked their way laterally across the mountain.

"Th-thems Major Chapman's Indiana boys," stammered Heaton.

"Yup, moving to turn the enemy's right." Custer shot the private a look of suspicion. A bead of sweat cut a path down the man's face, and the pupils of his eyes loomed wide. Something about Heaton felt wrong. "Private, have you been under fire before?" he asked.

"Once ... well, sort of," replied the shaking Midwesterner.

Custer blanched. "Once, sort of? What in God's name has Medill gotten me into by sending *you* along? Well, don't get any ideas about running off on me, you hear?"

"I—I won't, sir," Heaton sputtered, his eyes darting nervously from ahead of them to their right. "Where're we going, sir?"

Custer pointed his Colt at the foliage-covered hillside. "Up there to find Johnny's left flank. Now keep calm and follow me."

Rising from his crouch, Custer stalked around a tree and pushed through a stand of laurel. Heaton clicked back the hammer of his carbine and followed as quietly as he could. Creeping low through the underbrush, the two men made their way toward the cracking musket fire. It sounded so loud now that Custer expected any second to stumble onto the Rebel line. Then, without warning, a man wearing a brown slouch hat and gray cavalier's jacket appeared out of the underbrush some ten yards to their left. The Rebel picked his way carefully downhill, his gaze locked on the Indiana troops off to his right.

Custer spotted Heaton drawing a bead on the Butternut, his finger sliding down to the trigger.

"Wait!" he hissed, pushing the muzzle to the ground. "You damned fool! That man's a skirmisher. The main Reb line is farther up. You shoot him, and you'll bring the whole bunch of 'em down on us."

"I'm sorry. I didn't know," Heaton shuddered.

Scowling at the quaking carbine barrel in his hand, Custer released it to pat the man's shoulder. "Don't worry about it, Heaton. Just keep quiet and stay on my right. I'll tell you when to fire."

Heaton nodded and crouched closer to the ground. The enemy trooper eased himself farther to their left and disappeared once again into the trees. Then a twig snapped up ahead, and Custer pulled Heaton to the ground. Pressing his forefinger to his lips, he nodded up the hillside. Heaton's eyes widened when he spotted a second Rebel sporting a soiled hodgepodge of a uniform, including a gray short coat with Union sky-blue cavalry pants topped by a black kepi. The Reb leaned backward, feeling his way awkwardly down the incline. A carbine in his left hand, the man used his right to steady himself against the passing trees. He was headed almost straight toward them. Custer took note of the man's riding boots.

Another cavalryman. Must be Lee's rearguard, he concluded.

Cocking the hammer of his Colt, Custer leaned over to Heaton. "I'm gonna take that Johnny prisoner," he whispered in the man's ear. "Look out for others."

Custer rose from his crouch and stepped forward when suddenly he spied a line of Rebels farther up the hillside. "Aw, hell," he spat, returning to his place behind the tree.

Studying the enemy line, he realized that no man could be seen farther to the right. They had found the Confederate left flank. "Too many to take prisoner," he griped, "but we got what we came for, Heaton. Ease back to the horses as quietly as you can."

The private nodded and took a step backward while Custer kept his attention focused on the Rebels closing the distance between them. Adrenaline coursed through his veins, and he could hear his heart beating in his ears. Recklessness had held him in place for too long. Custer slipped back in Heaton's direction, realizing that the man had gone only thirty feet, and stopped. Motioning for Heaton to keep moving, Custer began to follow. Then disaster struck the unfortunate private. Stepping on a pile of scree, he lost his balance. Custer froze as the carbine dropped from Heaton's hands onto the rocks. The cocked hammer snapped home and a shot reverberated through the woods. Swinging his head faster than his blonde curls could follow, Custer saw the enemy lock eyes onto them.

"Goddammit!" he swore, and raising his pistol, he fired at the nearest man. The shot struck a tree next to the trooper's head, sending bits of bark flying into his face.

"Sonofabitch!" the Johnny shouted, "There's Yankees here, boys! Git 'em!"

"What the hell are you waiting for?" barked Custer, who had already leaped over the loose stones on a sprint downhill. "Get on your feet and run!"

The hapless private scrambled for his fallen carbine as a lead round pinged off a stone inches from his hand. For a moment Heaton thought he would piss himself out of fright, but before he realized it, he was on his feet and scrambling down after the captain. Thirty seconds later, they had put enough tree and brush cover between them and the enemy to make further shooting pointless. Custer paused to catch his breath as Heaton drew up beside him.

"Captain, I—"

"I don't want to hear a damned word out of you!" snapped Custer, his cheeks gone red. He scooped a fistful of Heaton's blouse and shook it with fury. "You nearly got me killed!"

Tears glistened in Heaton's eyes, and Custer felt a knot of disgust in his gut. "You're pathetic," he growled, pushing the man away. "I promise Major Medill will hear about this."

Without speaking another word, the pair reached the thicket where they had tied off their horses. Custer led Wellington back to the road and mounted, with Heaton keeping a respectful distance behind him. The gunfire near the mountain's summit had by now escalated into a continuous roar. When Custer arrived back at the Eighth Illinois's position, he discovered the men huddled along the embankment, ready to storm the enemy position. Medill stalked the ground behind them, encouraging everyone to check their weapons and stay patient.

"Captain!" he exclaimed as Custer drew up. "Where's Private Heaton?"

"He'll be along shortly," Custer growled. "Sir, the far left of the enemy's line is up there." He pointed uphill. "If you deploy your men to the right, you'll overlap it."

"Bully for you, Custer!" beamed Medill. "Tell me everything."

Custer explained what he had seen, including a few choice words about Private Heaton, while Medill listened. "Sir, what's the situation here?" Custer asked after he had finished giving his report.

"The Rebels have brought up reinforcements," explained the major. "General Pleasonton sent word that there may be as many as a thousand men defending this pass. Major Chapman's advance is pinned down on the left. Mine," he added, motioning toward his men, "is about to get underway." Medill glanced uphill and then back at Custer. "Can you confirm the only Johnnies you saw up there are cavalry?"

"I can, sir. It looks to me like we've hit Stuart's rearguard."

"Then we'll drive them soon enough," Medill snorted. Calling for Heaton, he turned to regard the sheepish private when he walked up. Custer glared at Heaton through smoldering blue eyes. "What happened up there?" asked the major.

"I—I made a mistake, sir."

Medill shot a glance Custer's way. "Is that so? What do you mean?"

"I mean that—"

A burst of artillery fire drowned out Heaton's voice as enemy shells shrieked toward a section of Pleasonton's rifled guns. Captain James M. Robertson's Battery of the 2nd U.S. Horse Artillery scrambled to unlimber as the rounds exploded in the air above them. Battery horses reared in their harnesses, but the gunners quickly controlled them. Swinging around their guns, they rammed home powder charges and the rifled shells before sighting the fieldpieces. One of the men at each gun placed a friction primer in the vent hole and backed off with a lanyard in hand. When all was ready, Robertson gave the order.

"FIRE!"

Custer could hear the man's cry from where he stood. The bucking guns rolled backward, belching rings of smoke. Their rounds screamed toward the Rebels on the heights, exploding in geysers of dirt.

"I could watch those boys work all day," proclaimed Medill with satisfaction. Turning back to Heaton, he waved the man off. "Private, I'll deal with you later. Dismissed!"

"Looks like we have a real fight on our hands," glowed Custer.

"It sure does," nodded Medill. "It's been two hours now, and the Rebs are getting stronger. They don't want us up there, do they?"

"No, sir, they sure don't. What do you think that says about their forces in Middletown Valley?"

"Can't know for certain, captain, but if I were General Lee—" Medill leaned in, drawling in a mock Virginia planter's accent, "I'd keep Stuart real close. My guess is the main body can't be too far off."

Custer folded his arms in frustration. The battle he had been waiting for was unfolding around him, and he had no role to play. "Major, you've got to let me into this fight," he insisted, his visage flushing red.

Sighing heavily, Medill shook his head. "I can't, Custer. You know that as well as I. General Pleasonton attached you to my regiment to observe the enemy and report what you see to army headquarters. Hell, I could get my ass chewed just for letting you scout that flank! Now, you wait here while I get this attack underway. Clendenin, sound the advance!" he yelled, stomping toward his waiting line with saber in hand.

The brassy notes sent Medill's men scrambling up the embankment while Custer, turning away in frustration, yanked the hat from his head and flung it on the ground. Leading Wellington by the reins, he picked up his dusty headgear and sulked to the roadside. His horse began pulling at weeds as Custer dropped onto a large flat rock. The clamor of battle rose around him, making his heart pound. "I'll find a way to get in," Custer vowed to himself. "No man's going to keep me from a fight while others have a chance to win glory. By thunder, I swear it!"

4

Saturday, September 13, 1862
(Mid-Morning)
Residence of Emma Wilson, formerly of the U.S. Sanitary Commission
East Patrick Street, Frederick, Maryland

slender middle-aged woman peered out of her parlor window between lace curtains yellowed by years of sunlight. The woman's sallow complexion contrasted strongly with the darkness of the thick hair she wore, parted down the middle, and pulled tight with a blue ribbon that dangled messily from the bun on the back of her head. Pursed lips gave the woman the appearance of a teenage pout, but aging skin highlighted the grooves of time that creased the edges of her mouth.

Beyond the glass of her parlor window, a raucous procession of blue-coated soldiers strode past behind an army band. The flower of the nation's youth beamed proudly in their ranks, the barrels of their rifled muskets packed with white and yellow blossoms passed out by the Unionist residents of Frederick City. Emma Wilson did not share this effusion of glee, watching the soldiers with a gloomy expression on her face. Their pounding drums rattled her china teacups, every sonorous beat causing the corner of Emma's right eye to wince involuntarily. She had awoken that morning with a headache and her right temple still throbbed despite the powder she had taken for the pain. Pressing a fingertip to the spot, she rubbed it in a circular motion.

As she watched the marching troops outside, Emma felt a familiar rush of hopefulness in her heart. Then, inevitably, a voice in her head told her that she, of all people, had no reason for optimism.

Stop it, you old fool! it whispered. *He is not among them.*

Tears welled up in Emma's eyes, and she thought she might burst with grief. Instead, she blew out a mighty sigh and turned away from the glass, her hand dropping to let the curtains come back together.

Months earlier, Emma might have stood outside throwing flowers, offering food, and waving a small flag with a deep sense of national pride. Now she felt only an emptiness that words could not express. All-consuming in its depth, it robbed her of any lust for life.

My poor Amos.

Lowering her gaze, Emma peered down at the gold locket dangling around her neck. She snapped it open to look at the face of her beloved son staring back at her. Emma stifled a sob. The photographer in town, a man named Byerly, had managed to capture a wonderful likeness of Amos in his new uniform. Fresh-faced and full of patriotic vim, the boy went off to war in the summer of 1861. Willingly had Emma let him go, thinking the war could not possibly last for long; and yet for more than a year since that time, the bodies of local boys killed in action were still coming home.

Emma's family had proven less fortunate than many in Frederick City. After one of Stonewall Jackson's loathsome Rebels shot and killed Amos near Front Royal, Virginia, in May 1862, the boy's remains never returned. Bile rose in Emma's throat as she thought of the filthy ruffians. Not only had they murdered her son, but they had also come to Maryland and infested *her* town! Singing their wretched songs and hallooing at her Secessionist neighbors—Emma cursed them all to hell.

Foul smelling, lice-ridden Rebels had filled the streets of Frederick for days, knocking on doors to beg for food. Some of them even strolled the sidewalks with their hindquarters showing through indecent holes in their trousers. *Those* seedy creatures were the latter-day knights of Southern chivalry? Men with bare feet blackened by dust, mud, and blood? Emma shook her head in disbelief. How in God's name had they managed to defeat well-equipped army after army sent by the national government against them?

By the time Emma had managed to cross the Potomac and reach Front Royal the previous June, she found Amos's body long since buried. She asked passing locals after fallen Union soldiers, but most had only shrugged. Then a man she met on the road whispered that Yankee remains lay in unmarked graves. Emma might find Amos among them, if she cared to dig through a pit of decaying corpses.

Her stomach turned at the memory.

Faced with an impossible task for a woman her age, and deep within Rebel country, Emma had returned to Maryland empty-handed. Losing her only son stripped her life of joy, leaving Emma a shell of the patriotic mother she once had been. Numb to the outside world, and embittered by Amos's fate, her heart grew as cold and hard as a tombstone in Frederick's Mount Olivet Cemetery.

A child shouted, shaking Emma from her thoughts. Gently, she closed the locket and glanced back through the curtains. A pack of small boys in the street wove like howling banshees through the marching soldiers' ranks. Tiny flags and sticks waved in their hands as they fired imaginary weapons at one another. When the column lurched to a stop, as it often did, a large infantryman with tossed one of the lads over his shoulder. Towering above everyone else, the boy raised his arms wildly into the air, his voice screaming with delight. Then his terrified mother arrived on the scene to claim her son and the soldier lifted him down. With a pat on his head, the man sent the lad on his way, his comrades chuckling at the prank.

Amos would have done that, thought Emma. *He would have played with that boy and made him happy. Boys love guns and war and playing soldier. Amos had been no different than any of these young ones when he was their age.*

She could still see her son playing in the street with his friends, broomsticks and tree branches propped on their shoulders. Charge and countercharge swept across the road, leaving the army of innocents soaked in sweat until calls to supper prompted them to disperse. For a moment, Emma almost smiled at the memory. Then she caught herself and shook her head at their foolish enthusiasm for war—as silly and as dangerous as her own once had been.

Real war had come to Frederick. Real flesh and blood soldiers with rifled-muskets, pistols, sabers, bayonets, and murderous artillery pieces rolled through the streets laughing as boys cavorted around them and gawping maidens made fools of themselves. Young Amos had been one of those young men, recalled Emma. Just eighteen-years-old in the heady days of April 1861, he became swept up in the torrent of popular enthusiasm for war. Most of the boys in his part of Maryland felt a need to fight for the Union, despite the proximity of their homes to Virginia, where everyone believed the war would be won. Those for secession, including several of Amos's friends, went south to join the Confederacy and fight for what they called the Second American Revolution. Those like Amos, who supported President Lincoln's call to arms, went to Baltimore to sign their papers for the First Maryland Regiment and suppress the rebellion. "I'll be home before Christmas," Amos had assured his mother. "You won't even know I've been gone."

Foolishly, Emma had believed him.

Unable to sit home and do nothing, she joined the Sanitary Commission to care for the wounded and, just maybe, have the chance to be close to her son. Her husband Jonathan joined the Commission, too, and all went well for the first few months—until suddenly it did not. Seated in the back of a wagon with several other men, the vehicle carrying Jonathan had careened down a steep embankment and overturned, crushing his spine beneath a load of heavy wooden crates.

Losing her husband devastated Emma, but she stayed at her work, determined to do her part until the word of Amos's death arrived. This second loss broke her beyond mending and Emma resigned from the Commission soon thereafter. The long months since that time blurred together in a grim tapestry of heartache, loneliness, and rage. Emma ate little and rarely stepped outside, even though she knew proper nourishment and sunlight would do her good.

Then the news arrived that General Lee's Army of Northern Virginia had entered the Old Line State and everyone scrambled home to prepare for the next bloody clash, sure to take place on their doorstep. Emma remained unmoved. She mourned for her lost family and pondered what might lie ahead for a widow well along in life.

Again, she let the lace curtain swing closed.

"Oh, Auntie, is it not marvelous to see the army here in Frederick?" inquired a melodious female voice behind her.

Fumbling for a handkerchief, Emma dabbed at the corner of her eye before turning to face her guest in the parlor's best red-velvet chair. Walking silently to a sofa of green damask along the far wall, Emma lowered herself onto it.

"I suppose it is, Lucy," she whispered, "but I'd give every last one of them to have my Johnny and Amos back."

Lucy Settle rose to comfort her aunt, sliding onto the sofa next to her and placing a consoling hand on her shoulder.

"How could I let Amos go?" asked Emma, trancelike. "I am his mother. I knew the danger. I should have kept him here, safe and with me."

Lucy's lips wrinkled into a grimace. No answer she could offer would comfort the older woman.

"Auntie," she began softly, "Amos didn't need your permission. Do you think he would have stayed home if you forbade him to go?" Emma stared back at the girl as if seeing right through her. "You are not responsible for his death," Lucy continued. "Amos was fully grown when he volunteered. He was patriotic and serving his country—responsible for his own life and his own decisions."

Emma's eyes focused on her niece. "I thought this accursed war would be over by now," she spat. "I never dreamed it would go on for so long and take so many lives. And Johnny, too, in such an awful way."

"No one did, Auntie," cooed Lucy while patting her aunt's icy hand.

A boom like thunder rumbled in the distance, jarring the teacups. Emma jumped to her feet and stared at the window, the handkerchief twisting nervously between her fingers. "Is there rain coming? It doesn't feel like rain," she asked.

"Not at all," said Lucy, who rose from the sofa to push apart the lace curtains. "It's odd, Auntie. I see nothing but blue sky and a few white clouds."

Boom! Boom!

Emma hurried to her niece in a rustle of skirts and grabbed her arm. "That isn't rain, Lucy! It's cannon fire. I remember hearing it in Virginia. Thunder is what it sounds like."

"I had no idea," pouted Lucy with a shake of her head. "I think it came from the mountains to the west." Then Lucy's face lit up, and she turned to Emma with a grin on her lips. "There must be fighting close by! Oh, hallelujah, our army has found the Rebels."

Boom! rattled the windowpane.

"So, more men will die for no purpose," growled Emma bitterly. "It is all so much wasted blood."

Lucy's face darkened, and she scowled at her aunt. "You are impossible to be with," she barked. "I'm leaving."

"Leaving? But why? And where will you go?" asked Emma, astounded by the sudden change.

"Outside, Auntie," said Lucy. "I can't bear to listen to you any longer!" Emma stared silently at the floor; her eyes moist with tears. Lucy, though, felt she must go on. "I mourn the loss of Cousin Amos and of Uncle John—not like you, of course, but my heart aches, nonetheless. I refuse to feel bitter about the war, though. Our family's sacrifice is for a greater purpose. I believe this with all my heart, and so should you."

"Is that so?" asked Emma, her eyebrows arching in surprise.

"Yes, it is!" snapped Lucy, stomping her foot to emphasize the point. Her back stiff and chin jutting out with resolve, Lucy thrust a quivering finger at the parlor window. "I believe the men out there are doing the Lord's work. They are righting a wrong that ought to have been corrected a long time ago. I intend to go outside and wave to them and show support for their cause. I even brought fresh bread to give them, though it cost me dearly to buy it. The basket is on the porch and handing it out to those heroic boys is just what I intend to do."

Spinning on her heels, Lucy left the room, returning a moment later with a round loaf in her hands. "Here it is," she said, holding it up like a prize for her aunt to see. "I am going to feed those men. They need—no! They *deserve* our support—mine and yours, too! If they aren't victorious in this war, then the slave power will be, and that cannot be allowed to happen. If the black man is not free, how can we ever expect our own sex to earn *its* equality?"

"Ah, yes, your *work* for women's rights," mocked her aunt resentfully. "Praise be you haven't spoken about *that* in some time."

Stunned by the slight, Lucy's cheeks flushed red. "There have been more pressing matters of late, *Auntie*, as I am sure you have noticed. But I'm still as convinced a follower of Elizabeth Cady Stanton and Susan B. Anthony as I ever was. We will see this war won first. Then we can return to the subject of equality for our sex and securing the right to vote."

"To vote? Why, in God's name, would a woman want to vote?" puzzled Emma. "Politics is a dirty game for drunken men in smoky parlors, not for respectable society ladies like us. You are condemning yourself to a life of spinsterhood, Lucy. No man with an ounce of self-respect will have a mouthy suffragette for a wife!"

The loaf in her hands shook with rage, and Lucy wheeled to leave the house. Then she thought better of it and turned back. "Pettiness does not suit you," she scolded, her finger pointed at her aunt. "Uncle John supported giving women the right to vote, and *he* was a decent man."

Emma stiffened at the mention of her dead husband's name, but Lucy went on. "I refuse to value my life based on what *men* think of me," she growled, "and I'll be content, come what may. If there is a man in the world for me, then I will meet him, and if not, then I won't. It is in God's hands."

Fuming, Lucy fell silent, her eyes studying the portraits of long-dead men on the wall above the sofa. Her aunt's remark had cut her to the core, and the older woman knew it. Despite her talk about being an independent woman, Lucy craved male companionship and a family, but she lived without those things. Being nearly twenty-five, the passing years had opened a gaping chasm of loneliness within her. She longed desperately to share her life with someone in a bond of love and mutual respect. "Maybe one of those soldiers marching by outside is the man I am looking for," she added wistfully.

"Lucy, you are a grown woman and will do as you wish," replied Emma, her voice softer now. "I no longer care what happens, but you must. I also know," she added, stopping for a moment to choose her words carefully this time, "that I love you and cannot afford to lose you, too."

Boom! ... Boom! Boom!

The teacups clattered, reminding Lucy and Emma of the extraordinary events taking place outside of the house. Both of them returned to the parlor window.

"How do you intend to return to Middletown?" asked Emma. "If there is fighting on the mountain, then the Rebels are on the road. There is no way you can get through the lines. Nor should you try, my dear."

Lucy watched the soldiers tramping past. "I don't know, Auntie. Perhaps our army will drive the Rebels back," she sighed.

"Dearest niece, stay with me," replied Emma, touching Lucy's arm in a gesture of reconciliation. "I let Amos walk out that door back when the war was far way. Now it is here in our town, and I am not about to let you stroll right into it. Besides," she added, forcing the first smile that Lucy had seen in weeks, "I prefer not to be alone."

Lucy felt her heart soften, and with a trembling lip, she reached out to embrace her aunt. The boniness of Emma's shoulders felt hard under her hands. "As you wish," she said. "I'll be happy to stay the evening. We will see what tomorrow brings."

Lucy gently pushed back at arm's length and mustered a smile for the forlorn widow. "First, I need to go outside and wave to our brave boys who chased the Rebels out of town. Join me?" Emma hesitated, prompting Lucy to add defiantly, "I'll leave town this minute if you don't!"

Heaving a sigh, Emma surrendered. "Very well, child. For your sake, I will come."

"Thank you, Auntie. I appreciate it very much and so will they. Now take my hand."

Entwining her fingers with the younger woman's, Emma noticed their warmth compared to hers. She allowed herself to be led out of the door and into the bright light. Lucy smiled at her aunt, who squinted in the sun, gesturing for her to follow down the steps. Emma hesitated for a moment as the roar of her cheering neighbors washed over them. A few seconds later she nodded and let her niece lead her into a street jammed with waving citizens and singing troops.

5

Saturday, September 13, 1862
Mid to late Morning
Headquarters, Army of the Potomac
Frederick, Maryland

McClellan pulled Dan Webster to a stop near the long-covered bridge over the Monocacy River. Wagons belonging to the Second Corps under General Edwin Vose Sumner crowded the turnpike, rolling across the bridge in single file. His ears awash with the braying of mules and cussing of army teamsters, McClellan scowled at the delay. The rumble of cannons on the heights of Catoctin Mountain, where Alfred Pleasonton's cavalry had engaged J.E.B. Stuart's Rebel horsemen, gnawed at him.

Each ominous boom set McClellan on edge. He needed to reach Frederick City and the headquarters of Ambrose Burnside; the commander of the Army of the Potomac's right-wing. Burnside would know what was happening. His Ninth Corps, under General Jesse Reno, had followed Lee's Graybacks across central Maryland, and now the two armies had made contact. McClellan believed the looming clash with Lee to be one he must win to save both the Union and his own imperiled career.

"General Williams is there no other place where we can cross?" he asked the officer beside him.

"Not that I know of, sir," replied the balding Assistant Adjutant General as he surveyed the bustling road jam. Having served with McClellan since early in the war, Seth Williams remained one of Little Mac's most loyal followers. "I can ride over and ask if a ford is nearby," he volunteered, directing McClellan's attention to a stone mill on the right.

McClellan dismissed the suggestion. "There is no time. I need to see Sumner's boys on the way into Frederick and then find Burnside. Pleasonton has met the enemy. We must learn what it means." McClellan scowled, his dark brows knitting together beneath the brim of his cap. "Please ride ahead and stop these wagons, so we may cross."

"Yes, sir," nodded Williams, who spurred his horse toward the bridge.

McClellan fidgeted impatiently with his reins for a full two minutes until the wagons creaked to a halt. Expletives filled the air as Williams reappeared at the bridge's edge. Standing tall in his stirrups, he waved that the way was clear.

"At last! Come along, gentlemen," snorted McClellan to the staff officers around him.

Dan Webster clopped across the bridge to meet regiments of blue-coated troops on the far side of the river crowding the pike and adjacent fields. Some waited in column, while others reclined in the grass. Saluting as he passed a small collection of officers, McClellan caught the eye of a haggard soldier in a uniform so dusty it almost looked Confederate gray.

"Why look here, boys, it's Little Mac! Hurrah!" yelled the man, his hat waving wildly in his hand. Others joined, their cheers cascading down the road to Frederick. McClellan forced himself to remain composed, acting as if the cheering amounted to nothing more than standard army protocol. Inwardly, however, he swelled with conceit. These ranks might wear the national government's uniform and serve under the national flag, but this was *his* army. These were *his* men.

Carried on the wings of vanity, McClellan slowed his horse to a walk and twirled his hat in salute. Even louder applause broke out. Word traveled swiftly about the general's approach as he made his way toward Frederick, now visible in the distance. Troops clogging the road parted ranks to stand at attention. McClellan nodded at them as he passed.

A colonel on the roadside met McClellan's gaze. His saber held out stiffly in salute, the man stood stock-still with the ranks of his command in file behind him, their weapons at present-arms. McClellan brought Dan Webster to a halt. "What is your name, colonel?" he asked.

"Hincks, sir. Edward Hincks, Nineteenth Massachusetts."

"Very good, Colonel Hincks," nodded the general. "Your men look splendid!"

"Thank you, sir!" bellowed Hincks in reply. "We do our best."

"You have succeeded, sir! I know your regiment. You were on the Peninsula with me."

"Proudly, sir. With the Second Corps."

"Of course," nodded McClellan, lifting his gaze this time to more closely study the men. "Are you boys ready to whip the Secesh here in Maryland?" He asked loudly.

"Hurrah!" cried the sons of the Bay State, volunteers to a man.

The roar warmed McClellan, who grinned. "That's very good. Very good, indeed. Carry on, Colonel Hincks!" Hincks snapped a smart salute that McClellan returned before cantering off.

Riding past a cemetery at the southern end of town, McClellan entered the dusty streets of Frederick City. Children at play in a connecting alley spotted him and came out into the street to follow the general's horse. The shouting and stray dogs barking as he passed called attention to his arrival. McClellan urged Dan toward the town center, where people milled about in the wake of two Federal infantry brigades that had just passed. A middle-aged civilian with a black bowler hat spotted him and did a double take. "It's General McClellan!" he yelled at the top of his lungs. A crowd of citizens suddenly converged around Dan Webster from every direction.

"My God, be careful George! There may be Rebel sympathizers about!" hissed General Marcy, riding next to his son-in-law.

Marcy's words drowned away in the swell of shouting townspeople. Hands reached up to grasp McClellan's coat and touch the legs of his trousers. Dan pulled back at the commotion, offering a high-pitched whinny. McClellan did his best to calm his own racing heart while keeping his horse in check.

"Easy, boy. Easy, Dan! These people mean no harm," he called out, pulling the reins with his right hand while leaning down to pat the thick equine neck with his left.

A bearded man in a fine brown suit pulled at McClellan's coat sleeve. "General, those filthy Rebels took everything we have! We thought ourselves lost, but now you've come and driven them away. Oh, praise God, we are saved!"

McClellan shook the man's hand and looked up to see a local woman brazenly shove through the crowd to a spot directly in front of his horse. Clutching her bosom melodramatically, she announced, "thank Heaven you've come!" before resting a forearm across her brow as if on a stage. "You've rescued us from those horrible Rebels!" she blurted, collapsing theatrically into the arms of a man standing beside her.

A wreath of flowers landed in his lap, and petals began fluttering onto the general and his staff, covering them in white, red, and yellow. A lady inserted a flag into Dan Webster's bit, and McClellan choked up. *These people, true Marylanders loyal to the nation, believe me a hero! How delightfully different this is from the hateful glares of those traitorous Virginians on the James River peninsula!* Little Mac reached down and accepted a rose from a lovely lass.

An officer with McClellan's personal escort grew increasingly worried about the size of the crowd. His alarm exploded when he realized that some civilians were carrying side-arms. He urged his horse through the milling masses. "General, we ought to get you out of here!" he shouted.

McClellan's eyes, glinting with a curious light, settled on the man. As if suddenly regaining his senses, the general nodded. "Captain Mann! Yes, I agree. Can you push us through?"

Mann waved for McClellan's guard detachment to clear a path, shouting for the people to make way. Troopers used their horses to push ever so slowly toward the main intersection. The dazzled populace fell back grudgingly until a path opened ahead. Then the riders went east on Patrick Street and passed by fine brick houses and stores on their way to Ambrose Burnside's headquarters at the new city fairgrounds.

McClellan slid down from the saddle as the army's right-wing commander emerged from his tent. "Welcome, sir. It's good to see you," said the Rhode Islander as he shook McClellan's hand.

"Good day, Burn," replied McClellan, noting the sweat sparkling on the man's bald pate. Still half an hour before noon, the sun already blazed hot in the clear sky above. Little Mac pulled at his collar, too, realizing for the first time how warm the day had become.

Boom! . . . Boom!

A distant thunder echoed across the valley. Both men peered west. Then Burnside broke the silence. "Come inside and refresh yourself, George. I'll have my orderly fetch some cool water while I brief you on the situation."

Burnside followed the general, whom he had known before the war, through the large flaps. Little Mac removed his sweat-soaked kepi and black gloves, tossing them onto a cot as an orderly arrived with a pitcher and a cup. McClellan drank deeply of the well-drawn water and cannon fire rumbled distantly as they spoke.

"Burn, I hear guns on the mountain. What's happening?"

Burnside reached for a dispatch he had received from the army's cavalry commander. "General Pleasonton struck the Secesh rear-guard on the Catoctins soon after sunrise this morning. Stuart's men hold a commanding position and have kept our cavalry from advancing."

McClellan raised an eyebrow. "What about our infantry?"

"Pleasanton requested support after the Rebs brought up artillery to strengthen their position. I sent him the two brigades of General Rodman's division and have General Cox's Kanawha boys standing by west of Frederick—if needed."

"What of the First Corps? Where is General Hooker?"

Dropping Pleasonton's dispatch, Burnside gestured to a large map on his camp table, over which both generals towered. Burnside tapped a spot east of the Monocacy River. "At last report Hooker's column was about here, near New Market."

"So, some twelve miles away?"

"Yes."

"Do you have a plan, sir?" asked Burnside expectantly.

McClellan thought about this for a moment and exhaled through his thick mustache. "I do, Burn. I intend to concentrate the army around Frederick and exploit Pleasonton's breakthrough when it comes. Sumner is the closest, so his corps is ready to support you first. I will order him to advance through the city and take position northwest of the National Road, here." Little Mac pointed to a spot near the town reservoir on the map. "That way, if any of Lee's army is in Middletown Valley, Sumner can push over the Catoctins north of Frederick and come up on your flank. The Twelfth Corps is coming up from Ijamsville and will be here soon as well. Have a message sent that I would like General Williams to stop on the east side of Frederick City after his command crosses the Monocacy."

"I'll send the dispatch right away," acknowledged Burnside. "What of the rest of my wing?"

"Have the remaining Ninth Corps divisions east of town proceed through Frederick to support Pleasonton's push. If we discover the Rebels in force on the far side of the mountain, Pleasonton will need all the help he can get dealing with them."

"And the First Corps?"

"Send word to Hooker that he is to march on Frederick immediately," urged McClellan. "Further orders will be waiting once he arrives."

Burnside nodded as he reached up to stroke his massive salt and pepper-flecked sideburns. "Sir, where do you think Lee is?" he asked.

Staring at Burnside's map, McClellan shook his head. "Likely on the far side of South Mountain, but we have several reports of enemy columns on the move, so I'm unsure what he's up to. If I were him," he paused, "I would move as fast as possible with my entire force and capture the garrison at Harpers Ferry."

Burnside's mouth dropped open. "Colonel Miles is still there? I would have thought him evacuated by now."

"Halleck gave me command over Miles only yesterday," grumbled McClellan, "and I could not reach him. Pleasonton has regiments fanned out as far as the Potomac to find a way through, but I am not optimistic. I've ordered his men to fire their cannon intermittently to alert Miles to our presence. I have also sent orders to General Franklin to halt his Sixth Corps at Buckeystown in case I find an opening to exploit. At present, I only know that Jackson's troops marched back into Virginia via Williamsport. Scattered reports put some Rebel forces north of here and near Hagerstown—but not all the information coming in makes sense. Our scouts have not turned up anything solid that I feel comfortable acting on."

"Could Lee be making his way into Pennsylvania?"

McClellan pulled absentmindedly at the tip of his goatee. "I think not, but can't be sure," he said after a moment. "I've seen no evidence he is moving north in any strength, but if he does, General Reynolds is ready with the state militia to slow him some."

"Militia isn't going to fare well against Lee's army, sir."

"Of course not. They won't stand long, if they stand at all."

Burnside looked perplexed, prompting Little Mac to wave away his concern. "Do not worry, Burn. At the first sign of Lee moving north, this army will move quickly to cut his line of retreat at Hagerstown!" The general turned the large map, thrusting the side of his hand across it like a knife. "This will force Lee to turn and fight me in Maryland."

"That would be the logical move, but—"

"But," interrupted McClellan, "it won't be necessary. That's what you were going to say, right?" Burnside chuckled uneasily while rubbing his neck.

"Lee intends to take Harpers Ferry. I am certain of it!" continued the army commander. "But it is also possible he is moving his army back to Virginia in retreat. We will press ahead and see what develops before deciding on a final course of action."

"Of course," nodded Burnside. Dipping a cloth into his washbasin, he wiped his head and face, muttering, "damn, it's hot." When he finished squeezing out the rag, the Rhode Islander used the palms of his hands to massage his tired eyes. "And so, the army gathers around Frederick while we wait for Pleasonton to break through?" he asked.

"Yes," nodded McClellan, referring again to the map. "Earlier reports noted two columns of Rebel troops leaving Frederick. One headed northwest toward Hagerstown," he pointed, "and one southwest toward the river. I'll wager Lee is going to sneak around Miles and take the Ferry from the rear. That's what I would do."

"As usual, sir, you have matters well in hand," grinned Burnside. "Excuse me while I have orders drawn up for Hooker and Reno. I must send the message to Williams, too."

"Yes, of course," waved McClellan. "When you finish, let's return to the center of town to review the men. I worry that this is not the same army I led on the Peninsula, Burn. Pope's troops joined us near Washington after a serious defeat."

"I understand, sir," replied Burnside.

"Some still carried their muskets, dragging them through the rain and mud to the fortifications around Arlington. I have never seen men so broken. I must do what I can to buck them up! We have won a bloodless victory by taking Frederick. The citizens are ecstatic. It will do the men good to look upon me when they advance."

"Indeed, it will," nodded Burnside, casting a sidelong glance at McClellan. While they had known each other for years, Burnside sometimes found the general's vanity difficult to swallow. "Ah, here is my orderly," he blurted out, grateful for a chance to change the subject. A private bearing a ceramic pitcher and basin appeared at the entrance with a clean wash towel draped over his arm. "Come in and place that here," commanded Burnside, gesturing to a small vanity mirror beside his cot.

Turning to McClellan, Burnside invited him to refresh himself while he handled the paperwork. McClellan stood before the mirror and pulled off his dusty frock coat. Cupping his hands, he splashed water onto his face and across the back of his neck. The cool liquid soothed his sunburned cheeks. Then he returned the coat to his shoulders, buttoned the front, and strode confidently into the sunlight, carrying his gloves and kepi.

Boom!

Another burst of cannon rumbled in the distance. The general called for a courier, telling the man to ride for Sumner's Second Corps and have him advance through the city. "Tell him he is to assemble his corps on the northwestern side of Frederick," McClellan added. "Do you understand?" The courier nodded, snapped a salute, and spurred out of the encampment.

Pausing once more to listen to Pleasonton's fight atop the Catoctin Mountains, McClellan scowled. *Damn it. Why has Pleasonton not pushed through? Patience, George. He will clear them out soon enough.*

An animated conversation a few yards behind the general caught his attention. He placed his forage cap on his head and turned slowly to see one man listening while the other told a lively story.

"And then part of our advance chased the Rebel horse through the streets. They rallied on the far side of town and came thundering back with sabers drawn," explained the fast-talking raconteur. "Our boys drew back then, it being their turn to play the rabbit. We exchanged a few shots and then we lost Colonel Moor."

"Lost Moor?" interrupted McClellan.

"Both men looked over, surprised to see the army's commanding general. "Sir, I—we didn't see you there!" stammered one of the pair with a sharp salute.

"Do you mean to say that Colonel Gus Moor is dead?" inquired a surprised Little Mac.

"Oh no, general," assured the trooper with a vigorous shake of his head. "The colonel's not dead. He got captured by Reb cavalry during their counter-charge in Frederick."

"As you were," waved McClellan. "When did this take place?"

Relaxing, the man lowered his hand. "Yesterday, sir, when we first entered the city."

"Ah," nodded McClellan. "Then we can expect the colonel to be paroled soon. That is a relief. I know him from our time in western Virginia, before I came east." The two men glanced at each other and then back at the general. The storyteller looked as though he was about to speak but remained silent.

"Is there something else?" inquired Little Mac.

"Yes, sir. It's just that in the fight we was talking about, one of our guns went off in the middle of town. A retreating trooper on horseback ran into the man holding the lanyard."

It took a moment for McClellan to grasp what he was saying. "Firing a field piece in the midst of these fine people?" he waved. "That is shameful! Why, someone could have been killed—a child, perhaps!"

"Yes—but no one we know of got hurt, sir."

Burnside emerged from the tent behind McClellan with a handful of notes, called for a courier, and ordered the dispatches sent.

"General," he announced to Little Mac, "all of your arrangements are in place."

"Excellent, Burn. I am going back into town to watch the men pass. Shall we depart?"

"Certainly, sir. I'd be delighted."

McClellan called loudly for his horse, squeezed the pommel of his saddle with his left hand, and pulled himself onto Dan Webster. Burnside pulled around beside him atop his bob-tailed gray.

Together, they rode toward the cheering heart of the city.

6

Saturday, September 13, 1862

Early Morning to Around Noon

Twelfth Corps, One-Hundred and Twenty-Fifth Pennsylvania Volunteers

Southeast of Frederick, Maryland

Jacob C. Higgins rocked in the saddle as his horse stumbled over a deep hole hidden in the grass. The sturdy 36-year-old ironworker and veteran of the Mexican War glared down past his stirrups to mumble a word of gratitude that the misstep had not broken his mount's leg. Then he spoke the less elegant thought swimming in his head. "Damned groundhogs! Why on earth did the Creator ever make such an accursed thing?"

A handsome, sandy-bearded lieutenant colonel riding beside Higgins stifled a laugh. "Why, they're fine eating, sir!" he replied. "Our Heavenly Father must've thought they'd be good for the pot."

"What are you going on about, Szink?" growled Higgins, casting an irritated look in his lieutenant colonel's direction.

"Cook 'em up with vegetables and potatoes and one hog can feed a whole family, colonel," grinned the round-faced Jacob Szink. A year younger than his commander, and a blacksmith by trade, Szink had volunteered for army service. Now, he found himself in the middle of a real shooting war and the second-in-command of a large infantry regiment called up less than one month earlier. "My mother makes a delicious stew from groundhog meat," Szink continued. "The key is to shoot 'em late in the summer after they've grown fat."

Grim-faced and dark-haired, Higgins blanched at the thought, his mouth twisting into a frown as he ran a gloved palm over his thickly bearded cheeks.

"Look out there, boys—watch your step!" yelled a man behind Higgins.

The colonel glanced over his shoulder to see the front ranks of his regiment approach the patch of groundhog holes and open around them, two men to one side and two to the other. Closing again once they had passed the dangerous obstacle, the column trudged on. The sweat-slick faces of his boys, every one of them a volunteer from the mountainous counties of Blair and Huntingdon in west-central Pennsylvania, stared back at him through tired eyes. The tramping regiment formed but a small part of the much larger First Brigade of the First Division in Alpheus Williams's Twelfth Corps. Three other Pennsylvania regiments, together with a regiment from New York and another from Maine, marched toward Frederick in brigade column.

Their journey from the village of Ijamsville that morning had not been long, but it also had not been easy. Wagons and guns crowded the road, their wheels cutting ruts into the reddish soil, still wet from an overnight downpour. Thousands of hooves churned the clay into slop, tossing it in every direction. "Bloody mud," some men called it. Clinging to everything it touched, the mud dried into a crunchy substance that made walking or sitting a chore.

The stickiness of the muck prompted General Williams's infantry to march alongside the road instead of on it. His soldiers even used farm fields to keep moving, although doing so meant taking down stout fences. Whenever they encountered one, the column would lurch to a stop and stand in formation, some men swearing, others nearly asleep, for as long as ten minutes while pioneers chopped down the sturdy post and rail structures. Once the order to march echoed down the line, the men heaved back into motion. Colonel Higgins himself had long since ordered his drummers to stop beating out time, because every time the men achieved something approaching a steady step, a fresh obstacle would bring them to a halt.

Higgins turned back from his column at the sound of a rifled gun booming in the distance. "What do you think that cannon fire means?" he asked his subordinate, knowing full well that Szink, an inexperienced captain just a month ago and an inexperienced lieutenant colonel today, had no idea.

Szink shrugged. "I reckon it's our cavalry after the Rebs. Gotta find 'em sometime."

"Probably," grumbled Higgins. "The thought of meeting the enemy now gives me no pleasure. No indeed," he added dourly. "They're not like the Mexicans we fought in forty-seven. Them poor bastards could hardly load their muskets. These Rebs, though—I tell you there's nothing quite like 'em." Higgins leaned in close to his lieutenant colonel, who did likewise until their heads were but a few feet apart.

"Szink, we are too green!" he whispered. "We're not ready. Not even close."

Szink nodded, but held his tongue, knowing it would not do for the men to overhear the colonel's doubts. Higgins, well, he knew what he was talking about. He had served with the Second Pennsylvania under General Winfield Scott in Mexico and got wounded storming Castle Chapultepec. Refusing to remain behind, Higgins had returned to the ranks to join his comrades when they entered Mexico City the next day.

"I long to get into the fight, Szink," continued Higgins, "but part of me hopes it never happens—at least not anytime soon with these boys—until they're ready."

Thinking back over the last month, Szink recalled mustering in on the sixteenth of August before traveling by a modified cattle car from Harrisburg to Washington. Three days later, the regiment entered the fortifications in northern Virginia and began training. Eight hours of drill per day consumed their time and every ounce of energy they had until orders arrived two weeks later, calling them into Maryland. They had marched with other members of the Twelfth Corps for the next seven days straight and were now approaching Frederick City.

Could fourteen days of drill possibly be enough when the time came to fight?

Szink pushed the thought from his mind as the lumbering column crested a lush hilltop. Below them curled the Monocacy River, winding its way through the valley like a thick silver thread. Higgins and Szink took in the spires of Frederick beyond the river, framed beautifully by the heights of Catoctin Mountain. Both men breathed deeply of the late summer air. Only the unsettling thunder of Alfred Pleasonton's fight for Hagan's Gap west of the city marred the otherwise glorious view.

"Well, now we know where the fighting is," observed Higgins dryly.

Ahead of them a long column of Bluecoats—other regiments of the Twelfth Corps—waded the Monocacy's shallows. Thousands had already crossed over, their ranks covering the fields before Frederick. Higgins motioned for the regimental column to continue as the pair of officers sat atop their horses. Neither officer had seen so many men at the same time.

"My word!" exclaimed Szink. "It looks like the entire army is here."

The colonel grunted as he raised a pair of binoculars to study troops off to the left camped apart from the members of his own corps. "Second Corps there," he informed Szink, pointing to the dark mass in the distance. "Sumner's men." Then he pivoted his glasses to the right. "Hmm. I think that's the Ninth Corps over yonder."

"Burnside?" offered his lieutenant colonel.

"Nope," shot back Higgins. "He may be there, but I hear he has some grand command now. Bigger than a corps."

Szink frowned. "I hadn't heard that. Who has Ninth Corps?"

Higgins shrugged. "Who knows? You think they call me in and tell me what's happening in the other corps? I barely know what the hell is happening in ours. Let's cross the river and join them."

Down the long grade, the Pennsylvanians trudged, dodging dislodged fence rails along the way. Within a few minutes, the soldiers slid down a steep embankment into the water. Once the regiment emerged on the far side, Higgins organized his command and a courier arrived with orders where to lead his men. The colonel pointed the way, and the troops marched into a stubble field of wheat hemmed in by the other regiments of General Williams's command.

"Fall out!" shouted Szink. The captains of the companies repeated the order, and the regiment broke into companies. The colonel, meanwhile, climbed off his horse with a scowl on his face. His men occupied a narrow area between regiments that was nowhere near large enough to conduct maneuvers. Higgins heaved a sigh. At least the men could refresh their practice of simple commands and mock firing drill.

"Szink! Have the company commanders report to me, if you please."

The lieutenant colonel set about gathering the captains in command of the regiment's ten companies while Higgins fished out his watch. Using the pad of his thumb, he clicked the side and popped open the cover: ten past twelve. It had taken them over five hours to cover the seven miles from Ijamsville to Frederick. Higgins closed the timepiece and stuck it back in his pocket. Shading his eyes, he glanced at the sun hanging directly overhead. A few wispy clouds moved lazily across the azure sky.

It's going to get even hotter, he thought as he removed his hat and used a yellowing handkerchief to wipe perspiration from his ample forehead.

"Sir! The company commanders are assembled."

With his hat back in place, Higgins clasped his hands behind his back and turned to face the line of captains. Szink strode up to take a place by the colonel's side.

"Gentlemen!" exclaimed Higgins. "We are going to drill."

A chorus of groans rang out. "Begging your pardon, colonel," replied Captain Gardner of Company K, "but the men have been marching all morning. Drilling them is going to feel like punishment." The others looked at one another, nodding in agreement until a burst of cheering in a nearby field interrupted them.

"Sir," spoke up Captain Gregg of Company H. "I heard that Colonel Knipe of the Forty-Sixth is letting his men go into town a bit for refreshment." He paused before adding, "hear too the townsfolk are mad with joy that we are here, and the Rebs have skedaddled."

Unmoved by this, Higgins stared daggers at the man, sensing a whiff of insubordination.

"Sir," whispered Szink, adding kindling to the embers glowing in the colonel's heart, "it might do the men some good to do likewise."

Higgins edged over until his face was just inches from the nose of his second-in-command. "Never contradict me in front of the men," he hissed. "Ever!" Stunned by the rebuke, Szink cast his eyes downward. "I'm sorry, sir," he whispered, "that was not my intent."

"The hell it wasn't," shot back the colonel before returning to face his captains. "I recognize your concern for the well-being of the men. I also appreciate your desire to celebrate with the inhabitants of this place," he began firmly, albeit more calmly than Szink or any of those listening had anticipated. "But the Hundred and Twenty-Fifth has yet to accomplish anything. What is there for *us* to celebrate?" The colonel's voice grew louder. "Have we earned the accolades of anyone—of our loved ones at home or of our great nation?" he continued, his gaze ranging from captain to captain. The once-hopeful look on Captain Gregg's face melted away. "Not a man in this regiment has fired a shot in anger," Higgins continued, "but the enemy sure as hell has—and think of what *he* has accomplished this past spring and summer while every man here was still wearing civilian clothes!"

Waving his finger back and forth, the colonel's voice rose in both pitch and volume. "This army was at the gates of Richmond, where our noble General McClellan led it—and Lee and his demons threw us back! Then they kicked John Pope's sorry western behind all the way back into the fortifications around our beloved capital where we, gentlemen, sat safe in earthen forts."

Higgins paused to wipe spittle from the corner of his mouth. Then he drew in a deep breath, exhaled, and began again, although softer now, in an almost fatherly tone. "Two weeks of drill is all our men have had. Do any of you believe this is enough?" Not a captain met his gaze. "Let's be honest with one another. In our present state, does this regiment stand a chance in a fair fight against the Rebs?"

"No, sir," replied one captain quietly.

Nodding like a professor who had just stumped his best students, Higgins scanned the sweating faces before him. "We will drill this afternoon before I grant a single one of you leave to attend what's taking place over yonder," he concluded, tilting his head toward the noisy regiment nearby.

"Bugler!" A young man with the brass instrument hurried to the colonel's side. "Blow assembly, corporal."

The metallic notes carried across the field, cutting short conversations and catnaps. Nine hundred exhausted men, most of them groaning or complaining, struggled to their feet, and, after some confusion, they formed into lines. Higgins swung himself back atop his black horse and walked it out in front of the collected regiment, noticing as he did the amused look of spectators from the other regiments sprawled nearby or leaning on fences to watch the Pennsylvania boys suffer under the hot sun.

"Count off!" The men did as ordered, calling out "one, two, one, two, one, two!" until they reached the last man, who shouted, "end of file!"

"Right shoulder arms!"

Szink walked his horse next to the colonel's and together they watched as the captains put the men through their paces.

"Company front!" yelled Captain Gardner. The men of K Company twisted about, half of them confused by the order. "Mother of God—front, damn you!"

"Not that bad," offered Szink nervously. Higgins chewed his lower lip, a ponderous silence hanging around him.

A musket clattered to the ground. Several men ran into one another and two nearly came to blows. "What the hell is this?" screamed another of the regiment's captains. "Dress this line!"

Higgins urged his horse down the front until he stopped before a young man facing entirely the wrong direction. "Look at this, Szink," the colonel complained. "This greenhorn has no idea what to do."

The youth's face glowed with sweat, his ruddy cheeks smudged with dirt and blonde hair sticking out like straw from under the brim of his blue kepi. When he finally realized his mistake, the boy pivoted in the proper direction, his eyes locked on the man beside him. The mounted officers watched as he executed each of his captain's commands an instant too late.

"Stop!" shouted Higgins in frustration. "Private, what is your name and rank?"

"Pree-vat Johann Steiger, Herr Co-lo-nel!"

"Son, every man in the regiment has been through these steps. Why are you having such difficulty?" Captain Gregg trotted up to watch the exchange.

"Excuse, please, Co-lo-nel. *Alles ist für mich ... um ... verwirrend.*"

Higgins glared at Szink. "What is this man saying? I don't understand Dutch." Szink shrugged.

"Sir, he says he's confused," volunteered the private by Steiger's side.

"What is he confused about?"

"About the drill orders, sir. Johann doesn't speak English too good."

"I know many of these men were not born in this magnificent country," barked Higgins, "but English or otherwise, he's been hearing the same handful of commands for a while now!"

"He's not the only one, sir," offered Captain Gregg.

Again, Higgins chewed his lip, biting harder this time. "How many more like him are there?" he sighed.

"At least a half a dozen in my company," continued Gregg. "Maybe a dozen? All recent immigrants from central Europe. This man here is from Bavaria, for instance."

"Ja, ja, Bayern, Herr Co-lo-nel!" smiled Steiger eagerly.

"I wasn't aware we had so many in the ranks who still could not understand simple drill instructions," commented Higgins. "You there," he pointed, addressing his question to the man next to Steiger. "You speak Dutch, correct?"

"Yes, sir," he began, before catching himself. "Well, no, sir. Sir, it's German, not Dutch."

"Fine. Translate the commands for Private Steiger here so he understands what to do. And you will do it in battle as well—clear?"

"Yes, sir. I'll inform him."

Higgins gazed at the rows of blue before him, crying out, "are there other men here who do not comprehend my words?" Walking his mount slowly along the line and then between companies, the men remained still. "Come now," he added. "I know there are more here from other lands! By a show of hands, are there men here who cannot speak English?" Several soldiers in the ranks turned and mumbled something to the man standing next to him.

Five hands rose into the air.

"Ah, you are revealed at last! We will remedy this right now. Those of you who can translate the drill instructions, do so for their comrades," ordered the colonel. "No man will remain ignorant of our commands. Pair up, and you will go into battle with your man next to you. Understood?" Heads nodded in the ranks. "Good. Now, Lieutenant Colonel Szink, carry on!"

Drill resumed as Higgins walked his horse back through the companies to the front of the regiment. He watched their every move under the scorching midday sun as they progressed from front-changing maneuvers to mock loading and bayonet drills. An hour passed. Then a second. When the colonel finally gave the order to fall out, the exhausted men collapsed into the trampled wheat to the mocking cheers of other Twelfth Corps troops watching them from nearby.

The colonel climbed down from his horse and called for Szink to reassemble the captains, who were told to issue passes into the city for men who had excelled in drill. "I'll allow the others to enter as well," he added, "but not until those who truly earned the reward have returned."

An orderly pulled the saddle and blanket from the colonel's horse as the exhausted officer removed his hat and gloves. Taking a gulp of warm water from his canteen, Higgins wet his handkerchief and wiped the perspiration from his forehead before reclining against his saddle.

Szink slumped down beside him. "The commissary wagons have just arrived. I've told the men to secure whatever food they can."

"I could use some myself," admitted Higgins, who waved over an orderly and asked him to fetch something to eat. "On second thought, not yet," he yawned. "I'm more tired than hungry. I'll get something later."

Szink pulled off his own gauntlets as he gazed across the large field of Pennsylvanians kindling fires, boiling coffee, and heading into town. "Colonel, you were right drilling the men today," he acknowledged. "I thought the decision harsh at first, but I'm glad we put them through the paces."

Higgins grunted low, his booted foot twitching in reply. Already he lay sound asleep, snoring softly under the brim of his well-worn cap.

7

Saturday, September 13, 1862
Around Mid-Afternoon
Eighth Illinois Cavalry Regiment, Army of the Potomac
West of Frederick, Maryland

Armstrong Custer could barely contain his frustration. For most of the morning, and now into the afternoon, he had waited beside his horse while Major Medill's troopers with the Eighth Illinois Cavalry worked their way toward the summit of Catoctin Mountain. Eavesdropping on the reports sent to Medill from the front kept Custer apprised of the situation, but the news also made him edgy. The fighting between Pleasonton's command and J.E.B. Stuart's Rebel rearguard had grown more intense as the morning progressed, leading Pleasonton to send for infantry support from Ambrose Burnside. None had appeared, though, despite assurances from the army's right-wing commander that men were on the way.

Pleasonton, in the meantime, brought up all the artillery he could collect to blast the Rebels from the mountain's eastern slope. Batteries topped the hillsides below Custer, their salvos shaking the ground beneath his feet. Rebel guns on the summit replied by dropping shells among Pleasonton's men, and the stalemate continued.

"How can this be taking so damned long?" Custer hissed.

And then, in the space of only a few minutes, the situation turned abruptly in Pleasonton's favor. Hope rose in Custer's heart when Medill received a report that his troopers had forced back the Rebel left. A second dispatch arrived on the heels of the first, claiming that Major George Chapman's Indiana boys had reached the summit on the right side of the enemy line. Reveling in the news, Custer raised his field glasses to follow the progress of the Hoosiers. Through wisps of smoke, he spied the Stars and Stripes flapping by a stone wall and several men in blue waving their caps. A second later, their cheering met Custer's ears. The enemy's fire petered out, cannons first, followed by muskets. Then only clouds of powder smoke remained, floating softly down the hillside.

"We've done it!" cried Custer, pulling down his glasses. "Major, we've won!"

Returning Custer's grin, Medill peered up the road through his own binoculars in the hope of glimpsing the Rebel withdrawal. For a moment, he thought he spotted a crimson battle flag in the afternoon light, but it disappeared in a flash over the mountain's crest.

"Bugler, blow the call for assembly!" cried Medill, sliding his glasses back into their case as a rider pelted up the road toward him. Yanking his mount to halt just a few yards away, the messenger cried out, "Major, the enemy is running off! General Pleasonton says you are to gather your command for the pursuit."

"Report to the general that we are doing so now," shot back Medill before sending off the courier with his reply.

The shrill call of assembly filled Custer's ears, swelling the excitement in his heart. "Here's our chance now, Wellington!" he announced to his horse. "At last, we'll get into this fight!"

Medill walked up to Custer, his boot heels crunching the gravel of the National Road. "Well, captain, opportunity beckons," he chuckled.

"It does indeed, sir," laughed Custer. "If you're not opposed, I'd like to ride to General Pleasonton before we move out. He may have instructions from headquarters that I should know."

"You have my leave to go, Custer, but if there is anything important afoot, I ask you to come back and tell me as quickly as possible."

"I will, major. You have my word."

The officers exchanged salutes before Custer reached for Wellington's reins, jumped into the saddle, and spurred down the crowded road to the base of the hill. Nudging Wellington into a hollow behind a low hilltop, Custer approached the general.

Pleasonton himself, one gloved hand on each hip, spotted Custer and called out to him in a voice brimming with enthusiasm. "Captain, you are here at a good time! Wait just a moment while I dictate this message for General McClellan."

Pleasonton turned to a captain standing beside him. "Take this down," he ordered. "'General, we have carried the Rebel position with my cavalry and artillery. Infantry too late. Will pursue.' Do you have that?"

The man nodded, carefully tore the page from his dispatch book, and handed it over. Pleasonton folded the message and extended his hand to Custer, still in the saddle.

Custer shot him a confused look, tinted with disappointment. "You want me to deliver the note?"

"I do, captain. You are McClellan's emissary, and this information is important. He will want it as soon as possible."

Custer could feel blood rising into his cheeks. "General, I must protest!" he snapped. "Major Medill kept me out of this morning's fight and now you want me to play courier rather than pursue the enemy! I can be of greater service in the field, sir."

"Now, now, don't be cross," chided Pleasonton. "This is vital business."

Swallowing his disappointment, Custer nodded slowly. "I understand, sir. General McClellan must know of our success. It's just—I'd hoped to join in the hunt. Your command is going after the Johnnies, isn't it?"

"It is, and you may rejoin us in Middletown Valley. Just get this message to General McClellan first. Every decision he makes from now on depends on it."

Custer, left with no choice but to submit to his fate, grudgingly accepted the note. "As you wish," he grumbled before swinging Wellington around and spurring him out of the hollow toward Frederick.

Heavy columns of troops clogged the road into the city, forcing Custer to weave his way through the formations. Each time he spotted an officer, Custer called out, "McClellan? Do you know where I can find the commanding general?" Heads shook and shoulders shrugged until a colonel with a heavy beard riding a white horse looked across the top of the marching men and called back, "I heard General McClellan is in the center of town, captain."

Nodding thanks, Custer urged Wellington toward Frederick, guiding his mount around, and sometimes through, throngs of cursing men who did not take kindly to an unfamiliar horseman shoving them aside. A band playing the "Battle Hymn of the Republic" tramped past him, flowers protruding from their hat bands and muzzles. When he reached the town, Custer turned down a side alley until he found a quiet route running parallel to the crowded main street.

Onward Wellington carried Custer toward the main thoroughfare until a wall of civilians waving hats and small flags blocked his way. Pulling up behind the crowd, Custer peered east down the street to see if he could spot McClellan, but a regiment tramping toward him with its musicians in front blaring out "Yankee Doodle" blocked his view. With a scowl, Custer looked west toward the main intersection. At last, he spotted the general.

Little Mac sat atop his black horse half a block away, flanked by several officers. Flowers fluttered down around the general, and a bright wreath of white and yellow blossoms hung from the pommel of his saddle. When the head of the regiment filling the street reached McClellan's position, the general straightened his back and returned the commanding officer's salute.

Custer reached down and tapped the shoulder of a man standing beside his stirrup. The townsman looked up. "What can I do for you, general?"

"General?" Custer choked. "Not yet, but thanks for the encouragement. I need to get through this crowd to General McClellan. Can you help me?"

"Sure, we can," replied the man. "Hey, Henry! Can you get the boys here to open a path for this officer? He needs through."

The man called Henry looked up at Custer and gave him a quick nod before passing the word to a pair of men standing beside him. Together, the four men called out for the spectators to step aside and within a few seconds, they had pushed open a gap in the line of ecstatic civilians.

"Much obliged!" shouted Custer with a tip of his hat. Pulling alongside a marching regiment, he spotted a gap in the column and used it to cross the street toward McClellan. Colonel Key saw Custer coming and swiveled in his saddle to greet him. "Captain!" he shouted above the tumult. "What can I do for you?"

Custer drew the note from his pocket. "I have a message for General McClellan from General Pleasonton. He broke through the Rebels on Catoctin Mountain and is in pursuit."

"Ah, that's excellent news!" exclaimed Key with a smile. "The general will be well pleased."

Plucking the paper from Custer's fingers, Key passed the message to the man beside him, who repeated the process by handing it to General Marcy, until the paper finally landed in McClellan's hand. Little Mac unfolded it and grinned. When he caught Marcy's eye, the older man pointed to Custer, whose crisp salute McClellan speedily returned. A few moments later, men with the general's security detachment halted an approaching regiment to allow McClellan and his mounted escort to move into the street. The commanding general spurred Dan Webster to the west, his entourage in pursuit. Satisfied he had done his duty well, Custer followed along through the flag-waving populace.

Stopping on the road amidst the crowded fields outside of Frederick, the general addressed a bearded officer sitting his horse next to the road. Custer walked Wellington close enough to hear the conversation.

"General Cox, it is good to see you again, but the hour is approaching two o'clock!" exclaimed Little Mac. "Why is your command not underway?"

"Sir, my compliments," replied Cox, an acquaintance from Ohio who sat taller in the saddle than the general. "My leading regiments are forming up, but some men are still in Frederick. They have been patrolling for Rebels. I anticipate we will all leave shortly."

"Very well," nodded McClellan. "But if you see General Rodman on the way, pick him up and take him with you. General Burnside sent him this way hours ago to support Pleasonton, but he hasn't been heard from since. I fear he may have taken the road to Harpers Ferry instead of this route ahead."

"As you wish, sir," saluted Cox. McClellan promptly returned the gesture and guided Dan Webster off the road toward a low hillside carpeted with clover. A cluster of hastily erected tents stood among the field of green. McClellan climbed down from the saddle in the center of the busy, but sparse, headquarters and called out for his maps. Lifting a canteen, he drank deeply for several seconds before turning to face Custer.

"Captain, it's good to see you again," he said, shaking Custer's hand. "Tell me about the fight this morning."

Custer recounted his narrow escape with Private Heaton and the details surrounding Pleasonton's effort. McClellan listened patiently until Custer commented that no infantry had arrived to support the cavalry.

"The general mentions that in his note," scowled Little Mac. "Burnside sent General Rodman to assist Pleasonton, but word has it he took the wrong road. At least part of his command is south of here, near Jefferson." McClellan waved his hand as if to brush away the mistake. "No matter. Pleasonton is through, and I must plan the army's advance into Middletown Valley."

"Sir, your map is ready," announced Marcy, who had spread it out on a nearby table. McClellan yanked off his gloves and strode past two soldiers carrying a piece of furniture into his tent.

"Now that Pleasonton has cleared the Catoctin pass, I will order him to open the road to Harpers Ferry," he declared, while tapping his forefinger on the map. "Captain Custer, did Pleasonton have any news of the Secesh in Middletown Valley?"

"Not the last time I saw him, sir. Our men had just driven off the Rebels. None of our boys, except maybe those in front, had time to see what lay over the mountain."

McClellan nibbled gently on the tip of his thumb. "Until we receive more information, I will proceed as planned. General Marcy, send word for Burnside to push into the next valley with General Reno's Ninth Corps." Marcy nodded as he scribbled in his dispatch book.

Colonel Key, who stood next to the general, quietly pointed out an approaching courier.

The group watched the rider rein in just beyond the circle of tents, vault from his saddle, and hurry into the encampment. "General McClellan, sir!" he saluted. "General Williams sends his compliments!"

"Acknowledged, corporal. Do you have something for me?"

"I do, sir." The man dug a folded piece of paper out of the satchel hanging at his side. "Colonel Pittman, General Williams's adjutant, assures me it is important." Major Albert Colburn of McClellan's staff snatched the document from the courier's hand and handed it to his chief.

"Let's see what has Williams so worked up," said Little Mac and, unfolding the paper, he began to read. After a few seconds had passed, he turned the document over to study the reverse side. "Curious," he mumbled, flipping back to Williams's note:

> General, I enclose a general special order of Gen. Lee, commanding Rebel army, which was found on the field where my corps is encamped. It is a document of interest and is genuine. The document was found by a corporal of 27 Ind. Regt., Col. Colgrove commanding, Gordon's Brigade.

"Hum, very curious indeed!" said McClellan, louder this time as he studied the enclosed document more carefully. His eyes moved rapidly down the page.

The men around McClellan looked at each other as they shuffled in place. Custer noticed Little Mac's hand shaking.

"Sir, what is it?" asked Marcy.

"Never you mind, general," said McClellan. "I will reveal all in good time. First, I need to send a message to General Pleasonton." Handing the paper to Colburn, McClellan ordered him to make a copy of it. Then he turned to his chief of staff. "Marcy, take a note for Pleasonton."

Marcy opened his dispatch book and picked up a pencil. "Ready, sir."

McClellan clasped his hands behind his back and paced around behind the table as he dictated. "General, the following order of march of the enemy came into my hands today," he began in a measured tone of voice. "It is dated September nine. I desire you to ascertain whether the enemy has thus far followed this order. Be warned that the passes through the Blue Ridge may be disputed by two columns, so you are to exercise great caution in approaching them." He paused to look at Marcy. "Do you have that?"

Marcy, who was still scribbling, nodded as the tip of his tongue poked out from the corner of his lips. "I do, sir."

"Good. Then add this postscript. Colonel Sanders's cavalry reported yesterday that an enemy force of thirty thousand men was at Burkittsville in Middletown Valley. Is there any truth to this report?"

"Is . . . there . . . any . . . truth," muttered Marcy. "I've got it."

"Excellent!" exclaimed Little Mac. "Now write that up properly and have it sent to General Pleasonton posthaste."

Marcy left to find a pen and ink while McClellan waved for Colonel Key and Major Colburn to come in close. "Gentlemen," he began, leaning forward on the table, "General Williams forwarded to me a copy of General Lee's operational orders dated nine September. They provide a detailed account of the Rebel army's positions—if the orders have been followed to this point. Verification of this is what I hope to receive from General Pleasonton." He paused, glancing at their stunned faces. "If the Rebels have followed Lee's orders, and I see no reason why they would not, then Harpers Ferry is in grave danger. It also means that Lee has divided his army into multiple columns, offering me the opportunity to strike him and potentially destroy his command. Providence has delivered a great gift into my hands."

Colburn and Key began muttering to one another, leading McClellan to call for silence. "You must keep quiet about this!" he hissed. "Go about your duties. I will call on you as needed. Dismissed!"

As the staffers dispersed, McClellan retreated to his tent to ponder the stunning intelligence and weigh its truth. Did he really have a copy of Lee's orders, or was the document a ruse designed to send him off chasing wild geese?

"Pleasonton will tell me," He mumbled while staring at the pen and ink before him. Then the general grinned and rubbed his chin. "Bobby Lee," he whispered, "you have made a gross mistake, and I will make you pay dearly for it."

8

Saturday, September 13, 1862

Noon to Evening

Twenty-Third Ohio Infantry Regiment, Kanawha Division, Ninth Corps

From West Frederick to Middletown Valley, Maryland

Two men in dark worn uniforms wolfed down scrambled eggs and strong black coffee as the dumbfounded family that took them in that morning looked on.

The idea to knock on doors until someone fed them had been Tom Kelly's, accustomed as he was to beg for food back in famine-stricken Ireland. David Parker, muttering something about pride, initially refused to participate. Kelly dismissed his moaning with a wave of his calloused hand.

"I reckon you're as hungry as I am," he grinned. "Let's see what we can get."

As if on cue, Parker felt his stomach roll and bubble. Falling sheepishly into line, he determined to let Kelly do the talking. The pair moved from one door to the next after being turned away at each. It was not until the fifth house that a man with a long, kindly face and a dark chin beard finally took pity on them. Kelly explained they had been detailed to patrol the city for Rebels before politely requesting something to "quell the pangs of hunger."

"Far be it for me to refuse the heroes who liberated our dear town," said the man, pausing as he looked down, "but you can't enter here with those dusty boots. The missus would have my hide for it. Go around to the back and I'll let you in the kitchen entrance."

"We're much obliged," mumbled an embarrassed Parker, hefting his musket before following Kelly around the house to a small yard enclosed by a wrought-iron fence. A brass angel poised atop a plume of water occupied the center of the quaint and well-tended garden. Kelly paused a moment to admire it, inhaling deeply of a flowering vine on a trellis of slatted wood that offered small pink blossoms, which threw off a delicious scent. As the essence filled his nose, he closed his eyes and thought of life far from the war. Then the door of the house creaked open, snapping him back to reality.

"Alright, boys, you may come in now," said the older gentleman.

The two friends removed their kepis and entered the house. Both noticed that their dirty brogans left faint prints on the plank floor. A plump woman in her forties stood quietly at the far side of the room, her arms crossed and a wary but warm look on her face. She wore her thick brownish hair parted down the middle and pulled tightly into a bun that rested just above the back of her high-collared gray linen dress. Beside her stood a dark-haired girl of seventeen, her hands clasped anxiously before her.

"Good morning, ma'am, sir, young miss," bowed Kelly politely. "Our thanks to ye for taking pity on us."

"Yes, thank you kindly," added Parker. "We don't eat regular on the march."

"You're quite welcome, gentlemen," said the matron of the house. "My name is Dorothy Grafton. This is my daughter, Emily." She tilted her head at the girl. "You've met my husband, Jed. I must say you're a welcome sight compared to those rotten Secessionists who were just in town." She gestured toward a table in the center of the room. "Take a seat and I'll whip up some breakfast for you."

Jed motioned for Kelly and Parker to lean their muskets against the wall and tuck their caps into their belts. Within minutes, the aroma of frying pork sausage, eggs, and potatoes filled the air. Kelly's mouth watered with anticipation and he wiped his moist lips on his sleeve. Emily sat opposite the two men while Jed poured them coffee.

"Where are you fellows from?" she asked.

"Ohio," replied Parker, "but my friend here hails from Ireland, 'riginally."

"Ireland? My goodness, that's a long way to come," gasped Jed. "Whatever brought you here, and in an army uniform, no less?"

"Davey left out that I been here going on ten years," replied Kelly. "Come over to escape the famine." Jed offered a grim smile at the mention of the plight suffered by the Irish. "Since then, I've been working a riverboat on the Ohio and Mississippi. America offers the opportunity for a man to make his own way. That's not so in me own land. The war ended me job on the boat, though, so I joined up to fight. Simple as that."

"Makes sense," nodded Jed. "And you, Mister Parker? You're native born, I take it?"

Parker leaned back in his chair. "Yes, sir. In Cincinnati. But some years back, my father moved me and my mother to a small place called Portsmouth. That's on the Ohio River. They raised me up there, and there I was when the war came. Tom and I worked the river together until all this began and trade with Kentucky stopped."

"Have you seen a lot of fighting?" asked Emily shyly. Dorothy shot her daughter a sharp glare as she set fresh coffee on the table.

"Could say we have, I guess," replied Kelly, catching Dorothy's eye to nod thanks. "Mostly bushwhackers in western Virginia. We've only been east a few weeks."

"They brought us here to put some backbone into the eastern army," grinned Parker. "Seems these Potomac boys need some instruction on how to fight Rebs proper. We're here to show 'em the way."

"Mm-mm, ma'am, this coffee's grand," announced Kelly after taking a deep slurp from his cup. "It's good and strong. Just the way I like it."

Parker sipped his, adding, "it beats boiling it in the field, too."

"I'm glad you like it, gentlemen," called the lady Grafton from the stove. "Now get yourselves ready to eat because the vittles are just about cooked."

Parker and Kelly tucked cloth napkins into their collars and waited impatiently while Dorothy heaped their plates full.

"Mmf. This is mighty fine, mithhus," muttered Parker, coming up for breath between bites.

"Aye! Seconds to that," added Kelly, biting down on a hunk of sausage.

"Best slow down or you'll make yourselves sick!" advised Dorothy, smiling at the favorable reaction to her cooking.

Kelly gulped down the rest of his coffee and held his cup out for more. "Ahh! Tis not likely, ma'am. If ye only saw what little we usually get."

"What do you men eat?" asked Emily.

"Lately corn off the stalk and green apples," replied Parker, "and maybe some beef here and there, or a little pork, if we're lucky. No salt, though. Most of the time we break our teeth on hardtack."

"Accent on the *hard*," winked Kelly. "Those tooth breakers will send ye to the camp dentist right quick if ye don't soften 'em in coffee or water before bitin'."

"That's awful," frowned Jed. "You boys serving our flag ought to be eating like kings."

"On that, we agree," grinned Parker, lifting his cup in a toast. Jed raised his to meet the gesture. "Truth is, we ain't."

Scraping his plate with his fork, Parker asked for a second helping. Dorothy graciously provided more food to both men until they had consumed their fill. Then Kelly sat back with his hands folded across his belly. "Oh my," he belched. "Apologies, ma'am. It slipped out." Emily stifled a laugh. "That was something special, Missus Grafton. You make one heck of a breakfast fry."

A muffled voice from outside the house reached Parker's ear. "Tom, do you hear that?"

Kelly paused. "I do. What's he saying? Can ye make it out?"

His friend wiped his mouth with his sleeve and then remembered his napkin, pulling the cloth from his collar. Jed opened the kitchen door and all three men stepped outside.

"Men with the Twenty-Third Ohio! Report to Colonel Hayes!" The voice rang out clearly in the morning air above the clopping hooves of his horse. "Regiment's forming up, boys. Report in!"

Sighing, Kelly turned back to the kitchen. "We're sorry to eat and run, ma'am, but duty calls. A thousand thanks for the breakfast. It set us right."

"You boys are welcome," replied Dorothy with a warm smile. "It's the least we could do."

Jed retrieved their muskets and handed them to the friends, who hefted their weapons and stepped off the porch. Pulling on his kepi, Parker looked back at the family gathered outside the door.

"We're grateful for your hospitality," he said.

"May God be with you boys," waved Jed as Kelly and Parker walked back to the street.

Thirty minutes later, they strode into the regimental encampment to find their comrades standing in formation, knapsacks in place and rifle stocks resting on the ground.

"It's about damned time you two showed up!" griped Sergeant Lyon. "We've been standing here near an hour. I was just about to report you for desertion. Now grab your things and fall in. The entire division's got orders to move out."

Sam Carey and the others in Company C chuckled, while Parker and Kelly retrieved their possessions and slung their knapsacks onto their backs. Pulling the straps tight, Kelly slid into the company's second rank on the outside, with Parker taking his place just in front of him. Bugles blared, drums rapped, and one after the other the regiments merged into a long column heading west on the gravel road toward Catoctin Mountain.

Kelly shot a glance at Carey. "Sam, what's happening? We could hear cannon fire from town. Did the cavalry clear the way?"

"That they did, after several hours," nodded Sam as he fidgeted with his belt buckle and pushed his canteen farther onto his back. "You didn't hear the fighting stop?"

"I can't say I did. Davey and me got lucky. A family in town fed us breakfast and coffee. *Good* coffee! Am I right, Davey?"

"That's right, boys. We're marching on full bellies," announced Parker loudly enough for men several ranks away to hear.

Sam shook his head with envy. "Lucky sons-a-bitches. We got orders to fall in and support the cavalry on the mountain while you were on patrol." When Kelly shot him a quizzical look, Sam added, "the colonel couldn't send us. Too many had gone into town."

"You shared our good fortune, then, Sam," laughed Parker.

"I guess. Wish you'd brought something to eat, though. I've had no more than sheet-iron crackers this morning."

"Ye waited in formation for us to come back?" asked Kelly, changing the uncomfortable subject.

"You and a bunch of others," nodded Sam as he turned and spat. "Then we heard the Johnnies had up and run," he continued, wiping his mouth on his cuff, "and orders came to march."

"Shit. We're in front of the division again?"

"Appears so. Like the colonel says, these eastern boys have got nothing on us. If there's a mountain to climb or a Johnny to whip, we're always the first ones in." Sam felt a trickle of sweat run down his neck. "Damn, it's hot."

The conversation fell away as the men trudged on and the road became steeper. Once near the summit, signs of the clash that morning came into view. Dead Rebels, no two dressed alike, littered the side of the road, their limbs already stiffening in the bright sunlight. Kelly stared at one—a bearded, grizzled man whose white hair caked in dried blood made him look too old to be in uniform—before turning abruptly away. It did a man no good to stare at death for too long. Better to focus on taking the next step in life. So, Kelly ogled the back of the man in front of him and trudged over the mountain crest. The road sloped down the other side into a broad green valley. South Mountain loomed hazily in the distance ahead. The low rumble of cannon fire caught everyone's attention, and the men craned their necks to see what awaited them. Marching on the outside of the column, Kelly spotted a line of battle along the crest of a low hill about a mile off.

"Our boys, Davey?"

Parker peered over the shoulder of the man ahead of him, squinting to make out the tiny figures. He shrugged and shook his head before spotting the national flag as another boom rang out. "Yep, ours." A third boom filled the air, followed by a fourth a few moments later.

A company of blue-coated horsemen emerged on a hilltop near four guns straddling the National Road. With drawn sabers glinting in the sunlight, the riders charged over the crest and disappeared. More cavalry appeared on a hill farther to the west.

Probably Rebels in retreat, thought Kelly.

The guns thundered again, but before the Buckeye column had closed the distance, they limbered up and pulled onto the road, rolling toward the spires of Middletown poking just over the hills.

Onward they marched, the column snaking west under the blazing sun. Unsure what to expect, the men around Kelly bantered back and forth about Rebel horsemen. They were close by, but beyond that, no one knew much of anything. Kelly scratched at a patch of skin itching from the sweat under his uniform. The band of his cap felt hot and wet. Fortunately, the gunfire echoing ahead grew fainter, and within another few minutes a column of black smoke rose ominously into the western sky.

"What do you think is burning?" asked Sam of no one in particular.

"Looks like that village up there," replied Parker, with a glance over his left shoulder. "Damned Johnnies probably set it on fire."

The men of the Twenty-Third slogged up a long hill, over its crest, and down the far side into Middletown. Just as the inhabitants of Frederick had done, the people here greeted them like liberators. Kelly and his comrades picked up their step, standing tall as they entered the village to loud cheering and smiling faces. Red, white, and blue bunting flew from open windows and flags appeared everywhere. Best of all for the men, the town's female population lined the streets with all manner of food and drink. A gleeful young miss thrust a thick slice of bread covered with butter at Tom Kelly. He seized it with a hearty grin, took a massive bite, and chewed happily until, in a pang of conscience, he glanced over at the famished man marching next to him. Staring hungrily at the bread, Sam met Kelly's eyes and looked away.

"Here, Sam," said Kelly, extending the bread to his comrade. "You take it. I had me fill earlier."

"Bless your heart, Tom!" grinned Sam, who promptly devoured what was left in two large bites.

Kelly watched as a jug of cider made its way down the column, rising and falling as it passed hand to hand. Captain Skiles stalked after it, peering intently into the marching column.

"You men, hand that over!" he demanded, reaching through the ranks.

"But, cap'n, it's just cider!" rose a complaint.

Pulling the stopper, Skiles sniffed and raised the jug to his lips. "Ah!" he smiled broadly. "You're right, boys, this is just cider! I thought it was applejack. You know how the colonel feels about intoxicants. Alright, carry on." A dozen men cheered when he handed the jug to the man walking beside him—just in time for Kelly to grab himself a swig. The sweet juice flowed down his parched throat, washing away the dust of the road.

Onward through the village they marched until the booming of cannon died away and the sun slipped behind South Mountain. Cresting a tall hillside just west of Middletown, Kelly looked over his shoulder to see a solid column of men in dark blue flowing down the western face of the Catoctins. A sense of relief poured over him then. He and his comrades would not have to face the Rebels alone, although to be fair, not a man in the regiment had spied a Grayback up close that day. The Irishman uttered a silent prayer of thanks as he strode on, grateful that another day had passed without the loss of Buckeye blood.

The column descended another long slope to a winding creek that flowed slowly near the bottom. Beside the creek stood the smoking ruins of a large barn and several outbuildings. An acrid stink floated through the column, burning eyes and parching throats. Colonel Hayes trotted alongside his men, directing them into a pasture on the left that ran down gently to the creek. Orders arrived to fall out and Kelly, Parker, and the rest slipped off their knapsacks before slumping to the ground. Foraging parties fanned out across the area to collect wood and stones for fire rings while others prepared coffee and whatever edibles they carried with them. By the time dusk slipped over the valley, Kelly and his comrades sat around a crackling blaze, swapping tales, writing loved ones, and puffing on their pipes.

"Colonel's coming!" someone hissed out of the darkness. A bottle of whiskey slowly making the rounds disappeared just as Hayes stepped into the flickering firelight, his small staff in tow. "How are you boys doing?" he asked in a deep voice.

"Fine, colonel," replied Sam. "What brings you around?"

"Mind if I sit?"

"Not at all, sir. Make yourself comfortable."

One of the officers behind Hayes handed the colonel a folding camp stool with a canvas seat. Hayes methodically set the stool in the grass, lowered himself onto it, removed his cap, and ran his fingers through his brown hair. When he was ready, he peered through narrow-set eyes at the quiet faces surrounding him.

"I'm out checking on you boys," he said after several seconds. "And want to tell you that I expect we'll meet the enemy tomorrow."

"But we didn't see a single Johnny today!" said Parker.

Hayes gave a slow nod. "That's true, but I'm sure of it, private. General Cox tells me the Rebel rearguard is posted atop that mountain. Just before sundown, General Pleasonton spotted Secessionist infantry up there, too. We're the tip of the spear, gentlemen. No regiment is farther advanced than we and the other Kanawhas."

The news triggered uncomfortable glances, but no one spoke. "I thought it best to come among you boys and ask that you remember why we are here," continued Hayes. "These last few days have been extraordinary. I expect we're all feeling mighty important after the warm greeting we've received from the folks in these parts."

Heads nodded. "Well, boys, tomorrow the reality of why we are here comes home," commented the colonel soberly. "I don't know what we'll find up there, but General Cox says he has the utmost faith we'll get the job done. Remember, we are *Ohio* men," he added with emphasis. "We've only ever seen the backs of the enemy—leastways since General Cox led us in western Virginia. If it comes to it, I know you'll fight well tomorrow. No need to remind you of that. I just wanted you to hear from me personally that I'm proud of each one of you. Now, let's make short work of the enemy tomorrow and go home! Who's with me?"

Kelly lifted his voice with the others in his company, some of whom had gathered around the fire from other campsites nearby. The men waved their caps and cheered. When the shouting fell away, Hayes thanked them with a simple nod, rose to his feet, and moved on with his staff.

"I guess I'd better write my family, seeing as how we might glimpse the elephant in the morning," said Sam.

"Yeah, that would be wise," nodded Kelly as reached for a pouch of tobacco.

"You writing to anyone, Tom?" asked Carey, digging into his knapsack. "I've got enough paper for you, too."

Kelly stared into the fire as a swirl of bluish smoke rose from the bowl of his long-stemmed pipe. "No, Sammy, I'll not be writing. Skilled in letters, I'm not. Me mother taught me to read a bit, but I can't do much writing. Can sign me name, though!" Sam, Davey, and a few others chuckled at this. Kelly shrugged, adding quietly, "besides, I've no one to write to."

"Aw, Tom, that can't be true. Must be someone waiting to hear you're alright," offered Sam.

A sad smile creased Kelly's face as he stared off into the darkness. "Once, there was Sam, a long time ago, but no longer." With that, the Irishman reclined against his knapsack and folded his hands behind his head. Sam turned to his writing, leaving Kelly alone with his thoughts. "There was someone," the Irishman whispered, quickly wiping away a tear that drifted down his cheek. "Long, long ago."

9

Saturday, September 13, 1862
Early Evening
Headquarters of the Army of the Potomac
West of Frederick, Maryland

rocked back on the legs of his camp chair with a stem of grass clenched tightly between his teeth. The initial excitement attending the revelation of General Lee's orders had long since worn off, leaving him stewing restlessly in its wake.

He had hoped McClellan would send him back to the cavalry in Middletown Valley, west of the Catoctins, but when the time came to deliver the general's missive to Pleasonton, McClellan dispatched two other men instead—a private from his security escort, and Lieutenant Nicholas Bowen, a topographical engineer on the headquarters staff. Custer knew Bowen from the spring Peninsula Campaign outside Richmond. He had liked the man then. Now he positively envied him.

Muffled footsteps drew Custer's attention, and he looked back over his shoulder to see Colonel Key striding toward him with a camp stool in his hands. Easing the front legs of his chair to the ground, Custer rose to his feet.

"As you were," said the informal Key. "May I sit?"

"Of course, colonel. I'm happy for the company."

Dropping his stool to the ground, Key cinched up his light-blue pant legs and eased down onto the seat. Custer scrutinized the officer with the dull, saw-tooth summit of Catoctin Mountain silhouetted behind him, its heights framed orange by the setting sun.

"Idleness doesn't suit you," said Key.

Custer pulled the frayed grass stem from his mouth. "No, sir, it does not. I'd rather be in the saddle chasing Johnnies than sitting here at headquarters."

"You should welcome moments of rest during a campaign," consoled Key, his face etched with fatigue. "You'll be back in the field soon enough. I guarantee it."

Custer cast a sidelong glance at the colonel. "Back in the field, sir?"

"The general has plans for you, Custer. He's writing them up as we speak."

Custer peered past Key at the thin triangle of lamplight spilling from the general's tent. McClellan sat inside with a thoughtful expression on his face. Framed by the tent's canvas flaps, he dipped his pen into a well of ink and resumed scratching on the piece of paper laid before him.

"I sometimes wish he would move faster," admitted Custer, looking back at Key. "Don't misunderstand me, colonel, I don't mean to be critical, but the general acts too deliberately for my taste. Take today, for instance. He received information about the enemy that would be the envy of any commander, and yet he has done nothing."

Key's eyebrows arched in surprise as he pushed his pince-nez glasses back onto the bridge of his nose. "Hasn't he?"

Custer eyed the officer, deciding to choose his next words more carefully. "As far as I've been able to tell, that is."

Key studied the twenty-two-year-old with a knowing smirk on his face. "You'd have done things differently, I take it?" He asked in an unmistakably patronizing tone.

Custer blundered past the affront. "Colonel, I'd have gotten this army moving as fast as possible with myself in the saddle at the head of it!" he shot back. "The enemy is out there," Custer urged, pointing a finger west before gesturing around him at the tents and troops huddled around their cookfires. "Not here!"

Key pursed his lips in a tight grin and gently shook his head. "Spoken like a green commander. Captain, do you honestly believe General McClellan has not taken any steps in response to reading General Lee's orders? Did you miss the couriers coming and going all day? The traffic on the National Road? You can see it clearly from here."

Key pointed in the direction of the gravel turnpike leading west out of Frederick, where wagons, guns, and troops trundled along, as they had been the entire day. Now, with darkness nearly upon them, the winking light of bobbing torches marked their progress. "There is General McClellan's reply, Captain Custer—the trailing elements of the Ninth Corps."

"I see them," Custer acknowledged. "But why is Reno the only one in motion? What about all these boys around us?"

"These are General Sumner's men of the Second Corps. They'll receive orders soon enough. The general intends to hold them here until he knows where they'll be needed.

Big doings are afoot, Custer, bigger than you can conceive." Custer shot Key a quizzical look in the fading light. "Custer, our dear commander is preparing to whip General Lee's army."

Fired by the prospect of battle, Custer's eyes sparkled in the lamplight, spilling from McClellan's tent. "So, a big fight's coming?" he asked.

The colonel nodded. "General McClellan is drawing up orders to bring it about as we speak, but they are merely the second part of orders already given. You asked why he hasn't ordered Sumner's men to advance." When Custer remained silent, Key continued. "He wants General Hooker's men to come up first to support Reno's Ninth Corps in Middletown Valley. They are both part of the army's right-wing."

Custer scowled at the news. "But Hooker's corps hasn't even reached Frederick, has it? The last I heard, he was at New Market."

"The general sent him orders earlier today, soon after reading Lee's orders."

Custer shrugged as if to apologize. "I didn't know."

"How could you?" countered Key. "As I said earlier, you can't know everything that transpires. Even now, Hooker is approaching Frederick. General McClellan intends to reunite his corps in the vanguard with General Reno's command, unifying General Burnside's wing of the army, which became separated during the advance. Reno's men marched quickly to get here."

Custer leaned in, grinning as comprehension of McClellan's plans took shape in his mind. "So, Hooker will pass first, and Sumner will move next," he paused before adding, "the question is where will he go—follow Hooker? That would make the most sense."

"It would," confirmed Key, "and he may do that, but that part of the plan is what the general's writing up now."

"Can you share it with me?" inquired Custer.

The colonel considered the request, scratching the side of his face thoughtfully. "Very well, captain. I'll fill you in. The plan General McClellan is now devising will be General Franklin's responsibility. It looks like the Rebs have split their army into multiple columns to capture the garrison at Harpers Ferry. The general will order Franklin's Sixth Corps to advance from its position south of Frederick toward the gap in South Mountain at Burkittsville."

"Burkittsville? I'm not familiar with it," said Custer.

"It's in the next valley, several miles southwest of Middletown. A road there traverses South Mountain into the valley beyond, and that valley opens the path to Harpers Ferry."

Custer nodded slowly as the colonel continued. "McClellan intends to use Franklin's corps to seize the Burkittsville Gap, and push into the heart of Lee's scattered forces. With General Longstreet's command at Boonsborough, and McLaws on the Potomac north of the ferry, we can turn and crush the pieces one by one. He will throw back this invasion," insisted Key, "and when he does, the general will be the hero of the nation. Then he will have the opportunity to act on my political advice."

Custer shot another glance in McClellan's direction before looking back at Key. Shadows cast by the firelight flickered across the man's thin face. "Sir, you said he has plans for me."

"Of course he does," laughed Key, reaching out to pat Custer's forearm. "You'll learn all about it soon enough."

"Colonel, about that advice you just mentioned?" Custer lowered his voice, even though there was no one around them. "Is this what I've been hearing about using the army to bring about a political settlement to the war?"

Key nodded. "Yes, quite probably it is. I know the general trusts you, so there is no harm in letting you know. Indeed, several of the army's senior commanders speak freely of it."

"They do? Which ones?"

"General Franklin, for one. General Porter does also, but he isn't with the army currently." Key thought for a moment. "General Sykes, General Keyes—and even Baldy Smith."

Custer shook his head in amazement. "I had no idea. What is it they discuss?"

Key leaned closer to the captain. "They talk about the folly of the current administration in pursuing this bloody conflict. They think the fool running the War Department—Stanton—has no idea what he is doing, and they suspect the president himself of taking acts that border on illegality. Rebellion against the Constitution is wrong, captain," he insisted, "but radicals have the administration's ear. They seek nothing short of the abolition of slavery as one of the war's primary objectives."

"Abolition!" spat Custer with a shake of his head. "That will force the South to fight harder and longer. There will be no hope of peace, short of the utter destruction of one side or the other."

"Precisely my belief," nodded Key. "The bloodshed we have already seen is nothing compared to what will come." The colonel scanned the hundreds of campfires that had popped up as darkness descended. "Our Southern brethren will fight to the last man against us, and who could blame them? Freeing the slave is not why we are here. It is not why *we* are at war. We in this army with General McClellan are fighting because Southerners rebelled against the lawful election of Abraham Lincoln as president."

Even in the low light, Custer could see that the colonel's face had flushed with a passion that matched his choice of words. "They turned their backs on the compact made by our forefathers—to form an indissoluble Union of States—to form a United States. There is no separation from this union unless it is agreed upon by all the states and decided procedurally through a vote in Congress. No state can simply declare the union dissolved and walk away from it, as South Carolina and the others have done."

"I swore an oath to defend the Constitution and I am here to see that through," declared Custer. "But I have many acquaintances in the Rebel army. It was old Jeff Davis himself who recommended me for West Point—did you know that?" He paused to take in the look of surprise on the colonel's face. "He and the others are men of conviction.

They think secession is just and consider their property rights inviolable. If the administration is truly moving to make abolition a war aim, as you say, well, that's a step toward the abyss. If the government can declare one form of property illegal," continued Custer with a wave of a hand, "then what is to stop it from taking everything else a man has?"

Key slapped his knees with delight. "Exactly, captain! I am glad to see you understand the importance of what is happening!" The colonel shot a furtive glance toward McClellan's tent and lowered his voice. "This is why several of us have urged the general to turn the army back on Washington and force the administration to negotiate an end to the war. We'll throw out that scoundrel, Stanton, and gently persuade Lincoln to bring the war to a peaceful conclusion on the basis of how things were before the Rebs fired on Sumter. We can work out our differences like proper Christians, and not like heathens slaughtering one another on the field of battle."

This stunning revelation left Custer speechless. Then, after several seconds, he spoke up. "With respect, sir. Turning the army on Washington sounds like treason. Does the general agree with this?"

Key dropped his gaze to his lap while he contemplated the consequences raised by Custer. After a few moments, he looked up and locked eyes with the captain. "The general knows, but he is cautious. He has many enemies in Washington who would see him destroyed or replaced by radicals like the late John Pope. There are many in the army who share our sense of things, Custer. Certainly, the men don't believe they're fighting to free the negro, nor will they ever willingly agree to do so!" Key's face turned from animation to scowl. "If this administration makes ending slavery the war's goal, the men will desert *en masse*—"

"And the war will be lost," blurted Custer. "I've only met one man—a Quaker—who thought abolition a cause worth dying for. He made himself a pariah in his own regiment."

"Exactly my point," continued Key. "Slavery must end someday, on that all reasonable men agree, but it must not be eliminated at the point of a bayonet. The men fight to preserve this nation, which is the greatest experiment in republican government ever attempted. We cannot allow our own government to be turned into that despotism we, as Americans, naturally despise. We also cannot get there at the moment."

Custer's brow furrowed. "Sir?"

"This army needs to throw the Rebels off Union soil and stabilize the front in northern Virginia," explained the colonel. "We will keep the armies in the field until the people become exhausted by war. At that point, we can open negotiations based on how things were before the war and restore the nation. Slavery will then die a natural death over time."

Just as Key finished speaking, McClellan emerged from his tent with a sheet of paper in his hand. Stopping, he peered into the darkness, waiting for his vision to adjust. "Ah, captain, there you are," he announced, striding to the two men. "You are just the man I require."

The officers rose and saluted. "I am at your service, sir," replied Custer.

Folding the note, McClellan handed it over. "I need you to take this to General Franklin. His command lies at Buckeystown on this side of the Catoctins."

"Would you have me say anything to the general, or just deliver these orders and return?"

"These orders instruct Franklin to move his command to Burkittsville in the Middletown Valley," replied McClellan. Custer shot a glance at Key, who nodded back at him. "There is a pass over South Mountain that General Franklin can take to push into the valley beyond. You will tell him I desire that he force the gap at all hazards." The general paused to lock eyes with Custer. "Pleasant Valley is the best way to get this army into the middle of Lee's scattered command and relieve the garrison at Harpers Ferry. This must be done as soon as possible. Do you understand?"

"I do, sir."

"Good!" nodded the general. "I would ride to see General Franklin myself but think it best to be with Burnside when he carries the gap at Boonsborough. Ride with Captain Albert here and report back to me once Franklin has achieved his objective."

"Yes, sir. We'll leave right away," answered the cavalryman, snapping a brisk salute.

"Custer," added McClellan, "there is one other matter I want to discuss with you. Your hair, sir, is well beyond regulation length. You should get it cut."

"I—respectfully, sir, I cannot," Custer stammered. "I have made a vow that I would not cut it until we have won a victory. To cut it without one would make me look a fool."

A corner of Little Mac's mouth slanted into an unbalanced grin. "I would never wish to see you embarrassed, Captain Custer. Leave your Arthurian locks intact for the time being, but keep your shears close. I'll give you reason to shed your ringlets soon enough."

Custer bowed in relief. "Thank you, sir."

Colonel Key watched as the two captains stalked off into the darkness. "Sir, I was under the impression you intended to wait for word from General Pleasonton before issuing the orders to General Franklin. Did you receive it?"

McClellan shook his head. "No, but I cannot wait any longer before deciding to attack Lee's army."

"Do you know with certainty that the orders are authentic? They could be a ruse to draw us into a trap."

McClellan watched Custer and Albert spur out of the encampment. "General Williams believes the orders are genuine, and I trust him," he answered. "Based on what we know of Rebel movements so far, Jackson's command has been following the orders. Think about it, colonel," he continued. "We know that Harpers Ferry is threatened and, according to the orders, Jackson is moving to bring about the surrender of Miles's command there while Lee waits with the rest of his army behind South Mountain. I don't require confirmation from Pleasonton. The time to strike is now, while Lee's army is divided. I will achieve a victory worthy of mention in the same breath as Napoleon's triumph at Castiglione."

"Castiglione?"

"Alas, Key, your poor knowledge of history fails you again!" cracked McClellan. "In 1796, the great Napoleon defeated an Austrian army at Castiglione after Field Marshal von Wurmser divided his forces. Bobby Lee has made the same mistake in front of me, and so help me God, I will make him pay for it."

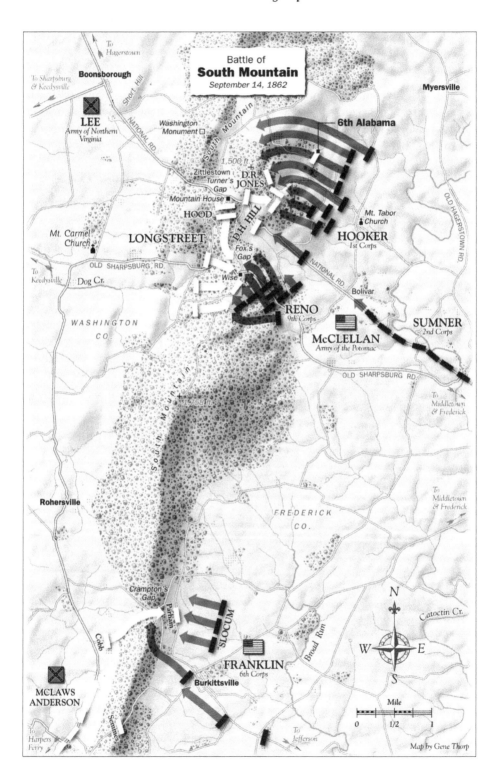

Battle of
South Mountain
September 14, 1862

Map by Gene Thorp

10

Sunday, September 14, 1862
Early Morning
Encampment of the Twenty-Third Ohio Infantry Regiment, Kanawha Division, Ninth Corps
Middletown, Maryland

strand of blue and black rosary beads clasped loosely between his fingers; Tom Kelly knelt in the dewy grass to whisper his morning prayers. Reveille had long since sounded and the men around Kelly moved like shadows through the pre-dawn darkness. Some boiled coffee on coals they had banked during the night. Others rolled their worldly possessions into blankets that they would secure atop their knapsacks when the order came to move. Kelly had packed his meager belongings like the rest of them and slipped away to wash and offer his thoughts to God. His comrades, in the meantime, devoured a wedge of cheese thrust into Davey Parker's hands the day before by a grateful resident of Middletown.

"Heavenly Father, please watch over me and me comrades today," pleaded Kelly, restlessly kneading the beads between his fingers. "Shine your face upon us and always keep us in yer favor." He sought God's presence in his mind, but the clamor of men around him made quiet contemplation impossible. Sighing, Kelly crossed himself and muttered "amen" before rising to his feet. He kissed the tiny crucifix at the end of his strand of beads and pocketed them as he walked back to his company.

When Parker spotted his friend approaching, he rose from his spot by the fire and held out a battered cup that looked like half a tin can with a handle welded to its side.

"Coffee?" he asked.

"Sure, Davey, that would be grand," nodded the Irishman.

Handing him the cup, Parker asked mischievously if Kelly had put in a good word for him with the Lord. "Of course not," he winked, raising his voice as he spoke. "Yer a Protty, Davey Parker, and while I count ye among me best friends, you're going straight to the hot place after this life, along with all the rest of these sinners." A chorus of hisses called back to Kelly in the pre-dawn gloom. Parker, meanwhile, accustomed to his friend's testy sense of humor, merely laughed and gave Kelly's lean shoulder a squeeze.

The warm coffee slid agreeably down Kelly's throat and the heat spread through his limbs like a procession of small torches. He gulped another hot mouthful and savored the sensation. It felt good to be warm again after the chill of his cold-water bath. Parker handed him a chunk of the hard cheese he had saved and Kelly, nodding thanks, popped it into his mouth before digging a piece of hardtack out of his haversack. Swallowing the milky smooth cheese, he eyed the hard flour biscuit with dismay. "These damned things are tougher than a gold coin."

"You complain about that every morning," chuckled Parker as he sipped from his cup.

"I know," sighed Kelly. "What's a poor wretch like me supposed to do?"

Breaking apart the stale biscuit, he silently dropped the pieces into his coffee. Then the rising sun brought out the regimental bugler and the first notes of assembly carried through the morning air. Groans went up across the field as men, stiff from sleeping in the grass, staggered to their feet. Captain Skiles ordered Company C into line for roll call. Kelly, still chewing his hardtack, followed Parker and the rest into place as Skiles rattled off their names. He had just finished calling the roll when Colonel Hayes and his staff arrived with the widely despised bugler.

"Company C, all present and accounted for," saluted Skiles as Hayes reined to a stop.

"Thank you, captain." Hayes turned to the bugler and was about to issue a command when a thunder-like boom rolled out in the distance. The ominous sound drew all eyes west toward the sun-bathed heights of South Mountain. When a second gun roared a moment later, Hayes wheeled in the saddle to greet an approaching courier.

"Sir, General Cox sends his compliments," announced the messenger as he slid his horse to a stop. "You are to get your regiment on the road immediately. The Twelfth Ohio is already underway." Pointing behind him, the courier directed Hayes's attention to a column striding down the gravel road. The men in the first rank splashed across the shallow creek near the charred ruins of a wooden bridge.

"Did the general say what is happening?" inquired Hayes.

"He did not, sir, but I overheard that last night our cavalry ran into a Rebel battle line on South Mountain. General Pleasonton cleared off this morning to give our corps a crack at them."

Hayes, who was now holding a map handed to him by one of his staff, shot a puzzled look at the man. "At the main gap?"

"No, sir. At another gap south of the road to Boonsborough. You can see it from here." The rider directed Hayes's attention to a cut in the wooded mountain left of the main pass directly ahead of them. "We didn't know it was there until this morning," he added. Hayes studied the terrain and nodded. "I understand, lieutenant. Tell General Cox we will march directly." Then he turned to Captain Skiles and ordered him to get his men moving.

"You heard the colonel!" roared Skiles. "Grab your things and get ready to move out!"

The order sent the men scrambling to pour out their coffee dregs and pack loose items before hustling into formation. Soaring bugle notes carried across the field, announcing the pending departure, and Skiles shouted for Company C to shoulder arms and face right. "Forwarrrd . . . march!" The men lurched into motion behind A and B companies, tramping ahead of them.

Kelly and his comrades crossed the pasture onto the gravel road, traversed the icy cold creek with curses and muttered complaints, before climbing a tall hill. The sun rose hot behind them and within a short time sweat had once again soaked through Kelly's cap and blouse. Onward, the column trudged through the hilly countryside, the lush summit of South Mountain looming before them. Throughout their advance, the Ninth Corps' artillery kept up a hot fire on the Rebels manning the mountainside gap, each round filling the air with reverberations that echoed across the valley.

Once they were well down a long grade, Kelly spied the brown-bearded and tidy-looking Jacob Cox. The brigadier general rode up to Lieutenant Colonel Hayes, who had started the march near the head of the regiment and, as he made his way along the companies, engaged in a rapid exchange of words with various men in the column. Cox caught up with Hayes near the front of Company C.

"In God's name, Hayes, remember to be careful!" he shouted as he lashed his mount rearward.

"Did ye hear that, Davey?" asked Kelly.

Parker nodded. "Sure did. We've got a mess of Johnnies up ahead."

Kelly remained silent, his typically buoyant nature troubled by the prospect of a fight. He swallowed hard to tamp down the fear and stared at his dusty boots as he and his comrades climbed yet another grade. The Buckeyes make a hard left at a rural crossroads enclosed by a handful of modest houses and continued marching a short distance down a winding road before encountering a dirt track that cut across their path. The head of the column turned right onto the dirt course and slogged a bit farther before Hayes called for a brief rest near an idle sawmill.

As the men fell out of the column, Hayes met with Brigadier General Eliakim Scammon and the commanders of the other two Ohio regiments in the First Brigade. Scammon, a thin, tight-lipped officer sporting a black tuft of hair on the end of his chin, pointed up the mountain road as the officers engaged in an animated discussion.

"Looks like Old Granny's got a plan," muttered Parker, jerking his thumb in the direction of the group. The brigade commander was not the most popular officer in the division.

Within a few minutes, the regiment was back on its feet and climbing an even steeper grade. They were moving toward a small schoolhouse on their left when a Rebel gun fired a solid shot that bounded down the mountainside and hissed past the Twelfth Ohio, whose front ranks immediately broke in every direction.

Raising a gauntleted hand, Hayes bellowed "Twenty-Third, halt!" as boys from the Twelfth streamed into the field on their left. Colonel White, the Twelfth's red-faced commanding officer, cantered past with a saber in hand, cursing for his men to stop and form up.

Kelly guffawed at the sudden chaos. "You lads seen a ghost?" he cried, eliciting chuckles from his comrades.

"Regiment, file left!" shouted Hayes, sending the column into a ravine where it halted to dress ranks.

Grateful for the pause, Kelly pulled out his canteen to fill his mouth with warm water when Sam Carey smacked him lightly on the shoulder. "Here comes General Cox," he said, pointing behind them.

Visibly furious, Cox reined in his horse, bellowing, "What in God's name is going on here?"

"Sir, there are Rebel guns at the top of this ridge," answered Colonel White sheepishly.

Standing tall in his stirrups, Cox peered up the road. "I don't see anything of the enemy. Are you certain they're up there, and that close?"

"I am," nodded White. "They threw a solid shot at us that broke the front ranks of my regiment."

While Cox scanned the high ground, General Scammon and Lieutenant Colonel Hayes joined the gathering. Kelly and the others stood by silently, out of earshot. Repeated gestures toward the mountain's summit, however, communicated the general idea.

"Well, boys, it looks like we're going in," muttered Parker, as he studied the surrounding terrain. "Kind of reminds me of western Virginia around here."

Kelly nodded in agreement. The fields adjacent to the road main road up the mountain, and the heavy forest beyond them, did resemble the bushwhacking country out west. He swallowed hard again to keep the bile from climbing into his mouth. Who knew what waited for them beyond the trees.

Hayes yanked his horse away from General Cox and cantered back to the Twenty-Third. "Attention, boys!" he shouted. "We're going to search for the flank of the Rebel line up top of this mountain!" His horse danced in a circle as he pointed toward the heights. "They have guns up there and if we find them, we are to take them! The other regiments in First Brigade will move up this main road while we take the lane here on the left. Company A will deploy as skirmishers on our left, Company F in the center and Company I on the right. The rest of the companies will follow in line of battle. Now fall out!"

"You get all that?" asked Parker as they moved into position.

"Aye. A fight's coming," shot back the Irishman.

The bugler blared out the call to advance and Kelly watched the skirmishers spread out in a semi-circle before melting into the forest. Once they had vanished, the rest of the regiment waited for the order to follow. It came shortly thereafter, sending the ranks ahead on both sides of the road. Stepping into the trees muffled the cannon fire that echoed across the mountainside, and with visibility less than a hundred yards, an eerie silence fell over the advancing Buckeyes. Kelly and his comrades stalked around limestone breaks, stepped across fallen tree trunks, and fought their way through laurel thickets that broke the regiment into clusters of men. Hayes followed behind them on the road, growling "close up!" as they advanced.

Upward, the Buckeyes climbed until the ground began to level out. A few of their skirmishers, shadowy figures at best, slipped carefully ahead of the main line. The sound of boots crunching through dry leaves, snapping twigs, and breaking small branches echoed in Parker's ears. *How could the Rebs not hear all of this racket?* he thought. The activity also flushed out rabbits and deer ahead of the men and Kelly lifted his musket to draw a bead on a fleeing squirrel. Mouthing the word "bang!" he smiled at Parker, whose nervous grin back at him disappeared almost as quickly as it had formed.

A shot rang out on the right, followed by several more in quick succession. Every head twisted toward the gunfire. The trees thinned there, allowing Kelly to see the forest give way to a field of wheat, beyond which stood a crop of corn. The ground rolled upward through the wheat before dropping into a swale, the corn standing tall on the left.

A skirmisher scrambled toward them through the woods, asking for Colonel Hayes. "Sir, there are Rebel skirmishers up ahead," he panted when he found the Buckeye commander.

"What do you know? Did you see the enemy's main line?" inquired Hayes.

"Part of Company I struck the Reb picket line in a small cornfield. Looks like more are in a line a hundred or so yards farther on. They look to be behind a stone wall over the crest of the hill."

Hayes scowled with concern. "A stone wall? How strong is the position?"

"I can't say, sir. I didn't see it myself."

Hayes called for the regiment to form a battle line on the logging road he had used to guide them up the mountain. More musket fire popped in the wheat field as the Buckeye skirmishers escalated the clash. Kelly and Parker stumbled into place over the broken ground and waited while Hayes weaved his mount through the trees ahead of them. Satisfied he could learn no more without moving his men into the open, Hayes ordered the regiment to load.

"Load muskets!" echoed Captain Skiles, sending Kelly, Parker, and the others reaching for their cartridge boxes.

Kelly tore open the paper tube with his teeth and immediately tasted the bitter tang of gunpowder upon his tongue. Dumping the ball and powder down the barrel of his Springfield, he rammed home the round and clicked back the hammer.

Hayes climbed down from the saddle and handed the reins of his horse to a private standing beside him. "Now, boys, remember you are the Twenty-Third Ohio!" he hollered. "Give the Rebels hell like you did in western Virginia and we'll come out of this alright! In these woods they don't know our numbers, so when we charge by God yell like we're ten thousand! Leave your knapsacks here. We'll collect them later!"

The men piled their gear and hurried back into line as Hayes yanked his saber from its scabbard. "Now give it to them!" he roared, pointing it toward the enemy. "Give the sons of bitches hell!"

With Hayes leading the way, the Buckeyes raised a cry and crashed out of the trees behind their commander. Sweeping into the field with the rest of his comrades, Kelly blinked his vision clear. Squinting and panting, he strode through the ripening wheat with the men around him bellowing like devils. Up the slope, they rushed until they came over the crest. There they found an enemy line of battle with a crimson flag hanging limp in the still air. When someone yelled "fire!" a torrent of small explosions rippled out from dozens of muskets. Lead slugs hissed through the ranks, stopping the Ohio men in their tracks. The sickening thud of rounds striking flesh and bone echoed down the line. Kelly hurried into place, with Parker on his right and Sam on his left.

"PRIME!" cried Hayes.

Kelly seated a percussion cap on the nib of his musket.

"AIM!"

A clattering wall of Springfields lowered toward the Rebels, who were furiously reloading their own weapons.

"FIRE!"

Pulling his trigger, Kelly felt the musket kick against his shoulder. Burning smoke clouded his vision, and he reached for another round. A minié ball sang furiously past his left ear, followed by a second that thudded into a man two paces from him on the right. Kelly watched the man stagger sideways into his friend, a fountain of his blood spilling across Parker's shoulder and neck. Turning toward the rear as his musket dropped to the ground, he took a step and collapsed face first into the wheat.

Shocked by the blood, Parker choked back a wave of vomit, frantically using the back of his hand to wipe the gore from his cheek. A deep-throated yell, low at first, but rising in volume and pitch, pulsed across the field. "By all that's holy, I hate that infernal caterwauling!" shouted Kelly, tearing off the end of another cartridge. The Ohio troops answered with a deep roar of their own. Kelly re-primed his rifle and clicked back the hammer.

"Fire by company!" cried Hayes as he walked along behind his men.

Captain Skiles stepped to the side when the lieutenant colonel stalked past. Then he gave the order. "Company C close up! Dress on the colors!"

Kelly eased to his left to take up the space beside Sam and steadied himself.

"Ready!" shouted Skiles.

"What're we shooting at?" screamed Parker. "I can't see 'em!"

"Just aim low!" shouted Kelly, as he tilted his head and looked down the length of his barrel.

"FIRE!"

The men of Company C pulled their triggers as one, their rifled muskets exploding like a clap of thunder. Hayes reappeared behind them, shouting for the men on the left to refuse their flank.

"Davey, turn which way?" asked Kelly in confusion.

"I don't know!"

"That way!" shouted Sam, pointing toward the smoke-obscured flank. Balls zipping past the friends reminded him of angry wasps. "We're angling the line, so we don't get turned!"

Panic-stricken shouts of "they're on our flank!" cut through the din.

"God damn it, don't worry about them!" barked Captain Skiles as he grabbed Parker by the shoulders and faced him forward. "Fire that way!" Skiles pointed his pistol toward the smoke-obscured stone wall. Nodding, Parker tore open another cartridge while Kelly, shaken by the moment of panic, did the same. Sam raised his musket, squeezed the trigger, grounded the butt, and reached into his cartridge box.

Out of the drifting haze came a glimpse of several Union companies advancing toward the cornfield on the left. Hayes called out "fix bayonets!" from his spot behind them.

Kelly finished ramming home his round, put the butt of his Springfield on the ground, and reached around his waist to draw the eighteen-inch length of steel from his belt loop. Lifting the bayonet into place, he snapped it onto the end of his musket. Everyone around him did the same, and within seconds, the sun glinted off a bristling regimental front. Kelly's sweating palms stuck to the smooth wood of his musket stock. His heart pounded in his ears and his lungs gulped for breath in adrenaline-fueled gasps. Every few seconds he thought he caught a glimpse of a Rebel battle flag hanging defiantly over the hazy field, but his eyes stung every time he tried to keep them open long enough to focus through the smoke.

He squeezed them shut for a few seconds before once again opening them wide. The crimson flag waved back and forth on the enemy's line, bringing out a maniacal expression on Kelly's face. "I'm gonna take that blasted banner!" he cried out.

"Not if I get there first!" contended Parker.

All at once, the firing fell off and an uncomfortable hush fell over the field, as if the battle itself were a living thing that had held its breath. "Twenty-Third Regiment!" yelled Hayes, his saber held high above his head. "Charge, bayonets!" The line surged forward with a roar that sent Rebels sprinting rearward in ones and twos. Most of the enemy stood their ground, though, lowering their muskets to unleash a murderous volley at the charging Buckeyes. A lead round struck the man on Sam's left, dropping him hard to the ground. Their line closed on the Johnnies and Kelly, now screaming at the top of his lungs, could clearly see the stone wall and the gray and brown men milling behind it. Some had turned about in fear to leave the protection of the rocks.

"The bloody cowards is running!" he yelled, noting that the flag remained in place as if mocking them to come for it.

The lines crashed together at the stone wall with a terrible clatter of metal, wood, bones, and flesh. Kelly's momentum knocked back the man to his front, who fell away in the chaos, leaving the Irishman to leap over the wall toward the flag-bearer on his right. A bear of a man in the color guard tried desperately to load his musket as Kelly approached but ran out of time. Kelly thrust his bayonet at the giant, missing him when the man stepped to one side. Raising the weapon with his ramrod still in the barrel, the Johnny swung it down to crush Kelly's skull. This time Kelly sidestepped the blow, which surely would have killed him, before spinning to drive the point of his bayonet into the man's midriff. Disbelieving eyes fixed on Kelly as a stream of blood burst from the man's lips.

Kelly tugged on his musket to yank the bayonet from the man's torso, but the stricken Rebel fell backward, taking Kelly with him. Losing his footing, Kelly collapsed onto his knees with his weapon still embedded stiffly in the man's body. Then a second Rebel stepped out of the smoke to drive his own bayonet into the Irishman's side. Kelly raised his hands helplessly to ward off the plunging blade when one side of the man's head exploded in a haze of red and white gore from a round fired by Davey Parker just ten feet away. "You owe me one, Paddy!" cried Parker as the headless corpse crumpled in the dust.

Climbing to his feet, Kelly pulled his weapon free and set eyes on the Rebel flag bearer, who now stood alone. Shooting his friend a glance, Kelly set out after him, followed by Parker, who yelled, "Oh, no, you don't, you ungrateful son of a bitch!"

The sandy-haired Butternut with grimy cheeks and a beard darkened by tobacco stains swung his staff hard and fast, missing Kelly, but leveling Parker with a sharp blow across the chest. Kelly saw his chance and with a howl he swung his own musket, catching the Rebel in the side of the head. The man stumbled to his knees, his flag dropping toward the ground. Sam Carey appeared at Kelly's side from out of nowhere and shot the prone enemy soldier through the breast. Kelly wrenched the staff from the man's hands, tore the banner off its mounting, and held up the flag in triumph. A wild look haunted his eyes as Parker rose to his knees, gasping for air.

"I told you!" shouted Kelly in a bout of battle fever. "This flag is me own!"

"If you live to carry it off the field!" shouted Parker back. "Look there!" He pointed at a cluster of Rebels in the trees some thirty yards away, lowering their muskets at them. By the time Kelly spied the puffs of smoke erupting from their line, whistling minié balls struck the ground around his feet and picked at his uniform.

"Sweet Jesus!" he cried, extending a hand along with Sam to pull Parker to his feet.

"I saved your life, you miserable bastard. Don't you forget it!" grunted Parker as more miniés sizzled past.

"Them Johnnies are mad as Hades, Davey!" bawled Kelly. "Here, you take the flag! I don't want it." Extending the banner to his friend, Parker wisely pushed it away. "Not on your life will I take that thing! Grab that musket and come on!"

Turning tail, Parker and Sam rushed back through the trampled wheat to where Hayes had formed a new line. Kelly came up hard behind them, bits of crimson cloth poking out from between the buttons of his tunic where he had stuffed the captured flag. In his hands, he grasped the new musket Parker had pointed to on the field.

Now hatless, Lieutenant Colonel Hayes stalked through the powder smoke shouting, "Twenty-Third! Dress on the colors!" Other regimental officers yelling the same order grabbed individual soldiers and turned them about.

Kelly and Parker converged near the national flag. Minié balls sang past them from the left, where the field sloped up to a stand of ripened corn. Just above it stood a new Rebel battle line, which had only now made its appearance.

"Ah, crap!" swore Sam.

"Company C, left face!" cried Lieutenant Sperry, his face slick with sweat.

"Where's Skiles?" asked Parker.

"He's down, damn you! Now, face left!"

Parker, Kelly, Sam, and the rest of the men within shouting distance turned toward the tall corn. Kelly looked about to see how many others in the regiment had followed suit, but he was unable to tell where their line began or ended. Enemy gunfire, meanwhile, continued knocking men backward or dropping them to their knees.

"We're going to drive them from the field. Get ready, boys!" shouted Hayes.

"Another frontal attack?" moaned Kelly, hefting his musket.

"Charge bayonets!"

Again, the Buckeyes surged forward, pushing through the stalks with their Springfields leveled and screams howling from their throats. When they exited the far side of the corn, a well-delivered volley ripped through their ranks, eliciting a collective groan from those struck by the murderous wave of lead. Kelly looked about to get his bearings and swore under his breath when he realized the Rebs were farther back than Hayes had thought. He moved closer to Parker just as a shell exploded above them. The concussion blew Kelly backward into the corn, knocking the new musket from his hands.

Lying on his back, the Irishman saw the stalks waving above him in the bright sunlight. Wisps of powder smoke drifted past, and he tried in his delirious state to touch them. Ringing filled his ears, and with both hands, he grasped his head. The wetness in his hair surprised him, and he looked at his hands to find them slick with blood. Tolling bells in his ears called forth shadows that closed in on all sides. Then a vortex opened beneath him, and Kelly's world faded to black.

Lying face down a few yards away, Parker cracked open his eyes. A loud ringing sound filled his head. Slowly, he pushed himself onto his hands and knees. He could see men opening their mouths and screaming, firing, and fighting, but everything sounded muffled, as if cotton had been stuffed into his ears. Dizzy, but aware of his surroundings, Parker ran his hands up and down his torso to confirm he was not wounded. Then he crawled on his hands and knees toward the new Buckeye firing line.

A cap lay on the ground in front of him, and thinking it was his, Parker reached for it. Sitting back to pull it on, he found it full of the former owner's blood and brains. Nausea washed over Parker, and he retched violently, splashing the remains of his breakfast and sticky yellow bile across his pant legs. He dropped the bloody cap and looked up when dusty boots appeared at his side. Major James Comly, the regiment's second in command, loomed above him, a scowl on his thickly mustached face.

"Get up, man!" cried the major, flecks of spittle flying from his lips.

Parker could barely make out the words and shaking his head, he gasped at the pain shooting behind his eyes. "I can't hear anything!" he yelled back. Or at least thought he did. Shaking his head at the private, Comly stalked ahead to the firing line.

Parker tried sticking his fingers in his ears and moving them about to clear his hearing. When that did not work, he reached over and grabbed an abandoned Springfield. Then he froze when he saw the blood on the tip of his forefinger.

"My ear. I'm hit!" he cried.

Staggering to his feet, he stumbled toward the firing line. Someone issued a muffled scream to "hold fast!" Was his hearing beginning to return? Unsure of what he was hearing or imagining, Parker wobbled into a gap in the line just as the man to his left pitched backward, his chest exploding in a shower of blood. Parker looked down at the man before turning about and raising his rifle.

Jesus, the Rebs are close! he thought as he pulled the trigger at the enemy standing only fifty yards away.

Reloading, he fired a second round, and then a third before the line of Buckeyes lunged forward with bayonets leveled. Parker, whose chest still ached from the blow of the flag staff, and head pounded from concussion, felt so exhausted he could barely stand. He hesitated, unsure what to do, until a hand in the middle of his back shoved him forward. He stumbled after the charging bluecoats as most of the Johnnies fled into the woods, leaving only a dozen or so to stand and fight. Bayonets cut down several of them, prompting the rest to drop their rifles in surrender.

An eerie silence fell over the position before a loud volley of rifle fire erupted off to the right. Cries of triumph rang out as the men of Hayes's regiment shook their fists, rifles, and caps. While the officers scrambled to form them back into line and check their ammunition, Parker turned back in search of his missing friends. "Tom! Where are you?" he cried, fearing the worst. "Sam! Sam Carey?"

A captain grabbed the back of his uniform, spun him roughly around, and mouthed "fall in!" Parker looked past the officer at the file closers, pushing men into line. The captain shoved him toward them, where he checked his musket and awaited orders. None of the men around him looked familiar. A fresh cloud of powder smoke filled the pasture to the right where another Buckeye firing line let loose a deadly volley into the trees. Parker sighed in relief when he set eyes on Major Comly, and decided he would watch the major as closely as possible to figure out what to do.

Thirst tortured Parker's throat, and he reached for his canteen. *Good thing I filled this at the creek!* he thought while pulling a long draught. *Where in God's name are Tom and Sam?*

When the major pointed his saber, the regiment faced right. Parker dropped the corked canteen to the end of its strap and pulled his rifle onto his shoulder. Moving by the right flank, the Ohioans stepped off at the double-quick toward another Buckeye regiment. They closed rapidly, drawing fire from Rebels in the trees on the far side of the field.

"Regiment, halt!" Parker stumbled to a stop.

"Left face!"

Parker mimicked the motions of the man beside him.

"Load!"

Dropping the butt of his Springfield to the ground, Parker reached around his waist to grab a paper cartridge. The weight of the .58 caliber ball felt reassuring in his hand. Emptying the paper tube into his barrel, Parker lifted his musket, set a percussion cap, and clicked back the hammer.

"Aim!"

Looking down the barrel at a line of the enemy, Parker focused on the belly of a thin, haggard-looking Rebel.

"Fire!"

"This is for Tom!" he grunted, squeezing his trigger. A tongue of flame and smoke stabbed out of the barrel. When it cleared, he saw several of the enemy crumpled in the grass. A man three paces to his right grabbed at his throat and sunk gurgling to the ground. Sweat poured down Parker's back as he loaded his next round. The sun blazed mercilessly hot. More Rebels moved up to fill the gaps in their line. Others fired. Men around them fell.

"How long are we gonna stand here and take this?" Parker called out to no one in particular.

The man beside him lowered his rifle a bit. "What's that?"

"Regiment! Charge, bayonets!"

The stranger next to Parker started forward before stopping to grab Parker by the front of his uniform. "Come on, dammit!" he yelled with a yank. Parker nodded, lurching ahead as a jolt of adrenaline coursed through his body.

The Buckeyes yelled as they advanced, causing the Rebels to falter, but this time, their line did not break. The combatants crashed together at the same low stone wall Parker and his friends had assaulted a short time ago. How they had managed to lose the position he could not imagine. Poking and stabbing with bayonets and swinging their rifle butts across the piled rocks.

Parker screamed as he jumped onto the wall and plunged his bayonet down at a seedy-looking fellow wearing a slouch hat riddled with holes. The Rebel easily sidestepped the thrust, striking Parker's left shoulder with the tip of his musket barrel. The blow knocked Parker onto the ground. Feeling panic surge inside him, he rolled onto his knees in time to use his musket to ward off the next blow. The Johnny's face contorted with frustration as the shock from the two muskets crashing together sent his Enfield clattering into the dirt. Scrambling to his feet, Parker lashed out with his right fist, striking the man squarely in the nose. Pitching backward, the Johnny crashed onto his rear end. Frantically, he drew a long knife from his belt and struggled to rise, but Parker, his blood up, fell on him too quickly, shoving his bayonet through the man's belly.

"Urgh!" gasped the man, his eyes going wide. Gore-covered hands clasped tightly around the barrel of Parker's rifle, making a weak attempt to push it away, but as the realization of his fate became clear, calm came over the man's face and he fell back dead, a line of crimson trickling from the corner of his mouth. Parker yanked the blade free and glared about. No more Rebels were within reach.

The victorious Buckeyes shouted triumphantly along the dirt road with the corpses of friends and foes alike strewn at their feet. Parker joined them, thrusting his bloody rifle into the air with a feral howl. Then the strength ebbed from his veins, and he stumbled backward against the stone wall. The man he had just killed lay on his back a dozen feet away, his sightless glassy eyes staring up at the sky.

Parker stared at the corpse and then looked away, unable to stomach it. He leaned his musket against the rocks and took a swig of warm water from his canteen. The sun hovered high above and Parker glanced into the bright light to clear his head. Heavy fighting rolled off to the right beyond a thick screen of trees. Once again, he thought of his friends.

"Tom! Tom Kelly!" Parker croaked, staggering shakily to his feet. "Sam!" He searched the dead and wounded for his friends. Then exhaustion overtook him, and Parker slumped again to the ground, a wail of grief erupting from his lips. The iron scent of blood filled his nostrils and tears began flowing freely down his face. Lying prone in the dirt, Parker trembled and wept as he never had before.

11

Sunday, September 14, 1862
Late Morning
Ninth Corps' Battlefront
Bolivar, Maryland

did what?" snapped Jesse Reno, commander of the army's Ninth Corps.

The general's aide nodded to confirm that Reno had heard him correctly. "Sir, General Pleasonton sent General Willcox's division north of the National Road and not to General Cox on the south side. His men are forming up now to attack."

"Damn it all to hell!" roared the fiery Virginian, his cheeks flushed and his dark eyes wild with rage. "I ordered Willcox to support Cox's attack on the gap up there!" The general pointed a gloved forefinger at the summit to the left of the main turnpike. "Not to strike the Rebel left!" The aide followed the general's finger as he swung it about, noting the long tendrils of grayish-white battle smoke drifting south from the Kanawha Division's fight. "What in God's name is Pleasonton thinking?"

"I don't know, sir," shrugged the aide. "All I know is that General Cox sent me to say he requires reinforcement as soon as possible. Rebels he has captured say they are from Sam Garland's North Carolina brigade, a part of General D. H. Hill's division."

A scowl wrinkled Reno's face. "Hill's division? But that can't be more than a few brigades."

"General Cox's point exactly, sir. But he says he has only two Ohio brigades and they've been engaged for hours. The general fears Hill will counterattack and overwhelm him."

"Where am I going to get troops on such short notice?" grumbled Reno to himself.

Pondering the issue, Reno failed to notice Ambrose Burnside and his staff ride up from the far side of the hill. Wearing a domed slouch hat and sitting atop Major, his bob-tailed gray, Burnside reined in before Reno. Immediately, he noted the vicious expression on the general's face.

"Why, Reno, what is disturbing you?" he inquired.

Reno looked at Burnside as if surprised to see him and raised his voice above the banging of Federal batteries on a hill three hundred yards to their front. "Sir," he saluted. "General Pleasonton's incompetence."

"Come again?" frowned Burnside.

"The damned fool has wrecked my plan to push back the enemy's right flank!" spat Reno. "I ordered General Willcox some hours ago to advance up this mountain spur to support General Cox. Instead, Pleasonton sent Willcox across the road to the north. Look there!" he pointed, stabbing his finger at a dark mass of troops in the distance. "You can see their line forming now."

Burnside followed Reno's gesture, releasing his field glasses from their case as he did. Raising the binoculars to his eyes, he trained them on the double line of blue-clad soldiers spreading out along the base of South Mountain. "I see them," he sighed. "Don't fret, general. All will come out right in the end."

Reno shook his head. "Sir, we must bring them back before the rest of the wing is up."

"General Rodman's division is only now arriving at Middletown after a long march," Burnside nodded. "It will take time to put him in. We do have Sam Sturgis's men at our disposal." When Reno pursed his lips, Burnside continued. "Order Sam to bring up his division immediately. I'll send to Willcox and have him move back this way to support the Kanawha's. We'll let Rodman rest for a moment before calling upon him."

"As you wish, sir," saluted Reno, his anger mollified by Burnside's composure.

Calling for an aide, Reno sent him pelting back to Middletown, where Sam Sturgis's Second Division camped near Catoctin Creek.

"Colonel!" shouted Burnside to William Goddard of his staff. He pointed to the blue battle lines forming in the distance. "Ride to General Willcox over there and tell him there has been a mistake. Tell him to bring his command back to this side of the road as quickly as possible and follow the same path up the mountain taken by General Cox earlier this morning."

"As you wish, sir. Is there anything else?" Goddard asked, pulling on his reins to calm his unsteady mount. "Yes, colonel," nodded Burnside, "tell Willcox he is to ask General Reno for guidance if he requires it—and no one else. Do you have that?"

"Yes, sir. I understand."

"Good man. Off with you, then." Burnside watched Goddard disappear down the hillside before walking his horse in a half circle to a spot beside Reno. He settled his gloved hands on the pommel of his saddle and scrutinized the mountainside for several seconds.

"Well, general, what do you intend to do from here?" inquired Reno.

Burnside lifted his nose toward the smoke. "I intend to bring up the rest of your corps and throw it against the Rebel flank where Cox made his lodgment. I've sent word to Hooker to hurry his corps from Frederick. When he arrives, I'll send him north to strike the Rebel left—wherever that is exactly. Like Pleasonton, I've seen no indication of defenses there. I think we can crush them between the two corps of my wing and win ourselves a resounding victory."

Reno pondered the answer. "It's a good plan, general," he replied slowly, "but what is taking Hooker so long to come up? I thought General McClellan instructed him to march at daylight."

"That is my understanding as well," said Burnside, pulling a small watch from his pocket. "It's ten o'clock now, but with only a single road behind us and a mountain range to be traversed, Hooker likely won't be up for some time."

Reno cast a sidelong glance at his superior. "Do you trust Hooker to make good time, general? Can he be relied upon to come to our aid?"

Burnside kept his gaze focused on the distant cloud of battle smoke. "I know what you are insinuating," he replied, choosing his words carefully, "but think in this case we can count on Hooker's vanity to work in our favor. He loves nothing more than the booming of guns and the chance to win himself a little glory, his personal contempt for me notwithstanding. This battle will draw him to us as honey draws a bear. I am not worried about it."

"And what of General McClellan? Have you heard anything from him this morning?"

The general shook his head. "No. Nothing from the commanding general yet, but I expect he will appear soon. Our orders are to carry these gaps and everything the general set in motion yesterday is intended to accomplish that end. Once he hears we have engaged—and he has surely heard our guns—he will come to us. My primary concern is to get Willcox back here to support the Kanawha's. Cox's boys hit 'em hard this morning and I hear the Rebs are back on their heels."

"Yes, and that's why I am so upset!" growled Reno. "We have an opportunity to crush their flank and drive them into Pleasant Valley! If Willcox had come up as I intended, he'd be preparing to enter the fight as we speak. Hell, general, we could have had this battle won by midday! God damned cavalier son of a bitch."

"Now, now, general," chided Burnside. "I'm sure Pleasonton didn't mean to thwart your efforts. He simply made an error that we must rectify."

"I hope so." Lifting his hat, Reno wiped sweat from his receding hairline. "If the Reb army is as large as General McClellan believes, Lee could be bringing up enough reinforcements to crush Cox even as we speak." Pulling the cap back onto his head, Reno punched one gloved fist into another. "We need to hit the Rebs while we have them at a disadvantage!"

Burnside pursed his lips at the warning. "Have you any indication of that occurring?" he asked. "I for one am not sure the Rebel army numbers are anything near the frightful horde General McClellan believes. At least, I have seen no evidence of it in Maryland thus far."

"Neither have I," shot back Reno. "The best information I have says Cox is facing Daniel Harvey Hill's division. Nothing more."

"If the Rebel force is limited to Hill's division, then we'll have the mountain passes in our hands this afternoon!"

"That's true, general," said Reno. "But if Hill's is the only command we're facing, we had better beat him quick and seize those gaps. Lee can't afford to lose them if his army is in pieces on the other side."

Burnside scratched at one of his giant sideburns. "General, you are, of course, correct," he said. "I'm going to return to headquarters and await McClellan's arrival. Keep me informed of your progress here."

"I will, sir," nodded the Virginian.

Touching the black brim of his kepi, Burnside guided Major back toward his headquarters camp just east of Middletown. Reno watched Burnside go before cinching up his reins and calling for his aides to follow him. The group of riders spurred downhill a short distance before cantering up the pitted wagon track leading to Jacob Cox's lines. By the time the group had passed halfway up the mountain, they spotted wounded men lining the roadside. The severely injured lay sprawled on the embankments. Many moaned in agony, but some, even those with horrendous, gaping wounds, did not make a sound. Some, in less pain, begged for water or simply stared off into space.

A grim-faced soldier, his head and half of his face wrapped in a blood-stained bandage, peered at Reno through one good eye. The general caught the man's gaze and held it firmly until the bloodied hero staggered unsteadily onto his feet and offered a salute. Reno nodded solemnly at the soldier, his chest swelling with pride. Returning the gesture, he turned to the colonel riding beside him. "Just look at that man there," he remarked. "With men like him in this army, we can never lose this war."

Spurring his horse onward, Reno and his staff passed a small column of Rebel prisoners moving past under guard. A few of the weary Southerners locked their eyes on him, though, whether out of curiosity or hatred, he could not discern. "Best be careful up there, general!" called out one. "Bobby Lee is coming to gobble up every last one of you Yanks."

Reno acknowledged the taunt with a cynical tip of his hat and kept riding. A short distance on, the rattling musketry near the summit fell away into a fitful silence, followed by deep cheering. Smoke crept down the hill like a light autumn fog as Reno rode past a field hospital jammed with wounded. He drew his mount to a halt and the rest of the riders clattered to a stop beside him. A handful of yards away, a surgeon in a bloody apron stood beside a rough table holding a bottle of whiskey in one hand. He poured some of the liquor onto the leg of a struggling man two others were holding in place and, as the injured man screamed in agony, lifted the bottle to his lips to take a deep swallow for himself. "Hold him now. Good and tight," directed the doctor as he set down the bottle and picked up a saw.

Reno looked away but could not avoid hearing the tormented screams until the stricken soldier fainted from the pain.

"You there," he asked a passing sergeant. "Do you know where General Cox can be found?"

"Yes, sir," saluted the man, pointing beyond the hospital. "General Cox is over yonder."

Reno spied Cox standing in a patch of trampled wheat amidst several of his aides and colonels. Kicking his horse toward them, Reno cantered over.

Cox looked up when he heard the hoofbeats. "Ah, General Reno, we were just discussing you!" nodded the Ohioan.

"Nothing bad, I hope," grunted Reno as he slipped to the ground.

"Not in the least, sir. I was just telling Colonel Ewing here you promised to have the whole Ninth Corps come up behind us in support."

A miffed look shaded Reno's face. "About that, Cox. It's why I'm here." Folding his arms, Cox braced himself for bad news. "I had Willcox underway to you," continued Reno, "but thanks to botched instructions, his division got diverted to the north."

"That is very unfortunate," frowned the Buckeye general. "We need his men here soon, sir."

"Damn it, I know that, Cox! General Burnside issued orders to fix this mess, but it'll take Willcox some time to come up." Scanning the mountainside, the general softened his voice. "Can you hold on until he arrives?"

Cox nodded he could before waving at rough map etched in the dirt. "I think the Rebs are here, sir," he pointed with the toe of his boot. "I've pulled back our lines to stronger defensive positions . . . here. If they don't hit us with several brigades at once, we can hold them for a while."

"That'll have to do," said Reno, peering up the mountain. "Why have the guns gone silent?"

"We drove the enemy into the woods north of the road here." blurted Colonel George Crook, the tall, slender commander of the Thirty-Sixth Ohio.

"We did indeed," cut in Cox, shooting an acid glance in his subordinate's direction. "Colonel Crook's command was instrumental in achieving that success. Once the Rebels fell back, I ordered our regiments to form a consolidated line."

"Why didn't you pursue them and drive the Rebs off of this mountain?" demanded Reno, his fist shaking in the air.

"It's not for want of will," assured Cox. "My command has been engaged for three hours and the men are low on ammunition and water. It's hard getting anything up there."

"Then there are Longstreet's men to consider," quipped Crook.

Surprised by this, Reno turned to Crook. "What's that you say? Longstreet is here, too?"

"No, sir, not yet!" exclaimed Cox. "It's just that some of the prisoners we've taken claim Longstreet's corps is coming to General Hill's support."

"If that's true, it would be most unwelcome news. Did they say when?"

"No, sir. All I know is that we drove off Garland's brigade and we command the road running west through the gap. If you can get me reinforcements before Longstreet—or anyone else—comes up, we can drive what remains of Hill's division off the mountain and hold the gap."

Reno exhaled heavily through his nose. "General Cox, my congratulations to you and your men for the good work. Hold your position for the time being. I will rush Willcox to you as quickly as I can. General Burnside and I also intend to send Sturgis and Rodman, but that will take longer." Reno removed his kepi and knocked it against his thigh, raising a small cloud of dust. "I will keep my promise, Cox. You'll have the Ninth Corps at your back."

"We appreciate it, sir," saluted Cox. "May I ask after the rest of the wing?"

Reno pulled his kepi back into place. "You mean Hooker? He's taking his sweet time coming up with First Corps. General Burnside intends to have him attack the Rebel left flank north of us when he arrives. That should take pressure off your boys, even if Longstreet comes up."

"I guess it's a race against time then," sighed Crook.

Reno stared hard at the man. "Isn't it always, colonel?"

*   *   *

General Burnside eased Major off the road and up an embankment to his sprawling headquarters in a picturesque apple orchard. Major lifted his nose in search of ripe fruit, prompting the general to pull back the reins. "Oh, no you don't! Not yet," he laughed. "Get me back to my tent and you can eat all the apples you'd like."

Touching his heels to Major's flanks, the animal walked on to a collection of large canvas tents. Burnside slipped off his horse and handed the reins to an orderly before pulling off his gloves. "The day is passing quickly, John," he announced. "Anything come in while I was away?"

Major General John Grubb Parke nodded as he rose from a writing desk littered with the day's endless paperwork. The 34-year-old native of Pennsylvania had known Burnside for some time. They served together along the coast in North Carolina, and Parke had even held a stint as the commander of a division in the Ninth Corps before becoming the general's chief of staff. Some in the army occasionally mistook him for his superior because of his own expansive sideburns, although, to be fair, Parke's wispier whiskers could not compare with the majesty of Burnside's.

"Something did come in, sir," replied Parke, handing a dispatch to the general. "Pleasonton reports that the pass at Burkittsville is defended by no more than 1,500 men, mostly cavalry and a few guns. We also received word that General Hooker should be arriving shortly."

"That's good news about Hooker—and about time as well," smiled Burnside, handing the paper back to Parke. "I sent for him hours ago. Pleasonton's news is very important. General McClellan will want to know about it immediately. Have we heard anything from him?"

Scratching his muttonchops, Parke replied, "no, general, but you can ask him yourself. There he is now."

Pounding hooves announced George McClellan and his staff. Weaving through the apple trees, the commanding general pulled Dan Webster to a stop and hopped down, yanking off his gloves as he strode toward Burnside and Parke. "Good morning, generals! Good to see you both."

McClellan returned their salutes and unbuttoned the top of his frock coat. "Warm for this time of year, wouldn't you say, Burn?"

"It is, sir. Will you take some water?"

"Please," nodded McClellan, who turned back to his mounted staff. "Gentlemen, we will be here for some time. Dismount and make yourselves comfortable."

Burnside and McClellan walked into the shade of the wing commander's tent. "Burn, what's happening?" inquired Little Mac. "I could see the smoke and hear the guns during the whole ride here, but now it's all gone quiet."

"Here is what I know," began Burnside, who took up a pencil and leaned over a large map spread atop a table. He pointed to a line marking the road Jacob Cox's troops had taken toward the summit. "Cox struck the enemy here," he tapped. "He has met only one brigade under General D. H. Hill so far, but there must be others lurking about."

McClellan puzzled over the map, his left hand drifting up to rub the lower half of his face. "Is that the Boonsborough Pass?"

"No, sir. The locals call it Fox's Gap. We didn't even know it was there until Pleasonton's troopers uncovered it late yesterday afternoon."

"We can use it to flank Hill at the Boonsborough Pass, then."

"My thought exactly. Reno sent Cox's division to the gap first thing this morning. He struck the enemy about nine and has been fighting ever since," confirmed the wing commander. "That is, until the firing tapered off a short time ago."

McClellan turned his head to look at Burnside. "What does the pause mean?"

"I don't know yet, general. Reno will send word soon. Cox has been sending back prisoners. He reports are that he has driven the enemy wherever he has met him."

"Bully for Cox!" exclaimed McClellan. "I knew he could be relied on from our time together in western Virginia. What of the rest of Reno's corps? Have they entered the fight?"

A scowl crossed Burnside's face. "No."

"But why not, Burn?" exclaimed McClellan with surprise. "You should have thrown everything you had at Hill and punched through his defenses! We must get through Hill and at Longstreet's command around Boonsborough while Lee's army is still divided. My plan is to destroy them in detail—you know that!"

Swallowing hard, Burnside nodded vigorously. "I understand that, sir, but there has been some confusion. Willcox went to the wrong place and is now retracing his steps to get into position. Sturgis is mustering his division along the creek west of here to support Cox, and Rodman is only just arrived." Little Mac stared silently at his friend. "George, the roads in this place are very confusing," continued Burnside, lapsing into the familiarity with McClellan that they had shared before the war. "Many aren't on any maps, and can't even be seen unless you stumble onto them! With the hills and trees and rocks—it's a mess getting through there. I assure you we are remedying the situation, but repositioning the divisions will take some time."

"You intend to renew the attack this afternoon, don't you?"

"I do, general. Here, let me show you." Burnside leaned down with his pencil. "As I noted, Cox made a lodgment on the enemy's right flank here," he tapped. "When Hooker arrives, I intend to push his corps north of the National Road and up South Mountain against the Rebel left here." McClellan nodded as he followed along. "The two parts of my wing will close on Hill like a vice and drive his command back on Boonsborough."

"Hooker is nearly up," observed McClellan.

"So General Parke has told me," acknowledged Burnside. "Reno will want Hooker to go in as soon as he arrives." He paused for a couple of seconds in contemplation. "Is there any news of Colonel Miles at Harpers Ferry? Will we be able to get to him in time?"

McClellan heaved a long sigh. "A detachment sent by Miles arrived at headquarters earlier this morning."

"Were those the men General Reno forwarded to you?"

"Yes. One of them, a Captain Russell, I think it was, told me Reno gave them fresh mounts to reach me as rapidly as possible," explained McClellan. "According to this same captain, Miles has foolishly abandoned Maryland Heights above the ferry. He reports having forty-eight hours of rations remaining. We have about two days to rescue them."

"Two days? Why, that should be plenty of time," exclaimed Burnside cheerfully. "Harpers Ferry is not far from here."

"True," replied McClellan, "but portions of Lee's army stand in the way, and we must dispose of them first. You must punch through his lines, Burn! It is imperative!"

Burnside stared down at the map. "We will do it, sir. The Reb defenses at Burkittsville Pass are especially light, too, so Franklin should have no trouble pushing through there, either."

McClellan's eyebrows knit together. "What do you mean, Burn?"

"General Parke, bring General McClellan the dispatch we received from Pleasonton."

Parke stepped over, handing a sheet of unfolded paper to Little Mac. "Sir."

McClellan read the brief message, a glow of excitement spreading across his face. "Franklin must have this at once!" he yelped. "Parke, allow me to use your desk."

"Of course, sir," replied the staff officer, moving aside so the commander could take a seat just inside the tent flap.

Pulling a piece of paper to him, McClellan dipped a pen into its well of ink and began scratching out a message. He finished, read it carefully, blew the ink dry, and folded the paper into a neat square. "General Parke, have this delivered to General Franklin immediately. Lose no time getting it to him." Parke took the note and hurried from the tent to call for a courier.

McClellan turned to back Burnside. "I have ordered Franklin to make haste through the Burkittsville Pass. Fifteen hundred Secesh! Burn, his corps can walk through them into Pleasant Valley. When he takes that pass and pushes ahead, Lee will be in serious trouble. We are on the verge of achieving something magnificent. It will be a signal victory! Miles needs to hold out, and you need to fight your way over that mountain."

McClellan set to pacing, his hands locked behind his back. Burnside assured him once again that he would get his part of the job done. "I must get a message through to Miles telling him to hold out to the last extremity. The question is how?"

"Send a local? They know the roads better than either we or the Rebels do."

"That is a capital idea!" McClellan stepped outside the tent and waved. "Colonel Strother, Mister Pinkerton, come here, if you please."

The two men loitered in the shade of an apple tree when McClellan hailed them. Pinkerton, McClellan's civilian head of intelligence, threw the apple he had been eating to the ground and wiped his fingers on his trousers.

"Gentlemen," said McClellan, "I need you to find me a local to carry a message to Colonel Miles at Harpers Ferry. He must inform Miles to hold out at all hazards until tomorrow morning, when I will come to his relief. Do you understand?"

"Yes, sir," replied Strother. The secretive Pinkerton merely nodded. Then the two men strode back to their horses and rode out of camp.

McClellan turned back to Burnside. "I must contact Hooker and hurry him forward. General Marcy," called the commander, "come here, please." The older man hurried over, red-faced from the heat. "General?"

"I want you to go down the road here to Hooker and urge him to hasten his march. He is not far away now. Tell him he is to pass through Middletown, and then west to the base of South Mountain. When he arrives there, he is to examine the country and consult with General Reno until Burnside and I come up to give him orders. Do you understand?"

Marcy raced off, leaving Burnside and Parke alone with McClellan. "It will take some hours for Hooker to get into position," said the former. "Do you think Franklin will get through the pass at Burkittsville in time?"

"He must!" barked Little Mac. "This could be the most important day of the war, Burn. Its outcome lies in your hands, and in Franklin's. Do what you can to achieve success for me. No, not for me. For the nation!"

"I will, sir," guaranteed Burnside, grateful for the army commander's confidence. "You may count on it."

12

Sunday, September 14, 1862
Mid to late afternoon
Sixth Corps, General Franklin's Headquarters
Near Burkittsville, Maryland

Custer smoldered under the brim of his hat. Propped against a locust tree some yards away from a collection of senior Sixth Corps officers, he ground a blade of grass between his teeth and wished furiously that Major General William Franklin would do something to get at the Rebels defending Crampton's Gap.

Instead, the general lounged on a camp chair with a cigar in his hand; his round, bearded face looming walrus-like in Custer's imagination. The officers seated around Franklin laughed heartily, cigars in their hands, too, as if on an outing. Behind Franklin stood the tents of his headquarters, set up in an orchard by the house of a prosperous local farmer named Shafer.

Custer listened to the generals, nearly all of them Democrats, exchange spiteful remarks about the irregular cut of Republican War Secretary Edwin Stanton's beard.

"If I'd known hogs could grow whiskers like that, I'd have bought a whole farm of them and charged admission!" roared Major General William "Baldy" Smith in a cloud of tobacco smoke.

"Admission! Why, Smith, that's a bully idea!" choked Franklin, wiping a tear from the corner of his eye. "You could add that Halleck creature to the exhibit, too, with a circus barker advertising him as the goggle-eyed man who can stare through walls!"

Smith leaned forward on his stool, the stogie in his fist pointed theatrically at Franklin. "Ah, general, but only after he peers at you through his bushy eyebrows first!"

Howls of laughter exploded from the gathering, drowning out the artillery fire that echoed down the mountain. Sighing heavily, Custer stared at the smoke rising above the spires of Burkittsville. Thinking back to when he had delivered McClellan's orders to Franklin the previous evening, he recalled telling the general the urgency with which Little Mac had sent him.

"Force the gap at all hazards! That is General McClellan's wish," he had said.

Franklin mumbled some perfunctory comment that he understood, and Custer had believed him. But after getting the 13,000-man Sixth Corps off to an early start that morning, the general paused at the hamlet of Jefferson to await the division of Darius Couch—something McClellan had urged him not to do, but which he ultimately left in the hands of his corps commander. The hours slipped away with no Couch in sight until Franklin finally ordered his men to resume their advance at around ten-thirty. Following a leisurely march of six and a half miles, Major General Henry Slocum's infantry division then arrived west of Burkittsville, pushed the enemy's pickets out of town, and promptly halted to take lunch.

"Lunch!" Custer snorted in disbelief. "He ought to have fallen on the enemy without delay. What in God's name is wrong with these generals?"

Custer peered sideways. Best to ensure he stood alone. No senior officer should hear him thinking such things aloud.

Mid-day passed, and the sun began its descent into the western sky. Now, the Sixth Corps' brain trust sat waiting for a young colonel named Bartlett to arrive from Slocum's division before they would decide how to attack the mountain gap. That there could be any question about the proper course of action evaded Custer. To him, the situation seemed clear, as it always did, and he had earned only average marks at West Point. General McClellan ordered the gap seized at all hazards. That meant an infantry assault. The only decision required was to determine the direction from which the attack should come. Troops from General Slocum's command approaching the village earlier in the day had drawn fire from Rebel guns posted close to the mountain's crest. Skirmishers sent out by Slocum had then encountered infantry posted behind a stone wall along the mountain's eastern base.

The enemy's position gave the appearance of strength, but Custer thought it a ruse. Observing the Rebel defenses through his binoculars, he could clearly see that the puffs of smoke from the enemy's muskets were widely dispersed. That suggested a thin line held by a few men. He also spotted no artillery on their front. The enemy's position looked quite weak, and could be easily swept aside if Slocum attacked with his entire division.

Stirring from his thoughts, Custer glanced down at his pocket watch.

One o'clock.

He had loitered around Sixth Corps headquarters for more than an hour, and still nothing had been done. Staring hard at Franklin, he kicked at the dirt until the sound of an approaching rider caught his attention. Custer looked up to see a youthful officer sporting a cavalier's goatee trot up with an aide.

Pushing himself from the tree, Custer strode up to listen.

"Ah, here is Colonel Bartlett," said Slocum, waving the cigar in his hand. "Let us hear his thoughts on the matter of our attack. Come closer, colonel!"

Sliding down from his horse, Bartlett approached his commanding officer. "General, sir, I understand you called for me?"

"Yes, colonel, I did. We here at headquarters are evenly divided on where to attack. You've reconnoitered the ground, have you not?" Slocum scrutinized the colonel with an eyebrow raised.

"I have. Quite extensively, and for some time now, I might add."

Custer smirked at the reproach. That's it, colonel, let the brass have it.

Slocum blundered past the affront. "That's very good. Tell us, then, how you would make the attack."

Bartlett clasped his gloved hands firmly behind his back. "General, I would attack on the right—the north side; where I believe the lay of the land serves us best and where I think the weight of our numbers can be brought to bear."

Great God! At last, someone has a plan! thought Custer.

Slapping his hands on his knees, Franklin blew out a prodigious cloud of smoke. "Well, gentlemen, that settles it. We will follow the colonel's recommendation and attack at once. Go to your commands and get them ready. General Slocum, your division will lead the assault."

Nodding to his commander, Slocum turned to the uneasy Bartlett. "Colonel, as General Franklin has allowed you to decide the point of attack, on the grounds that you are to lead it, it is fair that I should leave the formation to you."

Bartlett quickly shook his head. "General—I cannot."

"Spare us the modesty," retorted Slocum. "You've seen the ground. Tell us the tactics you will use."

Bartlett's Adam's apple rose and fell in rapid succession. "As you wish, sir. I would attack in a column of brigades with two regiments in the first rank of each brigade and two regiments following."

"Interesting. How great a distance between the regiments?"

"One hundred paces. This will give us six lines of infantry, a formation that will focus the division's weight against critical points on the enemy's line. I believe the Rebel position is vulnerable and undermanned. We will pierce it like a hot knife carves butter."

Excitement surged through Custer. Bartlett had seen what he saw—that only a few men stood between them and total victory.

"Is the Rebel position really so weak?" frowned Franklin. "The information I have estimates the enemy's number to be no less than four thousand men. I've written to General McClellan that we may have a rough go of it."

Bartlett turned to Franklin; his manner now thoroughly calm. "Respectfully, sir, if there are four thousand Rebels on that line, I will eat my hat."

"Bah! That's brash of you, colonel," gushed Franklin, wagging his cigar at the man. "I'll hold you to it in the event you are repulsed. But enough talk, gentlemen. Go to your commands and get the attack underway."

The gathering rose and strode off toward their mounts, cigar smoke lingering heavily in the air. Franklin rose as well and turned to enter his tent when Custer intercepted him.

"General, sir, a moment, please," he called out.

"Ah, Captain Custer. Still with us, I see."

"Yes, sir. General McClellan told me to stay and observe until you have won the pass. With your permission, I'd like to go forward and watch the First Division's attack."

"You have it, captain, and godspeed to you," waved Franklin. "Do be careful, though. I wouldn't want you to be hurt while McClellan has placed you in my charge."

"I'll do my best, general. Thank you," saluted Custer, before turning to retrieve his mount. Wellington nickered as he approached, acknowledging his master with a toss of his head. Custer loosened the straps that secured the Morgan to the tie-line and vaulted into the saddle.

"Come, Wellington," he called out, wheeling the horse west. "We're going to war."

*   *   *

Custer passed through a dense stand of corn and emerged to find a cluster of officers atop their horses near a copse of trees. At the center of the group sat the thin man with blonde hair and mustache that he recognized as General Slocum. Born a New Yorker, and an 1852 graduate of the United States Military Academy at West Point, Slocum let the chestnut mount below him graze on clover as he peered through his binoculars at the enemy. Sensing the weakness on their left, the Rebels had extended their position behind the stone wall targeted by Colonel Bartlett's pending assault.

Custer reined in near the group, saluting as Slocum lowered his field glasses. The general's eyes scanned him up and down, a scowl forming on his face as he took in Custer's longer than regulation locks.

"The name is Custer, is it not?" asked Slocum, returning the captain's greeting.

"Yes, sir. That's correct. We met at General Franklin's headquarters. General McClellan sent me to observe the attack. With your permission, I'd like to stay here with you. I'm sure the general would receive a report about your assault with great interest. Your men are about to go in, are they not?"

"They are, and you may remain," nodded Slocum. "The men directly in our front are those of General Newton. They are stout New York boys. To their right is the brigade of Colonel Bartlett."

Slocum pointed his field glasses at the line of blue regiments. "I see them, sir," said Custer. "Do you know the enemy's strength? They appear to have moved more men into the line."

"Earlier reports put it close to four thousand men, but Colonel Bartlett thinks they number considerably less. We shall see if he's correct. The Secessionists occupy that stone wall at the base of the mountain. More Rebels have been seen on the summit. Colonel Bartlett's brigade will strike their left. He holds the key position in our plan."

Peering at the First Division's three brigades, Custer sat, watching the ranks of each regiment form into the deep, narrow fronts that Colonel Bartlett had recommended at headquarters. To the division's left lay the village of Burkittsville, its shingled homes and church spires huddled close to South Mountain. A series of fences in the foreground straddled the rolling countryside between Slocum's men and the enemy. Field commanders moved in front of the ranks, gesturing for the men to shelter in a swale from Rebel guns, throwing shells at them from the front left. Skirmishers some yards ahead exchanged fire with Butternut pickets, their shots popping out in puffs of gray smoke.

Custer returned his gaze to Slocum. "Will the colonel be making his attack in column?" he asked.

"He will," nodded the slim general. "Bartlett believes the column formation will add weight to our punch. I have decided to give his advice a try."

Slocum turned to speak with the major beside him. Then he waved for his bugler. "Corporal, sound the advance!"

The musician blared the notes, bringing the long lines of Northern men to their feet. Officers moved out first, and with drums rapping, the brigades lurched up the hillside. Colors flapped in the sunlight and the formations glowed deep blue against the fields of emerald green. Slocum's men crested the hill to their front and paused to re-align as Rebel guns opened on them. Dark pillars of dirt and smoke erupted skyward, dropping men in the tall grass while volleys of timed spherical case burst above the ranks in flashes of white and gray, raining down a murderous hail of iron shards.

Transfixed by the scene, Custer peered through his binoculars with his heart pounding in his chest. Among the trees, he could see Rebel soldiers firing steadily as the Federal line rolled to a rail fence one hundred yards in front of the stone wall. Here Slocum's men halted to exchange fire. A wild, warbling howl wavered out from the Southerners' line amidst the crack of muskets and thumps of cannon fire. Heavy smoke drifted back from the front.

Time stood still for Custer. Wounded men limped rearward through the smoke, some carrying injured comrades. Then a man on a charger sped up to request a battery in support of Bartlett's advance. Custer realized for the first time that no artillery occupied the field in their vicinity. Slocum commented casually that he had hoped infantry alone could complete the assault. Shaking his head at the man's folly, Custer tugged at his watch chain, noting that the hour had already reached five o'clock.

Another courier appeared, followed by several more, each repeating the same request for ammunition. Custer scrutinized Slocum closely, but the general remained collected as he ordered the ordnance wagons brought up. Then the gunfire from his division slackened on the left, and Slocum stared hard at it. Barking for one of his staff to ride there and learn what was happening, Slocum began pacing his horse as the center also fell silent. Only Bartlett's command on the right continued exchanging shots with the enemy.

"What in God's name is happening?" growled the general.

"Sir, I'll go to Colonel Bartlett and find out!" volunteered Custer.

His blood up from observing the fight, Custer felt he could no longer sit still, so before Slocum could agree, he put his heels to Wellington's flanks. Speeding through the clover, he crossed the swale where the attack had stepped off and approached the indigo line. Shots whined past him, but Custer paid them no mind, his thoughts occupied completely by the thrill of battle. He called out for Colonel Bartlett along the line behind the stacked fence rails until the slim officer waved him over.

"You damned fool! Come down from that animal or you'll be shot!" cried Bartlett, his face aglow with perspiration.

Ignoring the advice, Custer danced his mount sideways. "Sir, General Slocum wishes to know why your men have stopped firing."

Stooping as a minié whistled past, Bartlett shouted, "Captain, I cannot tell if you are the bravest man on this field or the maddest. Tell the good general that we are preparing to charge along the entire line and drive the enemy. Colonel Torbert and the others have all agreed to it. The signal to go should come at any moment. Now, get yourself out of here!"

"Yes, sir!" said Custer, and wheeling Wellington, he spurred off at a gallop.

Returning to the copse where Slocum observed the fight, the general scowled when Custer rode up. "Captain, that was as stupid and reckless an act as I have ever witnessed," he scolded.

"I am sorry, sir," Custer fibbed. "But I got the information you need. Colonel Bartlett says the brigade commanders have agreed that they can no longer hold their position. They are preparing to drive the Rebels with the bayonet."

The color drained from Slocum's cheeks. "What! They are going to charge?"

"Yes, sir. They are."

A roar of voices rose from the left of the Federal line, carrying quickly to the center, and then to the right. Slocum's gaze snapped toward the sound and the general walked his horse a step forward. The men sheltering behind the rail fence rose to their feet and dashed into the field beyond, with flags waving. At a second fence some distance away, they stopped to clamber over the rails. Shots popped out from the stone wall, dropping men into the clover, but the greater mass moved on with bayonets flashing in the late afternoon light. The enemy's fire slackened, and Rebel troops could be seen bolting to the rear.

"General, they're skedaddling!" yelled Custer, unable to contain himself.

"By gum, they've done it! Go on, boys, and get after them!" yelled Slocum, grabbing the hat from his head.

Men in blue scrambled over the abandoned stone wall and into the forest after their fleeing adversary. Heavy firing erupted on the hillside, sending smoke billowing up through the trees. Slocum dispatched a rider to learn the situation, but before the man returned, a messenger from Bartlett pelted toward him from across the field.

"Sir, Colonel Bartlett sends me to say that our men have driven the Johnnies to the top of the gap!" he yelped.

"Where is Bartlett now?"

"Fighting near a ravine. The Rebs tried to hold on the mountainside, but Colonel Torbert's New Jersey boys got them surrounded. We've killed or captured almost the whole lot of them!"

"By God, we've won!" cried Slocum, balling his hand into a fist.

"Sir, congratulations!" said Custer.

"My thanks, captain! I'll be damned if Bartlett wasn't right. Custer, you may be of service to me after all. Go to General Franklin and tell him of our victory before you return to General McClellan. Tell Franklin that my division requires support to hold the gap. Nightfall will be here soon, but I wouldn't put it past Secesh to counterattack. We must consolidate our gains."

"As you wish, sir," replied Custer, and wheeling Wellington toward the rear, he sped toward the Sixth Corps headquarters.

*   *   *

Entering Franklin's encampment in the failing light, Custer spotted the barrel-chested general by his tent. He rode forward quickly, not bothering to dismount. Franklin, an old forage cap atop his head, turned to regard Custer with a troubled expression on his face.

"Ah, Captain Custer, you are still here. Will you return to the commanding general now?" he asked.

"Yes, sir, but first I have good news for you from General Slocum. His men have won a great victory!"

Franklin's brow furrowed. "A victory? How can that be? The reports I've received say the Rebel line is holding firm. Young Bartlett appears to have been mistaken in his advice. I should have known better than to follow the recommendation of a political officer and not a regular army man."

"But, general, that is not the case."

Franklin carried on, ignoring Custer. "I've communicated to General McClellan that we will suspend our attack until tomorrow morning. The Rebels here are too strong for us."

"Too strong?" shot Custer. "Respectfully, general, the information you have is incorrect. I have just come from General Slocum. His division—led by Colonel Bartlett's brigade—drove the enemy from his defenses. When I left him, they were fighting near the top of the pass. Sir, you've won the battle and the pass!"

Franklin stared at Custer; his visage contorted with disbelief. Then he turned to the officer beside him. "Major Greene, can this be true? Have we truly won?"

Greene glanced from Franklin to Custer. "I see no reason to doubt the captain, sir, but I'll send to the front for confirmation."

"General Slocum requested reinforcements as well, sir," added Custer.

Franklin's brow furrowed. "Very well, captain, I hope your report is correct. It would be welcome news."

"I assure you it is!" snapped Custer with barely veiled frustration. "Your men have carried the gap, just as General McClellan ordered. Now, you need to push forward. Harpers Ferry is in grave danger!"

"So, the commanding general reminds me," said Franklin, waving a recently received dispatch in his hand. "And you will mind your tone with me, captain. McClellan's errand boy or not, I can still have your bars. Is that clear?"

Custer's spine straightened at the rebuke, his narrow-set eyes regarding the general with barely veiled contempt.

"You young men are too full of fire," paced Franklin, "but you must not forget your place. Assuming your report is correct, I will push my command into Pleasant Valley. Do you understand?"

"I do, sir."

"Good. Ride to General McClellan and tell him of our success."

"Yes, sir, I'll leave immediately," nodded the captain. Cinching up his reins, he choked back the bile in his throat before steering Wellington out of the encampment.

A haze of powder smoke hovered over the saddle-shaped gap to the west, which had by now fallen into silhouette under the flaring orange sky. Touching his heels to Wellington's flanks, Custer sped northward into the gloom.

13

Sunday, September 14, 1862
Mid-afternoon to midnight
General Burnside's Wing, Army of the Potomac
Bolivar, Maryland

in God's name is taking Hooker so long?" A frustrated Ambrose Burnside sat atop his dappled gray, his brow furrowed with anger and his cheeks tinged in crimson.

Hooker's tardiness came as no surprise to Jesse Reno, who sat silently on the horse beside Burnside. He wished the good-natured Burnside would be more aggressive when directing "Fighting Joe's" movements. Instead, Old Burn exercised command with too kind a heart. His handling of Hooker, a pompous, conceited child of a man, served as a case in point. Burnside expected Hooker to act professionally; that is, to obey the orders he was given and do so promptly. Hooker, however, balked at every turn. If Burnside urged Hooker to hurry, he slowed to a crawl. When Burnside said go left, Hooker turned right. Worse yet, Hooker ignored the chain of command by communicating directly with General McClellan, bypassing Burnside completely.

McClellan proved no help with the matter. Far from discouraging Hooker's disobedience, he indulged the willful general's breaches of protocol. Now the Ninth Corps grappled with Lee's Rebels in a fight for the fate of the Republic and it seemed to Reno as if the latitude with which Burnside and McClellan handled Hooker was hindering the army's chance of success.

Fighting his corps alone atop Fox's Gap, Reno begged Burnside to order that Hooker make a diversion by bringing up his corps on the Confederate left, north of the National Road. Reno hoped an attack on the opposite side of the mountain passes would take the pressure off his men and enable him to capture Fox's Gap. Burnside saw the wisdom in Reno's request and issued the orders to Hooker, but the ingrate general from Massachusetts could not be found. Were Hooker under his command, Reno thought to himself, he would drive the man like an army mule and not spare the whip.

Chewing on the stub of a cigar, the Virginian peered at the high mountain pass where Jacob Cox's division held a twisted battle line. In the hour since Burnside returned from headquarters, General Wilcox had finally moved into position on Cox's right. Now General Sturgis had come up, too. The rattle of musketry on Willcox's front signaled that he had renewed the long-delayed attack. Had they beaten Longstreet to the punch? Reno could only wonder.

What remained to be done was keep the enemy off balance until the First Corps got into position. Headquarters reported that Hooker had scouted the ground north of the National Road some time earlier with General Marcy, McClellan's chief of staff. Hooker, however, had not bothered to report his findings to Burnside, so who knew if the information was correct. Old Burn grew agitated waiting for the leading elements of Hooker's corps to arrive. Looking at his watch, he sighed loudly and wondered again where the missing general could be. Reno met the question with a shrug and held his tongue. Burnside knew his low opinion of Hooker. There was no benefit in voicing it again.

At last, a messenger arrived to report the approach of General Meade's Pennsylvania Reserves from Hooker's corps. Burnside thanked the man and turned to his trusted subordinate. "Don't worry, general," he said, "I'll see to Meade's placement myself. You'll have your attack on the enemy's left, or my name isn't Ambrose Everett Burnside!"

Cinching Major's reins, the general traveled down the grassy slope toward the main road. There, he encountered a column of infantry tramping four men abreast over the crest of the hill. Ahead of the marching troops rode General George Gordon Meade, a dour-faced Pennsylvanian whom Burnside respected. Meade could be abrasive, but he also showed backbone in a fight.

Meade wore his graying beard short and kept his forage cap pulled down tightly upon his ears. Spotting the silhouette of Burnside in the late day sun, he pulled his horse off the pike and led it up the embankment to the wing commander's side.

"Greetings, general, do you know where General Hooker may be found?" he asked.

"Hello, George," nodded Burnside. "I haven't caught sight of General Hooker in days. He could be in Pennsylvania, for all I know, or care at this point. Your men are the first element of his corps to arrive and now that you are here, I'll position your division myself. Be a good man and ride with me."

"It'd be my pleasure, sir. Care for a smoke?"

Meade produced a pair of cigars from his coat pocket. Savoring the bite of tobacco on his tongue, Burnside cheerfully accepted the offer. "Thanks for this," he said. "I left my stock back at headquarters."

"When you're on the move as much as I've been these last few days, you've got no time to leave things behind," replied Meade, striking a wooden match. "Everything I need is in these saddlebags."

Meade held the match for Burnside, who puffed his stogie until a plume of smoke rolled out from under his brim.

"Ah, that's good! These from James River way?" asked Burnside, removing the cigar to spit out an errant bit of tobacco.

"Yes, sir. No sense making a trip to Virginia without sampling some of the local product."

"Well said, George. You're a man of discriminating taste. Now, come with me to the front."

Meade followed Burnside back onto the road and they walked their horses alongside the troops striding past. Equipment clattered amidst the tromp of marching feet and Burnside gazed down at the men. They appeared well-off, although dusty from days on the go. Tobacco smoke wafted from the ranks, mingled with the tang of sweat and leather.

"It's General Burnside, fellas! Give him a holler!" cried a burly sergeant. Cheers rose from the column as caps fluttered.

Tipping his hat, Burnside called out to Meade. "Your men look fine, general. Curious decoration on their caps, though. Are deer tails regulation?"

"I should think not," replied Meade, producing a handkerchief to wipe dust from his eyes. "These aren't regulars. They're Pennsylvania volunteers—Bucktails, they call themselves."

"Fascinating. The men are ingenious when naming their regiments," said Burnside, puffing smoke. "Their high spirits are to your credit, George."

"Thank you, sir. My boys are itching for a fight. That's Secesh ahead, I take it?"

Meade pointed to a rounded knob on the mountain where a battery of Rebel guns exchanged fire with Federal artillery positioned on a grassy knoll below.

"Some of them," nodded Burnside. "General Reno has engaged a much larger force on our left. That's the fight you hear at the moment. I have a different plan for your division. I want you to attack the Rebel left. Do you see this crossroads coming up?"

"I do," nodded Meade, picking tobacco from his tongue.

Burnside pointed with his cigar. "Off to the right is where I want your men to go. Follow that road north for a mile or so and spread out along the base of those mountain spurs. My scouts report a very thin Rebel presence on that side of the pass."

Burnside pulled his horse to a stop on the sloping roadside, prompting Meade to do the same. Meade signaled a brigade commander near them to keep moving while Burnside removed his hat to mop perspiration from his hairless pate. "My thinking, George, is to have your division crush the enemy's left while Reno occupies the right. Once you are in position, I will push a brigade at their center to keep them occupied."

"Classic double envelopment, eh?" nodded Meade, gloved fingers pulling thoughtfully at his beard. "Reno on the left, my command on the right."

"Something like that. Do you think you can get into position and start your attack before we lose daylight? It's past two now."

"I'll do my best, general," assured Meade.

Burnside flashed a smile and replaced his hat atop his head. "That's very good, George. You have my thanks. We have an opportunity to break the Rebel army here, I think. Cox gave us a good start this morning and Reno is following up on his gains. Now you must take up the work on the other flank. All I ask is that you do it as quickly as possible."

Meade tapped ash from the tip of his smoke. "I understand, sir. My men are up to the task."

"Excellent. Then I'll wish you Godspeed and good luck," said Burnside, and after shaking Meade's hand, he watched the general ride off to catch the head of his column.

*   *   *

Seated atop Dan Webster, George McClellan surveyed a column of troops striding out of Middletown toward the fight atop South Mountain. Cheers erupted from every regiment that marched by, the men's grimy faces shining with adulation for their beloved commander. McClellan basked in their applause, pandering shamelessly to them in return. To some regiments he tipped his cap. To others, he pointed his right hand dramatically toward the smoke-capped eminence in the distance. The men roared their approval, picking up their step as the general's gesture filled them with renewed purpose.

Little Mac's ability to inspire men impressed Joseph Hooker, who sat astride his horse near the general. A wide-brimmed slouch hat perched atop his head, Hooker and General Marcy had long since returned from their reconnaissance of the ground north of the National Road and reported to McClellan, without informing Ambrose Burnside.

Blonde-haired and blue-eyed, with lengthy sideburns, Hooker sat taller on his horse than did Little Mac, his expression betraying no emotion. Even when troops from his home state of Massachusetts marched past, Hooker merely nodded to them. He did not grin, wave, or make any other outward gesture of affection.

McClellan found Hooker's grim detachment puzzling, but he overlooked it in favor of the man's aggression. Hooker could be counted on to fight when the time came, and nothing mattered more than that.

Returning the salute of a passing colonel, McClellan glanced over at Hooker. "General, your men look splendid."

"Thank you, sir. They've marched hard today."

"Remind me, which division is this?"

Hooker shot a sidelong glance at McClellan, thinking it unlike him to lose track of details. "Why, these are the men of General Ricketts," he responded.

"That's right," nodded Little Mac. "They are following General Hatch's division?"

"Yes, sir, that's correct."

"I thought so. You must forgive me, Hooker. I have many things occupying my mind."

"That's understandable, sir. General Burnside requires more oversight from you than he ought. You need subordinates who can command without resorting continually to your intellect."

"Well said, general," commented the officer on Hooker's left. With a full brown beard and cheeks scarred from years of childhood acne, Major General Fitz John Porter competed openly with Hooker for McClellan's attention.

"You've only just arrived from some recent unpleasantness in Washington, haven't you, General Porter?" asked Hooker, his shark-like gaze landing on Porter.

Staring down at the pommel of his saddle, Porter set his lips. "Yes, that's right. That son of a bitch Stanton took my command from me after Pope's disgrace at Manassas. Thankfully, General McClellan was able to get it back and I am now in command of the Fifth Corps, the First Division of which is coming up behind your men."

"And we are glad to have you with us once again," said McClellan, glancing over at Porter.

Porter tipped his hat, but Little Mac had already turned to admire another passing regiment. Pointing west, he drew another cheer to fire his vanity.

"You know, sir, General Hooker is correct about Burnside," shouted Porter above the din. Scrutinizing McClellan's face for a response, he ventured on. "I don't believe he can be trusted to faithfully execute your orders."

Little Mac turned to Porter, his brows knitting together. "Fitz, what are you saying?"

"I'm saying Burnside can be treacherous and you ought to watch him more closely. Take General Hooker here. He should have his own command and not be under the thumb of a weak-kneed man like Ambrose Burnside."

Hooker swelled visibly at the comment.

"I admit I've never cared for the wing arrangement foisted upon me by the president," sighed McClellan. "It is too unwieldy."

"Why do you suppose Mister Lincoln demanded you take on Burnside as a wing commander?" probed Porter. "Do you suspect the president thought you could rely on him?"

"Who knows, Fitz? I haven't given it any thought. The army is mine to command, Old Burn's presence notwithstanding."

"Ah, but you ought to give it some thought, my dear general. Some real thought, indeed."

McClellan peered Porter's way. "What are you saying?"

Porter smiled inwardly. He had hooked his fish. "It's quite simple, sir. The administration had you put Burnside in a position of authority for the sake of convenience. The first time you make a decision with which they disagree, they'll recall you to Washington and give Burnside overall command."

"They would never!"

"They would, sir, and you well know it. You are aware, I take it, that Lincoln offered command of this army to Burnside?"

"Yes, of course, I know. Burn told me of it himself."

"That's kind of him, but it does not change things. The administration is hostile to you and to your supporters; good men such as myself, General Hooker, and General

Franklin. If Washington perceives Burnside is having more success than you, they will put him in your place before you can say Bob's your uncle and there is nothing that any of us can do about it."

"Perhaps there is," volunteered Hooker. "What if General McClellan were to assign me to independent command, as you have suggested? Burnside would be left with but one corps in his wing of the army and that is under General Reno. Burnside's position becomes extraneous, and he can take no credit for any victory this army might achieve, even though he remains technically in command. The administration's lapdog is rendered harmless, the commanding general is protected, and you, sir, can direct the army without concern for your hindquarters."

"That's a marvelous idea," grinned Porter to Hooker.

"General Hooker, you have a coarse way of putting things," sighed McClellan. "Burnside has been loyal to me and a good field commander thus far, but you gentlemen may be correct that his presence is a threat. I hadn't considered the prospect that whatever victory this army might win could be attributed to him and not to me. Now that I think on it, it does seem possible."

"It is more than possible!" nudged Porter, cultivating the seed of suspicion he had planted in McClellan's mind. "I'll say it again, sir, Burnside is not to be trusted. In the run-up to Pope's disaster in Virginia, he forwarded every missive I sent him to the War Department. Some of those messages were personal and written in the greatest confidence. Never in my life did I think Burnside would betray me so badly."

"He forwarded private correspondence?" gasped Hooker with mock indignation.

"He did, and it nearly cost me my command."

"Gentlemen, gentlemen, enough. Let us focus on the task at hand," said McClellan, waving away the conspiratorial chatter. "This army is engaged, and I expect General Franklin to begin his attack at any minute. In fact, I have not heard from Franklin for some time, and must find a better observation point from which to see if his attack has gone off. Let us move to the front and not linger here any longer."

Cinching Dan's reins, McClellan gave the order to move out. He spurred his horse through a gap in General Ricketts's line and galloped past the cheering ranks with his cap held aloft. One mile west of Middletown, the general and his entourage splashed across Catoctin Creek. Here, Hooker split off from McClellan, continuing due west to find George Meade's division.

Requesting an aide lead him to General Reno, Little Mac followed the man up a sloping road to the left. Across the rolling foothills, they rode to a high knoll where Reno and his staff observed the fight. The loyal Virginian spotted McClellan coming and turned in the saddle to greet him.

"General," nodded Little Mac, yanking Dan to a stop. "What's the situation here?"

"Sir, General Sturgis's division is on the road in front of us," said Reno, pointing to a column marching from right to left, some 300 yards down the slope below them. "His men are heading up the mountain to join Cox and Willcox in a combined assault on the Rebel right."

"Excellent," said Little Mac. "Burnside informed me that Cox's men did good work this morning."

"That they did. Casualties have been relatively light for the number of troops engaged, too, which is fortunate. Some regiments have suffered a good number of wounded, but despite his losses, Cox managed to push back the enemy's flank."

A hopeful expression formed on McClellan's face. "So, we hold the gap?"

Reno shook his head. "Not yet. Secesh is putting up a hard fight. Once my corps is fully engaged, we'll finish what Cox has started."

"I see. Very well, then," sighed the general, leaning forward to peer at the mountain. "What about the center of the enemy's position on the pike? Have you taken steps to pressure it?"

"No, sir. I know General Burnside plans too, however."

McClellan looked around. "Where is Burnside? I had expected to find him here."

"He went to speak with General Meade when his division came up, I believe he'll be back shortly. Ah, there he is now, in fact."

Reno pointed across the hillside at the approaching general. Burnside reined in opposite Little Mac and tossed him a salute, the stub of a cigar still smoldering between his lips. "General McClellan, it's good to see you."

"Greetings, General Burnside. Reno was just telling me that you went to speak with General Meade. Is everything in order with him?"

"It is, general. I went to see to the placement of his division on the Rebel left."

"I see. Is that not General Hooker's responsibility?"

Burnside's cheeks flushed a deep shade of red. "It is, sir, but I have not seen Hooker in days, and he does not respond to my orders. I called up his corps hours ago, but so far only Meade has appeared. I want his attack to take the pressure off General Reno's front. Time is wasting, sir."

"So it is," sniffed McClellan, looking up at the sun with his hand shading his eyes. "What of the Rebel center? Are you moving against it as well?"

"I am. When the next division after Meade's comes up, I intend to push a brigade at the enemy's line astride the main road. I have contented myself with shelling the position to keep the enemy's guns off General Reno's men."

McClellan muttered a word of approval and fell silent. Burnside appeared to have everything well in hand. Too well, perhaps. Porter's words came back to haunt him. If the army won here today, Burnside would be hailed as the victor, and not him. He must be seen by the men around them as fully in control.

"General Burnside, you must carry these mountain passes for me," he said stiffly. "General Franklin is forcing the pass above Burkittsville five miles south of here. If he captures it, my plan is to have you protect his right flank from General Longstreet's command at Boonsborough."

"Boonsborough?" blurted Reno. "But, sir, Longstreet's men aren't there. They are on the mountain."

McClellan turned sharply to Reno. "Longstreet is here?"

"He is. Captured Rebels report his men arriving on the field."

"Then I have the opportunity to destroy his command as well as that of Harvey Hill!"

"You do, sir," said Burnside. "That's why I've ordered Hooker to attack on the right."

"Sir, are you sure Franklin has begun his attack on the Burkittsville Pass?" inquired Reno.

McClellan stroked his mustache. "That is a good question, general. Major Myer, have you been able to establish signal contact with Franklin's command?"

"Not yet, sir," replied the bearded officer on a horse nearby. "I have a detachment trying to raise him now. Our present position is a good vantage point, with a clear line of sight. You see, general? There is smoke rising to the south."

Pointing down mountain, Myer directed McClellan's attention to a gray haze hovering in the distance. Thumping cannon fire echoed from that direction as well.

"Splendid!" exclaimed Little Mac. "My design to save Harpers Ferry is coming together. General Burnside, I concur with your assessment of things. We must get Hooker to launch his attack as soon as possible."

"I'm glad, sir," nodded Old Burn. "I've made it clear to General Hooker more than once already that he is to attack as soon as his men are up. Do you wish me to see to it myself?"

McClellan thought again of Porter, and he struggled to force the man's poisoned words from his head. If Hooker crushed the Rebel left, it would be a great victory and Burnside would get the credit. Yet maybe he would not. The victory would be Hooker's, not Burnside's. Uncertain for a moment, McClellan finally spoke up. "Yes, Burn, go to Hooker's front, and hurry him up. The daylight is failing."

"As you wish, general. I'll leave right away."

Insensible to the ominous blackening of McClellan's mood toward him, Burnside spurred away.

"Sir, with your permission, I'll go now too," said Reno. "I'd like to attend the attack by my corps personally."

"Understood, general. May God be with you," nodded McClellan.

Signaling his aides, the Virginian rode off, leaving Little Mac and his staff to observe the battle from atop the grassy ridge.

*　*　*

Weaving his mount through the crossroad hamlet of Bolivar, Burnside led a coterie of riders down a shabby road toward the army's right flank. A cluster of officers on a low hill caught Burnside's attention, and he guided Major toward them. The brigadier in the center of the group saluted as the wing commander rode up.

"Greetings, General Burnside, it's good to see you."

Burnside tossed the chewed remains of his cigar into the grass and brushed the ashes from his coat. "Hello, Hatch. Have you seen General Hooker?"

"I have, sir. He passed this way a short time ago."

"Headed which direction?"

"North, sir. To our right."

"Alright, then, I'm heading north, too. Before I leave, I want you to detach a brigade and send it back to the turnpike. I'm thinking John Gibbon's boys would be best."

"As you wish, general. With what orders?"

"With orders to move against the Rebel center at the top of the gap there. Do you see where I mean?"

Burnside pointed at a thin enemy battle line behind a stone wall on the hillside just below the gap.

"I do, sir. I'll send for Gibbon immediately."

"Thank you, general. I appreciate your attention to the matter."

Hatch called for a messenger as Burnside steered Major back onto the road. Cantering along, he passed masses of troops forming in the fields to his left. File closers shouted orders and bugle calls rang out. A regiment fixed bayonets as Burnside passed behind them, the click of steel scraping on steel filling the air. Up the twisted track and down another set of rolling hills rode the general until he came to a dip in the road by a low ridge. A battery of rifled cannon atop the height hurled rounds of spherical case and solid shot at Rebel guns on the mountainside.

Burnside surveyed the Pennsylvania Reserves. Arranged in two, and in some places, three lines deep, Meade's regiments spread out along the base of the mountain, flags peppering their ranks. Ahead of them, two mountain spurs, one to the left and one to the right, slanted down steeply from the heights, their slopes covered with cornfields, wood lots, and a latticework of low stone walls. A broad, steep ravine curved across the center of Meade's position, occupied by two modest farmhouses and outbuildings on the left and right edges of the hill. Just beyond the farmsteads fluttered the crimson battle flags of troops with the Army of Northern Virginia.

Focusing his field glasses on the banners, Burnside counted at least three enemy regiments. A fourth marched north before disappearing behind a dense mass of trees. The sound of pounding hooves filled Burnside's ears, and he pulled down the glasses to find General Hooker riding up to him. Fighting Joe reined in beside Burnside, offering a lazy salute. Burnside's temper boiled at the sight of the man.

"Ah, General Hooker, here you are at last," he said, struggling to keep his tone even.

"What do you mean, sir? I've been here all along," lied Hooker openly.

"Is that so?" spat Burnside, his rage rising to the surface. "Did you not think to communicate your movements with me? I am your superior officer, sir."

"I communicated them with General McClellan and assumed he would keep you apprised of my situation. Did he not tell you?"

"That is not procedure!" snapped the frustrated wing commander. "Your corps is under my wing of the army, General Hooker. You are to follow my orders promptly and without question. You do not report to General McClellan. You report to me. Do you understand this or did your service with Pope corrupt your comprehension of army protocol?"

Hooker's breath caught in his throat at the fury of Burnside's rebuke. Never before had any officer, much less the mild-mannered Ambrose Burnside, spoken to him in such a tone. Hooker stared at Burnside, his blue eyes cold and grim. "I am quite aware of protocol, sir. General McClellan deserves to know the movements of his corps."

"Indeed, he does, and it is my responsibility, sir, MINE to inform him. Not yours!"

Burnside lowered the finger he had shaken at Hooker. Taking a deep breath, he returned his attention to Meade's line. "Why hasn't General Meade initiated his attack? An attack I ordered him to make some time ago?"

"I told him to wait," replied Hooker. "The rest of my command is not up yet. I would go in with all of my men."

"Against four enemy regiments? My God, Hooker, you are a fool if I've ever seen one. Look up there. LOOK! Do you see an overwhelming Rebel force? Meade's division alone outnumbers the enemy on this part of the field."

Hooker remained unmoved, although his cheeks reddened a touch. Burnside did not wait for a response. "General Hooker, I order you to get Meade's attack underway immediately. It is four o'clock already, and the sun is setting fast. General Reno's men are dying over on the left flank. Do you hear me? They are dying to retain the advantage we gained this morning. Meade's attack can win this fight for us. Now get him moving!"

"General, I—"

Burnside held up his hand for silence. "Not another word, General Hooker. Give the order now or I will do it for you."

Shooting Burnside an acid glance, Hooker yanked his horse's reins hard to the right and spurred angrily toward Meade's line. Burnside looked on impatiently, feeling the ire in his veins as bugles finally blared out Meade's advance. Drums rapped, and the men stepped off with a vigorous shout, their bayonets shining in the late afternoon light. Blasts rang out from the Rebel guns, sending solid shot plunging toward the Pennsylvanians. The accuracy of the fire was so poor, however, that most of the projectiles bounded harmlessly to the rear.

The men in blue swept up the ravine and over the rightmost mountain spur. Gunshots from Confederate pickets popped out from behind a stone wall, then the Graybacks retired uphill toward their comrades. The lines engaged high above the fields of corn, exchanging fire with a rattle that echoed across the valley. At first the Rebels held fast, but Meade's line soon overlapped their flanks and Northern companies filtered into the gaps between the isolated Southerners. The Johnnies broke and fled rearward, prompting a roar from Meade's victorious men.

"They've done it!" yelped Burnside, shaking his field glasses with excitement. "Hurrah for Pennsylvania!"

Lowering the binoculars, he placed them into their case. "The commanding general must know of this success!" he exulted. The road south lay open before him, and he, Ambrose Burnside, rode down it with elation in his heart, having achieved what appeared to be the army's first decisive victory of the war against Robert E. Lee's Army of Northern Virginia.

*　*　*

George McClellan had clearly observed the events unfolding on the right flank. He saw Meade's attack sweep up the mountainside and heard the rumble of cannon fire from that quarter of the field. Reports also arrived from Reno, informing him that the Ninth Corps had pushed back Rebel defenders on the left. The road over South Mountain lay open there, just as Little Mac had hoped. Fading daylight would keep him from exploiting the gains won. Nevertheless, euphoria coursed through McClellan's veins. Victory had vindicated his rapid push toward the South Mountain gaps.

The general took a moment from his observations to shoot a glance at his chief of staff. "Marcy, we are on the cusp of a great triumph," he said.

"It certainly looks that way, sir. My congratulations," grinned the older man. "If General Franklin has pushed through the pass at Burkittsville, our victory will be complete."

"Yes, I wonder how Franklin is faring," said McClellan, turning in the saddle to peer southward.

Dusk fell, but the rumble of combat continued to echo from all parts of the field. Even the Rebel center on the National Road now found itself under assault from the brigade that Burnside had sent to attack it. McClellan peered at the flashing musket fire, his thoughts swirling at the possibilities lying open before him. His enemies in Washington would be silenced. He could have Halleck and Stanton removed. The war could be prosecuted as he saw fit, with honor and restraint, not with the brutality that the radicals in Congress wanted. His control had been restored and now everything would run his way.

"It is a capital day, gentlemen!" he beamed. "I'll be the toast of Washington."

"Washington? Sir, you'll be the toast of the whole country!" said Porter.

Twilight melted into darkness and the members of McClellan's security escort lit torches to illuminate the field. Word arrived of a house whose inhabitants had agreed to accommodate the general and his entourage. Tonight, they would sleep with a roof over their heads. McClellan climbed into the saddle, ready to depart when a rider coming up the hillside emerged from the dark.

"General, sir, I bear sad news," cried the corporal as he entered the torchlight. "General Reno is dead."

*   *   *

His body heavy with exhaustion, McClellan ran a hand down his face and dug out his pocket watch. It was eleven-thirty. The guns atop South Mountain had fallen silent over two hours earlier, but the day's work remained unfinished. Peering out of a large window, McClellan looked down at the lanterns moving like fireflies among wounded men in the grass. Earlier in the day, Dr. Jonathan Letterman, the army's medical director, had ordered straw brought to the yard for the injured. The Ambulance Corps carted in casualties all day and into the night until the ground around the brick house lay covered with men shivering under blankets, their heads propped up on knapsacks or bundled coats.

Surprisingly few complaints came from the boys lying hurt outside, unlike the howls of pain that echoed through the house from the downstairs parlor, where army surgeons hacked off damaged and bloody limbs. The cries of amputees had repeatedly interrupted McClellan during a gathering of his staff and corps commanders earlier that evening. One soldier had screamed out, "not my arm! Dear God, please help me!" just as Sam Sturgis recounted Jesse Reno's last words on the mountain. Shot under the ribcage by a ball that ricocheted off the hilt of his saber, Reno lay under a large oak tree when Sturgis came to check on him. The stricken general had greeted Sam with a "hallo!" and then calmly announced that he was dead before passing clean away.

Shuddering at the story, McClellan felt his stomach ball itself into a knot. His appetite fled the moment Sturgis told his tale, never to return. Of all the things that war forced a military man to witness, the sight of men suffering bothered Little Mac the most. He could never overcome the weakness it opened in him.

Fatigue gripped McClellan like a vice, its weight clouding his thoughts. Turning away from the window, he rubbed his eyes in the candlelight and walked to the room's only table. A map lay spread there beneath a pair of glowing tapers. Beside the map sat the bespectacled Colonel Key, exhaustion clear on his face. McClellan stopped before the colonel, his hands folded behind his back.

"It's been a difficult day, Key. We've won a hard-fought battle but losing Jesse Reno weighs heavily on me. He was a fine man and an excellent general. Having him at the head of the Ninth Corps made Burnside's assignment as wing commander tolerable. With Reno gone, I am not sure."

"I understand, general," said Key, his legs crossed and kepi resting in his lap. "Reno was a boon to this army and now he is lost, but you cannot let that stop you from thinking of the morrow. Lee's army is out there. Harpers Ferry is still in danger."

McClellan slumped into a chair beside the table. "Yes, Key, you are right. I must concentrate. The first order of business is to ensure that Franklin moves into Pleasant

Valley and cuts the road there from Boonsborough to Harpers Ferry. He must keep Longstreet's command from joining Jackson. I'll have orders written up to this effect."

"Captain Custer brought you the news of Franklin's victory, then?" asked Key.

"He did, a short while ago," nodded McClellan. "But Custer said that Franklin had seized the pass, not that he had moved his command beyond the mountain. Franklin's column is the most important part of my plan. If we are to rescue Colonel Miles, he must move over the mountain."

"And the rest of the army, general, what of it?"

Sitting up, McClellan traced Burnside's lines on his map. "I've given orders that the field commanders are to push out pickets at first light. If the enemy is still in position, we will renew the attack. If he has fallen back, we will pursue him—probably to Boonsborough."

McClellan tapped the black dot marking the village and slumped back into his chair.

"The question is how to restructure the army's commands so that I can maintain maximum flexibility and exercise personal command. General Hooker described a plan to me earlier today that could work. He suggested I release him from Burnside's authority without formally dissolving the wing structure of the army. With Hooker's corps acting independently, it would give me the ability to control his movements without going through Burnside."

Key scratched at his beard. "I see, and that would help you how, exactly?"

"It would ensure that any victory this army wins will be attributable to me alone. General Porter made an excellent point to me regarding this today. He said that under the current command structure, Burnside could take credit for our victory. After all, he directed today's fight almost entirely on his own, although under my orders. Even Meade's attack on the right stemmed from Burnside's orders, not Hooker's."

"And Burnside is a pawn of the administration?"

"Precisely," said McClellan. Leaning forward, his voice dropped to a whisper. "It is as Porter said. The administration offered Burnside command of this army more than once. After he refused, they insisted I take him on as wing commander, even though I did not want the army organized in that way. Porter thinks it possible that if I make one misstep—"

"The administration will oust you and put Burnside in your place!"

"Yes, colonel, but be quiet about it! You can see the reason for my concern."

"I can, sir, and I agree with General Porter. We are walking a fine line here. Winning a victory is crucial for us to dictate terms to the administration. If you are replaced by Burnside, all those possibilities will vanish. It cannot be allowed to happen!"

Again, McClellan ran a hand down his face. "You are right, Key. I was not thinking clearly when I had the orders drawn up this evening, formally recognizing Burnside and Sumner in their positions as wing commanders. It was a mistake, and I must correct it tomorrow."

Staring at the floor, Little Mac yawned deeply. "There is another thing that concerns me, Key. What to do about Cox."

"Jacob Cox? He is an associate of mine from Ohio," replied the colonel. "What's your worry, general?"

"His support for abolition," shot back McClellan. "He stands solidly behind Burnside, and he is a strident Republican. His rank and experience make him the logical commander of the Ninth Corps, now that poor Reno is gone, we must be careful with him. He does not share our political goals."

Key leaned forward in the candlelight, his hand resting on the tabletop. "Do not worry yourself about Cox. I will distract him. I'll—I'll tell him that we have both changed our positions on the question of slavery and that we completely agree it must be brought to an end if the war is to be won. He won't know a thing. In the meantime, you must remove Burnside from as much responsibility as you can or discredit him in some way. If that it too strong a step, then at least marginalize his involvement so that you can gain sole credit for our success."

"It pains me to take these measures," said McClellan, his dark eyes rimmed red. "Burnside has been a good friend. Now I cannot count on him."

"I understand, sir, but think of what is at stake—your future and the welfare of the nation itself. How different would history be if Caesar had discovered the conspiracy against him in time? His love for Brutus blinded him! Burnside is your Brutus, sir. Don't give him an opportunity to slip a blade into your back when you're not looking."

"You are correct as usual, Key, although I wish to God you were not. I'll issue the instructions, but now I have orders for Franklin to write up. Please send in Colonel Ruggles and get a good night's sleep."

Rising from his chair, Key placed his cap on his head. "As you wish, sir. I'll see you in the morning."

McClellan sat tapping on the table, his ears ringing with the cries of wounded men. A shiver passed through him. Why could things not be simple? Why could he not focus on fighting Lee's army and leave it at that? Key's comments, however, had clarified the situation. Burnside's authority must be curtailed, and quickly, if the glory of victory was to be his alone.

14

Sunday, September 14, 1862
Midnight
Encampment of the 125th Pennsylvania Volunteers
Near Bolivar, Maryland

Higgins stared vacantly into the flames of a small campfire, his empty stomach growling as he recalled the day's events. That morning, his regiment had joined the rest of General Williams's Twelfth Corps in the advance on South Mountain. They had not gone far, however, before receiving orders to stop and allow the trailing portion of General Sumner's Second Corps to pass through Frederick ahead of them.

For two mind-numbing hours, Higgins and his men stood in the dusty street under arms. Frederick's inhabitants made the situation more comfortable than it might have been by sharing food and drink, but in Higgins's experience, waiting in column was still one of the most tiresome things a soldier could endure. Better to march twenty miles than to stand for hours in one place or make only fitful progress. Boredom ate men up, making them tired and ill-tempered. Knapsacks and rifles felt heavier with each passing minute, contributing to disagreements that broke out among the ranks.

The scourge of liquor proved troublesome as well. After arriving in Frederick, Higgins had allowed his men to enter the town by company. The festive atmosphere of the place offered temptations that many could not resist, including prodigious amounts of rye whiskey. Much of this drink found its way into the bellies of the men, causing distress among the townsfolk and consternation in Higgins himself.

The first reports of public drunkenness reached him after dark, followed by men returning to camp with injuries received in brawls and accidents. Higgins responded to the torrent of black eyes and split lips by picking a squad of teetotalers from the ranks to act as his provost guard. They set off for town with bayonets fixed and rounded up as many of the intoxicated recalcitrants as they could find. Had time allowed, Higgins would have punished the worst offenders by making them ride a rail, but orders to march came early, and soon after sunrise, the One Hundred and Twenty-Fifth Pennsylvania filed back onto the road.

Reaching for his canteen, Higgins swallowed a mouthful of water. A shiver passed through him, and he rose to empty his bladder. The night air had grown chilly with fog in the short time since the regiment had finally fallen out of column. Higgins finished his business and looked over his men. Those who had not dropped immediately into the arms of Morpheus huddled around campfires, their sweat-soaked clothes turning cold in the damp air. With men cramming the National Road for miles, General Williams had led the Twelfth Corps on a torturous march over the Catoctins toward a hamlet named Shookstown.

The road they took hardly deserved the name. Pitted, narrow, and stony, the track wound up and down through heavily wooded heights, taking the lead brigades hours to reach Middletown Valley. Once his regiment had begun its descent, Higgins could see smoke rising from the Ninth Corps' fight at Fox's Gap. Cannon fire reverberated across the landscape, marring the idyllic beauty of the place. In times of peace, a painter of Rembrandt's caliber might make much of the view. In wartime, columns of darkly uniformed troops tramped over the roads and fields toward the battle smoke staining the horizon.

Images from the march faded in Higgins's mind as he returned to his place by the fire. Dropping cross-legged onto the ground, he warmed his hands and thanked God that his men had not been called on to fight that day. The drill exercises outside of Frederick had proved they were not ready. Spirit might make up for the lack of discipline in a pitched fight, but if they came up against a regiment of Rebel veterans commanded by an experienced officer, they would be hard-pressed to hold the field.

How he and his men came to be in these circumstances baffled Higgins. Was John Pope so incompetent that Lee could shatter his army so easily? And what of McClellan? Did the "Young Napoleon," as the press liked to call him, not have tens of thousands of veterans under his command on the James River peninsula outside of Richmond? Where were all those experienced brigades? Why did the task of pushing the Secessionists out of Maryland fall to his green boys, some of whom still struggled to load their weapons correctly?

Unable to come up with a suitable answer, Higgins yawned and let it go. Lying back on his saddle, he folded his hands behind his head, and peered up at the fog-dimmed stars. "Eighteen hours of marching," he muttered. "How did it take us so blasted long to get here?"

The colonel dozed under the firmament until a hand shook him awake. Rising with a snort, he peered into the face of Lieutenant Colonel Szink, his second in command.

"Sorry to wake you, sir, but we've had some trouble," reported Szink.

Higgins sat up. "Trouble? Is it liquor again?"

"Not specifically, colonel, although it is involved. It's this sort of trouble."

Szink extended a torn piece of paper to the colonel. Taking the battered sheet, one half dangling fragilely from the other, Higgins tilted it in the firelight to read the black print. "Free the negro! Oh, hell, Szink not this. What problem has this caused?"

Szink rose from his squat. "The problem, sir, is that whiskey and abolition talk don't mix. I took that broadsheet from one Private Collins, as committed an abolitionist as I've ever met in this army."

"What was he doing with it?"

"Preaching about freeing the nigger, of course. Turns out a citizen of Frederick passed these out while we marched through the city. Some men didn't take kindly to it, but Collins ate it up. He's got the fire in his eyes, sir, yammering on about Harpers Ferry and John Brown's martyrdom for the cause of liberty."

Higgins's brow furrowed into a scowl. "At this time of night, Szink? What's wrong with the boy that he's got to preach now?"

Szink lowered himself beside Higgins to warm his hands by the fire. "From what I've been able to piece together, the back and forth about slavery has gone on all day. Men on the march have a lot of idle time, you know, so they get to talking. Collins kept going on about fighting the war to end slavery and how shameful it is that the national government hasn't made abolition a political aim."

"Hold on, Szink, let me guess. Some of the boys didn't take kindly to that."

"Yes, sir. More than a few. Collins is definitely in the minority, but he's quite an agitator. Most let his talk slide, until they got tired, and a few started drinking. That's when the fight broke out."

Higgins ran his fingers through his hair. "Liquor! Damn it, Szink, I've got a mind to search every knapsack in this regiment and root it out."

"I've thought the same, colonel."

"So, some of the boys got liquored up and Collins started in with this talk?"

"They did. It came to fisticuffs and Collins took a hell of a beating. That's when I came up and put an end to it."

Higgins looked down at the paper. "This abolition stuff is poison. It's torn our nation in two and now it's tearing apart our regiment."

Szink remained silent, his tired eyes staring ahead at the fire.

"What is it, Szink? Don't tell me you agree with this Collins fellow."

Szink rubbed his chin. "I'm not what you'd call a true-believer, colonel, but I share his conviction that slavery must come to an end if this nation is to be reunited. Don't you agree?"

"I guess so," nodded Higgins wearily. "I never thought it should end in the States where it currently exists, but it can't be allowed to spread west. On that, I've always agreed with the Free Soilers. A man has the right to make his own way where he wants and that means working where he sees fit. Slavery is patently unfair to the free working man. How is a wage earner supposed to compete with slave labor?"

"He can't. You're right about that, colonel, but that's not how the South sees it. They see it as a matter of property, not just labor. Slaves are property and they say the government has no authority to say where a man can and can't bring his possessions. Imagine you want to pick up and move to the Dakota Territory and the government says you can't bring your mule. You can see the problem."

Higgins nodded again. "Yes, Szink, I see it. We've got two forms of economy going on here and they can't co-exist."

"That's right, sir, meaning we can't achieve peace unless we let the South go and that don't work for us because we're all here to restore the Union. The only way forward is for slavery to end. Private Collins sees it as a moral issue—that a man's a man no matter the color of his skin. I don't have an opinion on that score. All I know is that as long as slavery exists, there can't be a Union as we knew it."

"You might be right, Szink. What you say makes sense, but that's an issue for the politicians to decide, not us. We're here to keep the Union together. A man can't just up and leave his wife because he doesn't like how she keeps house, and a State can't just leave the Union because it doesn't like how an election turned out. There are rules, Szink. We can't just toss them out when we want or we're no better than despots. Slavery is a maddening problem, but we ain't responsible for solving it."

"Aren't we, colonel? Don't we have it in our power to enforce the change and end slavery for good?"

Higgins stared into the fire, his fingers pulling thoughtfully on the end of his beard. "I reckon you're right, technically speaking. Once we put down this rebellion, we could force the South to give up its slaves, but that's not the government's policy. More importantly, it's not why these boys volunteered. They joined up to save the Union and to fight treason, not to free negroes."

"That might be changing, sir. There are rumors going around that President Lincoln intends to make ending slavery an objective of the war."

"Good God, Szink, that would be chaos!" said Higgins, throwing his hands into the air. "How many of our boys would stay under arms if that happens?"

"I honestly don't know, colonel. They're good boys and I think they'll do their duty no matter what Lincoln says."

"I don't know either," replied Higgins, "but I fear a lot of them will throw down their arms and go home. We wouldn't have an army left to fight with."

"So, you're saying is this isn't an army of liberation?"

"You're damned right this isn't an army of liberation! We're here to put down a rebellion against the Constitution, not to free darkies."

"Maybe it ought to be," ventured Szink. "Maybe our cause needs a moral objective above politics. Men dying to free other men sure sounds like a noble cause."

Higgins fell silent, his shaggy head wagging back and forth. "I don't know, Szink. Saving our nation—the only democratic republic in the world, mind you—is pretty noble, if you ask me. Ah, the whole subject makes my head spin. Even I could use a drink just thinking about it."

Also weary of the discussion, Szink changed the subject. "Do you think we'll see the elephant tomorrow?"

"I can't say, really. From what I've heard, Hooker's attack on the right went tolerably well today. We'll have to see if Bobby Lee's boys are still on that mountain come daybreak. Then maybe we'll see some action. I tell you, though, I'm awful concerned about taking these men into a fight. You saw them at drill."

"I did," nodded Szink. "They didn't all look bad, but a few of them need more work."

Higgins tossed a pebble into the fire, sending a shower of sparks floating skyward. "I'm hopeful we'll get another crack at drill tomorrow, or the next day, but now that we've engaged the enemy, who knows if we'll get the chance?"

Too tired to carry on the conversation, both men fell silent. Higgins yawned deeply again and slid down against his saddle. "I've had it for today, Szink," he said. "See you in the morning."

"Good night, colonel," murmured Szink, and reaching for his blanket, he lay down in the grass with his face to the fire. The yellow flames danced lazily among the orange embers, reminding him of the hearth at home. The face of his wife passed before his eyes, and he smiled before dropping into a deep slumber.

15

Monday, September 15, 1862
Morning
Field Headquarters, Army of the Potomac
Middletown, Maryland

McClellan—George, for the sake of our long acquaintance, I am begging you not to do this. It's unthinkable!" Standing beside the modest table McClellan used as a desk, Burnside, hatless and bald-headed, implored the army's commander and friend to reconsider his decision to give Joseph Hooker an independent command.

Dispatches, letters, and telegrams littered the floor and table-top map that McClellan used to plan the campaign in Maryland. Little Mac himself sat on an upholstered chair. Velvet drapes, burgundy in color and tasseled with gold, framed large windows that let in the new day sun. As dawn brightened in the east, shafts of light spread across the countryside, illuminating the heavy fog that enshrouded the summit of South Mountain. Men stirred outside of army headquarters, checking their equipment. Horses nickered and campfires crackled into life. The scent of boiling coffee filled the air.

McClellan rose early that morning to follow up the gains his army had won the day before. Verbal orders issued the previous evening instructed his field commanders to send out pickets at daylight and probe the enemy's lines. If the Rebels remained on the mountain, they were to be attacked. If they had retreated, they were to be pursued. No general engagement west of the mountain was to be brought on, however, until Little

Mac could get to the front and direct the fighting himself. No longer would he allow men like Burnside to steal his glory. He, George McClellan, would see personally to the army's movements, no matter the outcome.

Changing the army's wing structure meant informing Burnside that Hooker's First Corps would operate separately. The Ninth Corps would remain under Jacob Cox, its new commander after the untimely death of Jesse Reno, but Cox would answer to Burnside in a very awkward arrangement. Burnside knew, as well as McClellan, that this ridiculous situation rendered his presence superfluous. After all, what corps required two commanding officers?

Little Mac had summoned Burnside to tell him of the change. Now he grew weary of the man's pleas to reconsider. "I have made up my mind, Burn, and that's final. I'll hear no more argument about it," said McClellan, directing his gaze to a dispatch in his hand.

"But, George, listen to me!" implored Burnside, his tone slipping back to the first-name basis upon which he and McClellan had known each other before the war. "What have I done to deserve this? Didn't I win us a victory yesterday? Haven't I served you faithfully?"

Dropping the paper onto the table, McClellan looked up. "You have, indeed," he sniffed. "This has nothing to do with your actions. They have been commendable. It has to do with my comfort in directing the operations of this army. I have never cared for the wing structure. You know full well that President Lincoln forced it on me at the start of this campaign. Now that we have engaged the enemy, I would prefer to direct the movement of yours and Hooker's corps myself, at least temporarily. You did note that word in the order, didn't you? This is a temporary arrangement. When the time comes to reverse it, I shall."

"I saw it," grimaced Burnside, "but engaging the enemy is precisely why you still need me in command. This army is large and unwieldy, and the roads around here are narrow and confusing. Allow me to help you."

"Thank you for the offer, Burn. You have always been a steadfast friend, but I have determined to do this myself. Besides, you and Hooker fight like tomcats. Wouldn't you prefer to be rid of him? My decision gives you more freedom of movement. Think of it, Burn! You can direct Cox as you like. He is an amenable and competent officer, but he is new to corps command and needs a steady and experienced hand such as yours. I need you to be there for him. Help him and you will help me."

Heaving a sigh, Burnside slapped his hat against his leg. McClellan smiled inwardly, relishing the man's capitulation.

"I understand, sir," said the dejected general. "I do not agree, but I understand what you are saying. I can't help it if Hooker and I don't get along. The man is a burr in my trousers. But to lose this command after the success I have won! It doesn't feel right."

McClellan rose from his chair and walked around the table. Placing a hand on Burnside's shoulder, he stared intently into the Rhode Islander's eyes. "I know this comes as a shock, Burn, but it is for the best. Help me make it work."

"As you wish, general," sighed Burnside. "I will do my duty and serve as best I can in whatever capacity you require."

"There's a good man," said McClellan, returning to his chair after giving Burnside's shoulder a pat. "Now, shouldn't you go to your command? We have the Rebel army to get after."

Burnside slowly pulled on his hat. "Yes, general, you are right," he said. "I'll return to my corps straightaway." Snapping a salute, he strode quickly from the room.

*   *   *

In the yard outside, George Custer tightened the belly strap of his saddle and patted Wellington on the neck. "Good boy," he whispered to the stout Morgan. The horse let out a steamy snort, boisterously tossing its head at the sound of his master's voice. A trooper leading a chestnut mount walked up behind Custer, the saber at his side clattering against his leg. "Good morning, cap'n. Lieutenant Martin reporting for duty. You about ready to go?"

Custer turned to regard the young man. Sanderson Martin served on McClellan's sizable staff as an aide-de-camp. So did Custer, but Martin kept his brown hair closely cropped and his face cleanly shaven.

"Good morning, Sandy. I believe I'm ready," said Custer. "We're off to see General Hooker this morning?"

"Yes, sir. General McClellan told General Marcy that we're to find Hooker and keep an eye on things with him."

"Keep an eye on things? I seem to be doing a lot of that these days."

"What do you mean, Autie? McClellan have you playing nursemaid?"

Custer pulled himself into the saddle. "Something like that. Two days ago, the general had me ride all the way to Franklin's command to deliver an order and ensure the old blowhard knew how important it was. I stood around all the next day until Franklin got his fat hindquarters in motion and finally attacked the Rebels at Burkittsville Pass. It was a heck of a sight once the attack got underway, but boy, did it take a long time for that laggard to get up a head of steam."

"Maybe that's what Little Mac wants us to do this time with Hooker," suggested Martin.

"Most likely. It's almost as if the general doesn't trust these officers to do things themselves. If a man can't be trusted to command, how'd he earn his stars?"

"I've got no idea, Autie. All I know is we'd better get going."

Spurring ahead, Custer pitched into the morning mist, with Martin behind him. The two men rode west along the National Road, which was already crowded with troops from Sumner's Second Corps, and then up the mountainside. The road wound through the fog, becoming steeper as the pair climbed, and as they approached the summit, Custer drew his revolver.

"We're near the enemy's lines," he said to Martin, advising the lieutenant to ready his carbine in case they were fired on.

They passed the corpse of a dead Rebel soldier draped over a stone wall, his torso pointed downhill and musket lying beside him in the grass. Custer noted the ragged edges of the dead man's coat and holes in his trousers. No shoes covered his soiled feet.

A Bluecoat sentry appeared on the road in front of them and Custer asked if the Rebels were still ahead. "No, captain," replied the man. "General Hooker's troops have occupied the enemy's lines. The general himself is at a fine house atop the gap."

"Thank you," nodded Custer, re-holstering his pistol. Arriving a short time later at the crowded pass, Custer steered his horse around a column of troops in the roadway. The bodies of the slain peppered the fields; some in groups of two or three, some lying alone. Men also lay around the stone house on the left, their groans filling the damp morning air. Calls for water rang out, along with prayers and calls for God to put an end to their suffering. Yankee orderlies passed among the moaning Southerners, identifying the living from the dead and assisting where they could.

Custer and Martin rode to the hitching rail by the front of the house and slid down from their saddles. Tying off their mounts, they walked to the open front door. The blue banner of General Hooker's First Corps hung from a windowsill on the second floor. Custer stepped into the entryway and removed his hat. A group of officers and civilians stood inside, examining documents that lay scattered across the floor. The tallest of the men, his icy blue eyes set within a pale complexion, turned to regard the newly arrived troopers.

"General Hooker?" saluted Custer. "General McClellan sent us here as liaison officers. We're to keep the general apprised of your situation."

Hooker dropped the dispatch in his hand and stepped over. "You are spies, eh? Yes, I recognize you from headquarters, Captain Custer. Welcome to South Mountain."

"Thank you, sir," grinned Custer, shaking Hooker's hand. "What is this place?"

Hooker gestured to the room behind him. "This house was headquarters for Daniel Harvey Hill, the Reb general whose division I defeated yesterday. These papers, and the dead and wounded men lying around outside, are all that Hill left behind."

"So the Rebels have retreated?" asked Martin from over Custer's shoulder.

"They have indeed."

Hooker nodded toward the civilians standing in the room. "These men are from Boonsborough. They tell me General Lee's army passed through their village in a perfect panic on the way to Shepherdstown. Lee himself is reported to be hurt and was overheard saying that his army took a frightful whipping." The general turned toward the visitors. "Isn't that right?"

"It surely is, gen'rl," said the oldest of the three locals. "We heard the Rebels say they took fifteen thousand men killt. Boonsborough itself is terrible, crowded with injured. They're layin' everywhere."

"We have also taken more than a thousand Rebel prisoners," added Hooker. "But you must report all of this to General McClellan for me. You should write to him as well that I have allowed General Richardson's division from Sumner's Corps to pass through my command in pursuit of the Rebel army. Those are his troops on the roadway outside. Can one of you go to the commanding general for me?"

"We can," nodded Custer. "I'll write up the note and add that you need cavalry for the pursuit. General Richardson's men won't be able to move fast enough."

"Yes, Custer, you are correct. Send for Pleasonton's horse. We'll chase the Rebel army back across the Potomac."

"Very good, sir. Come on, Sandy. Let's use that table over there."

Custer pointed to a sideboard at one end of the room and waved for Martin to follow. The two men strode to the oaken set-piece and Custer took out his dispatch book. Composing the note in his mind, he scratched out the message and folded the paper in half.

"Sandy, take this to General McClellan and tell him I'm going to stay here to wait for Pleasonton."

"Alright, captain, good luck," said Martin, plucking the note from Custer's fingers. Tucking it inside his jacket, he strode from the room.

Custer waited for a time, listening to Hooker and his senior commanders. An orderly brought coffee and biscuits, prompting Hooker to mention that his men had not eaten, so rations had been called up. The National Road was so congested with General Sumner's corps, however, that the commissary wagons could not make any headway. Custer testified to the horrible crowding on the pike and impatiently slurped his coffee, the itch to be doing something more gnawing away in his gut. Then a cry went up outside and the assembled officers went to the windows to see what was happening.

"Make way, you men! Make way for the cavalry!" bellowed a trooper to the foot soldiers standing in the road.

Custer recognized the officer coming toward them at the head of the column. "That's Colonel Farnsworth!" he exclaimed, tapping his forefinger loudly on the window. "He commands Pleasonton's second brigade. The horse you requested is here, general."

"At last. I'll go out and meet him," replied Hooker. "Come along, captain."

Custer fell in behind the tall general and the two officers strode into the sunlight. The fog covering the mountain had by now burned off, revealing a bright blue sky above.

Farnsworth, tight-lipped, with no mustache and a long beard dangling from his chin, rode into the yard. A major behind Farnsworth called out "halt!" bringing the column of stamping, snorting horseflesh to a stop.

"Hello, colonel, you are a welcome sight," said Hooker. "There is important work to do."

"So, I hear, sir. General Pleasonton tells me Secesh is on the skedaddle. I am here to track them down."

"They are indeed. I've sent General Richardson ahead with infantry to keep up the pressure, but they can't move very fast. Do you have a large command with you?"

"It's big enough, I reckon," nodded Farnsworth. "General Pleasonton sent me with six hundred men. The rest of our boys he led over the gap south of here, where the Ninth Corps is. We're to meet in the valley beyond, depending on what we find. Any idea what's down there?"

"No, colonel, but I reckon Lee's rearguard must be close."

"I expect you're right." The colonel's gaze strayed to Custer standing behind Hooker. "Look here, it's George Custer. Why am I not surprised to see you?"

"Hello, colonel," said Custer. "I'm here on orders from General McClellan."

"Of course, you are. Will the general mind if you come with us? I know you relish a fight."

Custer's face lit up. "I'm sure it will be fine, sir, if General Hooker no longer has need of me."

"I do not, captain, by all means go," waved Hooker.

"Thank you, sir. I wish you the best of luck," saluted Custer as he raced off to join Farnsworth's column.

The horsemen thundered down the winding road, catching up quickly with the tail of Richardson's infantry column. Cannon fire boomed at the front and Farnsworth called for the foot soldiers to make way. Indignant troops stepped aside, muttering expletives about cavalrymen. Farnsworth glared at them, but kept riding until he spotted a general officer and his staff on an embankment to the left. The mustachioed general held a set of binoculars to his eyes.

Farnsworth rode up with Custer close behind and announced his arrival. Israel Richardson, a grim Vermont man by birth, looked down at them before leaping from his perch and walking over to Farnsworth's horse. Gripping Farnsworth's hand, he shook it firmly. "Hello, colonel, I'm glad to see you."

"Thank you, sir. General Pleasonton sent me to pursue the Rebels. May I ask what the situation is?"

"Of course. There's a line of Secesh cavalry and horse artillery on the downslope ahead of us. They've shelled my column and forced me to halt. I've deployed a regiment of New Hampshire boys on either side of the road. We can easily drive them, but after surveying the enemy's position, I believe a concerted cavalry attack will break them to pieces with the least loss of life."

Farnsworth held his field glasses to his eyes. Surveying the hillside below, he saw the artillery pieces to which Richardson had referred and counted the dismounted Butternut riders supporting them. "I see the enemy," he said. "It looks like a single regiment."

"Can you lick them?" asked Richardson.

"I will hazard a try forthwith. Bugler, prepare to sound the charge. We're going in!"

"Good luck to you, colonel. I'll support your progress with my infantry once you've cleared the way."

"Thank you, general, I appreciate it," saluted Farnsworth.

Richardson stepped aside as the colonel wheeled his horse. Spurring it back along the column, Farnsworth yelled for the men to prepare themselves. "We're going to charge a line of dismounted Rebel cavalry! Sabers and pistols at the ready, boys. Give them cold steel or hot lead, as you prefer. Company commanders, pass the word to the rear."

Returning to the head of the column, Farnsworth drew his Navy Colt revolver and looked over at Custer. "You ready, captain?" he asked.

"Sir!" cried Custer, loosing his fine Toledo blade from its scabbard.

Sabers slashed free down the column, drawing cheers from the infantry as Farnsworth paced his horse in a circle. "Bugler, call the charge!" he bellowed.

The corporal's shrill notes carried across the hillside, lurching Wellington into a sprint. Custer's hat brim pushed back as the powerful horse heaved down the road, its hooves pounding with those of the others. Shots popped out from the Rebel line, bringing down horses and men in mighty crashes of dust, but the Johnnies numbered too few to resist the crushing weight of Farnsworth's charge.

Custer careened toward a man in the grass ahead of him. The Rebel rose from a crouch to take aim, but then fear filled his face and he tried to bolt away. Catching him after two steps, Custer brought down his saber across the man's back, tearing a bloody gash. The shrieking Johnny collapsed in a heap before the hooves of the trailing horses trampled him dead. A Yankee trooper to Custer's right cried out as a ball hit him in the chest, blowing a hole in his back. Blood flew in a crimson mist, and he threw his hands into the air, the pistol in his hand launching skyward. Drops of the man's blood splattered onto Custer's uniform, but in the madness of the fight, he took no notice. His heart pumped pure adrenaline now, leaving his head hot with battle fever.

A squadron of mounted Rebels approached from the left, their mounts coming on at full gallop to intercept the flank of Farnsworth's lead company. Custer spotted them out of the corner of his eye just as they crashed into the Federals. Sabers clashed and the man beside Custer shot a Johnny out of his saddle.

Custer parried a blow directed at him by a man who had appeared from nowhere on his right. Rage colored the man's face, and he foamed at the corners of his mouth like a rabid dog. Raining blows onto the upheld blade, the Rebel tried in vain to batter down Custer's defense. Custer blocked the blows in a clanging weave of steel while attempting to thrust the point of his own saber into the man's gritted teeth. The Rebel handled his sword with skill, though, denying Custer an opening. Custer let go of Wellington's reins and pulled his Colt from its holster. His enemy spotted the move, and for a moment, just long enough to give Custer an opening, his eyes filled with surprise. Custer raised his pistol and put a bullet in the man's chest.

Peering around at the melee, Custer saw the bodies of eight of the Rebel troopers that had attacked them lying in the grass. If they were dead or just wounded, he did not know. Several of Farnsworth's men also lay dead on the ground. The three remaining Rebels spurred their horses into a sprint for the National Road and the village of

Boonsborough. Farnsworth's bugler called the charge a second time, and the Bluecoat cavalry dashed after the now-fleeing enemy.

Custer spotted Farnsworth toward the front of the pack and urged Wellington to keep up. The fast-moving pursuit column crammed into the narrow street between the houses and dust rose so thickly into the air that Custer could not see ahead of him. A Rebel trooper on foot emerged from the cloud by the side of the road, his pistol pointed at Custer's face. Custer steered Wellington into the man, knocking him into a hitching rail.

Past the main crossroads in the middle of town, they rode. Then Custer heard cries at the front and saw blue horsemen riding back toward him.

"They're charging! The Rebels are charging!" came the shouts.

"Dammit!" yelled Custer as he yanked Wellington to a bounding stop.

A squadron of Grayback riders firing pistols thundered past him back in the direction they had come. Federal horses behind Custer slammed into Wellington and he reared with a scream. Custer fought to control the horse by pulling hard on the reins. Dust clouded the air, filling his mouth. Choking, he peered through watering eyes at the surrounding chaos. Riders crowded in on all sides, unable to maneuver their mounts. Sabers rose and fell; slashing, hacking, and stabbing murderously at anything that moved. Pistol shots rang out, and a bullet fired from God knows where zipped past Custer's head.

"What the devil?" he roared, turning to see a man in a second-story window take aim at a Rebel in the street. The civilian pulled the trigger and shot the Grayback's horse out from under him. Wellington stamped and snorted, still unable to push away from the crush of horses around him. Men swore oaths and Custer cried out as another man's mount momentarily pinned his leg.

A bugle blared out the retreat, and Custer spied enemy riders coming toward him again from the right. Charging past, the Rebels fled up the road toward Hagerstown.

"The Rebs are running! Get after them, boys!" cried a Yankee trooper.

Custer pulled out his pistol and took aim at the Rebels streaming past. Pulling the trigger, he struck a man in the shoulder. The wounded Johnny hung tight but kept going, slumped over his horse's neck. More of Farnsworth's men appeared in pursuit. Custer tried to follow them, but the crush of horseflesh would not set him free.

"By thunder!" he roared. "Get out of the damned way!"

No one could hear him in the rumble of stampeding horses. Frustrated, Custer pushed and kicked at the men and animals around him. Then the crush gave way, and he slipped free.

"H'yah, Wellington! Git up!" he shouted, galloping off in pursuit of the Secesh riders until Farnsworth's bugle call brought him to a halt. Reining in, he returned to town as Boonsborough's inhabitants emerged from their houses to raise a cheer. An old man reached for Custer's hand.

"I'm sorry about almost shooting you," he laughed. "I was aiming at the Rebel to your front, but he moved too fast for me to draw a good bead on him."

"So that was you!" Custer snarled, his cheeks going red.

The man blanched with alarm. "I—I'm real sorry, mister."

"Let him be, Captain Custer," called Colonel Farnsworth. Shooting the colonel an acid glance, Custer grudgingly shook the old man's hand.

"That enough action for you today?" grinned the colonel, his face gleaming with sweat.

"I'll say!" Custer nodded. "Hottest fight I've been in yet."

Holstering his Colt, he gazed around at the carnage. Horses and men lay everywhere, a few dead, some only injured. House stoops and porches stood thick with men covered in blood and grime.

"These can't all be Confederate troopers, can they?" he asked, waving a hand at them.

"They aren't," replied Farnsworth. "Look around, captain. The whole town's a hospital. These men are the wounded from yesterday's fight."

Custer felt the heat drain from his blood. Victory felt good after the reverses they had suffered that year. He removed his gloves and took a swig from his canteen.

"Hey, Custer!" shouted someone standing nearby. Looking over, he spied Daniel Buck, Major Medill's adjutant in the Eighth Illinois Cavalry, weaving his horse toward him.

"Buck! Am I glad to see you're alright."

"Likewise, captain. Heck of a fight, eh?"

"I'll say. We whipped 'em good!"

"We sure did. After that licking, it's time to pay up on your wager."

"What?"

"Your wager, Custer. The one for your hair! You said you'd cut it when this army won a victory."

"Ah, you're right!" replied0 Custer, pinching tightly a blonde ringlet between his fingers.

"Yes, sir-ee, captain, you're due for a scalping," grinned Buck. "I'll get the shears."

16

Monday, September 15, 1862

Morning to noon

Ninth Corps, Army of the Potomac

South Mountain, Maryland

Burnside urged his horse toward the misty summit of South Mountain, his thoughts a jumble of confusion and anger. General McClellan's behavior was puzzling. Was there an example of a commander being relieved of responsibility after he won a battlefield victory? None came to mind. Technically, McClellan had not demoted him, but separating the First Corps from his now defunct wing of the army downgraded his authority.

What in God's name is happening? Burnside asked himself. *Whenever I see McClellan, he acts warmly toward me, but when we part, he issues orders that imply the opposite.* Burnside stared down at the pitted roadway. *Can all of this be Hooker's doing? Or Porter's? Is it both?*

His brow clouded with dark thoughts, Burnside continued up the mountain, encountering a growing number of dead along the way. Their bodies littered the roadside as he drew near the place where Reno had been shot. Peering through the thinning fog, Burnside surveyed the carnage. Slain rebel soldiers, some of their bodies already bloated and black, lay heaped along a fence line, their fingers gnarled into claws, grasping at the empty air. Burnside observed a burial detail digging a long trench and asked around for Jacob Cox, now commanding the Ninth Corps. Word spread of Burnside's search, summoning Cox to him from out of the mist.

"Good morning, sir," said the Ohioan, touching the brim of his cap. "I was just about to come to headquarters and find you."

"Good morning, Cox," replied Burnside, still taking in the grim spectacle around him. "I've saved you the trouble. Congratulations on yesterday's triumph. You and your men did a bully job."

"My thanks, sir. I knew the boys could do it. They haven't had much experience in large-scale fights like this, but they came through it alright. The question, general, is what you'd like me to do next. I haven't received any orders."

"Yes, Cox. That's why I'm here. McClellan wants us to pursue the retreating Rebels. Do you think your men can be underway soon?"

"They can, sir, but I'd prefer to move after they've had something to eat."

"To eat? Haven't they received rations?"

"No, general, they haven't had anything in two days. Our commissary wagons never made it here. These boys are subsisting on what they carried with them, or on what they've been able to gather from knapsacks on the field."

Burnside's stomach turned at the thought of rifling through a dead man's kit for food. "I don't understand. Colonel Goodrich assured me he had called up the commissary from Middletown. It hasn't arrived?"

"No, sir, it hasn't, and let me tell you, general, the food the men are finding isn't particularly appetizing. Have you ever eaten an ash cake, sir?"

"No, Cox, I haven't. But now that we've spoken, I'll go back to headquarters and find out what's happening. We'll get some beef for your men as soon as possible."

"Thank you, sir. In the meantime, what are your orders?"

"Well, we can't have the men marching on empty stomachs, so for the time being, have your boys bury the dead and send the wounded to the rear."

"Won't General McClellan be cross with us for not moving? You said he's given orders to pursue the Rebel army."

"Maybe, but I'll take responsibility for that," sighed Burnside. "General Pleasonton has already begun the pursuit and Hooker is moving on to Boonsborough. It will need to suffice for the moment."

"Yes, sir," nodded Cox. "I saw Pleasonton leading his cavalry through the mountain gap earlier. That's why so many of the dead are piled in these heaps. We had to get them out of the road."

Burnside's gut knotted even tighter. "I understand, Cox. Carry on. I'll be back as soon as I can learn what's happened to your rations."

"As you wish, general."

Burnside returned Cox's salute and wheeled his horse back onto the road. Calling for his staff to follow, he spurred Major into a trot toward Middletown, hoping to locate the commissary wagons of his corps.

*   *   *

A knock on the door roused George McClellan from his map. "Enter," he called, seeing his chief of staff walk in. "Yes, General Marcy, what is it?"

"Sir, Major Myer just received a message from General Franklin via signal. The general reports that the cannon fire from Harpers Ferry has gone quiet."

McClellan's eyes went wide. "What? Give me that paper!"

Handing over the message, Marcy stood silently as the general's eyes scanned the sheet. Then McClellan looked up. "This is bad news, Marcy. Very bad, indeed. If what Franklin says is true, then the ferry has fallen. We are too late."

"But I thought Miles had forty-eight hours of rations. He sent word of that only twenty-four hours ago. What changed?"

Dropping the dispatch onto the already littered floor, McClellan folded his hands behind his back and began pacing. "I don't know, Marcy. Perhaps Miles found his situation more compromised than he'd thought."

Falling quiet, McClellan walked to the window. For a minute, he rubbed his chin in thought. Then he spun around and returned to the table in the center of the room. There, he stopped and tapped his finger on the map. "I am going to stay the course," he said. "We have Lee on the run—in a perfect panic, I've been told—back to Virginia. Burnside and Hooker are pressing him, and Sumner is on the National Road waiting to advance. I have also placed the Twelfth Corps under his command so that he can bring it and the Second Corps up as quickly as possible. Hooker reported the Rebel rearguard thrown back from Boonsborough by Pleasonton and he has sent Israel Richardson's division in pursuit. His corps will move soon by Boonsborough and Keedysville toward the village of Sharpsburg. Then there is Porter's division, which I have ordered to come up behind Burnside on the mountain gap road. Everything is still well in hand, even if Colonel Miles has capitulated."

"I understand, sir," sniffed the older general. "Is there truly nothing we can do? Can't General Franklin still go to Miles's aid?"

"I don't know, Marcy. We'll need to wait until Franklin reports what's happening on his front. If I were Jackson, I'd pull the men in Pleasant Valley back to Virginia, but in case he stays put, I'll keep Franklin where he is. Burnside's orders, however, will need to be modified. He'll need to march toward Rohrersville to link up with Franklin. That way, he can provide the Sixth Corps with support if McLaws elects to attack him."

"That makes sense," nodded the older man.

"The key now is to press Lee," said McClellan, stabbing the map emphatically. "We have the advantage and cannot let it go."

Thumping army boots drew Little Mac's attention, and an orderly loomed in the doorway. "General, sir, I have a message here from General Porter."

"Yes, come in and give it to me," said McClellan, beckoning for the man to approach.

Taking the note in his hand, McClellan read it, his cheeks flushing red. Then he crumpled the paper in his fist. "Damn it all, why can't Burnside do as he's told!"

"Is something wrong, sir?"

"Yes, there is. Porter has arrived at the mountain gap, but his division cannot pass over it because Burnside's command remains in the way. He is requesting permission to push through."

"The Ninth Corps is still on the mountain? How can that be? You ordered Burnside to advance hours ago."

McClellan pitched the paper ball into a corner of the room, disgust clouding his face. "That I have! More than once, in fact. I've sent two orders to Burnside to move, yet he remains in place. He hasn't even acknowledged receiving my commands. I don't know what's happening up there, but I need to see to it myself. Have Dan readied. I'll leave immediately."

"Very good, sir," nodded the general, and turning on his heels, he hurried from the room.

Minutes later, McClellan spurred out of the busy yard with a few aides and an armed escort in tow. Riding out of Middletown, and up the mountain, he passed regiment after regiment of U.S. Army regular troops with the Fifth Corps division of George Sykes. The men cheered him as he rode by, and McClellan lifted his cap in salute. At the top of the gap, he found Porter sitting astride his horse beside the road. Regiments of Ninth Corps men stood in the roadway itself, drawn up to resume the march west even though they still had not eaten.

McClellan steered his horse up the embankment. "General Porter, what's happening here?" he asked, yanking Dan to a stop.

"Sir, I am following your orders to move my division to support the Ninth Corps, but upon arriving here I found Burnside's men blocking the road. My men cannot move any farther."

McClellan peered angrily around him. "Where is General Burnside?"

"I can't find Burnside anywhere," shrugged Porter.

"Well, then, where is General Cox? This is his corps. He can get it underway without Burnside."

Porter shook his head. "I can't find Cox either, sir."

"By thunder, who is in charge here?" barked McClellan, gazing around him. "Someone find me Burnside, immediately!"

A lieutenant split off from the general's entourage to seek the missing Rhode Islander. Porter then walked his horse close to Little Mac. "Sir, I need to get my men underway. We cannot wait for Burnside to arrive. Give me permission to push past his command and get my division into the valley beyond. We'll take the fore, general. You won't need to wait."

Fuming for a moment, McClellan agreed. "Very well, General Porter, permission is granted. Get your command underway. Hooker's command is already on the Rebels' trail, and he will need support. I cannot have you sitting here waiting for Burnside to arrive."

"Thank you, sir," grinned Porter. "May I request a formal, written order authorizing the change? Your earlier orders stated that my command was to support Burnside's. Since those orders have changed, I would prefer it to be put on the record."

"I don't have time for this, Fitz, but I know what you are after, given the late unpleasantness with Pope," replied McClellan. "General Marcy, write something for me, please."

"Yes, general," nodded Marcy, pulling out his dispatch book. "I'm ready, sir."

"Good. Write this, then, for General Porter. Burnside's corps has not yet marched. Should the march of Sykes's division be obstructed by Burnside's troops, he is to direct General Sykes to push by them and to put his division in front. Do you have that?"

Marcy scribbled on the page, the pad resting on his thigh. "I do, sir."

"Sir, may I suggest an endorsement from me to give it a little more weight?" asked Porter.

"Yes, that is fine," sniffed McClellan. "Marcy, take down General Porter's endorsement of my change in orders and the reason for them."

Marcy cocked an eye at McClellan, bewilderment on his face. "That is rather irregular, sir. Shouldn't General Burnside have the chance to respond first before you put anything in writing? After all, this amounts to something of a rebuke."

McClellan stared daggers at his chief of staff. "You will do as I command, sir! Take General Porter's endorsement and be done with it."

"As you wish," sulked Marcy. "What is it you wish to say, General Porter?"

"Thank you, General Marcy. Please add the following statement: Burnside's corps was not moving three hours after the hour designated for him, the day after South Mountain, and he obstructed my movements. I, therefore, asked for this order, and moved by Burnside's corps."

Marcy scratched out the words. "Is that all?"

"Yes, I am satisfied," replied Porter smugly. "With your permission, General McClellan, I'll get underway."

"By all means, Porter, get moving," waved Little Mac.

Cinching his reins, Porter called for his men to resume their march. Drums set to rapping, and the men pushed past the Ninth Corps regiments, some staring in astonishment at what had just taken place.

McClellan observed the procession for a moment before calling for his officers to follow him back to headquarters. Sometime later, he strode into his makeshift office, finding Colonel Key, Colonel George Ruggles, and an aide gathering papers off the floor.

"I don't know what Burnside is up to," raged McClellan, "but whatever it is, he is keeping me from following up my victory!"

"I'm not sure what you mean, general. Is there a problem with General Burnside?" asked Key.

"Yes, there is! Burnside's command has still not advanced despite the orders I gave him to do so. He is frustrating my plans. I have ordered General Porter to push past him, but Burnside must be informed of this and provide me with an explanation for his dereliction of duty. Colonel Ruggles, take a message for me. It is to be sent to General Burnside immediately."

"Yes, sir." Ruggles dropped the bundle of papers in his hands and sat down at the general's map table.

"Write this, colonel. General Burnside, you will let General Porter's command go past you. You will then push your own command on as rapidly as possible. I demand to know the reason for your delay in starting this morning. Do you have that, Ruggles?"

Ruggles nodded that he did, and McClellan commanded him to have it sent. Key watched Ruggles leave and went to close the door. Coming back to the table, he detected an odd expression on McClellan's face; something akin to glee with a touch of shame in it. "Sir, has General Burnside really not moved his command?" he asked.

"Yes, Key, that's correct. He hasn't budged an inch. In fact, I couldn't find him at all."

"Why, general, that is remarkable good luck. It provides an opportunity to issue him a reprimand. His reputation will be tarnished despite yesterday's performance."

McClellan nodded slowly as the colonel caught on. "Indeed, it does, Key. The chance fell into my lap as if Providence willed it to happen. I could not have planned things better myself."

17

Monday, September 15, 1862

Morning to afternoon

Ninth Corps, Twenty-Third Ohio Volunteer Infantry Regiment

Fox's Gap, South Mountain, Maryland

God!"

Davey Parker was standing in the center of a long shallow trench that he and his comrades were digging when he heard the words cut through the air between the grinding scrapes of the shovels. Sam Carey doubled over and retched, choking and heaving until there was nothing left in his belly. The nauseated man sat back in the grass and wiped his mouth on a filthy sleeve.

A mischievous grin spread across the face of Sergeant Lyon. "You find a ripe one, Sam?"

The chuckling Buckeyes received a hateful stare from Carey in return. "I sure did," he spat, gesturing to the corpse lying a few feet away. "This man's been gutted. I rolled him over and his insides spilled out all over my boots. It's damned disgusting!"

Parker wiped sweat from his forehead. Their work that day had been too trying to laugh, especially on an empty stomach. Whatever food any of them had eaten came from the knapsacks of the dead. Now poor Carey had choked up even that. He would pay for it later, unless the commissary trains happened somehow to find them.

Stripped to the waist and covered in glistening sweat, Parker returned to swinging his pickaxe into the dirt. He and his comrades had already buried or carried off their own dead and wounded. Now they had just started to put dead Confederates in the ground, too. Putrefying corpses lay strewn across the fields and along the low stone walls that the Rebels had used as cover during the previous day's fight. The Ohio boys collected some of these in a pile that they could throw into the trench when they had finished digging. The rest remained scattered in the grass.

"Some victory," muttered Parker bitterly to himself. "Them that holds the field gets to do the dirty work afterward."

"Yeah, I reckon the Rebs have been planting our boys all over Virginia," remarked Sergeant Lyon as he paced the edge of the deepening pit. "This is the first field this army's held after a fight."

Swinging his pick into the soil, Parker struck a large stone. The blow sent a shiver up his arms that numbed him to the elbow. He dropped the tool into the dirt. "Dad-blast it! This ground is too hard to dig much deeper."

Lyon looked over at Parker's section of the burial trench and shook his head. "Tsk, tsk, Davey. That's only a foot down. Hogs will be at these boys before we even get off this mountain."

"What the hell's that matter to me? We didn't care enough to kill 'em, why should we care enough to bury 'em?"

"You'd want someone to do it for you, wouldn't you? It's the Christian thing to do."

Parker clapped dirt from his hands. "You're wrong there, Sarge. The Christian thing to do would've been not to shoot 'em in the first place. Then we wouldn't be in this fix."

"I heard some boys camped closer to the road have been throwing dead Rebs down a farmer's well," said George Love, stretching his back.

"Can't say I blame 'em," nodded Parker. "It's a damned sight easier than digging this trench."

"Well, the farmer stopped them from doing it," added Love. "Said they were ruining his water."

"That's the truth," commented Lyon. "He'll never be able to use that well again, the poor bastard."

Parker stuck a filthy finger into his right ear. Hearing had returned only in his left. The right remained silent as a grave. Shaking his head, he looked up at Lyon. "Sarge, you heard anything about Tom Kelly? I didn't see him when we were clearing the field. Has anyone reported him wounded or, God forbid, killed?"

"No, Davey, I haven't. I asked the major about him, too. Seems our regiment has seven men missing from yesterday's fight. Tom Kelly's one of them."

"Missing? How's a man go missing on a small field like this?" Parker waved his hand around him. "Tommy was behind me on my right. Then that shell went off, and I lost sight of him."

"You think it hit Tom directly?" asked Carey, climbing back onto his feet. "It could have blasted him to Kingdom Come, if it did."

"I can't say, Sam. I sure hope we find him, though, the miserable Irish son of a bitch."

"Don't worry, Parker, Tom will be alright," replied Lyon. "He's a tough one. You'll see. Now get back to digging!"

Parker resentfully hefted his pick. "I hope you're right, Sarge," he muttered. "I surely do."

*   *   *

Voices echoed in Tom Kelly's head. He saw flashes and heard an explosion, but the reverberation of it came from down a long tunnel. A dusky face appeared above him, swimming in and out of focus. It spun and shifted in the dim light. The man wore a slouch hat pinned up in the front and black stubble covered his chin.

"Here's one, Luther! This man's still alive," said the stranger, his words barely registering in Kelly's ears. Hands pushed under his armpits and a second pair grabbed him by the boots. Kelly felt himself being jostled, as if he lay in the back of a wagon. Then darkness took him again, and he sensed nothing until a cool cloth touched his brow. Droplets of water trickled down the side of his face and a melodious feminine voice came to him. The woman hummed softly like a mother would when bathing her child. Kelly struggled to open his eyes, but pain filled his head. His strength failed and again he fell into the gloom.

The next time he awoke, Kelly opened his eyes with ease. The blackness that had engulfed him dropped away, and he felt strength returning to his limbs. Peering up, he saw painted white wooden ceiling beams and a plastered wall on his left. Sunlight streamed in through a paned glass window opposite his feet, illuminating a case of books and newspapers beside a roll-top desk. Kelly lay in a narrow bed, his clothing gone, except for his union suit. A thin blanket lay over him, pulled up to the chest. He looked around, expecting to see an army orderly or a nurse, but got a start when his gaze settled on the handsome woman sitting beside him with a book. A white apron covered her dark dress, and she wore a length of lavender ribbon tied in her hair. Behind the woman stood a sturdy black man with a chin beard and canvas jacket, clutching a slouch hat in his hands.

The woman's eyes rose to meet his. "Ah, you're awake," she smiled, her teeth full and white. "We were afraid you'd never come back."

"Oh," said Kelly weakly. "Where am I?"

"You're in my home ... in Middletown."

"Middletown, Maryland? So, I'm still near me regiment?"

"I reckon so, but you can't go anywhere just yet. You're still not well."

Kelly pushed himself onto his elbows. "I'm fine. Ye can't keep me here!" he complained, pain shooting through his head.

The black man gently pushed Kelly back onto the bed. "You best lie still, mister. You ain't fixed up yet," he said.

"Get yer filthy hands offa me, nigger!" Kelly growled.

The man drew back as if a rattlesnake had bitten him, but it was the woman beside Kelly who spoke out. Her eyes narrowed and an angry shadow spread over her face.

"You'll watch your language in this house, mister! We've done our best to make you comfortable. The least you can do is show some gratitude."

Kelly stared at the ceiling, his chest tight with dismay. A door opened and a second black man stuck in his head, his hat held politely to his breast. Kelly thought he recognized this man's face, too. Had he seen it in a dream, or was it somewhere else?

"We heard shouting, Miss Lucy. Everything here alright?" he asked.

The woman stared coldly at Kelly. Then she rose to her feet and smoothed her skirt. "Yes, Luther, everything is fine. Our guest here had a start."

Stepping into the room, Luther closed the door behind him and walked over to the foot of the bed. Kelly gazed uneasily at the man's grinning face. "How you doing, Mister Soldier Man? Everything alright?"

Pulling a frown, Kelly turned to the wall. "Where's me clothes? I've nothing on but me knickers here."

"Hey, y'all! He sure talks funny, Don't he?" Luther laughed.

"That he does," sniffed Lucy. "He's from Ireland. Isn't that right, Mister Irishman? You come all the way across the ocean to fight in the war?"

Kelly rolled to face Lucy. "I've nothing to say to ye, and even less to the likes of those two. Now where are me trousers? And where's the Rebel flag I captured?"

"Why, the trousers is outside in the pot, Mister Irishman. We're bileing out the lice and such. We didn't find no flag wit you."

"The trousers are outside, Simon, not is," said Lucy, admonishing the man in the canvas jacket. "And you are boiling them, not bile-ing ... understand?"

The grin faded from Simon's face. "Yes'm, Miss Lucy. I forgot."

"Well, from now on, don't forget," replied Lucy, turning to fetch a pitcher of water. "Remember what I taught you, Simon. A man earns respect by the way he speaks. Your situation might keep you from looking proper, but that doesn't mean a man should speak poorly. He must show the world that he is a man every time he opens his mouth."

"Geez-o, ye talk like an old school marm," marveled Kelly. "What in the devil kind of place is this?"

Lucy wheeled toward Kelly, her eyes dark with wrath. "My rules go for you too, Mister Irishman. You're a guest in my house and by God, you'll act like one."

Again, Kelly pushed up on his elbows. Pain filled his head, but this time, he fought to stay upright. "I'll be damned if I ever heard a woman talk that way! A white woman teaching niggers to speak proper? Where's the master of the house? I want to see him."

"Ain't no masta here," said Simon. "This Miss Lucy's house. She an independent woman."

Kelly glanced from Simon to Lucy and back again. "An independent woman? Ha! Bah, ha, ha!" Falling back, Kelly gasped for air. "Oi, that's rich. Me first time wounded and I end up in the care of an independent woman and niggers with book learning! Wait, ain't that against the law? What are the odds?"

Lucy flew to the bedside in a rustle of skirts with cheeks flushed as she stuck her finger in Kelly's face and shook it within an inch of his nose. "You listen here, mister, and you listen good. You'll stop using that word in my house straightaway! This is my home you're in. I'm no delicate housewife you can hurl insults at, and my sex doesn't limit me no how. I can read and write, and I take care of myself. This place is rightfully mine, left to me by my Pa, who built it himself, and if I wanted to, I could have left you lying in the yard when Simon brought you in." She drew a deep breath and continued. "No one here wants anything from you, or of you, for that matter. Simon brought you here because he has a good heart and because we want to help the boys in blue, however we can. Simon's still in bondage. He has a master, like you said, and even though the man is good to him, for a slaver, he still owns Simon, and by all that's holy that isn't right! So, we're behind the national army all the way and do what we can to help, but you'll show gratitude for what we've done and hold your tongue while you're here, you understand? Or so help me God, I'll throw you into the road, wet clothes and all!"

Kelly wiped away the spittle that had flown onto his cheek when Lucy scolded him. Chastened, he lay staring at the ceiling of the room. Simon fiddled nervously with his hat brim, like he always did when Lucy grew wrathy. Her independence and fierce personal pride had forced her into a life of solitude. Most folks would not tolerate her education, thinking it improper for a woman, but the isolation suited her most of the time. She did what she could to support her own household and Simon came to visit her every so often, sometimes bringing his brother, Luther, with him.

"I'll get some fresh water and check on the mister's clothing," offered Simon, breaking the uncomfortable silence.

Lucy nodded to him. "Thank you, Simon. I'll put out something for you boys to eat when you come back."

"We'd sure be grateful, Miss Lucy," grinned the man, pulling his hat back onto his head. "Come on, Luther." The two of them walked out of the room.

"What about you, Mister Irishman? Would you like something to eat, too? I've got a hot stew on the stove. You may have some, if you mind your manners."

Kelly had already caught wind of the stew when Simon opened the door and his stomach growled for a taste of it. Pride nagged at him, though, and the word "no" rang out in his mind. How could he take charity from someone like this haughty spinster? How dare she shame him like she did? Kelly lay there agonizing with himself, but with hunger too much to bear, he gave in.

"Your stew smells good, and I could eat ... if you're willing to share," he admitted.

Lucy Settle placed her hands on her hips and peered down at Kelly. He looked up at her, feeling as if she could see right through him. Shaking her head, she strode from the room without saying a word. Kelly heard her clattering in the kitchen and then coming back up the stairs. When she reappeared, she carried a large porcelain bowl, a spoon, and a cloth napkin.

"Sit up a bit," she commanded, placing the bowl on the bedside table. She tucked the napkin into his collar and sat down. Kelly glanced uneasily at Lucy while she made herself comfortable. Her thin nose stood above high cheekbones and strands of darkly colored hair dangled enticingly from under the ribbon that held it tight. Haughty or not, Kelly had to admit her beauty.

Taking a spoonful of stew, Lucy raised it to Kelly's lips. He looked down at it and let her push the spoon into his mouth. The heat scalded him a touch, and he blanched, but the exquisite taste quickly distracted him.

"Oh, my word, that's grand!" he bubbled. "I've never had a better tasting concoction."

"I'm glad you like it. You have a name, mister?"

"Kelly. Thomas Kelly."

"I'm pleased to meet you, Tom Kelly. My name is Lucy Settle. Simon is my neighbor's man. Luther, too."

"I see," muttered Kelly through a mouthful of soup. "I'm grateful for the help, Miss Settle. Did you say it was Simon who brought me here?"

"It was," Lucy nodded, offering Kelly another generous spoonful. "He went up the mountain early this morning after a call went out for the local folk to come help. There are wounded men like you in houses all over town after that fight yesterday. I thought the shooting was never going to stop."

"I don't hear any of it now, is the army still here?"

"It is, far as I know. The National Road is filled with you boys as far back as Frederick City. Those still at the top of the mountain have been sending the injured all over the valley. Simon went up there and found you near a stone wall with blood running down the side of your head. You've got a nasty gash in your scalp, but I think you'll live."

"A stone wall? I don't recall that," frowned Kelly.

"What do you remember?"

"I remember driving the first line of Rebels we met. Davey Parker and I—Davey's me best friend—fought over a Rebel banner and I tuck it. Then we got orders to go back into line and we ran through a cornfield. That's when I heard the explosion. I got hit and went down. I must have crawled to the rear before losing consciousness. There was a stone wall behind us, as I recall. Hey, may I have more of that lovely stew? I feel better already."

Lucy rose to refill the bowl. Returning to the bedside a short time later, she fed Kelly until he had eaten his fill. Then she offered him a cup of water, which he drained, and sat back, a curious expression on her face. "An Irishman in the national army. Tell me, Tom Kelly, how'd you come to be here?"

"Not much to say," Kelly shrugged. "I came to this country some years ago and became a citizen a few years after that. Naturalization, they call it. A funny term, if ye ask me. In any case, they gave me papers saying I'm an American. I thought jining up was the right thing to do, especially with the riverboat trade drying up when the war came. They offered a hefty bounty. Thirteen whole dollars to take up arms. I made me mark and here I am."

"Hmpf, a citizen," snorted Lucy. "Here I am, born and raised in this country, and I can't call myself a citizen. You come from a faraway land, and they call you an American. When will the degradation of my sex, and of Simon's people, end?"

"Look here, now, Miss Settle. No man I know jined the army over slavery. We jined to put down rebellion and to fight treason."

"Is that so? Did they also make you a fool when they made you a citizen?"

"Now, wait just a minute!" balked Kelly.

"No, you wait a minute and listen. Did it ever occur to you that the rebellion, and slavery might be connected? That the men you and your friends are fighting against are fighting to keep people like Simon in bondage, and that's why they rebelled?"

Kelly pursed his lips thoughtfully. "I—well, no, I never gave it a thought. Fighting to keep me new homeland together seemed reason enough to take up arms."

"Your homeland?" scoffed Lucy. "What homeland do I have? What future does Simon have, or any of the colored folks in the South? They have a future of hardship the likes of nothing you've ever seen. The whippings, the back-breaking labor in the hot sun for sixteen hours a day, having your kin sold out from under you, families torn apart. Does any of that sound just to you?"

Chewing the inside of his lip, Kelly stared down at his lap, an uncomfortable sense of shame spreading through him. "No," he said, finally. "None of that sounds just. A lot of it, in fact, sounds like the life I left behind. The English don't practice slavery in Ireland, but they might just as well. Irish people can't own land, use their own language, or worship the Lord as they see fit. They can't hold political office and families are thrown off the land at a landlord's whim. People are starving and they've got no money. No future, either."

"Things in Ireland sound bad, Mister Kelly, almost as bad as for the colored folks in Dixie."

"Well, not quite that bad, I reckon, but bad enough," admitted Kelly.

"Hard to feel like a man under those circumstances, isn't it?"

"Aye, Miss Settle, I reckon it is."

"But you deserve to be treated like a man, don't you?"

"I do. A man's nothing if he's got no self respect...."

The words tailed off as they left Kelly's lips. Echoing Lucy's earlier statement to Simon, he found himself faced with a revelation that had never dawned on him until that moment.

The plight of Irish and that of American blacks did seem strangely similar. He himself had experienced the prejudice of some native-born Americans against Irish immigrants when he arrived in Baltimore. No dogs or Irish read signs on some of the shop fronts. It confronted him again when he had gone to find work on the Ohio River. Foremen would glare at him and spit streams of tobacco juice before grudgingly taking him on at the lowest possible pay. The only laborers who made less money, in fact, were the free blacks who plied the river trade. Never mind the Kentucky side of the river where an Irishman stood no chance of making even the meager wage that Kelly had managed to secure. Too many slaves worked on the docks and the riverboats. The labor of free white men was just not in demand. Free Soil slogans made sense on the river.

A knowing smile formed on Lucy's face. "Do you understand the war a little better now, Mister Kelly?" she asked gently. "Do you understand how important it is for a man to be seen as a man, and not as an Irish mule or a negro slave? What makes you better than me or Simon? Is it book learning, or land owning, or wealth, or a big family? Does religion make you a man, or is it something else?"

"I never thought about it before, Miss Settle. It sure ain't book learning, as I don't have much of that."

"Oh, so you can't read or write? Well, I can. Does that make me better than you?"

"Lord have mercy, I should say not!"

"Why not? I can figure and write, and read the Bible. You can't. What good are you in this world other than as a mule for some rich man? What can you make of yourself without an education?"

"I—I can do what I want and go where I please! When opportunities all dried up, I can move on."

"Because you're a white man. That's why. Your sex is the only difference between us, isn't it? I'm considered less than you because I'm a woman. I can't vote. I can't work in most professions. I can't hold public office! Should I command less respect than you, a louse-bitten immigrant?"

"Now wait just a minute! I won't be insulted by a woman! Even a—an independent woman, like yerself. I didn't make things the way they are and there's nothing I can do to change them," protested Kelly.

"You're right about that. We can't change the world, but we can change our hearts and that's where the difference comes in. It's like the Psalm says: create in me a clean heart, oh God, and renew a steadfast spirit within me. Change your heart, Tom Kelly, and in your own small way, you can make the world a better place."

Kelly lay quietly in bed while Lucy got up and took his empty bowl to the doorway. "Do you need anything else?" she asked.

"No, marm," he pouted.

Lucy walked from the room, leaving Kelly dumbstruck. The things she said about the world made his head spin. When she returned, she brought a new cup of water and set it down at Kelly's bedside before taking a seat.

"Miss Settle, where'd ye learn to talk like you do," he asked meekly. "I've never met a woman like you."

An ironic grin formed on her lips. "Why, thank you, Mister Kelly. That's the kindest thing I've heard you say. I owe my thinking to Elizabeth Cady Stanton and her colleague, Susan B. Anthony. They've long argued that women ought to be equal to men in society.

They've argued, too, that slavery is an abomination and that it must be stamped out in a nation which claims to call its people free."

"Oi, that's trouble there," commented Kelly with a shake of his head.

"Only to the small-minded, Mister Kelly. It comes down to basic human dignity. If we are all men, in the philosophical sense, then the fundamental principle of our existence must be self-respect. It is as you said. Without it a man has nothing. We must all have the liberty to live our lives and to dream our dreams—to make something more of ourselves. If we do not, then what kind of a land are you and your friends fighting for?"

Kelly fidgeted uncomfortably with his blanket. His thoughts urged him to get away from this odd woman as quickly as possible, but the dizzying ache in his head immobilized him. For the time being, he was as good as caged. "I don't know, Miss Settle. I hadn't thought of it like that before," he said at last, hoping to bring the conversation to an end.

Lucy would not be put off. For many long months, she had longed to speak with someone about these matters; to find out why a man would rather take up arms for some nebulous political cause than for an obvious moral good. Tom Kelly struck her as a disappointment. Poorly educated and unsophisticated in his beliefs, he spouted the same platitudes that she read in the papers. Saving the Union! Suppressing rebellion! These were all well and good causes, she supposed, if one came at the war from a narrow perspective, but for a working man like Kelly, and an immigrant as well, how could those things count for more than the idea of freedom for all?

"Well, Mister Kelly, I'd advise you think hard on it now," she said at last, "or for as long as you are laid up in my home, at least. These are times that try men's souls. The war is a furnace, burning away the impurities in this land. The scourging brings pain, but in the end, it is worthwhile. Is securing the Union enough of a purpose for you? It isn't for me, but then I can't take up a musket and fight for what I believe."

Rising to her feet, Lucy smoothed her skirts and strode to the door, her posture ramrod straight. She paused there for a moment, looking back at the man in her care. "You have taken up a musket, Mister Kelly. Think on what I have said to you and make your sacrifice a conscious one. Then will it be righteous in the eyes of both the Lord and your fellow man."

Closing the door behind her, Lucy's footsteps faded down the staircase. Kelly sank down into his bed and threw an arm over his face. His head swam with the things she had said, and he regretted losing his battle trophy, but the throbbing of his wound made it difficult for him to think. Resolving to contemplate the woman's words after he had gotten some rest, Kelly willed himself to sleep.

18

Monday, September 15, 1862
Afternoon to nightfall
Field Headquarters, Army of the Potomac
Middletown to Boonsborough, Maryland

McClellan frowned at the message Randolph Marcy had just thrust into his hand. Received from General Franklin, it reported two enemy battle lines stretched across Pleasant Valley several miles above Harpers Ferry. The Rebels, continued the dispatch, outnumbered the Sixth Corps by two-to-one. Instantly, McClellan recalled his last estimate on September 12 putting the size of Lee's force at 120,000 men. With that many troops, the Army of Northern Virginia remained extremely dangerous, despite being split in two.

Jackson.

The name tolled ominously in McClellan's mind. Lee's misplaced orders had put Stonewall in command of the effort against Harpers Ferry. Would he stay in Virginia with his command, or would he cross into Pleasant Valley and attack Franklin with his entire force?

Then there was Lee himself to contend with. Only a short time earlier, Major Myer's signal station atop South Mountain had reported the advance of General Richardson's division toward a speck on the map called Keedysville. McClellan received that news gratefully, but then he read the ominous postscript—the Rebel army was drawing up in line of battle on the heights behind Antietam Creek.

Little Mac paced the hardwood floor, his thoughts in a jumble. The victory atop South Mountain had appeared to be decisive, but if Lee was whipped, why would he pause north of the Potomac instead of retreating across the river? Lee on one flank of his army and Jackson on the other? McClellan shuddered at the thought of it and yet here he was, facing that exact scenario.

Pacing to his map, McClellan studied the roads of Washington County for routes the Rebels could take. "Franklin reports a large force on his front," he said to Marcy, "a force too powerful for him to reasonably attack. He says he is outnumbered two-to-one."

"Two-to-one? That's troubling, sir. If Franklin is attacked, we will need to come to his aid."

Scrutinizing the map, McClellan's finger traced the length of Pleasant Valley from Harpers Ferry in the south to Boonsborough in the north. "Indeed, we will," he muttered, his gaze settling on a spot near Boonsborough. "Franklin's predicament requires not only that I keep him where he is, it demands that I move Burnside's corps closer to him for support. A place like Rohrersville will do." Little Mac tapped the map and stood, folding his hands behind his back. "My concern now, Marcy, is the Rebel army at Sharpsburg. With Elk Ridge between Hooker and Franklin, neither will be able to reinforce the other if Lee turns to attack."

"What makes you think he will attack, general? His army has suffered a great defeat."

"Here at South Mountain, yes, but Harpers Ferry may have capitulated, so our victory is not clear. Lee's numbers give him the ability to turn on us and lash out with overwhelming force on either side of Elk Ridge. Why else would he halt his retreat and remain in Maryland?"

Marcy nodded thoughtfully. "I see what you are thinking. You suspect Lee is inviting you to further divide your army. Then he will fall upon one or the other with a superior force."

"Yes, Marcy, that possibility concerns me greatly, particularly with Jackson on the loose near the ferry."

"Then what will you do next, sir?"

McClellan gestured to the map. "The best I can do now is to concentrate the army around Keedysville. It will be close to Sharpsburg there and accessible to Rohrersville. Both flanks—Hooker's or Franklin's—can be supported if the Rebels attack one or the other. What I need is confirmation that Lee intends to remain in Maryland. Until I have it, I can make no further plans. It's critical now that we move headquarters to Boonsborough. The town's location will give me the ability to direct the army's movements as required. I cannot oversee them from here."

"Very good, sir. I'll give the orders."

"Yes, Marcy, do that," nodded McClellan. "And please be quick about it. We need to get underway as soon as possible."

Proffering a salute, Marcy hurried from the room, leaving Little Mac to his thoughts. The general stared down at his map, his teeth gently grinding his lower lip. "Your actions confound me, Bobby Lee," he mumbled. "What are you planning?"

*   *   *

Informed thirty minutes later that the headquarters staff stood ready to depart, McClellan walked outside. Grayish clouds covered the sky and humidity moistened the air more than usual for late summer. Looking around him, the general pulled on his gloves and nodded to the dozens of officers and escort troops waiting to depart.

"Good afternoon, gentlemen," he called out. "Mount up. We are leaving." He climbed atop Dan Webster and clicked his tongue to get the horse moving. Dan carried the general down the National Road, which was packed with marching troops from the Second Corps. The heavy blue column wound over the countryside for as far as the eye could see and McClellan's escort moved ahead to clear a space for the general. Up the road they went, past ranks of men cheering whenever they laid eyes on their commander.

Eventually, McClellan arrived at a house on the roadside. Raising his hand for them to stop, he ordered Marcy to come with him and dismounted. Men lay strewn across the grass nursing wounds and McClellan walked up to them.

"Good afternoon, son. Are you badly hurt?" he asked, squatting beside an injured soldier.

The young man's eyes lit up. "No, sir, general. I took a ball in the arm, is all. The surgeons tell me it missed the bone, so I'll be able to keep it."

"That's very good. Are you one of General Gibbon's boys?"

"I am," replied the man. "The name's Macy, Private William Macy, Nineteenth Regiment Indiana Volunteers."

"I am pleased to meet you, Private Macy. Will you allow me to shake your hand?"

"I—I'd be honored, sir," said the astonished Hoosier, taking the general's outstretched palm.

"You and your comrades did good work yesterday, private. Your courage and bravery won us an important victory that has thrown back the Rebels. Please accept my congratulations on behalf of a grateful nation."

Macy glowed at the praise and thanked the general. Little Mac patted Macy's shoulder and rose to his feet, every eye in the yard upon him. "Your nation thanks you boys for your courage and sacrifice," he called out. "You are all to be commended. I am humbled to have such brave men as you under my command."

The wounded raised a cheer, and McClellan lifted his cap to them before striding up to the house. Inside the narrow rooms lay more injured men. Furniture had been pushed to the corners to make space for the bodies lying on the floor. McClellan and Marcy walked slowly through the place, speaking softly to the injured and offering gentle nods. Those who could acknowledged the general's presence with grins and salutes. The more seriously injured merely stared.

McClellan moved among them for a time, stopping finally in front of a soldier with particularly grievous wounds. Both legs had been amputated at the knees and he lay on the floor with his arm thrown over his face. Tears welled up in McClellan's eyes at the sight of the blood-soaked bandages and he opened his mouth to speak, but no words would come.

"Do you wish to say something, general?" whispered Marcy.

McClellan stretched a hand toward the injured man. "I do, Marcy, but what do I say to a poor, brave boy such as this?"

How about "God bless you, son, and thank you?"

"Yes, Marcy, that will do," nodded Little Mac, and bending down, he whispered the words into the stricken man's ear. After, he rose and quickly strode outside, unable to hold back his tears any longer. "All right, gentlemen, come along," he choked, and pulling on his kepi, he climbed into the saddle while wiping his eyes.

McClellan soon crested the gap behind his escorts and continued down the opposite slope. Artillery thumped ominously in the distance and McClellan stopped to observe it from a shelf on the mountainside. Raising his field glasses, he saw clouds of powder smoke drifting skyward. At such a distance, however, the details could not be seen.

"Sounds like Hooker is getting after them," commented one of the general's staff. Distracted by the noise, McClellan nodded. He dropped his glasses into their case and cantered on.

Regiments at the base of the mountain covered the fields that General Longstreet's Rebel command had occupied only hours earlier. McClellan noted the debris left behind by the fleeing Confederates; the dead men on the roadside, the wounded silently eyeing him, the broken wagons, shattered gun carriages, and wrecked caissons bearing abandoned ammunition. All about him lay the signs of an enemy thrown back in haste, and yet Lee remained in Maryland, his army drawn up like a viper just to the west.

The wood-framed houses of Boonsborough hove into view and McClellan looked for the scouts that Marcy had sent ahead to locate a suitable headquarters. Peering over his right shoulder, Little Mac spied a squat stone tower atop a distant hill. A signal flag wagged there, communicating with General Hooker. Best to find a location on this side of town, he thought. Pleasant Valley lay to the left and the signal station to the rear.

McClellan spotted a white clapboard house on the right. Steering Dan into the yard, the general slid down from the saddle and handed his reins to an orderly. An aide appeared, leading a civilian, who approached McClellan with his hat in his hands.

"Sir, this is Mister Raestrouse. He's volunteered his house for headquarters," said the aide.

McClellan shook the man's hand. "I'm grateful for your hospitality, sir. With any luck, we shouldn't need to bother you for too long."

Raestrouse offered McClellan a toothy grin. "That's fine, general. As long as the Rebels are on the run, I'm happy to see you. They were here until just this morning."

"So, I've heard. My boys ran them out, though, didn't they?"

"Yes, sir, general, they surely did. Right quick, too. You and your men may make use of my house for as long as you need."

"Thank you, we will. Please let me know if there is anything I can do for you."

"I'll do that, but you won't be seeing much of me. I'll stay with my cousin up the road a piece until you go. It's been a pleasure meeting you."

Turning toward the door, McClellan climbed the steps, removing his cap when he entered the front parlor. A table stood in the center of the room with his map spread out on top of it. Staff officers and aides passed correspondence and reviewed reports coming in from the army's numerous corps and divisions. Little Mac tossed his cap onto the table as a man rushed in from outside.

"Sir, dispatch from General Hooker; just received by signal."

McClellan took the note, scowling as he read it. "Colonel Ruggles, bring me a pen, ink, and paper right away!"

Several officers gathered around the general. "Is something amiss, sir?" asked Marcy.

"Yes, general, there is. The gunfire we are hearing is Pleasonton's artillery replying to Secesh guns. Hooker confirms Longstreet's command is drawn up in line of battle on the heights west of Keedysville. Lee is not retreating to Virginia."

Marcy and the other officers shot bewildered glances at each other. "But, general, that doesn't make sense," blurted Colonel Key. "After the thrashing our boys gave him? What could Lee be thinking?" McClellan stared hard at his confidant. "I don't know, colonel, but right now I need to communicate with General Burnside. General Franklin still has the enemy in front of him, so Burnside had better move the Ninth Corps to Rohrersville and provide Franklin with support. If the two of them can throw back the Rebels in Pleasant Valley, I'll order an attack. If Franklin thinks his position is defensible, however, and an attack is ill-advised, I'll have Burnside march on Sharpsburg to cooperate with us."

"And Sykes's command with General Porter? His men are ahead of Burnside. What about him?" asked Marcy.

"I'll send Porter to support Hooker at Sharpsburg. If that is where Lee is, then that is where the largest portion of our force should be assembled. I'll take my chances with Jackson, but Lee is too dangerous to overlook for even a minute. We must keep this army in front of him until he goes back across the river. Now, give me a few minutes, gentlemen. I need to write up all of this."

Colonel Ruggles brought McClellan a pen and well of ink to write out his orders for Burnside, whose column had finally gotten underway at two o'clock after Porter's division cleared the road. Scratching out the note, McClellan worked while couriers came and went. An aide brought bread and cheese, along with a pitcher of water, and McClellan nibbled in silence while waiting for news of events on Hooker's front. The cannon fire in the distance reverberated across the landscape, making the general edgy. At last, a man arrived from the signal station atop South Mountain.

"Message from General Franklin, sir!" he said, snapping a salute.

McClellan glanced at his pocket watch. Four-fifteen. Hours had crawled by while he waited for information. Taking the paper, the general opened it.

"Ah, clarity at last!" he exclaimed, hurrying to the table where Marcy worked. "Marcy, here is good news. Franklin reports that Jackson is withdrawing from Pleasant Valley. My guess is Lee has called him back to Virginia, where he intends to rejoin him. Write orders for Franklin to hold his position, without attacking, unless he should see a favorable opportunity. Tell him I am going to concentrate everything we have on Longstreet's force near Sharpsburg. If Franklin can keep the enemy in his front without doing anything decisive until matters are settled at Sharpsburg, he should do it. Do you have that?"

Marcy scratched on the paper, dipping the nib in black ink. "I do," he nodded, "and will have it sent immediately."

"Good man," nodded McClellan. "Colonel Ruggles, come here. I have work for you as well." Little Mac turned to the colonel, ordering him to take a message. "This is for

General Burnside. Tell him he is to move his command to Sharpsburg at once, via Porterstown, to assist in the attack on the place. Inform him as well that I will be there in person. Understand?"

"Yes, sir. I'll get this out directly."

"Excellent, colonel. Before you send a rider, be sure and contact Major Myer to ask if he has established contact with Burnside by signal. We should get this order to the Ninth Corps as quickly as possible to keep Burnside from marching too far out of the way. I pray it's not already too late."

"As you wish, sir. I'll find out," nodded Ruggles.

His plans set; Little Mac ordered his staff to gather their things. Hooker's front and the thumping of artillery beckoned to him. The opportunity to strike Lee's fragmented army now presented itself clearly and McClellan intended to see it through.

19

Monday, September 15, 1862
Late afternoon to nightfall
Ninth Corps
The Road to Keedysville, Maryland

Burnside rocked lazily in the saddle beside Jacob Cox. Lost in thought, he stared into the distance as Major plodded past fields rich with the late summer bounty. Endless acres of corn, wheat, clover, and other crops surrounded them on all sides, promising a rich harvest once the war had passed by the region.

Ahead, beneath the gray-bottomed clouds of a lowering sky, Burnside could see the trailing regiments of General George Sykes's Second Division, the only portion of Porter's Fifth Corps up that morning from Middletown. Behind Burnside and Cox flowed the Ninth Corps in a long blue column, now independent of the army's dissolved right-wing. The corps crawled snake-like down the western side of South Mountain, an immense haze of beige dust rising from under its many feet.

Inhaling a breath of the swirling dust, Burnside sneezed mightily into his handkerchief. "God bless you, general," commented Cox. The morose Rhode Islander nodded thanks, but said nothing, tucking the handkerchief back into his tunic.

Cox eyed Burnside closely. Ever since his re-appearance that afternoon, the good-natured general had acted strangely withdrawn. Something of importance was clearly bothering Old Burn, but Cox, being new to the responsibilities of his command, and to Burnside personally, shied from asking what it might be. After a time, however, his curiosity became too much to resist, and Cox worked up the courage to speak.

"Um, general?" he inquired, "you've been awfully quiet. May I ask what's troubling you? It might help to get it off your chest."

Burnside's right cheek twitched at the question. Staring down at his reins, he sighed and spoke up. "My apologies, Cox, I am not myself. There are certain matters on my mind."

"I am happy to listen, sir, and to offer counsel, if it might be of assistance," volunteered the Buckeye.

"Thank you, general, I may avail myself of your company," Burnside replied. "This day has been quite unpleasant. It disturbed me to learn that your men had thrown the bodies of dead Rebels into a farmer's well. The man was justifiably furious about it, and he told me so in no uncertain terms."

"He was irate, general, but you worked out an agreement with him, didn't you? The government will be compensating him for the loss."

"I did, Cox. I promised him one dollar per body. Your men didn't know how many they had already disposed of in that way, but from the wretched pile of corpses lying nearby, it looked as if many more were still to come." A shudder passed through Burnside. "A distasteful task. Most awful."

"Indeed, sir," agreed Cox, "but I cannot blame the men. They found a way that eased their work. Not only did they have a shortage of shovels and pickaxes to use, but the soil on the mountain is also as hard as rock. Most of the trenches my men dug were less than three feet deep. They couldn't go down any farther. I think they did the best they could, under the circumstances."

Burnside heaved a sigh. "Perhaps, Cox, perhaps. Alas, I wish the farmer's well was my only distraction. A portion of my thoughts are also on poor Reno. He was a good friend and an excellent corps commander."

"Oh," said Cox, his tone betraying disappointment. "I hope you will find me equally competent."

Realizing that Cox might interpret what he had said as a slight, Burnside moved quickly to correct it. "Please, Jacob, do not trouble yourself about it. I am grateful to have you with me. You have done nothing but good work since I've known you. I meant no insult by commenting on General Reno."

Relieved, Cox shot Burnside a grin. "I understand, sir, and took no offense. It's hard to lose a friend."

"It is, Cox. I fear I may have lost more than one, too."

This comment took Cox by surprise. His decision to pry open Burnside's thoughts had borne unanticipated fruit. Being a trained attorney, he elected to pursue the matter. "What do you mean, general? Was someone else close to you killed yesterday?"

"Oh, no. That's not what I mean," waved Burnside. "I mean General McClellan. We have been on good terms since before the war, but his recent conduct toward me has grown peculiar. Take, for instance, the reprimand he issued at midday." Burnside paused before continuing. "He's never done anything like that before to me or to anyone else in the army. I understand we're supposed to be underway, but the couriers he sent couldn't have known to look for me east of Middletown. Neither could you have directed them there because I didn't learn about your commissary train until after I returned to headquarters from visiting your command. Your men had not eaten for two days, general, so I went to the rear to find your wagons. I never thought I would need to go back so far. The roads from Middletown were entirely blocked by Sykes's division and Sumner's corps. There was no way I could bring up rations for your boys in a timely manner."

"I understand, sir. Have you explained that to General McClellan? He may withdraw the reprimand."

"No, not yet," replied Burnside with a shake of his head. "The commanding general is no doubt occupied by more important matters. This is my fault, in any case. I ought to have informed McClellan of my difficulties finding your train. It took much longer than I expected."

A dark expression shaded Burnside's face and, falling silent, he resumed staring into the distance. Then he blew out another sigh and turned back to Cox. "I am sorry as well, general, that your men have still had nothing to eat. By the time I could bring up your train, we had no choice but to march."

"Don't let it trouble you, sir. The men will live. It isn't the first time they've had to subsist on whatever they can find. Besides, the day is already more than half gone. Once we reach our objective, the train will come up and the men will eat their fill."

Cox peered at the low ridge ahead of them, cannon fire thumping in the distance beyond it. "We shouldn't need to march much farther, should we? That artillery is growing louder."

"I don't think it's too far ahead," said Burnside. "Our orders are to march to Porterstown, over the lip of this ridge, and then on to Sharpsburg."

"Are we headed back to Virginia, sir?"

"It appears that way. Lee must be crossing the Potomac by now. Those are probably our guns hurrying him along."

Conversation between the two men dropped until a rider came up. Yanking on his reins, he threw Burnside a salute and held out a folded piece of paper. "Orders from General McClellan, sir!"

"Thank you, corporal," replied Burnside, taking the note. Steering Major to the side of the road, he pulled it open as Cox walked his horse alongside. "The news is bad, Cox," Burnside frowned. "It seems we are not bound for Virginia after all. Longstreet is at Sharpsburg in force, drawn up in line of battle behind a creek."

"So Lee isn't retreating?"

"It appears not. The commanding general also informs me that General Franklin is facing a sizable Rebel force here in this valley." Burnside pointed south. "He says we're to communicate with Franklin and move in that direction, toward a place called Rohrersville, if the Sixth Corps requires assistance. If Franklin responds that he can handle the enemy on his own, we are to continue to Sharpsburg as originally ordered."

"It sounds like we need to call a halt," suggested Cox.

"Yes, general, that would be a good idea until we know what to do."

"I'll see to it right away," nodded Cox, and cinching up his reins, he called for a bugler.

Burnside watched Cox go and waved to a courier. Giving the man instructions to ride south for Franklin's headquarters, he told him to inquire after the Sixth Corps' need for reinforcement and return as quickly as he could. Meanwhile, Cox's bugler blared out the notes to halt and the lumbering column lurched to a stop.

"Fall out and rest!" cried the brigade commanders, sending the men to the roadsides where they settled down to wait.

The sun sank slowly in the western sky, its face peeking every so often through the overhang of clouds. Guns thumped in the distance and men tightened their belts against the churning of their empty stomachs. Having exhausted their supply of hardtack crackers, famished soldiers drifted from the column into the neighboring fields and orchards to consume whatever ripe fruit and corn they could find. Those at the rear benefited from being close to the trailing commissary train, and they filled their bellies with tins of beef. The much-needed supplies did not find their way to all the men who needed them, however, and most continued to suffer while lolling in the heat.

Burnside and Cox consulted a map, marking out the roads that would lead them to where they might be needed most. Of concern to Burnside was the ridge that lay between them and the rest of the army. If the Rebels attacked one or the other portion of the army, it would be difficult to reinforce either flank. Surely McClellan saw this, too, and would do what he could to mitigate the risk. At long last, another rider approached from the west, bearing a note from headquarters. Burnside rose from the grass to consult his watch and found it to be well after five o'clock. He read the note and told Cox its contents.

"Well, general, it seems the situation has changed. We are now to move immediately on Sharpsburg."

Cox rose, brushing dust from the seat of his trousers. "So, the danger on Franklin's front has passed?"

"I assume so, but do not know. This note says only that we are to march on Sharpsburg via Porterstown. There is no mention of what is happening with Franklin."

"All right, then, general. I'll get the column underway."

"Very good, Cox. Once we have the men back in hand, I am going to ride ahead to learn what is going on. Not knowing is driving me to distraction."

"May I come with you, sir?"

"Of course, I'd appreciate the company. Get the men going so we can be off."

Cox snapped a salute and bawled out the orders while Burnside waited. He assembled his staff, and a short time later, the massive blue column crept back into motion. Cox communicated the marching route to the lead brigadier and informed the man that he and Burnside were riding ahead. They took off at a trot toward Porterstown, and the place where McClellan's note said he would be directing the attack personally.

The sun had dropped well toward the horizon by the time Burnside and Cox located McClellan in a pasture off the main road from Keedysville. Dismounting where orderlies held the reins for the command staff's horses, the two generals approached where McClellan and the others had gathered. Little Mac spotted them coming and pushed through the throng to greet them.

"General Burnside, welcome. You are here at last!" he grinned, grasping the Rhode Islander's hand.

Taken aback by the warmth of McClellan's greeting after the tension between them that morning, Burnside stammered, "I . . . I thank you, sir," in reply.

"And here is General Cox as well," said McClellan, turning to shake the Ohioan's hand. Clutching Cox by the back of the arm, he led him to the officers loitering about. "Gentlemen, for those of you who do not know him, I'd like to introduce Brigadier General Jacob Cox of Ohio. General Cox is now in command of the Ninth Corps, after poor Reno's unfortunate passing." Cox nodded to the men as McClellan went on. "Cox served admirably with me in Ohio and western Virginia at the outset of the war. He is a capital officer and I expect all of you to pay him every professional courtesy."

"Thank you, sir, I appreciate the confidence," nodded Cox. "It's good to see you again."

McClellan patted Cox on the shoulder and turned to the assembly. "Now, then, let us go to the top of this hill and see what we can make of the enemy, shall we?"

The group climbed to the crest. Trailing behind McClellan, Burnside noted the presence of Joe Hooker and Fitz John Porter, neither of whom acknowledged him. Old Burn felt his temper rise at the sight of Hooker, but he forced himself to remain composed. A broad view of the countryside opened before them.

To the front and right of the turnpike lay the men of General Richardson's division, which had pursued Lee's army from South Mountain since daybreak. In the fields to the left, and still partially occupying the pike itself, could be seen the regular troops of George Sykes's division from Porter's Fifth Corps. Beyond them, a series of hills climbed westward to summits crowned by the ranks of Lee's army. The enemy front, peppered with batteries and regimental flags, stretched north and south in the distance, puffs of smoke erupting from rifled guns that engaged in a fitful long-range duel with the four field pieces of Captain John C. Tidball's Second U.S. Artillery and six Parrott guns of Captain Rufus Pettit's New York Light Artillery. Still farther to the west, the spires of Sharpsburg peeked above the tree-dotted landscape.

The sun lay low on the horizon as Little Mac raised his spyglass. After surveying the hills in the distance, he lowered the glass and pointed to the right side of the panorama where a tiny, whitewashed church stood framed against a thick expanse of forest. No Rebel troops could be seen in its vicinity.

"General Hooker, you've been here the longest, do you think Lee has refused his flank there?" he asked.

Pulling down his own spyglass, Hooker nodded his agreement. "A portion of the Rebel line on the hills in front marched for that wood lot before you came up. They disappeared into it before I could see where they deployed. I assume they are still there."

McClellan plucked thoughtfully at his mustache. "What do you estimate the enemy's strength to be?"

"I'd guess about thirty thousand men. It's not the entire Rebel army, that's for certain."

"Nonetheless, they are strongly posted," said McClellan, drawing out his watch. "It is six o'clock, gentlemen. I had hoped to attack the enemy today, but the evening is too far gone."

"Sir, a Rebel gun has opened on us!" cried one of McClellan's staff, observing a puff of smoke in the distance. The deadly shell shrieked through the air over their heads.

"Find cover before they get our range!" commanded McClellan, sending the clutch of officers scrambling down the hillside.

Assembling near their mounts, Burnside looked back to see McClellan still on the summit with Fitz John Porter. Another shell flew past, exploding in a shower of dirt. Spooked horses whinnied, pulling against their orderlies. Unfazed, McClellan and Porter remained where they stood.

"What in God's name is the general still doing on that hilltop?" asked Marcy of no one in particular.

Burnside shrugged, bending to pluck a stem of grass. Gnawing on the end, he watched McClellan gesture with his hands as more enemy shells flew by. The general pointed to the west and then motioned from left to right, as if describing the lay of the land. Porter nodded, replying with an expansive wave of his own.

Burnside spat the sour tang from his mouth. Peering about for Cox, he saw the Ninth Corps' commander walking toward a cluster of trees with Colonel Key of Little Mac's staff. Curious, he thought, but not out of place, given that Key and Cox had known each other in Ohio before the war.

Trailing Burnside down the hill, Cox had felt a sudden tug on his sleeve, and found it to be Key. "Jacob, it's been a long while since last we met!" grinned the colonel. "Can you spare a minute?"

"Certainly, Judge Key," replied Cox, using Key's title from before the war. "Shall we find a place to sit?"

"An excellent idea. I see a fallen tree over there. It will make a good spot."

The two men crossed the hillside and took a seat. Key removed his cap and mopped perspiration from his brow before replacing the kepi and resting his palms upon his knees. "Well, Mister Cox … forgive me, General Cox, we've come a long way since the war's early days, have we not?"

"That we have, judge. A long way, indeed."

"Do you recall events back in Columbus when the legislature learned of the war's coming?"

Cox's brow furrowed. It was a strange subject to raise while in the field, and under fire, no less. Oh well, he thought, best to humor the man.

"Of course. How could I forget? If I recall correctly, Judge Thurman and others in the Democratic Party held that two hundred thousand of their supporters would stand in the way of any armed force sent south from Ohio. If the Democrats had things their way, there would be no war. A compromise with the slave power in the South would have been achieved and the differences that led to this unfortunate conflict set aside yet again."

Key stared down thoughtfully at his boots. "That's true, general. Your memory is sharp, but Fort Sumter changed all that, and here we are."

"Do you still hold the same opinion of the war and the gradual dissolution of slavery, Judge Key? It would put you in an awkward position, considering you are wearing the uniform of the national government."

"No, Cox, I do not. My opinion has changed with the times. General McClellan's has, too. We are both satisfied that the common tie of slavery is what binds the disloyal states together. The war must end with slavery's abolition. Support for it is clearly the soul of the rebellion."

Shaking his head in disbelief, Cox stared hard at Key, suspecting the man of some subtle deceit. "Frankly, judge, I am surprised to hear you say that. Do you really mean you no longer wish to placate the South?"

"Yes, Cox, that is what I am saying. If the abolition of slavery will help our cause, then we are behind it all the way."

"We?" Cox peered at Little Mac, still atop the hill with General Porter. "Even General McClellan, you say? I find that singularly hard to believe. The general's differences with the administration over the matter are widely known. Some officers speak freely of it, in fact, almost as if it is a point of honor with them."

"They do?" replied Key in apparent disbelief. "No, no, Cox, I assure you that General McClellan stands fully behind the administration. If President Lincoln chooses to make abolition a war aim, Mac will back him."

Cox stared hard at the colonel, letting the conversation lapse. His eyes narrowed with suspicion, but after a moment, he let it go.

"That's good to hear," he responded, "and a weight off my mind. A lack of unity among the army's commanders makes me fear for our cause."

A Rebel shell screamed past, exploding in a flash of smoke and fire among some nearby trees. Key flinched, the color draining from his cheeks. "We had better change position, Cox. I'd rather not be hit in the back by one of those confounded things."

"That's just as well, Judge. Here comes General McClellan."

Key and Cox rose to meet McClellan and Porter, striding down the grassy slope. Stopping before the collected officers, McClellan announced that he had seen enough to issue preliminary orders. "Gentlemen, I am inclined to advance against the enemy's left, as the terrain on his right is not sufficiently open for maneuver. I'll need to confirm that before coming to a final judgment, however."

"We don't know the lay of the land, either," volunteered Porter.

"Nor of the creek itself," agreed Hooker. "The Rebs appear to have concentrated their guns in the center to stop an effort to force the turnpike bridge. I ordered Major Houston of my staff to survey the creek for other crossing points to the north. He's found a bridge and several serviceable fords. My men are already moving to cover them."

"Mm-hm, that's good, General Hooker," nodded McClellan. "And to the south? Do you know what is there?"

"I don't, sir.'"

"General, our scouts report another bridge in that direction," volunteered Colonel Farnsworth, the only representative of the army's cavalry present. "I am still waiting for details concerning its placement and accessibility."

"I see," nodded McClellan. "General Burnside, your command is coming up from that direction, is it not?"

"It is, sir, but my men are heartily fatigued. They still haven't eaten today."

"That does not matter to me now," waved McClellan impatiently. "Fatigued or not, general, I want you to take your command to the left, south of the turnpike, and secure the army's flank in that direction. Your men can eat after they have arrived."

Burnside frowned but remained silent.

"Good. Then it is settled," said McClellan. "Tomorrow morning, we will see what the enemy's disposition is before making final plans to attack. Right now, I will content myself with having your command, General Hooker, on the enemy's left, and yours, General Burnside, on his right. General Sumner, your corps and that of General Mansfield's, now commanding Twelfth Corps, will occupy the center. It will take time to bring up the rest of the army, so my thoughts on this are subject to change." Little Mac drew a breath, held it for several seconds, and exhaled loudly. "It is my belief," he continued, "that if we coordinate our attacks we should be able to crush Lee and Longstreet between our flanks. General Sumner and General Porter can then follow up with a direct assault on the Rebel center. This is my initial plan, gentlemen, but I will think on it overnight and issue final orders in the morning. For the moment, that is all."

When the assembled officers broke up, Burnside moved to speak with McClellan, but Porter and Hooker were uncomfortably close. Motioning for Cox to follow him, the two men walked to the orderly holding their horses. Burnside thanked Cox as both men mounted. They spurred toward the turnpike packed with Union troops, Burnside saying nothing and Cox sensing the general had fallen into a black mood. Cox thought to speak, but reconsidered. There would be time to discuss matters. Awaiting them were hours of marching on empty bellies.

20

Tuesday, September 16, 1862
Mid-morning to noon
Center of Union Lines, Army of the Potomac
Near Keedysville, Maryland

Rumbling behind him drew George McClellan's attention over his right shoulder. Glancing back, he saw a column of twenty-pounder Parrott rifles thundering toward him down the turnpike, the riders on the lead horses lashing their eight-animal teams with leather whips. McClellan ordered his entourage off the road and pulled Dan aside to watch the battery clatter past. A lieutenant with a thick mustache trotted by, saluting the general.

"That's Sam Benjamin, Second U.S. Artillery," observed the short-bearded general atop the horse beside McClellan. "He shows real promise with his guns."

"That's all well and good, General Hunt," grumbled Little Mac to his artillery chief, "but weren't those guns supposed to be in place yesterday evening?"

Stung by the general's criticism, Hunt anxiously chewed his lip. "They were, sir, but the turnpike was too choked with troops to bring them up. We've had a devil of a time getting men and supplies onto the field. The roads in this place are entirely unsuited for the movements of an army."

"So others have also told me," grumbled McClellan, recalling Ambrose Burnside's similar complaint the previous evening.

Dismissing the bothersome memory, the general surveyed the blue-clad regulars with Israel Richardson's infantry division camped in a nearby meadow. Tendrils of smoke rose from their fires as the men boiled coffee and ate the meager rations they still possessed. Very few had received fresh food in days. Perhaps today provisions would arrive.

Shifting his attention to the west, McClellan scrutinized the grassy ridge stretching north along Antietam Creek. Three-inch ordnance rifles from Alfred Pleasonton's horse artillery still crowned the heights after taking position the previous day. Now they began to withdraw as the army's formal artillery reserve took their place. The larger guns rolled into line with drill-field precision. At least the army's long arm would be in place without further delay.

McClellan sniffed the moist air, wondering when the heavy fog that lay over the land would burn off. Warmth on his shoulders suggested the mist would not remain in place for long. Already, the sun glowed dully through the haze, promising heat in the afternoon. Once the fog cleared, he would see if Lee's army remained on the heights across Antietam Creek.

In his heart, Little Mac hoped to find the hills empty. If Lee withdrew, he could set Pleasonton's cavalry on the Rebel army's trail and declare Maryland and Pennsylvania delivered from the Secessionist menace, as he had telegraphed his wife earlier in the morning. His victory at South Mountain would be complete and with Burnside neutralized, he, George McClellan, would be a national hero. Alas, preliminary reports suggested that at least some Rebels had stayed put overnight. They might be a rearguard, but McClellan would determine that for himself once the fog dissipated.

Waving his small entourage back onto the road, Little Mac rode toward the front. Benjamin's guns rattled down the long grade ahead of them, approaching a pronounced gap in the ridge line along Antietam Creek. At a farm lane to the left, the young lieutenant directed his men up a steep hillside and onto the heights. McClellan and his staff followed at a walk, alighting on the hill's crest as Benjamin barked orders for his guns to deploy. One-by-one the crews unhitched the Parrotts above the wall of misty gray swirling along the creek.

The fog lay thick in the near distance, but on the hills above it had thinned enough for McClellan to make out some details. Grassy fields split by stone walls and rail fences rolled upward to a height crowned with Rebel guns. Removing his field glasses from their case, McClellan peered at the enemy. Some portions of Lee's artillery that he had seen yesterday remained in place, but other parts had shifted. The masses of infantry, evident the day before, also could not be found this morning. A few regimental flags hung limply in the air, but most of the Confederate commander's men appeared to have withdrawn behind the safety of the hills.

"Well, general, what do you think?" asked Henry Hunt.

McClellan pulled down the binoculars. "I don't know yet, general. This mist is hiding some of the field from observation."

"Should we send a few rounds at them to stir the hornet's nest?"

"Yes, general, I believe we should," nodded McClellan. "Let's wake up the Secesh and discover the extent of their resolve."

Hunt touched the brim of his cap and turned to Benjamin, whose crews stood at attention beside their guns, with rammers and other implements of the artillerist's trade in hand. Pointing at the Rebel line, Hunt shouted, "as you please, lieutenant, fire at will!"

Benjamin spun to his cannoneers, barking orders. "Sight that enemy battery at the left, boys, and give them spherical! Range two thousand yards. Two second fuses. Quickly now!"

The men at the caissons scrambled to retrieve the proper ammunition from the chests. Carrying the shells in leather satchels, they handed the projectiles to gunners who placed them and powder charges into the Parrotts' muzzles. Rammers pushed the shells home and stood aside while firing pins were fixed into place. Lanyards pulled tight and Benjamin raised his hand to give the command.

"FIRE!" he shouted, his arm chopping downward.

Shafts of flame and smoke stabbed out from the four guns. McClellan put his field glasses to his eyes, watching the shells explode above and beyond the Confederate line. Benjamin called for an adjustment of barrel elevation and set his men to re-loading their pieces. Rounds now erupted from the batteries on the right, blowing dirt and rocks skyward along the enemy's front. Smoke enveloped the field and McClellan smelled the tang of burning gunpowder.

Scanning the far ridge through his binoculars, he watched shots roar out from the Rebel guns. The shells plunged over Antietam Creek, landing in front of Benjamin's battery. Dirt showered through the air and Dan Webster stamped nervously. McClellan yanked the reins tight and dismounted. Handing control of the horse to an orderly, he resumed peering at the Rebels. More than a dozen guns boomed out now from the distant heights in a concave pattern that revealed the shape of Lee's defenses. McClellan remained calm, moving his glasses from left to right, while more enemy shells sailed overhead.

"Sir, hadn't we better find cover?" asked Major Colburn, one of the general's closest aides.

Little Mac shot Colburn a grin. "Why, major? Is the fire not thrilling?"

Colburn gulped; his forehead beaded with sweat. McClellan resumed his investigation of the enemy amidst the murderous barrage. A shell intended for Benjamin's guns struck the ground close by, its fuse sputtering in the furrow it had plowed up. Hunt glanced at the shell and then at Little Mac, who had lowered his binoculars. Locking eyes, the two men laughed.

"Faulty ammunition! Those boys send over a lot of duds," said Hunt.

"Thank goodness!" shouted McClellan in reply. "Alright, General Hunt, I've come to a conclusion. I don't like what I see."

"I agree, sir. Bobby Lee's still got plenty of fight."

"That he has. I had thought he might retire during the night to meet Jackson in Virginia, but now, I can only assume that Jackson is on his way here."

"All the way from Harpers Ferry, sir?"

"Yes, general. Franklin reported yesterday morning that the guns around the ferry went quiet. I assumed then that Colonel Miles had capitulated, but only knew for certain when a dispatch arrived from Franklin confirming it. Miles surrendered the garrison to Jackson around nine o'clock yesterday morning. It's shameful, Hunt! If he had only held out for another day, I could have delivered him. Instead, he gave in. Thousands of men have been lost. Men this army could have used."

"So many?" gasped Hunt. "It is disgraceful!"

"So it is," nodded McClellan, directing his gaze back to the smoking hills in the distance. Gesturing toward them with his binoculars, he hollered, "and we still have Lee to contend with here. I'd like to get at him this morning, but I fear a direct approach will be costly." Little Mac swept the binoculars from right to left. "You see the enemy's positions there? They cover this bridge and all the approaches to his line. Getting across the creek will be difficult, and if we attack those hills head on, it will be flat suicide."

"Even with our guns here, sir? Give my men some time. They'll sweep the Rebs from the hills. Just wait. You'll see."

"I appreciate your confidence, general, but there may be other options," replied McClellan, sliding his glasses back into their case. "I must scout the line to find them."

A shell exploded on the hillside, dropping McClellan into a crouch. Pushing his cap down onto his head, he braced as dirt pattered down around him. He stood and brushed the dust from his coat. "Alright, major, now it's time to retire," he chuckled at Colburn. "Let's go and see General Hooker."

Mopping sweat from his face, Colburn turned his jittery horse to the rear while McClellan climbed back into the saddle. He waved for his men to follow and trotted back down the ridge. Rebel shells whistled over the hill behind them, landing among the troops encamped there. Shouts went up and groups of men scattered from the explosions.

McClellan cantered past down the pike to a lane that intersected the road on the left. Turning Dan onto it, he continued over a hill toward a two-story brick house perched prominently atop an eminence. The horses of Hooker's staff stood along a fence rail. McClellan rode to the front gate, part of an extensive picket fence that enclosed the yard, and slid from the saddle. Commanding his orderly to take Dan with the other horses, Little Mac pushed through the gate and up the steps.

Joe Hooker emerged into the sunlight as McClellan reached the stairs to the house's front door. His boot heels thumping down the wooden steps, Hooker shook McClellan's hand. "Good morning, sir. I'm glad to see you."

"Thank you, General Hooker. I've come to discuss our operations for the day."

"Very good, sir. Walk with me to the yard over here. There is an excellent spot where we can observe the enemy's line."

Gesturing right, Hooker led McClellan up the steep lawn to a knoll beyond the fence, where they peered out over the valley of Antietam Creek.

"It sounds like Lee is here to stay," offered Hooker, folding his arms over his chest.

McClellan pulled his field glasses from their case. "Perhaps, Hooker. I've set Hunt's gunners to pummel his line. Lee has taken up a devilishly strong position. It is impervious to frontal assault, so I am seeking a way around his flanks. What have you been able to learn from here?"

"Not much more than we already knew, sir. The enemy's left appears to be near that large patch of trees on the far plateau, but most of his line is hidden from sight."

McClellan squinted through his binoculars at the distant woods. "Do you have a spyglass, Hooker? These field glasses will not let me see that far."

"Certainly, general. Just a moment." Turning back to the house, Hooker called for an orderly to bring his spyglass. A man ran up from the back door with a brass telescope in his hands.

"Thank you, corporal," nodded McClellan, raising the glass to his eye. Pushing it in the direction he wished to see, Little Mac spied Grayback troops near the distant wood lot. "I see them now," he muttered. "They are right where you said they would be, but only a few regiments are visible. Lee must have more men concealed behind those trees."

Sighing heavily, McClellan lowered the glass. Hooker eyed the general while waiting for him to speak. Little Mac tugged at the end of his mustache; his lips clamped tightly together. At last, he spoke. "My present inclination, general, is to have your corps cross the creek north of here and move against the Rebel left near that white building by the forest. Do you believe your men can carry the enemy's position there?"

"Of course, sir," nodded Hooker confidently. He paused briefly before resuming, "although without better knowledge of the enemy's number, I cannot say for certain. Gibbon's brigade suffered in the fight on South Mountain, but he can go on. The rest of my boys are in high spirits and can be ready to move in short order."

"That's good," replied McClellan, his fingers tapping thoughtfully on his thigh.

"Would we have support for an attack, sir? I blanch at the thought of my corps crossing the creek against the whole Rebel army alone."

The general shook his head. "I am not sure yet, General Hooker. There is only one way to find out where the enemy's flank rests, and that is to send your command against it. The ground in the center is unsuitable for an attack without causing excessive casualties."

McClellan gnawed the inside of his lip until finally his breath hissed out between his lips. "For the time being, general, hold your position here," he said. "I've ordered Sumner to call up the Twelfth Corps, which is now under the command of General Mansfield, but I haven't decided where to send him."

"You mean to support an attack here, on the Rebel left, or to engage the enemy's right?"

"The choice is not clear to me. Scouts reported this morning that Lee's troops are covering the bridge south of here, but I haven't gone there to examine the ground. Then there is General Burnside to consider. That is his part of the line."

Hooker's eyes narrowed. "You lack confidence in him, sir?"

"Not exactly, but since our last discussion of this subject with General Porter in Middletown, I have determined to direct Burnside's movements myself. I will push him where he needs to go."

"A wise decision, sir."

"Thank you, General Hooker. Directing Burnside requires, however, that I see his sector of the front with my own eyes, and that takes time. I can't leave anything to chance. I want to get at Lee, but there's no telling how many men are hidden behind these heights, or even where his line ends. Hence my hesitation."

"I understand, sir. It's a tough nut to crack."

"It is indeed. In any event, general, hold your place while I ride to the left and see what is happening there. Once I have a better understanding of the situation, I will give you your final orders."

"As you wish, sir. My corps will be ready."

McClellan placed the field glasses into their case and strode back to his horse. He commanded his aides to mount and steered Dan back to the main road before continuing southwest toward the creek. The command group attracted the attention of Rebel batteries and puffs of smoke blew out from their barrels, sending shells screaming at them from across the valley. Little Mac remained calm and arrived a short time later at the first encampment of Ninth Corps troops closest to the creek. Alternating between nods and salutes to those shouting their greetings, he continued over the rolling countryside past the end of Burnside's line until he had reached a high knoll overlooking a sharp westward bend in the Antietam. There he stopped and turned Dan to survey the countryside.

The hills on his left rolled off toward the Potomac River. To the front, beyond the creek's sluggishly churning water, rose a steep bluff crowned with trees and Rebel battle flags. The enemy's position loomed ominously over both the creek and the triple-arched field stone bridge below them that crossed it.

"That's a damned strong position," muttered General Hunt. "I don't envy attacking it."

"Yes, it is, general," replied McClellan, scowling at Hunt's use of profanity. "What concerns me is this road behind us. It leads to Harpers Ferry and General Burnside has not covered it. If Jackson comes up this road with his command, he will take us in the flank before we know what hit us. The hills themselves would hide his advance."

"Do you think he will approach on this side of the Potomac, sir? The countryside is quite broken that way."

McClellan shook his head. "I don't know, Hunt. With Jackson, I cannot take any chances. The man is as dangerous as a rattlesnake. These hills to our front screen the rebel army's movements. We may not see him coming. Burnside must know this. Come along, gentlemen, I need to find him."

Spurring Dan back in the direction he had come, McClellan cantered behind a hill to evade Rebel sharpshooters and back through the ranks of the Ninth Corps. Then he climbed another hillside and stopped on the crest.

"Captain Duane, come here, if you please," he called out to a heavily bearded man on his staff.

Duane steered his horse forward. "Yes, sir. How may I help?"

"Captain, take a note. Look back at the hillside to our rear."

"Just a moment, general, allow me to take out my book."

"As you wish, captain, but be quick about it," snapped McClellan.

"Yes, sir, I just need a pencil … ah, here it is. I'm ready."

Duane looked up to find McClellan swatting at a fly that had landed on his cheek. "Be gone, blast you!" bawled the general, as the buzzing insect circled his head. Landing on the general's cap, the fly rubbed a hairy arm over its greenish eye. Duane smirked, but quickly lowered his gaze when he noticed McClellan glaring at him.

"Is something amusing, captain?"

The smirk evaporated from Duane's face. "Ahem! No, sir, not at all. Please, continue."

Staring hard at the man, McClellan pointed back at the ridge they had traversed. "That tall hilltop, captain. Make a note that Burnside is to invest it with artillery; at least two batteries, if not more. It commands the entire creek. If the enemy attacks this flank, our guns on that eminence could repel him. Write as well that I want Rodman's division down here, covering the road to Harpers Ferry and supporting the guns. Oh, and have that young Lieutenant Benjamin we saw earlier bring his battery down here to this side of the line. Do you have all of that?"

Duane peered off at the hill while scribbling in his book. A rough sketch emerged of the landscape with notes written atop the features. "I do, sir. Please go on."

"Very well. To our rear, I want Orlando Willcox's division brought up and placed behind this hill. He will support the center of the line. Burnside is to throw Scammon's division ahead of it and closest to the creek, to the right of that orchard, do you understand?"

Duane glanced up from his writing to make notes of McClellan's gestures. "Yes, sir, I see the orchard. Scammon's division to the right of it. Understood."

"Good. Burnside's final division, that of General Sturgis, is to take position behind the hills to our right. His right flank will rest on the left of General Sykes's. The general alignment of Sturgis's line should be to the south-southwest."

"Sturgis south-southwest . . . I have it, sir," nodded Duane.

"Sir, General Burnside is approaching," called out Henry Hunt.

McClellan watched Burnside come up the hillside on his dappled gray. The Rhode Islander reined in, throwing a salute.

"Hello, General Burnside, I was just coming to find you," said Little Mac.

"Good morning, sir. I caught word that you were on my part of the line and thought I should come to meet you. Is something here amiss?"

"It is, Burn," nodded McClellan, attempting to rekindle a modicum of warmth. "Your corps is too far from the Rebel right. Lee has moved troops to this bridge, but your men are a mile behind our line. I want you to move your corps from its present camp near Porterstown and place it closer to the bridge. We need to cover the road from Harpers Ferry in case the enemy appears in force from that direction."

"As you wish, general," replied Burnside. "My corps is where it camped last night. The men did not come up until well after nightfall. I've also had no orders from you until this moment. Now that we have spoken, I'll have Cox come up and direct the deployment."

McClellan shook his head at this. "No, Burn, that won't be necessary. I have chosen the locations for your corps myself."

"Oh?" Burnside's eyebrows arched in surprise.

"Yes. I had Captain Duane here make note of where I wish your divisions to be placed. He and members of my engineering staff, whom I'll send forthwith, will guide your division commanders to their desired positions."

Burnside's countenance darkened. In the space of two days, he had been demoted from commander of the army's right-wing, to having his own troops deployed without consideration for his thoughts. The air grew tense between the two men, and for a moment, the reddening Burnside looked as if he would explode. Lowering the brim of his hat to hide his face, Burnside swallowed his ire.

"Very well, general," he choked. "Would you care to enlighten me as to your plans? You do intend to attack the Rebels, don't you?"

"What? Of course, I intend to attack!" sputtered McClellan. "Lee has offered battle, and I am going to give it to him."

"That's good to hear, sir. What would you have me do?"

McClellan eyed Burnside closely. The man smoldered with impertinence, and Little Mac thought to give him a proper dressing down. Burnside stared hard in return, his gaze alight with anger.

"General Burnside, my design is to make the main attack upon the enemy's left, or at least to have that attack create a diversion in favor of a main attack, potentially on Lee's center. If something more can be gained by assailing the enemy's right on your flank, then I will order it. If either General Hooker or you are successful in your flanking movements, I will order an attack on Lee's center with whatever reserve I have on hand."

"Hooker, eh? So, the dissolution of my wing is still in effect?"

"It is, general. My orders are still in place."

"How could I forget, sir? You've made that perfectly clear."

"Humph!" snorted McClellan. "I thought so. You have your orders, General Burnside. Wait here for my staff to deploy your corps, and do not move it until commanded. It is—just a moment." McClellan fumbled for his watch. "It is just noon now. I'll send them back to you as soon as I am able."

"I understand, sir," nodded the Rhode Islander.

McClellan spurred Dan into a trot downhill. Burnside watched him go, shaking his head. He had tossed on his pallet for hours the night before, wondering what had turned McClellan against him. For the life of him, though, Burnside could not reckon what it was. The faces of Porter and Hooker loomed large in his mind. Now Hooker was to lead the army's primary attack after McClellan had removed him from Burnside's command? The situation reeked of intrigue, and Burnside suspected it had all played out at his expense.

"Hooker, you damned snake!" he growled. Leaning over the side of his horse, he spat the bitter taste from his mouth, and wiped his lips on his sleeve. Someday, Joe Hooker would pay for his perfidy and when that day came, he, Ambrose Burnside, would drink a hearty toast to his destruction.

21

Tuesday, September 16, 1862
Noon to mid-afternoon
Field Headquarters, Army of the Potomac
Keedysville, Maryland

fuming after his exchange with Burnside, George McClellan trotted back the way he had come. Rebel shells flying over the hills to his left exploded in plumes of smoke and fire among the meadows and wood lots, crushing trees, splitting branches, and throwing jagged bits of stone skyward. McClellan warily directed Dan along the backside of the ridge, riding among the men of George Sykes's division, sheltering from the cannon fire. Stopping occasionally to chat and take measure of their spirits, McClellan eventually made his way to the camp of General Sykes.

A dispatch in his hand, Sykes tugged thoughtfully on his short ginger beard, the outer ends of which hung longer than the center. Then he noticed McClellan approaching and rose from the folding chair on which he sat. Behind Sykes stood a canvas tent and several other stools occupied by the members of his small staff. Touching the brim of his cap, Sykes stepped up to greet the general. Little Mac leaned down to grasp Sykes's hand, but remained mounted, pleading a need to depart quickly.

"Sykes, how are your men doing?" he asked.

"Well enough, I reckon," replied the brigadier. "None of us likes lying idle under fire, but at least we have the ridge here to protect us. May I ask what your plans are for the day, sir? Should I ready my men for an attack?"

McClellan shook his head. "No, Sykes, not yet. I am going to throw Hooker's corps over the creek and develop the Rebel army's flank. Only after Hooker has made contact, will I consider ordering your division forward."

His bottom lip poking out as he thought, the brigadier offered a nod. "It's a sound plan, general. My boys will be ready when you need us."

"Thank you, Sykes. I'll be sure to call upon them." Little Mac peered around at Sykes's troops and then leaned forward in his saddle. "Tell me, general, do you still hold a regiment west of the bridge?"

"I do, sir, the Fourth U.S. Infantry. Captain Dreyer commanding."

"Good, good. Regulars are just what I need at the moment. If we are going to attack Lee's center, we must be able to get over the creek, so do what you can to retain that foothold on the western side. Don't let your men go too far, mind you, just secure a perimeter."

"As you wish, general. Dreyer has reported taking Rebel picket fire all morning. Sharpshooters have pinned his men close to the creek."

McClellan straightened in his saddle. "They'll withdraw if Lee retreats. Don't fret over them. Now, listen closely, I have another task for you that Captain Duane will explain. Captain, please come forward."

Waving to the prodigiously bearded engineer, Duane walked his horse to McClellan's side. "Good morning, General Sykes. Reconnaissance by some of my men has uncovered a dam by the mill on the other side of this ridge. As the commanding general wishes to make an assault over the creek to the north, we believe it would be best if you could have your men dismantle the dam, lowering the water level."

"That makes sense," nodded Sykes.

"Break it up, Sykes!" exclaimed McClellan, glancing skyward as a shell shrieked past. "And let it be done by this afternoon at the latest. The day is passing, and Hooker must get into position."

"I understand, sir. I'll get men on it right away."

"Excellent, general. I know I can count on you. Now, I'll be off. Keep me informed of things here. My headquarters is two miles or so behind us on the road to Keedysville."

"Very good, sir. Godspeed to you, general," saluted Sykes.

Cinching his reins, McClellan spurred Dan to the pike. Entering the road behind the ridge, he took off at a trot, with the thunder of his army's artillery roaring behind him. He crossed over a hill and passed the lane that led north to Hooker's headquarters before cantering into a sloping field where Pleasonton's cavalry had bivouacked. The division's horse artillery stood parked in a long row north of the roadside, close to the horses tethered to a line of staked rope. The division's mounts cropped at the tall grass beneath their feet, nickering every so often as a shell thrown by Lee's artillery exploded nearby. When the threat had passed, they simmered down to resume pulling at the vegetation beneath their feet.

Yanking Dan to a stop before Pleasonton's tents, McClellan swung down from the saddle and handed his reins to an orderly. Pleasonton, his dark-brimmed hat perched cockily atop his head, rose from the camp chair on which he had been seated. A smoking cigar stub in one hand, he walked to meet the commanding general. Other officers gathered around the men, hoping Little Mac's sudden appearance would bring news of some action. Boredom festered in the men's hearts after the events of the previous two days. It seemed no battles remained to be fought by horse soldiers once the armies had ceased moving.

George Custer counted himself among these listless observers. Rising, he tossed away the grass stem he had been chewing and walked to Pleasonton's side.

"Sir, it's good to see you," grinned Pleasonton, taking McClellan's hand.

"Likewise, General Pleasonton. Your men look well, but idle, I see."

Pleasonton glanced back at them. "Yes, sir, we're at a loss for what to do. There isn't much work for cavalry today."

"I hope to remedy that soon," replied McClellan. "General Hooker's corps will be sent across the Antietam to strike the enemy's flank."

Pleasonton's face lit up at the prospect of renewed activity. "Ah, very good! Sam Owens's regiment of mounted Pennsylvania boys is with Hooker already. What about the rest of us horse soldiers? Can we count on seeing action?"

"I am hopeful you can, general. I'll send orders to Hooker shortly, but we must wait and see how things develop. If the enemy takes flight, I'll call on you to pursue him."

"Of course, sir! We'll be ready."

Nodding confidently, McClellan turned to leave, but then he paused. "Captain Custer, is that you I see?"

"It is, sir. Good afternoon," replied Custer, stepping forward.

McClellan scrutinized Custer closely, his brows knitting together. "Captain, there is something different about you. So much so that I almost did not recognize you."

His cheeks flushing pink, Custer cleared his throat. "Yes, sir. I … ah, have cut my hair."

The surrounding troopers snickered. Custer shot them an irate glance.

"Yes, that's it. I see it now," laughed McClellan.

Pleasonton clapped a hand on Custer's shoulder. "Sir, I take it you've heard of Captain Custer's courageous exploit in Boonsborough?"

McClellan glanced from Pleasonton to Custer. "I did hear something, I think. You were involved in the fight there yesterday morning, were you not?"

Custer opened his lips to speak, but Pleasonton checked him. "He was indeed! Old Custer here tried to take on the whole Rebel cavalry himself. For his gallantry, he caught a haircut out of the deal."

Custer frowned with embarrassment. "The general here is telling wild stories, sir. I did what the moment required."

McClellan shook his head. "Humility, captain? That is unlike you. If General Pleasonton says you performed gallantly, he means it. Bully for you! Although I admit I'm glad to see your locks trimmed to an acceptable length. But now, gentlemen, I must return to headquarters. Major Colburn here informs me that General Marcy has moved to a field by Keedysville. Our tents have not arrived, but you can find me there if I am needed."

"Very good, sir," chirped Pleasonton. "We'll be ready and waiting for your orders."

McClellan turned to leave when suddenly Custer piped up. "Sir, wait! May I cross the creek with General Hooker?"

Little Mac thought for a moment. "I don't see why not," he said at last. "It's a good idea for you to go. I'll need you to keep me informed about what is happening with him."

Custer's face glowed at the prospect of seeing action. "Thank you, sir!" he bubbled.

"Think nothing of it, Custer. You've earned my confidence on more than one occasion. In fact, it just occurred to me that you should be the man to deliver Hooker my orders."

"As you wish, sir. I can go immediately. What would you have me say?"

McClellan moved in close to Custer and lowered his voice. "I'll tell you, captain. Say to General Hooker that I want him to cross the river with his corps and attack the enemy's left flank."

"Excuse me, sir, the river? Do you mean Antietam Creek or the Potomac?"

McClellan's brow furrowed. "Did I say the river?"

"You did, general. I just want to be certain I understand."

"Of course. Thank you for alerting me to the error. Yes, I mean the creek … Antietam Creek. Hooker is to cross the creek, locate the Rebel army's left flank, and attack. Tell him I said he should use the bridge that lies down this road behind us." Little Mac pointed to a narrow track some distance away that branched off from the main turnpike. "Is that clear enough?"

"Perfectly, sir."

"Alright, then, captain, get moving! The day is wasting."

Custer went to gather up his saddlebags as McClellan returned to Dan Webster. Climbing into the saddle, he wheeled the horse back toward the road, noting as he did an uncomfortable rumbling in his gut. He fell silent as he rode, and a light sweat broke out on his forehead. General Hunt, trotting along beside Little Mac, noticed the general's discomfort and asked if he was in distress. McClellan, however, waved him off. *My old disease again. Of all times, why now?* The previous June, malaria had nearly crippled him on the James River peninsula outside of Richmond. To suffer a renewed bout of it on the precipice of a tremendous battle would be disastrous.

He swallowed hard, intent on remaining in control as the tension growing inside him increased. Sending Hooker alone across the Antietam posed a significant risk. If Lee elected to fight, it would open the largest clash of the war and thousands of lives would be lost. Disturbing memories of the wounded boys he had visited the day before loomed fresh in McClellan's mind, souring his mood as surely as the illness had soured his bowels.

"Hunt, I must win this fight," he blurted out, sounding unsure of himself.

Hunt shot the general a puzzled glance. "Of course, sir," he replied, leaving it at that.

Cantering into a field of wheat some distance down the road, Little Mac saw Randolph Marcy coming to greet him. The army's chief of staff walked out from behind a table surrounded by several high-backed chairs that he had procured from the locals. Neither tents, nor wagons, nor any of the other accoutrements of army headquarters could be found.

Sliding down from the saddle, McClellan shook his chief of staff's hand. "Well, Marcy," he said, "I see you've found a suitable location for headquarters. Where are our wagons?"

"Good afternoon, general. They are still on the road. Last I heard, they had just cleared Boonsborough, but their progress is slow."

Frowning, McClellan pulled off his gloves. "Allow me to venture a guess regarding their tardiness. The roads have been too full for them to come up?"

"Precisely, sir," nodded the older man. "General Mansfield's corps has blocked the way of late. There is only one road here from the east, and that is via Boonsborough. There is another road that comes in from Nicodemus Mill over the hills here, but General Burnside's corps has been strung out along it for more than a day."

Marcy noticed a tic in the general's cheek at the mention of Burnside's name. It passed quickly, though, as the two men walked to the table.

"There is a telegram here for you from Washington," said Marcy, drawing the folded paper from under a fieldstone weight.

McClellan took the note. "This is undoubtedly from that fool, Halleck." Unfolding it, he read the contents, a sneer of disgust on his face. "And so it is, Marcy. Think of it! The idea of Halleck giving me lessons in the art of war!"

McClellan crumpled the paper in his fist and tossed it to the ground.

"What did it say, general?" probed Marcy cautiously.

"It says that I should be wary of the Rebel army crossing back over the river, turning my left, and menacing the capital city. Lee will do nothing of the sort. His army is here to stay, unless I am able to push him back across the river." Raising his hand, McClellan pointed to the west. "Do you hear those guns, Marcy? That is Lee standing his ground!"

"I understand, sir. What is the plan for dislodging him?"

McClellan circled the table holding his map. Peering down at the twisting black line depicting Antietam Creek, he tapped firmly upon it. "The plan, Marcy, is to strike Lee's left flank while holding his right in place along the creek; which reminds me, I must send Captain Duane back to Burnside. Captain Duane, come here, if you please!"

Duane corked his canteen and strode forward.

"Captain, gather two assistants to help you with the placement of General Burnside's divisions," commanded McClellan. "Get on your horse and go now. We need to get him underway."

Duane hurried off, leaving the general staring down at his map until beating hooves drew his attention. Looking up, he watched Joseph Hooker ride into the encampment with an aide. Hooker stopped near McClellan's table and dismounted.

"Why, General Hooker, I am surprised to see you here," said Little Mac. "Did Captain Custer not communicate my orders?"

"He did, sir. My divisions are already on the move with General Meade in the fore."

"That's good to hear, general, then why have you come?"

A frown formed on Hooker's face. "Sir, I am here to see if you have any further orders to give me. All I learned from Captain Custer is that I am to move my command across the creek, find the enemy's left, and attack."

"Yes, General Hooker, that's correct. Has something happened to prevent you from doing it?"

"Well, no, sir, but I'm a bit confused. Is there anything more that I should know about this movement? I must repeat my concern about confronting the entire Rebel army with my corps alone."

A new spate of rumbling shuddered through McClellan's gut. "You need not be worried, General Hooker," he said in a strained voice. "You are at liberty to call for reinforcements if you need them."

Hooker's expression relaxed visibly. "Thank you, sir. That's a relief. May I assume command of those reinforcements, if I should need them?"

"Yes, of course, General Hooker. Any reinforcements called for will be under your command. Does that satisfy you?"

"It does, general, very much. I'll return to my corps now and see to its advance."

"Very good, Hooker. Godspeed to you," nodded McClellan.

Hooker tossed a salute and strode back to his horse. Little Mac watched him go, his hand still pressed against the mounting urge in his belly. "Marcy, have you arranged for a sink?" he asked.

"I haven't gotten around to it," replied the older man, "but there are sufficient trees around to hide you. I have an old newspaper you can use. Should I fetch it?"

"Yes, Marcy, do that," groaned Little Mac, the color draining from his face. "And quickly!"

Marcy ran to his horse to dig the paper from his saddlebag. Returning to McClellan, he handed it over and called for an orderly to stand watch over the copse of trees into which the general disappeared. After a space of time McClellan emerged from the bushes, his face gray and wet with perspiration. Dropping the newspaper onto the table, he leaned down, knuckles first, onto the map.

"Hooker must find Lee's flank," he muttered.

"Sir?" asked Marcy.

"I said Hooker must find Lee's flank here, north of Sharpsburg." Little Mac tapped the map between Antietam Creek and a large u-shaped bend in the Potomac River. "When he does, I am hopeful that Lee will see he has been flanked and withdraw back across the river without further bloodshed. In the event that he does, I'll send Pleasonton's cavalry after him."

"Sounds sensible if Lee retreats, general, but what if he decides to stand and fight?"

McClellan looked up from the map, his eyes dark with apprehension. "Then there will be the devil to pay, Marcy. The very devil himself."

22

Tuesday, September 16, 1862
Mid-afternoon to nightfall
Ninth Corps, Left flank of the Union Line
Near Sharpsburg, Maryland

Cox eyed Burnside carefully. Loitering in tall grass atop an eminence that sloped in a long, graceful curve down to Antietam Creek, the general surveyed a column of troops through his field glasses. A regiment below them marched into place under the watchful gaze of three men on horseback—the unit's commander, a member of Burnside's staff, and the guiding engineer sent by General McClellan to position the Ninth Corps' men. Meanwhile, for the first time that afternoon, the pounding guns in the distance fell silent, portending exactly what, no man could say.

Sighing heavily, Burnside pulled down his field glasses. "Cox, this is madness. General McClellan is the army's commander and of course, he has the authority to order my men where he wants them to go, but to place them himself, without asking my opinion, or transmitting the orders directly through me, instead of subordinate officers, smacks of an affront."

"My sympathies, sir, I don't like to see you troubled," replied Cox. "Why don't you take personal command of the Ninth Corps? I'll gladly return to the command of my division alone."

Burnside shook his head vigorously. "No, General Cox, I will not do that. I appreciate the wisdom in your suggestion, and know that our arrangement is inconvenient for you, but President Lincoln himself requested I assume command of the army's right-wing. General McClellan has suspended my responsibilities, but he assures me it is temporary. The right-wing is made up of two army corps, not one. If I take direct command of the Ninth Corps, it would acknowledge an alteration of the president's direct wishes and I will not do it! I will not accede to the lessening of my authority just because that conniving snake, Hooker, wants an independent command."

Burnside grew red in the face as he spoke, the hand holding his binoculars shaking visibly. Cox fell silent, uncertain how to respond. Returning his gaze to the troops ahead, he watched as a blue-clad brigade formed up beside an orchard on low ground at the base of the hill. Casting his gaze to the right, Cox saw the brigades of Sam Sturgis's division moving into position across a rolling field. To their left, behind Cox's back, he knew that Hugh Ewing's brigade, yet another part of the Kanawha Division, was filing slowly into position as well. A battery of guns clattered across a hillside near Ewing's men. Rolling onto a commanding plateau, it unlimbered beside the others already collected there. Beyond them could be seen parts of the line occupied by Isaac Rodman's division guarding the Harpers Ferry Road, as General McClellan had ordered. Musket fire from Rebel sharpshooters popped on the heights beyond Antietam Creek.

"Well, general, at least we have young Benjamin's guns with us again," Cox ventured. "I know he is a favorite of yours."

Burnside peered at the guns. "Yes, indeed. Lieutenant Benjamin is a fine artillerist. It is reassuring to have him on our part of the field. Now, about your staff, general; you can make use of mine since yours is suited for divisional and not corps command. I have no direct command, and with Hooker due to move across the creek on the extreme right, he is beyond my control."

"Hooker's corps is moving across the creek? I had no idea."

"Yes, general, it is," snorted Burnside. "All of Hooker's scheming for an independent command has paid off. General McClellan has seen fit to let him advance on our extreme right and strike Lee's left flank."

Confusion furrowed Cox's brow. "His corps alone, sir? But the Rebels will eat him up!"

A grim smirk appeared on Burnside's face. "Yes, Cox, they will consume him, and he well deserves it. I fear for his men, though. Meade, Hatch, and Gibbon are good officers. They and their men deserve a better commander than Joe Hooker." His expression souring, Burnside spat into the grass.

Again, Cox fell silent. The nastiness of the Army of the Potomac's politics had not ceased to amaze him since he came east. Intrigue infested the upper echelons of the officer corps, often manifesting itself as personal animosity, such as that between Hooker and Burnside, or even as a malicious disdain for the national government. Rumors whispered among the officer corps suggested turning the army on Washington. Cox could only shake his head at this, unable to wrap his mind around the thought of such a treasonous act. What man wearing the indigo uniform of the government could conceive of such a thing?

Judge Key.

The colonel's face hovered in Cox's mind. What was it Key had said; that he and McClellan now believed in slavery's abolition as a war aim? If true, Key's change of heart represented one of the most unusual about-faces Cox had ever witnessed. Key had always ardently supported the pre-war state of things and Cox had heard McClellan express the same. What could have changed in the last few days to alter their opinions? The victory at South Mountain? Some other event of which he knew nothing? Cox let go of the thought. Only the Almighty could know the sentiment hidden in the hearts of men.

"General Burnside, a rider is approaching!" announced General Parke, Burnside's chief of staff.

Turning in the saddle to watch the man approach, Burnside slid his binoculars back into their case.

"General Burnside, sir, I'm sent by General McClellan," said the aide. "The commanding general desires that you stop the deployment of your men at once."

"Stop the deployment? What in God's name are you talking about?" puzzled Burnside. "Did the commanding general say what he has in mind?"

"No, sir. I was told only to come here and have you halt the re-positioning of your troops pending further consideration."

"Pending further— Look around you, captain!" exploded the Rhode Islander. "My men are on the move in every direction of the compass. No movements are pending. They are underway!"

The captain gulped hard, his Adam's apple rising and falling rapidly in his throat. "I—I am sorry, sir. I merely used the language spoken to me. I can see your men are in motion."

"But you have no further orders to communicate? No details from the general informing me of his thoughts?"

"No, sir. I have none."

Frowning, Burnside tilted backward in his saddle, the leather creaking underneath him. Then he took out his watch. "It is presently four o'clock, General Cox. Do you see what I am required to deal with?"

Cox nodded silently, preferring to remain silent in front of McClellan's aide. The last thing he needed was a rumor of insubordination flying about.

Burnside, however, vented his ire freely. "Damnation! This is highly irregular. How am I to get my command into position for an attack under these circumstances? I'll need to speak to the commanding general myself, since we can make no further moves here. General Cox, see that the elements of your command stay where they are until I clear this up. I'm riding to headquarters."

"As you wish, sir," nodded Cox. "I'll give the orders and wait for your return."

"Alright, captain, lead me to the commanding general," demanded Burnside. "I don't know where the army's headquarters have been set up."

Saluting, the man wheeled his horse about and kicked it into a trot. Burnside cast a final furious glance at Cox and spurred Major in pursuit. Traveling to and from headquarters would take precious time, and Burnside fretted over it. The sun had already begun its downward journey to the western horizon and the Ninth Corps was in disarray. God forbid an order came for them to attack because in the corps' present state, any assault it might make would take hours to get going. Burnside rode off, his thoughts as dark and confused as the long, difficult night to come.

* * *

Walking Major into the headquarters encampment near Keedysville, Burnside pulled to a stop and dismounted. The captain peeled off toward a small group of officers sipping coffee around a campfire. Randolph Marcy looked up at Burnside from the table filled with papers that covered General McClellan's map. Peering around the encampment, Burnside saw it consisted of little more than a table and a few chairs. He did not see McClellan. Tugging off his gauntlets, he strode up to Marcy.

"Good evening, General Burnside. What brings you to headquarters?" asked the chief of staff.

"Good evening, General Marcy. I've come to speak with the commanding general. Is he about?"

"I'm afraid the general is not here. He's gone to see how General Hooker's movement across the Antietam is progressing."

Burnside slapped his gauntlets against his thigh in frustration. "Well, that is extremely unfortunate. I received an order not long ago telling me to suspend the movement of my corps pending further consideration from General McClellan. Now I find him gone, without any idea how he wishes me to place my men."

"I see, general, that is indeed unfortunate," nodded Marcy. "The general left here thirty minutes ago. There's no telling when he'll be back."

Burnside paced in a circle. "Marcy, you've been here all day. Can you tell me what McClellan is thinking regarding my command? Have you overheard him commenting on it in any way that might give me some direction? The light is fading, and it will be nearly nightfall by the time I return to my men. Do you realize how difficult it is to place troops in the dark, and in the rain?"

Marcy looked up at the iron gray sky, suspecting it could begin pouring at any moment.

Marcy shook his head. "I'm afraid General McClellan has told me nothing of his plans. If he believes changes should be made to your line, I am not aware of them. In fact, I was not even aware a courier had been sent to you."

"That's curious, General Marcy, don't you think? You are, after all, this army's chief of staff."

"It is unusual, general, but not unheard of. General McClellan does not tell me everything that goes on around here."

"I knew of the courier," said a voice to Burnside's left. Spinning toward it, Burnside saw Colonel Key, his pince-nez glasses propped tightly on his nose. "General McClellan told me he was sending a man to see you."

"I'm glad to hear that someone knows," snorted Burnside. "Do you know what his plans are for my command, Colonel Key?"

A cryptic smile formed on Key's lips. "I don't," he responded with a shake of his head. "All I know is that the commanding general wished to halt your movements for the time being."

"This makes no sense," muttered Burnside, glaring at Marcy. "The day is nearly gone."

"I am sorry, general. There's nothing we can do but wait for General McClellan to return," replied the chief of staff.

Slapping his thigh again, Burnside began pulling on his gloves. "Very well, gentlemen, I'll return to my command and wait. When McClellan returns, please tell him of my visit and my need for orders as soon as possible."

"I'll be sure to, general," offered Marcy with a shallow bow.

Burnside returned to his horse, leaving Key and Marcy behind. Shooting a final glance as he took his reins, Burnside shook his head and spurred Major out of the encampment. Thirty minutes later, he appeared under the shelter of an oak tree where Jacob Cox awaited him. Twilight had closed in, and a torch flickered weakly, its flame sputtering in a light shower of rain. For more than an hour, the clamor of heavy cannon and musket fire had been banging in the north, but it began drifting away as Burnside arrived.

Dismounting, Burnside handed his reins to an aide. "Well, Cox, General McClellan is nowhere to be found," he said, removing his gloves. "I looked for him at headquarters, and elsewhere on our line, but he has gone to the right to check on Hooker. He is directing Hooker personally, it seems."

Cox shook his head. "So, we have no orders, general? The men have been standing in formation for hours. Where are they supposed to go?"

"I don't know, Cox. The situation is maddening. We must get these men into position if we are going to attack tomorrow."

"Are we going to attack, sir? We've received no orders to that effect." Cox held out his hands plaintively before him.

"I don't know that either," grumbled Burnside. "General McClellan told me earlier today that we might be required to take the bridge here and carry the enemy's works on the heights behind it, but I've heard nothing from him since."

Lowering his voice to a whisper, Cox walked in close. "Sir, with all due respect for General McClellan, this is no way to command an army. Even I can see that, and I'm new to military affairs."

"I know, Cox, I know, and I agree with you," sighed Burnside wearily. "Now night has fallen, and we still don't know what to do."

"We need to decide, general. The men cannot remain where they are."

Burnside stood silently for a moment. Then he looked up, his tired eyes glistening in the torchlight. "Alright, general, I am going to make this decision on my authority. As we have no new orders, we will continue with the placement of your command based on General McClellan's earlier orders. Send word to the engineers from McClellan's staff that they are to resume the deployment immediately."

"Very good, sir," saluted Cox, who spun and barked out instructions to his staff.

Stepping further under the oak, Burnside turned and folded his hands behind him to watch Cox go about his business. His stomach growled emptily at that moment, and he realized he had eaten practically nothing that day. Filling it must be his next priority, but the commissary trains had still not arrived, so they did not even have coffee to sustain them. Misery clouded Burnside's brow as he pondered their predicament. The enemy lay less than a mile away, his line bristling with guns. Yet, here sat McClellan's army, its line still in disarray after a day of confusing counter-marching.

The brief roar of combat to the north confirmed Lee's intention to fight. Burnside hoped earnestly for the sake of his friends in the First Corps that Hooker would prove more competent than he had at South Mountain. He also hoped that George McClellan would show himself up to the task of confronting Lee. Doubts about Little Mac had never entered his thoughts before, and Burnside struggled to dismiss them. However, now they nagged like a bad habit, drawing his attention back to the general's oddly sloppy approach that day.

"May God help us in this fight," he whispered.

===============

23

Tuesday, September 16, 1862
Mid-afternoon to after sundown
First Corps, Right Flank of the Union Line
Near Keedysville, Maryland

Orderlies rushed about Custer as he waited for Joe Hooker to return from army headquarters. Upon conveying General McClellan's orders to old Fighting Joe, Custer had watched Hooker's lips twist into a scowl.

"Captain, allow me to understand this correctly," he asked. "I am to take my corps across the Antietam, find, and strike the enemy's flank? Is that really all the general said?"

"It is, sir," nodded Custer. "General McClellan gave no additional instructions."

Staring down thoughtfully, Hooker paced the ground, one hand rubbing his forehead, the other pressed against the small of his back. Suddenly, he looked up. "That doesn't seem at all prudent. My corps will be isolated on the far side of the creek against the entire Rebel army. We will have no support."

"Sir, perhaps the commanding general wishes you to make a reconnaissance in force," volunteered an officer on Hooker's staff sporting a prodigious mustache.

"You may be right, Major Dickinson," replied Hooker, turning to face the First Corps' Assistant Adjutant General, "but I must make certain of it. Captain Custer, I am going to General McClellan's headquarters to ask if he has anything more to tell me."

"As you wish, sir," sighed the frustrated Custer. McClellan had given orders, and they should be followed, he thought, not questioned, or reflected upon. The time had come to attack and Custer's heart beat faster just thinking about it. No more dallying! Boredom be damned! His mind churned with anticipation, but he got hold of himself, held his tongue, and quietly thumbed the hilt of his saber while Hooker returned his attention to Dickinson.

"Major, send word to my divisional commanders to get their troops underway. Inform Meade and Ricketts that they are to use the upper bridge across the Antietam. Doubleday is to use the ford below this house. It is after two o'clock now, so we have precious little of the day remaining to us. Tell them to hop to it! I'll be back as quickly as possible to supervise their movements."

"I'll see to it immediately," confirmed Dickinson.

Looking back at Custer, Hooker told him to wait where he was until he had returned. Then he spun on his heels and strode down the lawn to his white horse.

Custer watched the general go before he stooped to pluck a long blade of grass. The bitter taste of it spread on his tongue as Custer spun to face west. Clouds hung above the countryside, prompting Custer to conclude that it looked like rain. Would they have enough time that day to attack? He shook his head in doubt.

The army moved slowly, and Custer wondered how Hooker would find the enemy's flank before darkness descended on them. Attacking an enemy always involved risk, but in this case, Hooker's corps seemed to be blundering forward without properly scouting the field. Even General Pleasonton had not received orders to move ahead of Hooker's advance and locate the enemy. Custer shook his head, telling himself that General McClellan knew what he was doing.

Returning sometime later, Hooker quickly dismounted and hurried up to the house, barking orders. "All of you get moving! We are ordered across the Antietam immediately!"

The instructions sent the officers and men scurrying into action. Custer greeted Hooker as he approached, the scabbard holding his sword clattering against his leg. "Sir, did General McClellan clarify his intent?" he asked.

Shaking his head, Hooker's pale blue eyes revealed no more comprehension than they had earlier. "He did not. He said only that I am to take my corps across the creek and strike the enemy's flank. He did add, however, that I am free to call on reinforcements if I need them."

"That's reassuring, at least," Custer shrugged.

Hooker's lips pressed into a grim line. "It is, but I'm not sure what we are expected to accomplish today. General McClellan and I spoke hours ago about attacking the Rebel left, but we've only just received our orders." Hooker threw his hands into the air. "Ah, well, we must carry on. Come along, captain. It's time we caught up with the vanguard. I have already sent several companies from the Third Pennsylvania Cavalry ahead to feel for the enemy."

Pulling the well-chewed stem from his lips, Custer tossed it onto the ground. He followed Hooker down the slope to where Wellington waited near the general's horse.

Hooker ordered his staff to mount up and spurred toward the road that ran from Keedysville to the bridge over Antietam Creek. Striking the crowded track, the general steered left and ambled across a narrow stone bridge crammed full of Federal troops. Men stared as he passed, their eyes glassy with the tedium of fitful progress. Up the narrow road went Hooker and Custer, swooping over the uneven terrain before the track flattened out alongside a large brick mill house on the column's left.

Outriders, crying, "make way for General Hooker!" cleared a path for the First Corps commander as he approached and then crossed an arched span over the creek. The heavy column of troops on the far side labored up a steep grade that forked off to the right. Here, Hooker met General Meade, and after a brief exchange of words, he and the Pennsylvanian climbed the hill alongside the infantry. At the top of the ridge, Hooker halted his horse and drew out his field glasses. Silently surveying the countryside, he searched for signs of the enemy.

The landscape, broken into fields of corn, clover, fruit trees, and grazing pasture, dipped down in front of him before rolling upward again toward a plateau topped with forest. Off to the left he could see the columns of Abner Doubleday's brigades slogging across the creek and onto the rim of the vale before them. Squads of pioneers bearing axes fanned out in advance of the column to hack down fence posts and clear a path. George Meade's division, meanwhile, continued its march along the road that locals said led northwest to Williamsport and the Potomac River.

Sliding his glasses back into their case, Hooker continued ahead of his men until he had reached the crest of a second ridge. There, he pulled off by a farm lane to watch the column trudge past. General Meade joined him, tugging out his watch when he pulled to a stop.

"What is the hour?" asked Hooker.

"A quarter after four," sniffed the Pennsylvanian. "We've made less than a mile. This is slow going."

"It is, indeed," nodded Hooker. "The countryside here is too broken for rapid marching. Just look at Doubleday's column. He's had to chop his way through every cow pasture and meadow he's come to."

"How far up this road do you intend to go?" asked Meade.

"As far as the road to Hagerstown, if need be," replied Hooker, tossing his chin toward the west. "We'll guide due south from there."

"Sir, General McClellan is approaching!" cried one of Hooker's aides.

His head snapping to the left, Hooker watched McClellan ride up with his aides, a stern expression on his face.

"Sir, I'm surprised to see you. We've only just begun our advance," said Hooker as Little Mac reined in.

"So, I see," nodded McClellan, looking anxious. "Your column must move faster, general, and it must get off this road. Your men are marching in the wrong direction."

Hooker's brows knit together. "But, sir, this is the only road in the area. I thought we would stay on it until we hit the turnpike to Hagerstown and then go south."

McClellan shook his head. "No, General Hooker, that is not what I want you to do. You must swing more to the left before the turnpike and stay within range of the rest of the army. If you continue in the direction you are going, your flanks will be in the air and the Secesh will gobble you up!"

"I understand, sir, and will issue the orders immediately. But I must repeat that I am not happy with my corps being out here alone. I have only around ten thousand men after the fight on South Mountain. Can you not send General Sumner's corps across the creek to support me?"

Little Mac thought on this but shook his head. "No, general, I cannot. Sumner's men are needed to attack the enemy if he breaks for the Potomac."

"But, sir, Lee means to fight. He's not going to break, particularly if my corps is the only attacking force. We need support."

McClellan glowered at the First Corps commander. "I'll take it under advisement, general, and may be inclined to send you the Twelfth Corps, but I have not yet decided. For the time being, you are to proceed in a southerly direction with your corps and keep your left under the cover of our heavy guns. Your objective is to attain that ridge yonder. Understood?" McClellan pointed to the wooded high ground in the distance.

"It is, sir. Is there anything else?"

"Not at the moment. Give your orders, and I will accompany you for a distance."

Tossing a salute, Hooker barked instructions for his column to leave the road and move toward the distant ridge. "Shake out two regiments as skirmishers, General Meade!"

Responding with a nod, Meade ordered the Thirteenth and Third Pennsylvania Reserves to fan out ahead of the advance and form a strong skirmish line. Custer eyed the Keystone Staters curiously as they passed, noting the white deer tails they wore pinned above the brims of their caps. Equipment clattering, the men swung left toward a prosperous farm as other regiments filed into the fields behind them. The collection of generals and their aides watched all of this for a time when a local man accompanied by a lieutenant rode up to them.

The officer announced that the bearded man had just come from Harpers Ferry, where he had witnessed the surrender of Miles's garrison.

McClellan looked the man over, noting his worn brown jacket and tattered slouch hat. "Is that right?" he asked. "Do you expect me to believe you are not a spy sent by the Rebels?"

The man's eyes went wide. "No, sir, gen'ral, I ain't a spy," he gulped. "I work the canal near the ferry and was in town when the Rebs came in."

McClellan peered at the man, his eyes narrowing. "Very well, then. Is there something I ought to know?"

"Well, sir, for one thing, the colonel in charge lost a leg in the fight. We heard he surrendered five thousand men, too."

"Five thousand men. How would you know a number like that?"

"Word travels fast, gen'ral. We also heard that a bunch of horse soldiers, near two thousand, broke out across the Potomac and rode up to Williamsport, where they captured a mess of Rebel wagons and supplies."

McClellan's jaw fell open. "Why, that's splendid news! You say the column was two thousand strong? How many wagons did they capture? Do you know the details?"

"I do, sir. Heard they captured one-hundred and twelve of General Longstreet's wagons. Sixty-two of those carried ammunition. They destroyed them and sent fifty more into Pennsylvania. I think those wagons beared flour."

"Sir, this is fortuitous! The Secesh might be short on ammunition," marveled Hooker.

"That they might," said McClellan. "This man's information has proven useful, after all. Thank you for bringing it to me."

"My pleasure, gen'ral," nodded the civilian, doffing his hat.

Little Mac turned back to Hooker. "Shall we ride on?"

Hooker steered his horse down the country lane where the tail end of Meade's column marched. The collection of officers rode through the yard of a farm, past the house, and up the ridge when booming cannon fire rent the air ahead of them. McClellan called for them to halt when a rider sped from the tree line to Hooker.

"Sir, Captain Jones sent me to tell you the cavalry advance has been fired upon by Rebels. His men have fallen back. The captain requests support."

"Very good, corporal," nodded Hooker. "Take me to Jones. I want to see for myself what he is facing. Sir, you will forgive me," he said to McClellan. "I need to attend to things on my front."

"By all means, general," nodded Little Mac. "I will return to headquarters now. Send word if you require something of me."

"Very good, sir, I will."

Hooker called for an aide and galloped into the trees with Custer in pursuit. They soon emerged into a field where Hooker called Custer to his side. "Captain, you know McClellan best among us. Did he appear unsettled to you?"

"Not that I noticed, sir," lied Custer. Remaining circumspect out of loyalty to his chief, Custer had to admit that McClellan did seem out of sorts. A light sheen of sweat covered his face, and he looked pale when normally a rosy color tinted his cheeks. Could it be a case of nerves? Coming to grips with the army of Robert E. Lee was enough to give any commander pause, so Little Mac could be forgiven for being jumpy. Even if fearful, however, it had not kept the general from ordering Hooker's attack, so Custer quickly dropped the thought.

Picking their way over the countryside, Hooker and his entourage struck a farm lane running perpendicular to their course. They turned left down the lane and walked their horses past fields lined with trees and underbrush. Ahead, Custer spied a squadron of horsemen sheltering behind a small stand of trees. Shots broke the stillness, and Custer noticed other riders had dismounted to take up a position along a fence. Hooker rode up to the troopers, meeting a captain with hangdog-looking eyes.

"Why, General Hooker. What are you doing up here? It's too dangerous," said the man.

"Don't worry about that, Captain Jones. I received your report. Are there Rebels about?"

"Yes, sir. We spotted several Secesh observing us from a distance. They let us alone initially, but then decided to give us a few shots, so I ordered my men to dismount and return fire. No reason we should just sit here on our horses taking lead."

"I agree, captain. It's a prudent move. Are your men the only part of the Third here?"

"No, general. Company H is somewhere in that direction." Jones pointed to his right where the deer tail clad men from General Meade's column could be seen advancing across a plowed field.

"Lieutenant Miller's in command over there," continued Jones. "If it's all the same to you, I'd like to hear from him first before moving forward. As broken and grown up as it is around here, this countryside is perfect for bushwhacking. I don't like being out here one bit."

Heavy gunfire broke out, snapping Hooker's head to the right. He rose in his stirrups to see if he could discern what was happening but sank back quickly in frustration. The firing escalated into a rapid exchange of shots, accompanied by a high-pitched Rebel yell. "Sir, those sound like Sharp's rifles," observed Custer, referring to higher-pitched reports nearby.

"The captain's right," nodded Jones. "Those deeper shots are muskets."

"Some of General Meade's men carry Sharp's Rifles. He must be engaged," said Hooker.

"What would you have us do, sir?" asked Jones.

Hooker walked his horse a couple of steps before wheeling him about. "Captain, I think the Secesh you've encountered are pickets, not outriders. You are to drive them in and make contact with the enemy!"

Yelping, "yes, sir!" Jones barked orders for his command to mount up.

Hooker rode off, calling for Custer to follow him. Spurring toward the gunfire, he passed through a plowed field and over a farm lane before entering a copse of trees. He reined in to use his field glasses. Up ahead, he could see the rear of several regiments in battle formation across a rolling field bisected by the dirt road he had just traversed. Flags fluttered in a light breeze while powder smoke rose from skirmishers posted beyond the main line of infantry. The volume and level of musket fire rose abruptly on Hooker's left.

A bearded officer with a single star on his shoulder straps rode up. "Sir! Colonel McNeil's men have driven in the enemy's pickets and struck their main line in yonder woods. Given the lateness of the hour, I've ordered McNeil to press them for all he's worth."

"Excellent, General Seymour! That's precisely what we need," nodded Hooker.

The gunfire grew to a roar as McNeil's men pressed forward. Then big guns opened on them from the right, sweeping the Pennsylvanians with canister. Puffs of dust rose around the men as dozens of iron balls struck the line. A groan went up from the right as volunteers tumbled to the ground. A second set of guns opened on the Keystone Staters from the left, sending limbs and shattered muskets soaring into the air.

"Those men need to get out of there!" cried Hooker in alarm. "They'll be cut to pieces."

"Look, sir, they're moving!" shouted Custer. The line lurched forward with a cheer, flags and rifles tilted at the smoke-filled trees. More men dropped into the dirt as the Reserves disappeared among the trunks. Cracking musket fire subsided for a moment, only to erupt with greater intensity deeper inside the woods. Meade's batteries joined the fray, and a courier arrived, informing Hooker of the general's deployment on the right. Meade had encountered Rebel infantry occupying a large field filled with ripening corn. Hooker sent Meade orders to secure his right flank and watch for an enemy movement against it. Reports came back from the front. Hooker glanced at one of them, crumpling the paper in his fist.

"Colonel McNeil is dead!" he shouted. "His men are heavily engaged in that wood lot."

The roaring gunfire rose to a crescendo in the building gloom. Projectiles trailing sparks and smoke cut through the sky and word arrived that the Rebel battle line, which had initially given way, suddenly firmed up, offering stubborn resistance. Custer felt a drop of rain on his cheek and gazed up at the iron gray sky. A misty drizzle began to fall, drawing curses from Hooker. Calling for his horse, the general climbed into the saddle and ordered his staff to follow him to shelter for the night. A scout had located a large barn by the Hagerstown Pike that would suit them, and Hooker rode into it before dismounting.

Reports came in from brigade commanders, and Hooker scanned them by the light of an oil lamp an aide had brought. Custer watched the man pace and bark orders, learning over time that confusion reigned throughout the corps. Whereas the general believed his entire command was engaged, it became clear that only the men under Meade and Seymour had seen action. Then darkness fell, leaving everyone ignorant of exactly where the main enemy battle line could be found.

"I can't make heads or tails out of this," growled Hooker, shaking the sheaf of papers in his fist. "Corporal, take these from me." The general thrust the dispatches into the man's chest and turned on his heels toward his horse. Climbing into the saddle, he spurred into the night.

The First Corps staff inside the barn chatted quietly among themselves. A man boiled coffee and Custer was sipping some when Hooker finally returned. Dismounting, the blonde-haired general slapped his rain-soaked hat against his thigh. He called for General Meade, and Custer approached to listen.

"Meade, the lines are so close in places that our men can hear the enemy talking," said Hooker, "but it's so dark that I can't make sense of where we stand in relation to the Rebel positions."

"I still hear the shooting out there, too," offered Meade, shaking droplets from his beard. "Our pickets and the Rebels must be right on top of each other."

Hooker ran his fingers through wet hair. "They are, general. They are damned close."

"So, what will you do tomorrow?" asked Meade.

"Obviously, I will attack!"

"Is that prudent? We don't know where the enemy line is, and I'm particularly concerned about our right flank. We don't know what's out there."

"We know the enemy is on your front, general, and for now that is sufficient. When daylight comes, we will attack south along the Hagerstown Pike as General McClellan has ordered. Understood?" Looking around, Hooker called for an aide. "I must write to him and communicate my plans."

Hooker ordered the man to tell Little Mac that his command had become engaged along most of his front. He paused for a moment; the fatigue clear on his face. "Add that I formally request General Mansfield's corps be sent as reinforcement," he said at last. "We drove the enemy before darkness fell and by God, we will drive them again when daylight comes!"

Custer grinned under the shadow of his hat. At last, he had found a man who would fight. Stepping forward to volunteer, Custer offered to carry the message to army headquarters.

"So be it, captain," Hooker nodded. "You are the general's man. Impress on him our need for support. I don't know what we are facing out there."

"As you wish, sir. I'll tell him," Custer saluted, and taking the note, he tucked it inside of his tunic before stepping into the rain-soaked night.

*   *   *

An hour later, Custer wearily steered Wellington into the yard outside of the large brick house where General Hooker had made his headquarters earlier that day. Beside Custer rode the spindly figure of Colonel Key, who had joined him in Keedysville. Army headquarters remained in the rear near the Boonsborough Pike, and Custer had ridden there first, but upon arriving, he found that Little Mac had elected to spend the night at Hooker's headquarters closer to the front.

"The general's nerves are on edge," explained Key to Custer, who was irritated because he had to retrace his steps. "He wants to be up close when the fighting opens in the morning."

Dropping from Wellington's back, Custer mounted the wet steps to the house. He and Key entered the front door and gazed around for the general, but did not see him. Colonel Ruggles noticed them and waved them over.

"Colonel, I have a message from General Hooker," reported Custer.

"Ah, very good, captain. The general will want to see it immediately. Please follow me." The colonel led them to a doorway lit with candlelight. Custer thanked the colonel and entered the room with Key close behind. McClellan sat at a table scratching out a message with maps and papers spread out before him. He looked up when he heard the two men approach. Dark circles ringed his eyes, hinting at the immense strain under which he labored.

"Ah, Captain Custer, it is good to see you!" he said, laying down his pen. "And you, Colonel Key, what brings you out on this rainy night? I'd have thought you'd find a nice dry tent to hide in."

"General," bowed Key.

"Sir, I have a message from General Hooker," said Custer, pulling the note from his pocket.

Taking the paper, McClellan unfolded it and read the contents. "Yes. Mm-hm. Excellent! Hooker is in control of the situation, I take it?"

"He is, sir, but things on his front are in disarray. Darkness fell before the general had an opportunity to make a proper reconnaissance of the field. He doesn't know what to expect in the morning."

"There is always fog in war," observed Little Mac. "Hooker will do just fine, I am sure."

"And the reinforcements he requests, general, should he expect them tonight?" asked Custer.

McClellan pushed himself out of his chair. "Yes, captain, he should. I sent orders for Sumner to have Mansfield move the Twelfth Corps over the creek several hours ago. He should be underway by now."

"Undoubtedly, sir," nodded Custer. "Will there be anything else you require of me?"

"Not that I can think of. Ask Colonel Ruggles to find you a pallet for the night so you don't have to sleep in the rain."

"I will and thank you," saluted Custer. Nodding to Key, he strode from the room.

"He is a good officer," said Key, folding his hands behind his back.

"Yes, Key, he is. I appreciate him more every day. Come, have a seat." Little Mac gestured to the chair opposite him.

"Sir, if I may say so, you look tired."

McClellan rubbed his eyes. "I am weary, colonel. Bone-tired, in fact. But there is too much to be done, and worries keep me awake."

"Concerned about the fight tomorrow, sir?"

"Yes, and mightily at that."

"But, general, are you not confident in Hooker? After all, you've already ordered him to attack."

McClellan leaned back in his chair. "I am confident enough, colonel, but the stakes are high. This battle could decide the war. I must win it and throw back not only the Rebels, but my enemies in Washington."

Key offered a thin smile. "I am with you, sir. We must be very careful to make the right moves and take advantage of the situation as it unfolds."

"Politics again, Key?" complained McClellan. "I must win this fight first."

"Indeed, you must. Are you ready?"

"I believe so. Hooker and Mansfield will initiate the offensive with Sumner and Porter as reinforcements."

"And Burnside, what of him?"

"I will order him to attack as well, if I believe there is a good opportunity to strike Lee a blow. I have also ordered Franklin to meet us with two divisions from the Sixth Corps as quickly as he is able. One division, that of general Couch, I will leave in Pleasant Valley to guard this army's left flank against any mischief from Jackson. With any luck, Hooker will crush Lee in the morning and force him to withdraw across the Potomac."

McClellan fell silent, his exhausted gaze dropping to the table. "If I am honest, colonel," he said after a moment, "I had hoped that Hooker's movement this afternoon would compel Lee to retreat. However, he seems determined to fight. Why he would do it evades me. How can a man with Lee's experience take as perilous position as he has? The river is at his back. If we break his lines tomorrow, he will have no place to run."

"Well, then, sir, you had better break him!"

"That's easier said than done, colonel, but you are correct. We must break Bobby Lee's army tomorrow and God willing, we shall!"

24

Tuesday, September 16, 1862
Mid-morning to evening
Middletown to Keedysville, Maryland

Kelly tossed pebbles outside of Lucy Settle's house while waiting for a wagon to pick him up. Earlier that morning, old man Sutherland, the owner of Simon, had informed Miss Settle that several lightly wounded men in Middletown were going to rejoin their regiments. Sutherland had arranged to drive them over the mountain, on the condition that Simon return the horse and wagon immediately to the farm. Kelly marveled at the leeway Sutherland gave his slaves. The Pennsylvania state line lay less than a day's ride away, yet Sutherland let Simon roam as freely as he pleased. It was an arrangement Kelly found unfathomable.

Lucy had, for her part, pronounced Kelly fit to travel that morning. After spending a second night in her care, he found himself rapidly regaining strength. The ache in his head disappeared and his equilibrium returned. He still wobbled if he moved his head too quickly, but mostly he felt well enough to go back. After their rocky start together, Kelly found being with Miss Settle a pleasant experience. She fed him well and kept him as clean as the limits of propriety would allow. He even wore a freshly laundered uniform free of lice, a luxury he had not experienced since joining the army more than a year earlier.

Now, Kelly waited in the yard while Lucy filled a sack with vittles for him to take on his journey. The dull thumping of artillery fire in the distance told him that the army had not gone far. He would be back with Davey Parker and the rest of the Twenty-Third by nightfall.

The door behind Kelly pushed open, and he watched Lucy come down the steps with a plump canvas sack. "Here you are, Tom," she said as she approached. "Here's something to take on your way."

Kelly peered into the bag to find a blue glass bottle, a loaf of bread, a wedge of hard cheese, and half a smoked ham lying at the bottom. "My goodness, Miss Lucy, that's grand of you," he grinned. "Are ye sure you don't need this food more than me?"

"I'm quite sure, Tom. You and your comrades will need all the sustenance you can find." Lucy looked off in the direction of the rumbling cannon fire. "The war's not far off. Trying times lay ahead for you."

"You're probably right about that," nodded Kelly, distracted as he dug out the bottle. "Is this what I think it is?"

"You mean fresh water?" Settle winked, crushing Kelly's hopes.

"I was rather thinking of some of that rye whiskey folks make in these parts," he admitted.

"Liquor is the devil's handmaiden, Tom. You'll get none of it from me."

Disappointed, and a little embarrassed, Kelly dropped the bottle back into the sack and spun it closed. "Oh well, it didn't hurt to ask, now did it?"

"I reckon not, but temperance should be the way of all God-fearing men. You do fear God, don't you?"

"Fear God? Why, no, I can't say that I do. I'm Catholic, Miss Lucy. We don't fear God. When we've erred in our ways, we go to Confession, and he forgives us. There's nuttin' to fear." Kelly shook a finger at Lucy. "You Protty's now. You've got something to be afraid of!"

The pair broke out laughing. The wagon arrived at the end of the driveway, and Simon waved his hat, beckoning Kelly to hop on board. Three men in blue uniforms sat behind Simon on the flatbed.

"That's me, then," said Kelly, peering first at the wagon and then back at Miss Settle. A sad expression had formed on the woman's face.

"Lucy Settle, you're the oddest woman I've ever met," said Kelly, "But I'm grateful for your kindness. Ye've been good to me despite my, um, medieval way of seeing things, as ye put it. Still, I'm thankful."

"You're welcome, Tom. It's been nice spending time with you even though we disagree on some things. I ask only that you keep an open mind about some subjects we've discussed. We women may be the fairer sex, but we're not weaker than you. We deserve better treatment than is our lot."

"I promise I'll give it more consideration," winked Kelly.

"We ask only to be given the same respect you'd give any man, Tom. There's a pamphlet in that sack for you to read. It's written by Susan B. Anthony, and it explains our position clearly. I believe you will find the ideas in it difficult to argue with."

"Ah, I dunno …" Kelly grimaced, thankful that he could not read particularly well. Ignoring him, Lucy went on. "More important still, Tom, I'd ask you to think on Simon. None of God's creatures is born in chains. It's men who put them there. You've told me how your people long to be free from oppression. Well, so do Simon and his ilk. Tell me, Tom, would you deny that Simon is a child of God?"

Kelly scratched his temple. "Em … no?"

"No, indeed, Tom. Ponder this. Who is man to bind what God made free? This is the madness of our time, and the real reason you and your comrades are fighting this terrible war, even if you don't yet know it. You are doing God's work. You are setting things right on earth. You, Tom Kelly, are an instrument of divine justice. Serve Him faithfully in your heart and fight this slave power rebellion with everything you've got. Make your sacrifice and the sacrifice of those with you mean something. Let it mean freedom for all men."

Struck dumb, Kelly stared down at his boots. Again, Simon called him.

"Just a minute!" Kelly shouted. Turning to Miss Settle, he took her hand. "I'll think on it, Miss Lucy. I've heard what you've said, and it makes sense to me. I can't understand why I didn't see it before, but I have now, I promise."

Mustering a smile, Lucy pulled him into her embrace. "Then, may God bless you, Tom Kelly," she whispered.

Kelly touched the brim of his hat when Lucy released him and threw the sack over his shoulder. Walking to the wagon, he climbed onto the driver's bench, where Simon told him to sit. The black man tipped his hat to Miss Settle and snapped the reins over his horse's back. Kelly glanced back a final time to see his friend standing in the road, her hands clasped tightly in front of her gray dress. He waved to her and she to him before Kelly turned to face the ominous rumble in the distance.

* * *

The sun had slipped low into the western sky by the time they arrived outside of Keedysville. Wagons, guns, and marching troops crowded the road ahead, forcing Simon to pull his cart into an adjacent field.

"Well, Mister Tom, this is it. I can't go no futher," he said.

"That's alright, Simon. We'll walk from here. C'mon boys. The army's a-waitin'," he called to the others in the back.

Climbing to the ground, Kelly watched Simon circle back the way they had come. He looked at the encampments covering the fields on both sides of the road, wondering how he was going to find his regiment. Reckoning it was best to start walking, he headed toward the sound of battle. The Kanawha Division was always at the front, so the closer he got to the action, the likelier it was he would find his friends.

Some distance on, the desultory booming to the northwest exploded into a continuous roar. Only a full-scale engagement sounded like that, Kelly thought, hoping his regiment was not involved. Troops seemed to be in motion everywhere around him the closer he got to the front. Asking passing strangers for General Burnside's command, he finally found Sam Sturgis's division, where a friendly sergeant directed him still farther to the left. He wandered through the fields in the fast-fading light until a familiar voice called out his name.

"Tom Kelly! Hey, Tom! Over here!" Glancing over, Kelly saw Sam Carey waving at him. He ran to Carey and took the man in his arms, crying, "Sam, boy! Yer a sight for sore eyes."

"Likewise, Tom. Where've you been? We ain't seen you since the fight on the mountain."

"Yeah, I got injured, Sam, as ye can see." Kelly pointed to his bandage. "Where's the rest of the boys?"

"Back here behind me. We've been called into column, but I had to heed the call of nature, so I'm out here. The rest of the boys are in line waiting to move again."

"Again, Sam? What do ye mean? What's going on?"

"Damned if I know, Tom. We've been all over the place. Now we're marching again. I guess we're heading closer to the enemy, but who knows?"

"Marching at night, Sam? It's nearly dark now. I'm lucky ye saw me. I'd never find you boys in the dark."

"You're right about that. C'mon, I'll take you to them."

Kelly followed Sam through the trees and into a field on the backside of a long hill. Shadowy figures standing in the grass emerged from the gloom, and Kelly realized they were troops from his brigade. Carey wove through them until he reached their objective. "Hey, fellas, look who I found!" he called out.

Heads turned in their direction and Kelly spied a tremendous grin on the one face he had hoped to see most. "Davey!" he shouted, rushing to embrace his friend.

"Tom Kelly! Thank God you're alive," cried Parker. "We left you for dead!"

Kelly shook other outstretched hands and explained what had happened to him. Then he recalled the food in his sack and divulged its contents. Hungry men converged on him from all sides begging for something to eat. Kelly pushed away from them, shouting, "stop crowding me, you bastards! What the hell is wrong with you?"

"We haven't eaten anything but field corn for two days," grumbled Sergeant Lyon. "The commissary train still isn't up."

"He's telling the truth," Parker added. "We've had nothing but corn and apples. The hardtack's all gone. Hell, even old Burnside's been seen roasting an ear, God bless him. I give the old general one thing, he knows how to suffer with his men."

Kelly shook his head in disbelief, but after seeing what he had behind the front, everyone agreed the army was simply too big for the place they were in. The wagons could not get through on such small roads. Kelly began handing out the food in his sack with instructions that each man was to take a single bite of the ham and pass it along. Same with the bread, cheese, and potatoes. He cut off hunks of each item for himself before handing them out. The rest he stuffed back into his sack. After this meager repast, Sergeant Lyon told Kelly that he should report to Major Comly. That way, he could receive a new musket and ammunition.

"As sure as I'm standing here, Tom, we're gonna see the elephant tomorrow," he said. "You're going to need a rifle."

Kelly agreed and set out in the direction that Lyon pointed. After locating the major and securing a new musket, cartridges, and bayonet, he made his way back through a light rain.

Orders soon arrived for the men to march and they promptly did so, tripping and cussing their way through the darkness until they reached their designated position. Once they fell out Parker and Kelly pulled a rubber blanket over themselves, exchanged a few words, and settled down to sleep.

The misery of lying on wet ground kept Kelly awake long after his friend had gone quiet. At least with him and Parker sleeping back-to-back, they could keep warm. At length his eyes closed, and Kelly felt himself falling asleep, the last sound passing through his mind being the voice of Lucy Settle admonishing him to keep his promise.

25

Tuesday, September 16, 1862
Late evening to after midnight
Twelfth Corps, Encampment of the One Hundred and Twenty-Fifth Pennsylvania
Keedysville, Maryland

in! Fall in!" shouted a man on horseback, thumping past Colonel Higgins's tent. The colonel fumbled in the dark for a match and lit the taper by his side. Then he pulled out his pocket watch. "Ten o'clock? What in God's name is happening?"

Rising from his pallet, Higgins stepped into the drizzly night. "You, there. What's going on?" he shouted, grabbing at a passing shadow.

"Sir, we've got orders to move out! General Mansfield is to take the corps across the creek."

Higgins let go of the man's tunic, allowing him to run off through the mud.

"Of all the blasted nights," he growled, returning to his tent.

Buckling on his saber, Higgins gathered a few personal items that he tucked into his pocket. He pulled on his cap and stalked into the torch-lit chaos.

"Orderly, bring me my horse!" he roared, hoping someone nearby would notice him. Fortunately, a private heard the call, and he appeared with the colonel's mount saddled and ready. Higgins wheeled the horse into the field where his men had arranged their small shelter tents into neat rows. Lieutenant Colonel Szink stood bawling orders in the rain and a portion of the nine-hundred men in the regiment had already formed up. Still more emerged from the darkness pulling on jackets and caps, their haversacks, knapsacks, and rifles in hand.

Higgins watched over the scene like a grim sentinel, the rain soaking through his collar and trickling down his back. At last the simple tents had been torn down, and the men stood in rank before him, rifles propped on their shoulders and rubber ponchos glistening in the flickering torchlight. Higgins rode along the first line, nodding to those he knew by name. Then he spied the German-speaking youth he had met outside of Frederick City.

"Son, are you ready?" he asked, drawing his horse to a stop.

"Ja, Herr col-o-nel!" shouted the boy.

Nodding sternly, Higgins walked his horse until a rider approached from the Boonsborough Pike.

"Sir, General Crawford sends his compliments," he said. "His orders are for you to move out. All torches are to be extinguished once we get onto the road. We're trying to get the drop on the Rebels."

"Acknowledged. Tell the general we are moving now," nodded Higgins. Turning in the saddle, he bawled out the order to face right and step off.

The column lurched forward unevenly, the men tripping on stones and splashing through puddles as they advanced. Stepping onto the pike did not improve matters. The formations marching ahead of them had churned the dirt into a pasty slop that clung tenaciously to the men's flat-bottomed brogans. Higgins rocked in the saddle at the front of his regiment, with Szink riding alongside him.

The column moved slowly through the rain until it turned down a roadway to the right, scaled a hillside, and crossed a stone bridge at the bottom of the opposite slope. Higgins thought the night as black as any he could remember and all around him men cursed as they crashed into one another. He struggled to make out the backs of the men ahead of him so that if they stopped, his horse would not trample them. Dark shapes shifted in the darkness like ghosts. He heard their footsteps, though, and let them guide him through the miserable trek that took them into open countryside. They tramped past gloomy farm buildings and up a grassy ridge line past fences cut down to make way for the army. At last, orders came for Higgins's regiment to file into a field. The colonel dropped to the ground among the plowed furrows and looked around him.

"Szink, where are you?" he called out.

"Here, colonel!" Szink pushed through the darkness toward the sound of Higgins's voice.

Higgins squinted at the man, just making out his face. "Have the men fall out where they are. We're not going any farther in this mess."

"Yes, sir!" Szink moved off to convey the orders.

Sighing, Higgins looked around him. "A damned fine place this is to spend the night, in an open field in the rain."

Szink returned, reporting everything in order, and the two men huddled at the corner of a fence.

"Well, Szink, here we are. We might as well make the best of this," said Higgins, running a hand down his wet face. "I'll put my blanket under us. You put yours on top. That way, we don't have to lie in the mud."

Settling down, the two men lay back-to-back.

"Sir, do you know where we are?" asked Szink.

"I haven't the faintest idea," yawned Higgins. "We crossed a bridge, though, which probably means we're on the Rebel side of the creek. I just don't know how close we are to the front line."

"So, we're going to see the elephant tomorrow after all," commented Szink, a hint of fear in his voice.

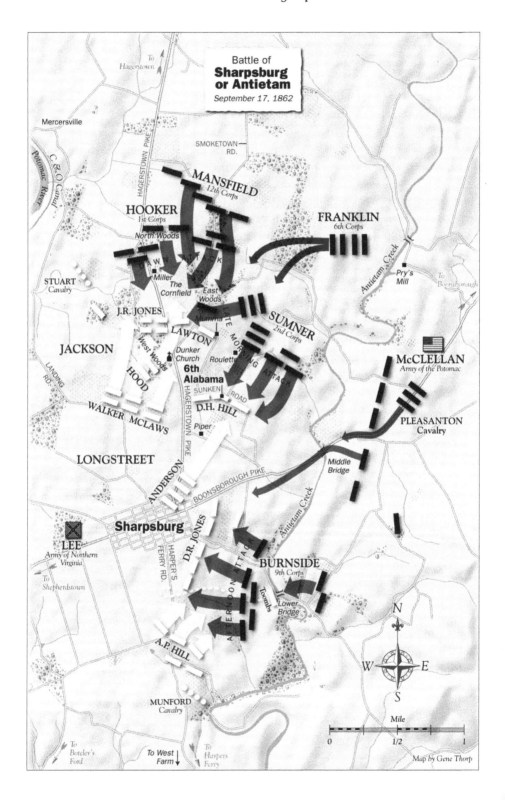

Battle of
**Sharpsburg
or Antietam**
September 17, 1862

Map by Gene Thorp

Higgins listened to muskets popping in the distance. "It seems so," he said after a moment. "The Twelfth Corps must have been called up to support General Hooker instead of the Second Corps. We're probably in for it come daybreak."

The two men fell silent, each lost in his own thoughts. Higgins fell into a light sleep, his veteran's mind less tormented than that of Jacob Szink, who had never seen combat. Szink stared into the darkness, feeling the rain pattering on his cap. He envied Higgins and wished that he too, could rest, but thoughts about the war plagued him. What would the morning bring? Would he acquit himself honorably on the field or would courage fail him? Szink shivered under the blanket, his arms wrapped around him and hands clutching the wet wool of his tunic. He lay there for a long while, visions of friends and family and the army haunting him, until finally he dropped off into an exhausted slumber.

26

Wednesday, September 17, 1862
Early dawn to 7:00 a.m.
First Corps, Right Flank of Army of the Potomac
Sharpsburg, Maryland

Joseph Hooker stirred awake. Lifting his hat from his face, he stared wearily at the corporal kneeling beside him. The man carried a tin cup filled to the brim with coffee that he placed in the straw upon which Hooker lay.

"Good morning, general. I brought this for you," nodded the orderly.

"What's the hour?" Hooker croaked, laying aside his hat.

"It's half past four, sir, exactly when you said to wake you. The sun's not up yet."

Rolling to his right, Hooker propped himself on an elbow. "Very well. Thank you," he said, reaching for the steaming cup.

Sipping gingerly, Hooker found the brew too hot to drink, so he set the cup down and sat up to rub the sleep from his eyes. The barn hummed with activity. Men came and went through the open doors and a small cooking fire smoked and sputtered behind the building, sending weak shafts of yellow light flickering through the cracks between the wall boards. Hooker wriggled uncomfortably in his uniform, still damp from the night's rain. How much sleep he had gotten he could not say—three hours, maybe four at the most.

He and Meade had spent much of the night moving guns and troops into place around them. The inky blackness hampered their efforts considerably and Hooker still did not have a clear notion of his lines. He knew, for instance, that Abner Doubleday's division had taken position along the Hagerstown Road on the rise behind Meade's men. James Ricketts's division lay on the left flank. Behind it waited the Twelfth Corps under General Mansfield, which had slipped across Antietam Creek after midnight. Beyond these few facts Hooker knew little about the alignment of his corps, and even less about the enemy.

Shaking the haze from his head, Hooker labored to his feet. He brushed the straw from his coat, his blonde hair askew on his head. His bladder urged him to empty it. Stepping through the hay, he found a dark corner and relieved himself before returning to gather up his hat, saber, and the precious cup of invigorating black liquid. Striding to the door of the barn, he found Meade looking outside, his back bathed in lantern light.

"Ah, General Hooker, I see you're awake. Good morning to you," commented the Pennsylvanian.

"Likewise, Meade," said Hooker, stretching his arms. Horses in the yard ahead of them stood tethered to a line on their right, while a row of wagons loomed shadowy on the left. Beyond that, all he could make out was a light mist in the air. "It's damned murky this morning," he shivered. "I say, Meade, this is the foggiest part of the country I've ever seen."

"It's the time of year, sir," replied Meade, waving at the darkness. "We're heading into autumn. It's almost always foggy in the mornings now. It'll clear soon enough."

Hooker looked up at the cloud-covered sky. "At least it has stopped raining. That alone is a comfort."

His coffee cooling rapidly now, Hooker swallowed the cup's contents in one deep gulp and poured the dregs onto the ground. "Orderly, bring me some more of this!" he called out, extending the cup to a man standing nearby.

The thump of hooves caught Hooker's attention, and a rider took shape in the mist. Walking his mount forward, he entered the weak circle of light cast by the lamp just inside the barn door.

"Ah, Captain Custer, you're back from headquarters," observed Hooker, his expression relaxing when Custer's features became visible.

"Sir ... General Meade," saluted Custer before climbing down from his saddle. "General McClellan gave me permission to come ahead and observe with you."

"As you wish, captain. I can always use another hand. Now, Meade, as I was about to say, with the Twelfth Corps a short distance behind us, we ought to be able to strike the Secesh a heavy blow."

Hooker shook his fist in the air. "If only McClellan had let us start earlier yesterday, we might have already finished them!"

"Perhaps, general," muttered Meade. The grizzled officer had hear similar confident claims from senior officers too many times to count, only to have their commands wrecked by Lee's Rebels. "Have you settled on a plan of attack?"

"I intend to drive them at first light! When General McClellan orders the attack on the enemy's right, we will crush the Rebels between us until an assault on their center can finish them. All the general requires of us is to hit Lee's flank and draw his attention until the rest of the army can be thrown upon him."

Hooker slurped boorishly from his freshened cup. "But now, Meade, let us consult the map and see what we can make of the situation. From the firing I hear on Seymour's front, it sounds like his skirmishers are already engaged. When I visited his command last night, his pickets were so close to the enemy, they could hear the Secesh talking."

Hooker turned back into the barn while Meade cocked an ear to the southeast where Seymour's Pennsylvania Reserves, a brigade in Meade's division, occupied an irregularly shaped stand of woods. Seymour's men, as well as the others on the line, had slept on their arms that drizzly night, a miserable situation for soldiers on the cusp of battle. The men would be ornery when daylight arrived. Perhaps it would be an advantage when the shooting started, mused the general. Irritable men fought harder.

Meade stepped to Hooker's side and Custer entered the whitewashed barn to listen, having tied off Wellington on a fence outside. The trio surrounded the map that Hooker had pondered the night before. Its rough outlines showed few details, but a man on Hooker's staff had at least marked it with lines estimating the positions of infantry and artillery. Hooker rubbed his stubbled chin while he scrutinized the chart. The same orderly who had brought him coffee arrived with a plate of salt pork and bread, which Hooker greedily devoured while Meade described the situation.

"My division is here in front of us—Anderson's brigade on the right and Magilton's on the left. Their men have taken shelter on the northern edge of this wood lot." Meade tapped a forest in the shape of an elongated triangle on the map. "Seymour's brigade is ahead of them on the left, in the wood lot here, southeast of us."

"Mm-hm," nodded Hooker, sucking his fingertips. "And Ricketts, are those his men here?" He pointed to a line to the left of Meade's men on the map.

"I believe so, sir."

Wiping his mouth on his sleeve, Hooker laid his plate on the barrelhead. "Well, general, we must go and find out for ourselves, and quickly at that. Daylight is coming."

Calling for his horse, Hooker strode out of the barn and propped his hat upon his head. An orderly ran up with the general's white stallion and he climbed into the saddle just as the world outside began taking shape. General Meade appeared on his mount with Custer in tow and together they fell in behind Hooker, along with several staff members.

The blonde general steered his horse around the barn, noting a battery of guns on the left. Still more guns stood on the rise behind them, their muzzles pointing west. Walking his horse some distance north, Hooker surveyed regiments going through roll call and preparing their weapons for the day's fighting. The line of troops ran along the

Hagerstown Pike and Hooker commented the men did not need to be so far from the front. No one knew where the Rebel left lay, however, so rather than face a potential attack on his flank, Doubleday had pivoted much of his command to face west.

Hooker barked for an aide to find Doubleday and hold his brigades in readiness to move at a moment's notice. He wheeled his horse about and passed back around the barn. Proceeding to a dirt track that crossed in front of him from right to left, Hooker spied the rear rank of Meade's men lined up in a wood lot. He saluted a passing colonel and looked up as the firing on Seymour's front picked up.

A cannon boomed on the right, the shell shrieking overhead.

"Where in God's name did that fire come from?" Hooker bawled.

His horse pranced in a full circle as all hell broke loose. Geysers of dirt and rocks erupted behind Meade's line, while the guns on the right flank let loose, taking under fire the flashes from Rebel guns the spotters had seen on a low ridge to the west.

Hooker spun in the saddle, his horse shifting nervously to the side. "Well, Meade, the ball has opened! Come along!"

Spurring his horse to the left, Hooker entered a grassy field where ranks of blue-coated boys from Massachusetts, Pennsylvania, and New York stood in line of battle. Steering behind them, Hooker stopped for a moment to survey the ground ahead of him through his field glasses. A plowed field covered with an ankle-high mist ran straight and flat for two hundred yards before sloping gently to a tall crop of tasseled corn. Smoke drifted from the wood lot left of the corn where Seymour's reserves were engaged. Beyond the plowed field and the corn, Hooker saw the ground dip down on the left. On the right, it ascended to a plowed rise beyond which lay another heavy field of corn about six hundred yards away. Past this farther field of corn, he saw Rebel soldiers in battle formation, their rain-soaked uniforms looking dark below the scarlet battle flags.

Hooker lowered the binoculars when Brigadier General James Ricketts, a stern-faced Empire Stater with a squarish beard, rode up.

"Good morning, sir," shouted Ricketts over the gunfire. "What are your orders?"

Hooker pointed at the enemy line in the distance. "Ricketts, I want you to push a brigade ahead to support Seymour's right. Do you see that field of corn in front of the enemy's line?"

Ricketts raised his field glasses. "I do, sir."

"Put your men in it. I'll order Doubleday to push his command forward on your right in support. Together, you will drive the enemy from that high ground! I also want you to help clear that neck of woods in front of us. Seymour is there now. Take your command forward and add weight to that point in our line. We'll push the Rebels back and advance on the small white structure that lies in that direction. That building is the objective. Do you understand?"

"Perfectly, general," nodded Ricketts. A shell shrieked close-by, prompting Custer to crouch in his saddle.

"The ones you hear are already past you!" shouted Hooker. "It's the ones you don't hear that will be your demise. Alright, General Ricketts, push on!"

Ricketts rode off as another shell careened into the ground near them. Hooker's cheeks flushed red. "Where is that goddamned fire coming from? It is enfilading our entire line!"

"Sir, it's from that hill to the west," shouted Custer. Hooker, following the captain's pointed finger, vented a stream of profanity.

"Custer, go back to General Doubleday and tell him to open the attack on his front! His division is to push down the Hagerstown Road in support of Ricketts's command, which will be pressing forward on his left."

"Yes, general!"

"And tell him to do whatever it takes to silence those blasted batteries. They are murdering us!"

Snapping a salute, Custer wheeled Wellington about and crammed his heels into the horse's flanks. The Morgan leapt forward with a whinny, carrying Custer past multiple explosions. A solid shot blasted a fence into bits, sending rails and part of a post soaring skyward. Custer pushed down his hat and kept moving. He called out for General Doubleday as he went and followed the gesture of a colonel pointing to a mounted officer behind the headquarters barn.

Doubleday turned as Custer pulled up beside him, his hollow, darkly bagged eyes taking in the hirsute captain.

"Sir, General Hooker sends me to say that you are to push your division at the enemy down the Hagerstown Road," said Custer, pointing a gloved finger south.

Doubleday nodded. "Tell the general his order has been received. I'll get my men moving immediately."

"Very good, sir. The general also asks that you silence those batteries on our flank."

"Tell General Hooker I am doing everything I can. My guns are fully in action!" The New Yorker pointed to the bucking cannons.

"I see that, sir, and will let the general know!"

Dodging scurrying troops and advancing batteries, Custer made his way back to where he had left Hooker and Meade. Neither was immediately visible. He spun Wellington around scanning the chaos. Off to his left, a line of General Ricketts's men had fallen into formation. Bugles blared and drums rapped just before the regiments stepped off toward the distant cornfield, their muskets propped on their right shoulders.

Custer turned to his right and rode ahead. He finally spotted Hooker on a knoll directing a battery of guns into place. He watched as its crew unlimbered and rammed home rounds. When the battery commander hollered the order to fire, spouts of flaming smoke erupted from the muzzles, drowning out every other sound on the field.

Custer felt himself twitch from the shock of the reverberation. The canister fired by the guns spattered across the landscape, raising a haze of dirt as it entered the cornfield in the near distance. Stalks of corn flew skyward, along with muskets and at least one arm that Custer could see. Once the smoke had cleared yards-wide sections of the field's mature corn lay strewn on the ground, along with the bodies of several Butternut skirmishers who had once stood among it.

Custer took hold of himself and led Wellington up to Hooker. "Sir, General Doubleday has promised to advance!"

"So, I see, captain!" replied the general, pointing at a line of troops pushing out of the woods to his right-rear.

The indigo lines of General John Gibbon's brigade dressed ranks and strode forward under the Stars and Stripes. Regimental flags bobbed to the cadence of drums above the curious plumed black hats favored by the boys from Wisconsin and Indiana. Custer watched them move in good order through the clouds of swirling powder smoke that drifted over the field. Rebel artillerists noted the movement as well and promptly took the brigade under fire. Balls of solid shot sliced laterally through the packed ranks, tearing off limbs and heads. A groan went up from the brave western boys. Custer thought for a moment that they might break, but Gibbon bawled for them to close ranks, and they kept moving south, a portion of their line disappearing into the field of tall corn.

A wave of exhilaration surged through Custer as he watched the spectacle unfolding before him. He buzzed like a plucked string, his breath coming in short gasps. Blood pulsed hot through his temples. Suddenly, the cacophony of battle went distant, and Custer heard only his own voice in his head, crying, "get at them, boys!" as Gibbon's men pushed through the corn. Cornstalks swayed between the rows of bayonets that glinted in the newly-risen sun. The fiery ball climbed through inky black smoke above South Mountain, its golden rays burning off the last of the morning's mist.

Peering to his left, Custer saw that General Ricketts's command had pushed into the cornfield on Gibbon's flank. Hooker had at last coordinated the advance along his entire front. Fire and smoke stabbed out from the Rebel line and a hideous warbling scream filled the air. Hooker's men in the corn greeted it with a deep roar of their own before leveling their muskets to reply with a murderous volley.

Custer sat transfixed atop his horse, watching what he could see of the fight through his field glasses. Gunshot men dropped to the ground singly and in clusters, opening gaping holes that their comrades closed by stepping forward over the bodies. Behind the Federal line, men reeled backward through the corn, their powder-streaked faces contorted in fear and pain.

"Captain Custer!"

The words reached Custer as if from far away.

"Custer!"

Blinking, Custer came to himself.

"Captain! What in God's name is wrong with you, man?"

Custer found Hooker glaring red-faced at him.

"Sir?" replied Custer, half in a daze.

"Captain, I said go to General Ricketts and find out what has happened to his third brigade! He has only one brigade engaged and one ready to go in. I want him to put in everything he's got!"

All Custer's senses rushed back to him. "Yes, general! Right away!"

Wheeling Wellington to the left, he sped across the field, spying heavy columns of Bluecoats standing on an expanse of plowed ground. Rebel shells exploded among and around the immobile men, who provided an easy target for gunners on a plateau well to their south. Custer steered Wellington in their direction and called out for Ricketts, thinking the general might be with these men.

A thin lieutenant colonel with muttonchops like Custer's hailed him. "Captain, General Ricketts is somewhere off to our left!" he cried. "You must find him and tell him we are without a commanding officer!"

"Without a commander? How can that be?" gasped Custer.

"Rank cowardice! We came under fire as soon as we left the trees and our colonel lit out like a scared rabbit."

"I'll be tarred if I've ever heard such a thing. You say General Ricketts is to the left?" Custer peered in that direction. "I don't see him."

"He's there, I tell you! He just sent Hartsuff's brigade into the fight. Do you see it?"

Custer shot a glance at lines of infantry pushing forward in the distance.

"Captain, please! Tell the general we need someone to take command now," implored the officer.

Nodding, Custer prepared to ride off when a general with a single star on his shoulder straps pulled up hard in front of them. Custer recognized the man from the evening before as General Seymour, an officer in whom General Hooker placed a great deal of faith.

"Richardson, why are these men just standing here under fire?" the general roared.

"Sir, we don't have a commanding officer! Colonel Christian has abandoned the field."

"Abandoned the field? During a fight? I'll have the coward shot!" Seymour thundered. He pointed a gloved finger at the idle men. "Goddammit, Richardson, you take command and get these boys moving! Form them into line and head straight for those trees ahead of you. My men are nearly out of ammunition and must fall back. We need your boys to reinforce us."

"Yes, sir!" saluted Richardson, turning to shout the orders.

Relieved of the need to find Ricketts, Custer pulled Wellington back toward General Hooker, who was still behind the battery of guns that he had earlier ordered to take the corn under fire. By now, the four three-inch rifles had elevated their barrels to exchange shots with a line of Rebel artillery to the south. Hooker moved his horse slowly from left to right, directing the gunners as miniés whipped the air around him. Custer felt one sizzle past his left ear.

"General, do you think you should expose yourself to enemy fire like this?" he cried out.

Hooker turned to him, a curious light in his eye. "A commander must lead from the front, captain! His men must see him taking the same risks as they are, or they won't follow him into battle."

"I understand, sir, but you might be hit!"

Turning back to the front, Hooker raised his binoculars. Rebel shells soared in sending geysers of smoke and fire skyward. A gunner on the right screamed out and fell to the ground, his body pierced through by a jagged shard of iron.

"My God, they are breaking!" cried Hooker suddenly. Bringing down his glasses, he stood high in the stirrups to see more clearly before sitting down again and pacing his horse out from behind the bucking cannons. A deep cheer erupted at the far end of the cornfield, but at the same time, a disorganized mass of blue-coated soldiers emerged in disorder from the rear.

"What's happening?" Custer asked Hooker. "I see our men in retreat, not the Rebels."

"No, captain, it is we who are driving them! Hartsuff's brigade has wrecked their line!" Hooker grabbed the hat from his head, crying, "get after them, boys! Push on!"

Custer peered through smoke at the battle line south of the cornfield where fresh Northern troops had taken up the fight. Loosing a tremendous volley at the thinning Rebel formation beyond the corn, they tore gaping holes in the enemy's ranks. Two other regiments from Gibbon's side of the field now wheeled left and loosed another torrent of lead upon the left flank of the hard-pressed Rebels. Still more musketry poured in on them from their right, where General Seymour had at last brought the absent Colonel Christian's brigade to bear.

Custer trained his field glasses on the beleaguered enemy. Tiny figures in butternut and gray loped rearward through the smoke. A scarlet battle flag went down. It came up again for a moment and then fell a second time for good. Another cheer roared out from the Federals as entire sections of the enemy position disintegrated.

"Press them, boys! Press them!" shouted Hooker, his horse prancing sideways.

Gibbon's regiments pushed forward on the right, over the lip of the plateau on which the enemy line had made its stand. Heavy firing erupted from that direction, sending clouds of smoke skyward. Another cheer rent the air, and Custer's heart leapt with joy at the sound. "General, are we victorious?" he asked.

"I believe so! We must be!" shouted Hooker in reply.

Custer hoped he was right. Peering around him, he saw more men streaming to the rear. Hooker himself took no notice; his gaze fixed on the fight. Gibbon's men also began rushing back into the cornfield, their ranks torn by Rebel cannon and musket fire. A new enemy line appeared on the lip of the plateau, causing Custer's heart to sink. Victory had eluded them, after all. In fact, their fight had only just begun.

27

Wednesday, September 17, 1862
Early Dawn to 7:00 a.m.
Philip Pry House, Field Headquarters, Army of the Potomac
Keedysville, Maryland

McClellan peered through the window of his room into a world of darkness. The night's rain had stopped, but a heavy mist hung over Antietam Creek. Below him, the general could hear the comings and goings of his staff, the footfalls of their boots echoing through the house. Soon, an orderly would call him to breakfast. Then he would depart to observe the front. No news had reached him of Lee abandoning his lines for the safety of Virginia, so a fight it would be.

His coat thrown sloppily over a chair; McClellan paced the room in his shirtsleeves. "An experienced soldier like Bobby Lee would never offer battle with a river at his back," McClellan mused out loud. "Or would he? When I sent Hooker across the creek, I hoped he could pry Lee from his foothold in Maryland. Instead, Secesh has done nothing but sit there." The general fell silent, puzzling over the motives of his opponent. "Were I in his place, I would withdraw to a more defensible line across the river. How can he be so confident? He must have legions at his command."

A shudder passed through Little Mac, recalling the chills he had suffered the day before. He recognized the sensation and fear of it grew in his heart. "It feels like my old Mexican disease," he hissed through gritted teeth. "Of all days, not this one. Not today!"

Willing the pang of malarial fever to leave him, McClellan faced the darkened window to regard his own reflection. "These are the moments that try men's souls," he muttered. "You, George, are called to rescue the nation from this tragic war. Men will die this day, but they *must* fight. God has willed this conflict to be, and he has put you in this place to act as his instrument." McClellan smirked at his own foolishness. "I should pray."

Dropping onto his knees, the general closed his eyes with his hands clasped before him. Silently, Little Mac beseeched God to be with him in his hour of need and to deliver his army a victory over their adversaries. Then a knock on the door interrupted him.

"Enter!" he called out, rising to his feet.

An orderly poked in his head. "Sir, breakfast is ready, if you'd like something to eat."

"Very good, corporal, I'll be right down," replied McClellan, and picking up his coat he cast one last glance at his reflection in the darkened window before blowing out the candle and striding from the room.

*   *   *

Taking a final sip of coffee, McClellan wiped his lips with a cloth napkin as the first light dawned outside. A cannon boomed, and the general looked up. Batteries near the house opened in earnest, rattling plates on the table. Anxiously, Little Mac pulled out his watch. "Five-thirty. General Hooker is as good as his word."

Pushing himself up, he took his cap from an orderly and hurried outside the back of the house, encountering a collection of his staff gazing at the smoke in the distance. Spouts of fire erupted from the guns along the creek. Someone had strapped a spyglass to a fence rail. McClellan strode up to it.

"Please, sir," offered the major, inviting Little Mac to gaze through the eyepiece.

McClellan stooped to the glass and pushed it to the right, where the most prodigious clouds billowed from the field. A dark line of Confederate troops met his eye in front of a piece of woods on their right flank. Their ranks stretched away from him toward another, larger body of trees. Volleys of musket fire stabbed out from their line in a northerly direction.

"I cannot see General Hooker's men from here," he commented. He looked at puffs of smoke coming from the enemy's line on the heights along the creek. Black spouts of dirt and smoke erupted near his army's batteries, and he peered in that direction. The artillerists rolled their guns to face the threat and hammered home fresh rounds before returning fire. McClellan pushed the scope back to the right as the volume of musket fire rose into a roar and smoke obscured the field.

Rising from the glass, McClellan paced with his hands folded behind his back. News from the front must arrive soon, he thought. Men covered the rolling fields behind him, the troops of Sumner's Second Corps, which he had ordered to be ready the night before. Turning back to the knoll, McClellan approached his chief of staff.

"Marcy, do you know if General Sumner pushed a portion of his corps' artillery over the creek last night, as I instructed?"

"To the best of my knowledge he did," nodded the heavily mustached general.

"Good, good. I want Sumner ready to move against Lee's center when the time is right. Now, though, I wish a message sent to General Burnside on our left. Tell him he is to form his troops for an assault on the bridge in his front. Understood?"

"Yes, sir. I'll send a man right away, but are there any further orders? Is he only to form up and wait?"

"Yes, Marcy. I want him ready to attack when the time comes. His command will make a demonstration against Lee's right to pin the enemy's forces there."

"Very good, sir. I'll let him know."

McClellan dismissed Marcy with a nod and returned to the telescope, which revealed little to him through the smoke. Heaving a sigh, he resumed pacing until a messenger ran up from the signal crew nearby.

"Sir, we've received a message from General Hooker," he said, extending the note.

McClellan took the paper and read its contents.

"Is something wrong, sir?" inquired Albert Colburn, McClellan's Assistant Adjutant General.

Little Mac shook his head. "No, major, not in the least. Hooker writes to say that his entire command is engaged against heavy Rebel resistance. He will call up the Twelfth Corps for support when they are needed."

"It's a good thing you ordered them to General Hooker last night, sir," said Colburn.

McClellan turned toward the fighting. "It is, indeed. Now I must consider what to do with Sumner. My inclination has been to hold him ready for an attack on the enemy's center, but with Hooker engaged, I may consider sending him the Second Corps, too." McClellan looked back at Colburn. "Has General Franklin communicated his whereabouts?"

"No, general, we've received nothing. Last we heard, he is making his way here from Pleasant Valley, but I have no further information on his progress."

A frown formed on McClellan's face. "That is unfortunate. I would feel better sending the Second Corps into battle if I knew the Sixth was up and ready to reinforce our center against a possible Secesh counterattack."

"Do you want me to signal the station atop South Mountain? They can see the entire valley from up there. Surely they can tell us where General Franklin's corps is."

"That's a capital idea, major! Tell me as soon as you receive a response."

"Very good, sir," nodded Colburn.

Returning to the glass, McClellan stooped to survey the fighting. The thunder of battle swelled to a new high on Hooker's front and the general fretted, his fingers tapping nervously on his thigh. He rose from the glass and resumed pacing, his mind hoping desperately for news of a triumph on the right. Instead, the opposite came to pass. An aide staring through the glass cried out suddenly that a new line of Rebel infantry had emerged from the forest near a small white building and was advancing toward General Hooker's line.

McClellan turned back to the scope, asking the man there to step aside. Spying geysers of black smoke and shells bursting above the enemy in the distance, the general watched the line move north. Then McClellan saw a second line of the enemy coming up on the first line's right flank. It also moved north toward Hooker's command.

The general took his eye from the scope, his face filled with alarm. "General Marcy, come here, if you please!"

Marcy rushed up to the general, and Little Mac peered grimly into the older man's eyes. "General, send word to Sumner that he is to immediately cross the Antietam and communicate with General Hooker. I had hoped to throw him in later, but Hooker's corps is in a terrible scrape. Tell Sumner he should leave Richardson's division on this side for now. I will send for Captain Custer from my staff to meet him at the creek. Custer knows the field and will show him which fords to use. Understand?"

"Yes, sir! I'll see to it right away!"

"Just a moment, general. Add that Sumner should cross his remaining artillery, too, and ascertain if General Hooker wants the assistance. I don't want him to go too far."

"Very good, sir. Is that all?" asked the older man.

"It is. Now, go!" nodded Little Mac.

Marcy scurried off to communicate the orders as McClellan turned back to the brass scope. A vast cloud of smoke rose in the distance, enveloping the enemy's forces, so he could see only parts of their line. The thundering cannons told him, however, that a mighty struggle prevailed there. He hoped only that Joe Hooker could hang on until Sumner had reached his beleaguered command.

28

Wednesday, September 17, 1862

6:45 a.m. to 8:45 a.m.

Attack of the First Corps, Right Flank of Army of the Potomac

Sharpsburg, Maryland

Custer stared in dismay at a new line of enemy infantry advancing toward the right front of General Hooker's command. Where once the black hats of John Gibbon's boys had dominated that part of the field, a new formation of yowling Rebels now approached, drums rapping and scarlet battle flags flying.

Custer scanned the enemy line from right to left, concluding after counting regimental banners that the men in it came from two or three southern states. One flag in particular caught Custer's attention—that on the line's right flank. Glowing red, white, and blue, Custer thought at first that the Rebels were flying the Stars and Stripes. He pulled down his binoculars to squint at the banner, then looked again through his glasses, realizing at last that the dark blue field was much larger than any national flag he had seen. Stretching from the top of the banner to the bottom, a single white star occupied the center of the blue, opposite thick bars of white and red.

"Texas," he muttered, pulling down the binoculars.

Ahead of him to the right, Gibbon's depleted brigade retired to form a thin line in the gently sloping center of the battle-ravaged cornfield. A section of guns rolled up the Hagerstown Road to support them, letting loose on the Rebels when they halted. The blasts of iron canister at close range tore holes in the enemy line, but the Butternuts coolly leveled their weapons and fired into the scrambling artillerists. A complete battery of guns now came up to support the beleaguered two-gun section and together, they began a pitched fight with the enemy. Too many muskets played on the gun crews from too close a range, however, and before long the Butternuts had entered the much-contested cornfield. They closed quickly on the guns, cutting down the crews with rifle fire until only a few men remained in action.

To the left of the guns, Gibbon's Wisconsin boys made a heroic stand among the tattered stalks of corn. How Gibbon's men could continue the fight after the heavy combat they had already endured bewildered Custer. His gaze remained glued on the remaining two-hundred or so Westerners. They fired with as much precision as circumstances would allow, but their resistance could not last long. The Rebels facing them dressed rapidly on their colors and raised their muskets to deliver a blazing volley that dropped a number of Gibbon's remaining men. Those not killed or grievously injured finally fled to the rear, filtering through a line of reserve troops that General Meade had moved to the edge of the plowed field. The regiment of Texans that Custer had spied earlier, perhaps a few hundred men, came on courageously, but recklessly, exposing both of their flanks. Closer and closer they pushed until Custer could see their powder-streaked faces through his field glasses.

One-hundred yards. Men dropped from their ranks with every step.

Seventy-five yards. A bearded fellow waving the Texas flag went down. His comrade picked up the banner, only to have a bloody hole blown in his chest. He, too, fell straight backward into the arms of a friend. This third man dropped his musket and hoisted the flag high, continuing forward.

Fifty yards! Custer's throat went dry. How could flesh and bone withstand such withering fire from so many directions?

Forty yards! A Napoleon on the right belched canister, blowing a dozen shrieking Texans off of their feet in a maelstrom of smoke and dust.

Thirty yards! Custer could see them very clearly now with the naked eye, their gaping mouths howling the Rebel yell. Federal muskets in front of them erupted with a deafening roar at close range and powder smoke blotted out the morning sky. Wellington tossed his head and Custer cinched the reins to bring him under control. Then he smelled the nauseating tang of spilled blood and blasted guts, and realized why Wellington had grown jumpy.

Behind the Texans came a second line of yelping Johnnies. Advancing on the Texans' right flank, they pushed over the bodies of their fallen comrades, striking deep into the corn. The tall stalks hid their advance until they hit Hooker's line and sent the men there reeling backward. Panicked Massachusetts boys broke in panic, flying out of the corn past General Hooker, who shook his saber at them.

"You men stop!" he bellowed. "I said stop and rally or damn you all to hell!"

Hooker slashed at a private speeding past him. The man ducked under the swing, continuing on without casting so much as a glance at the general. Hooker looked on helplessly as still more of his command melted away on the left. Men streamed back from the wood lot with cries of "the day is lost! Our line is broken!" echoing through the clamor.

Slamming his blade back into its scabbard, Hooker spurred to Custer. "Captain! Ride to General Meade and tell him to send a brigade to bolster our left!" he cried above the thundering guns. "He is to plug the gap in the trees where Seymour and Ricketts have been fighting. Go to him now!"

"Yes, sir," saluted Custer, kicking Wellington's flanks. The horse lunged across the plowed field strewn with the bodies of dead and wounded men. A frightened youth careened blindly into Wellington's left shoulder, spinning to the ground as if he had struck a wall. The horse reared with a shriek at the impact, nearly throwing Custer from his back.

"Whoa, Wellington! Easy!" he shouted, pulling at the reins. The Morgan stamped in a half circle as Custer glared down at the shaken man. "You damned fool! Where are you going?"

The youth hauled himself to his feet. "I'm real sorry, sir. I didn't see you coming."

"So you should be, coward! The fight's that way!" Custer barked, pointing back toward the shattered cornfield.

"Don't I know it. I was just there!"

"Well, get yourself back there, then. That's an order!"

The youth held up his empty hands. "Can't captain. I've got no musket and I'm no coward, either. The Sarge said retreat, so that's what I'm doing."

Custer shook his head at the soldier and spurred Wellington toward a battery of rifled guns. "Captain, where's General Meade?" he called out to the officer in command.

"I haven't seen him," replied the man with a shake of his head. "Try to our right. Colonel Magilton's brigade has just gone to the front. The general may be near him."

Nodding thanks, Custer plunged toward two long lines of Federal infantry formed up beyond a snake-rail fence on the northern edge of the bloody cornfield. Miniés whistled past and Custer realized a rider on horseback made an inviting target. Smoke clouded the field, hiding him for a moment, but the balls flew so thick through the air that he could still be struck. Ramrods rose and fell along the Federal line on the right, where boys from Pennsylvania slugged it out at close range with the few howling Texans who remained. The reek of burnt saltpeter filled Custer's nostrils and blinding smoke stung his eyes as he searched for Meade. He spotted a small group of officers near the tree line, some distance to the rear, and made for them. Meade saw him coming as Custer pulled up.

"Captain, is there something from General Hooker?"

"Yes, sir! The general wishes you to send a brigade to the left. He says that the line in the forest there must be reinforced; the wood lot where Seymour and Ricketts have been fighting."

"To the left, you say? But my men are already engaged here." Meade gestured toward the blazing front. "Marching across the enemy's front will invite disaster."

"I understand, sir, but those are General Hooker's orders!"

Meade peered sternly at Custer before turning at last to a young officer mounted beside him. "Lieutenant, you heard the order. Ride to Colonel Magilton and tell him to pull back his brigade. He is to march them to General Ricketts's support in the woodlot on the left."

The lieutenant sprinted off as another officer on Meade's staff questioned the general. "Sir, you can't seriously consider following those orders? Magilton's men will be cut to pieces!"

"I am quite serious, colonel," growled Meade. "Our flank is threatened, and General Hooker requires our assistance to make it whole. Magilton does not have the enemy ahead of him, as far as I can see. What choice do I have?"

A bugle blared out and faces in the line of Bluecoats looked back over their shoulders. Officers called for the men to shoulder their arms and face left. The regiments did so haltingly, confused about receiving such an instruction in the midst of a fight. Approaching Rebels, meanwhile, emerged from the tall corn, stacking up at the fence on the northern end of the field. Spotting Magilton's men moving laterally across their front, they lowered their rifles and let loose a fiery torrent of lead. The right side of one Pennsylvania regiment melted away in panic as gunshot men collapsed into the dirt, their surviving comrades fleeing for the trees. Another volley exploded from the regiments of Mississippi and North Carolina boys along the fence. Federal flags dropped into the dirt, only to be hoisted again and instantly shot down once more. Rebel troops grew more confident, scaling the low fence into the field where one of Magilton's regiments remained in battle formation. Officers cried for their men to face the enemy, and they wheeled the regiment to its left. The front rank lowered its muskets.

"FIRE!" bellowed the commanding officer, unleashing a rippling explosion that knocked dozens of Rebels from their feet.

The remaining Southerners pulled their triggers in response, loosing a ragged volley into Magilton's running men. Clouds of crimson mist flew as the miniés tore into the ranks. Men struck by the blazing bullets howled in pain, their comrades scurrying to escape the maelstrom of .58 caliber slugs. A battery to Custer's right blasted the shrieking Rebels with canister. Hats, rifles, limbs, and flesh torn loose flew grotesquely into the air. A cry of agony went up and Custer tasted bile in the back of his throat.

To the right, the Texas regiment Custer had spotted earlier withered away under a blizzard of gunfire. The Lone Star flag went down, rose again, and then fell for a final time as men struck by balls convulsed like marionettes. A Federal battery opened on them from the right, sending a swarm of canister into their ranks. Brave men, once vital and defiant, disappeared from the face of the earth, vaporized in gruesome billows of blood.

Soon, only a handful of the Texans remained. These men gave way grudgingly despite the licking they had taken. Backpedaling the way they had come, the vengeful Southerners turned to deliver a light volley at the Federals, who pursued them into the grisly field of corn, then they loped off through the smoke. Custer made a quick count of them as they ran. Of the hundreds that had begun the attack, only dozens remained on their feet. Their comrades lay sprawled in a tangled line of bodies. Among them, Custer spied the final flag-bearer, his grimy face peering lifelessly at the sky, the bullet-riddled flag of Texas crumpled woefully in his lap.

"Hurrah!" exulted Meade's exhausted men at their grim victory. Custer joined them by wheeling Wellington in a circle and swinging his hat wildly in his hand. Gathering his wits, he looked for Hooker and spotted the general atop his horse some distance away in conversation with a white-bearded officer. Pointing to the wood lot occupied by Seymour's troops and then the trampled field of corn in front of him, Hooker directed the man's attention to a new line of Rebels approaching in the distance.

Custer felt his stomach harden. The crisis had not passed after all. One assault had been beaten back, but only here in the center of the line. Now a new one was forming where the Massachusetts boys had earlier withdrawn, and still no one knew the state of things on the left where General Ricketts's men had retired from the woods. A roaring fight continued on the right flank, too, sending clouds of smoke skyward near the northern extremity of the western woods. Custer had no knowledge of affairs on that end of the line, either.

Riding up as Hooker gestured to a white-haired officer beside him, Custer watched the general sweep his hand in front of him. "My corps will not be able to hold this line much longer, General Mansfield. Your men must come up."

"I understand, General Hooker," replied Mansfield. "They are arriving on the field as we speak. I must warn you, however, my men are green. Some of my regiments haven't seen a drill field, much less a field of battle. I can't promise they'll be worth a damn under fire."

"That's quite unfortunate, but we have no choice. I wish for their sake that General McClellan had sent me Sumner's veteran corps instead of your boys, but there is nothing for it now. Green or not, your men must deploy in these fields before us and meet the enemy. I have no men left to put in. The Secesh are advancing on my left without any resistance."

"As you wish, general. I'll see to it right away," nodded the older officer, and wheeling his horse toward the rear, he cantered off.

Hooker leaned with both hands on the frontispiece of his saddle and glowered at the enemy line in the distance. Sensing his ill-temper, Custer remained silent until the red-faced general finally erupted. "We must have more men! General Mansfield's corps must come up as soon as possible. Without it, this fight is surely lost."

Hooker looked on anxiously as the shattered remnants of his corps filtered back to the shelter of the batteries collected at the rear. The wood lot on the left, where the first crack of rifle fire had opened the morning's contest, now stood empty, effectively relinquished to the enemy. For the moment, Meade and Doubleday's men continued their fight on the right, but a messenger from Meade reached Hooker with news that

Anderson's brigade, the last Pennsylvania Reserves on the front, was falling back. Hooker crumpled the note and tossed it into the grass. He raised his field glasses to peer at the field of corn, which had seen so much death already that day. Boys in blue surged rearward under their flags, their line driven by advancing Rebels.

Hooker rubbed at the stubble on his chin. "How many blasted men can Bobby Lee have on this part of the field?" he muttered.

"Sir?" asked an aide, sitting atop the horse beside Hooker.

"I said, how many men can Lee have here in front of us, Major Lawrence?" Hooker gestured at the Rebel formation in the distance. "We have broken his lines twice already this morning. Now a third line is upon us."

"Surely he is pulling men from elsewhere on his front, sir."

"He must be! That is General McClellan's plan, after all; to draw the enemy to us so that he may strike Lee's right, but I have heard nothing of another attack. I had hoped the commanding general would communicate with me by signal."

"Sir, a rider is approaching!"

Looking over his right shoulder, Hooker watched a lieutenant rein in. The man reached into his jacket to draw out a note. "General, I've a message from General Doubleday."

Hooker took the paper and unfolded it. Custer watched Hooker's already thin lips compress into a line of frustration. "General Doubleday reports the withdrawal of his men from yonder forest," Hooker commented, waving the paper at the tree line beyond the battered fences on the Hagerstown Road. "He says that the retreat of Anderson's brigade from the corn left his flank undefended. His position has become untenable, so he is pulling back."

The general heaved a heavy sigh. "It is a good thing that General Mansfield's corps is coming up. We need them very badly."

"Indeed we do, sir. There they are now!" said Major Lawrence, pointing to a column of troops approaching from the rear. The new regiments filtered through Hooker's frowning batteries and down to the northern edge of the cornfield where Meade's command had earlier made its stand. They passed over the bodies of fallen comrades before settling into line of battle. Hooker greeted them with a cautious sense of relief.

General Mansfield rode up, and Hooker received him like a guardian angel. "Your men are here just in time, general! Thank you for bringing them up so quickly."

"You are welcome, General Hooker. Do you have a notion where they ought to go?" asked the snowy-haired Mansfield.

"I do. Your men on the right are well-placed already. My line there has fallen back after heavy fighting this morning. As you can see, we have nothing to protect my guns from the Rebels on the far side of that corn. The men you are bringing up should go on the line in our front and off to the left in those trees. Rebels are in those woods, too, and must be pushed out."

"As you wish, general, I'll get my men into position. Then we will attack!"

"Bully, General Mansfield! May God be with you and your boys."

The elderly general touched the brim of his hat and rode off, shouting orders. A large regiment surged past Hooker at the double-quick under the blue flag of Pennsylvania. Passing through a stand of corn and a screening line of trees, the men proceeded into a grassy field just north of the battered cornfield. Officers bawled orders for the ranks to form in line of battle, and men scrambled into their places.

Just then, Rebels advancing un-noticed through the corn opened fire on them. The colonel in command went down, killed by a ball that smashed through the side of his head and showered blood onto the men standing near him. Shouts went up, and the line wavered. The lieutenant colonel, now in charge, stalked the front of the regiment, trying to restore order, but enemy bullets quickly brought him down as well. Then a solid shot thrown by a Rebel cannon to the west bounded across the ground from the right, smashing through the ranks. Faces gone pale with fright searched for cover back the way they had come. A man broke from the line and scampered back, his musket dropping to the ground; another followed, and then a third.

"They are breaking!" shouted Custer in alarm.

The officers prowling behind the ranks threatened to shoot any man who ran. The major in command roared the words "fix bayonets!" focusing his green volunteers on their weapons. Wheeling his horse to one side of the regiment, the major pointed his saber at the corn. "Charge!" he yelled.

The Keystone Staters entered the corn with a cry, throwing back the enemy's skirmishers. A much heavier Rebel line lay concealed in the vegetation, however, and these men leveled their muskets, delivering a vicious volley at the onrushing Pennsylvanians. The blast staggered the front rank. Screams rose above the gunfire and men milled about, some wounded, others clearly stunned by the violence of their first time under fire. Some shattered volunteers streamed toward the rear; their weapons lost in the chaos. Most men pressed on, firing sporadically at the enemy. The howling Rebels proved better disciplined and again, they blasted the attacking formation with a terrific volley. This halted the Keystone Staters for good, and with cries of "retreat!" they backpedaled through the corn.

Fuming at the failure of this poorly led attack, Hooker turned to Custer. "Captain, go to the left and find General Mansfield. Tell him he must put in all his regiments. These green boys will not stand against a veteran enemy unless they have the numbers. Go!"

"Yes, sir!" saluted Custer, grateful to have a task. Sprinting Wellington to the left, he searched for the white-haired general until he had reached the road to Smoketown that Hooker's corps had used to guide its movement south. There, he stopped and looked around. A heavy line of men prepared to enter the woods to their front. Custer scanned the area but saw no sign of the elderly general. Then two men bearing a stretcher scampered past him and he steered Wellington to stop them, demanding, "where is General Mansfield?"

"We heard he got shot and was brought to the rear, captain," replied one of the privates.

"Ah, I am sorry to hear that. Who is in command of the corps, then?"

"That would be General Williams. Captain, may we go? There are wounded men that need attention."

Custer walked Wellington to the side, clearing a path for the men. "Yes, of course. Be on your way," he said.

The stretcher team loped toward the trees as the long line of troops behind Custer stepped off. He moved Wellington out of their line of march, which took them into the trees on the left. Custer rode the field searching for General Williams, but he could not find him in the chaos of battle, so he went back to find Hooker near the battery of roaring guns. Once again, the enemy had pushed into the blood-soaked field of corn, but in doing so, they left open their right flank. A Bluecoat regiment appeared at the edge of the trees and promptly opened fire on them at the same time as the Federals on the Rebels' left. The beleaguered enemy regiment stood for a few moments and then melted away, its colors dropping into the corpse-filled cornfield. Hooker let out a cry of triumph, followed by the men around him. Custer waved his hat in the air, yipping and cheering for the third time that morning.

Attention shifted to the left, where the gunfire tapered off and a long line of Union troops stepped from the tree line onto the plateau. The Southern formations there withdrew to the western woods as quickly as their legs could carry them.

"Now we have them!" exulted Hooker. "We have broken the enemy's flank, gentlemen, and our path is clear to that white building in the distance. Major Lawrence, send word to Doubleday to push forward on the right whatever remaining force he has. Let us ensure this victory is complete. Lieutenant Candler, send a message to General McClellan by signal. Tell him we have crushed the Rebel army's left and require reinforcement."

"Right away, sir!" shouted the aide, bounding off on his horse.

Falling silent, Hooker surveyed the gruesome field. The thirty-acre expanse of corn lay shot to pieces. Entire sections of the ruined harvest covered the ground, stalks sheared off by hours of incessant musket and cannon fire. Amidst the fallen vegetation lay the bodies of men in both homespun and indigo; some motionless, but many twitching or convulsing. So many moved, in fact, that to Hooker it seemed as if portions of the field creeped like a scene from Dante's vision of hell. Cries for water and moans of grief carried through the air as stretcher-bearers searched for wounded men. Carefully, they picked their way through the corpses, which lay so thickly in some places that a man could not take a step without treading on a once vigorous soldier.

"It is a dismal field," muttered Hooker ruefully. "So many good men lost."

"It is, sir," agreed Custer. "It is, quite frankly, appalling."

* * *

George McClellan chewed his lip before stooping again to peer through his scope. Naught but smoke and the tiny shapes of running men caught his gaze. Sighing heavily, he relinquished the eyepiece to an aide and turned to the staff gathered around him. "Gentlemen, I am going to see General Porter on the turnpike. Have Dan saddled and get yourselves ready. Tell those remaining behind that I want all messages forwarded to me. We'll leave promptly."

His aides rushed off as McClellan strode up the hillside to the team of signal personnel wagging messages across the battlefield. "Sir!" saluted the man in command.

"Sergeant, I need to send a message to General Hooker," said Little Mac.

"Yes, general. Just a moment while I get a dispatch book." The man stooped to retrieve a pad and pencil. "Alright, sir, please go ahead."

"Very well. To General Hooker. General, you will release Captain Custer to go to Antietam Creek, where he will identify the fords that General Sumner will use to bring up his command. You will then communicate with Sumner once he is across and put in his men where they are needed most."

McClellan paused for a moment, as if intending to add something, but then he seemed to think better of it and asked only if the sergeant had copied the message correctly.

"I have, sir," nodded the man, reading it back.

Little Mac approved the message and ordered it sent before turning back to the house. Arriving at the open rear door, a rumble in his gut stopped him in his tracks, and he waited for a sign that he would need to find a sink. Nothing troubled him further, though, so he went inside to his map, which lay on the now cleared breakfast table. Ordering the chart rolled up, he strode outside and down the steps to his waiting steed.

Dan eyed McClellan carefully as the general patted his neck. "Don't worry, old friend," he said, "we won't be in any danger." The horse tossed his mane and McClellan climbed up into the saddle. Wheeling Dan about, he spurred to the pike that led from Boonsborough to Sharpsburg and cantered west for a short distance before steering Dan up an embankment to the left. The ground there rose to a rounded crest upon which someone had constructed a makeshift observation post of fence rails stacked in the shape of an open-sided triangle. Within this post loitered General Fitz John Porter and several members of his staff. The troops of Porter's single division from the Fifth Corps occupied the fields down slope in front of them.

"General McClellan, sir, it is good to see you," said Porter.

"Thank you, general," replied McClellan, climbing down from the saddle. "I've come to use your vantage point and to ask your advice."

Porter gestured to the stack of rails. "You are, of course, welcome here, sir. How may I be of assistance?"

Stepping up to Porter, McClellan took his hand and drew him close. "You may give me the benefit of your company, Fitz, and help steady my nerves," he whispered. "It pains me to say this, but I am at my wit's end. Today is the battle of the war and the responsibility for it weighs heavily on me."

"I'm grateful you would come to me, sir," murmured Porter confidentially. Then he stepped back to offer McClellan a place behind the rails. "I am afraid our quarters aren't comfortable," he said, "but the view of the fighting is top-notch."

Striding to the makeshift wall, McClellan peered through Porter's spyglass, which rested on the top rail. Hooker's fight roared on unabated, with no visible indication of the outcome.

Porter, stepping to Little Mac's side, produced two cigars from his jacket. McClellan selected a stogie and puffed it alight to the flame of a match held up by a member of Porter's staff. The swirling smoke seemed to calm McClellan, and he exhaled a thick stream of it. Looking carefully, however, Porter noticed the general's hand quivering with nerves.

"Hooker's gotten himself into a hell of a fight," nodded Porter toward the rumbling field.

"That he has," agreed McClellan. "I expect to hear soon that he has called up Mansfield's corps. A message I received earlier from him said his command is heavily engaged."

"And Burnside, what of him?"

"I have sent orders for him to ready an attack as a diversion to keep Lee from shifting men to his left."

"An excellent strategy, sir," mumbled Porter, stooping for a moment to peer through the spyglass.

"See anything of note?" asked McClellan.

"No, sir. Not yet. The smoke there is thick."

Little Mac squinted up at the milky sky and undid the top buttons of his jacket. "It's grown mighty hot today. This morning seemed as if it might remain cool. Now, it feels like August. Do you have any water?"

Porter turned from the rail and ordered a man to retrieve the canteen from his saddle. Returning a minute later, the aide handed it to Porter, who directed him to McClellan. Little Mac took the canteen and tilted a stream into his mouth. Glistening droplets cascaded down the front of his jacket. "Ah, that does it. Thank you, general," he said.

Porter also took a swig and handed the container back to the man who had brought it up.

"Anything now, Fitz?" inquired McClellan in a low voice as he brushed water from his chest.

Porter peered once again through the glass while McClellan puffed on his cigar.

"Not yet, sir, I—wait, I see Rebels flying to the rear! I can't tell how many yet, but a few are running."

McClellan stepped forward. "The glass, Fitz, let me see!"

Porter handed over the scope, which McClellan promptly put to his eye. He held silent there for a moment, smoke billowing lightly from his lips. Then a wide grin formed on his face. "You're right, general! They are skedaddling!"

McClellan looked up from the glass, noting the murmur that went up among the assembled officers around them who also had scopes. They, too, had seen what he saw.

"I see them!" cried Porter. "Look again, sir, they are coming out of the corn!"

Again, McClellan held the scope to his eye. A long, glinting line of bayonets pushed through the southern end of the wood lot on Hooker's front while Rebel troops emerged in a mass from the cornfield bordering the woods. "Those are Secesh, General Porter! Our boys are coming out of the trees on their flanks. They are driving them!"

The Rebels in the distance scattered toward the large forest in their rear. At the same time, a heavy formation of Northern infantry emerged from the cornfield alongside the blue line that had first come out of the trees.

McClellan shot Porter a glance, his face aglow. "He's done it, general! Hooker has broken Lee's left flank. I must send to Burnside. Courier! I must have a courier!" Little Mac stalked from the rails to the waiting staff. "Where is a courier?" he asked.

"I'll go, sir," responded a small man with cherub cheeks and a short beard.

"Ah, Lieutenant Wilson, very good. Come here!" Waving John Moulder Wilson to him, McClellan placed a hand on the man's shoulder. "Lieutenant, ride to General Burnside on our left. Tell him he is to carry the bridge on his front at once and gain possession of the heights beyond. Is that clear?"

"It is, general."

"Excellent, then make haste!" cried McClellan, stabbing his cigar into the air. He turned to the remaining staff around him. "I need someone to go to General Richardson. Volunteers?"

"I'll go!" replied Captain Duane of the army's engineers.

"Good, Duane, good! Do you know where the Second Corps is camped?"

"I do, sir."

"Very good. Go there to General Richardson and tell him he is to take his command across Antietam Creek as rapidly as possible. He is to rejoin Sumner's corps for an attack on the Rebel left."

Duane saluted and sprinted to his horse. McClellan watched him go, puffing triumphantly on his cigar. The smoke billowed up around his head as he took hold of himself and returned to Porter's side. "I have him, Fitz! I have Lee in the palm of my hand. If Sumner can come up quickly and Burnside can take that bridge, the day is ours!"

"Congratulations, sir! You'll be a hero after this," grinned Porter.

A wistful expression formed on the general's face, and Porter eyed the general carefully. He thought to speak but held his tongue. A moment of reverie had clearly come over McClellan. His eyes glinted and the tension in his aspect fell away.

Turning from Porter to gaze west, the general's imagination flew with fantasies of redemption. He would make good on the victory he had thought won at South Mountain. Crowds in Washington would cheer him.

HIM!

George Brinton McClellan, the savior of the Republic! Back to the august halls of the War Department, his mind's eye soared. Esteemed colleagues would slap his back and shake his hand while that blackguard Edwin Stanton groveled for forgiveness. Away he flew to the loving arms of his wife and the approbation of his family in Philadelphia. Away, as far from the terrible field of battle as the wings of vainglorious hope could carry him.

29

Wednesday, September 17, 1862

8:00 to 9:00 a.m.

One Hundred and Twenty-Fifth Pennsylvania Volunteer Infantry Regiment

North of Sharpsburg, Maryland

of cut hair floated past Jacob Higgins's face. Lifting his hand to catch the tiny strands, he watched them drift into his palm. "Why, this is mine!" he muttered, realizing just how close a Rebel ball had come to his head. He had heard it whip past, but took no notice of it in the clamor of battle around him. Now, he shuddered to think how it had nearly killed him.

Shaking the hair from his hand, Higgins returned his attention to his men. The ranks of his green regiment, packs on their backs and musket-butts at rest on the ground, stood in three rows just ahead and to the left of him. To their left lay the Smoketown Road, down which they had guided earlier that morning. To their right, stood a small patch of corn occupied by part of the Federal battle line. Wounded men streamed back from the fighting there, some carried by their comrades, others crawling painfully across the dirt with bloodied heads, gunshot arms, and blasted legs.

The extent of the carnage left Higgins nervous, and yet the ranks of General Tyndale's First Brigade, a part of the Twelfth Corps, stood toe-to-toe with the wolfishly howling Rebels beyond their line. Tyndale's brigade, comprised of Buckeye and Keystone State regiments, answered the Rebel yell with a manly roar of their own. Ramrods rose and fell in the ranks as men loaded and fired their muskets.

The minutes slowed to a crawl as Higgins watched the furious contest, wondering how long it could go on. Nothing he had seen in the Mexican War compared to combat such as this. The muskets rattled at a higher pitch than the bellowing big guns nearby, creating a cacophony so loud that he could barely think. National and regimental flags hung above it all on the firing line, jerking this way and that as balls tore through their silk.

A much larger cornfield than the small one in front of Higgins lay some distance away at approximately his two o'clock. Batteries stacked on the low rise to the north of it blasted the Rebels in the corn with charges of canister. Fighting roared on the left, too, within an expanse of trees. That battle Higgins could hear, but not see. He knew from earlier events, however, that General Mansfield had fallen in those woods while scouting the front line, and that his own men had carried the injured general from the field.

A shell shrieked in from the right, blowing dirt onto Company A. In all the marching and counter-marching that morning, the regiment's normal order had become reversed. Company G now stood on the far left in the place typically occupied by Company A. Hands flew to caps as the men cowered beneath the falling debris.

Lieutenant Colonel Szink trotted his horse to Higgins, smudges of dirt on his face. "Sir, we need to get out from under this artillery fire!" he shouted.

"I know it, Szink, but we have no orders! This is where General Crawford wishes us to be."

Another Confederate shell whirred past, exploding in a burst of branches and pulverized leaves. The Pennsylvanians ducked, some muttering fearfully among themselves. A third projectile frightened Higgins's horse onto its hind legs. Again, he felt the icy hand of death reach for him and come up empty.

"Colonel Higgins, Lieutenant Johnston's been hit!"

Higgins's head snapped to the voice. A soldier at the end of the line pointed to the stricken form of Robert M. Johnston, the acting adjutant for the regiment. The colonel dropped from his saddle and hurried to Johnston's side. Johnston lay on his back with a sucking chest wound in his upper right breast. A comrade cradled Johnston's head in his lap and in the injured man's hands he clutched a worn pair of gauntlets.

"Lieutenant, are you badly hurt?" asked Higgins, kneeling in the dirt.

"Ach," Johnston choked, "not hurt too badly, sir. I can go on."

"Let me see your wound."

Higgins pulled apart the tunic and blouse to find a jagged gash. Blood bubbled from the wound with every breath Johnston took. A punctured lung. This much Higgins had learned while on service in Mexico. "Son, you'll need to go to the rear," he said.

Johnston struggled to rise. "Respectfully, colonel, I can go on. I'm not hurt too badly."

"You *are* hurt badly, lieutenant," Higgins barked. "Shock is keeping you from feeling the extent of your wound. You will go to the rear and receive medical treatment. That's an order!"

Johnston's expression darkened. "Pardon me, colonel, but I'm not going to see those butchers in the rear! They'll kill me just as surely as the Rebels."

A murmur went up from the men around them, and Higgins shot them a stern glance. "No, lieutenant, I'll not allow it," he said. "You are going to the rear now."

Johnston fell silent and held up the gloves in his hand. "Colonel," he said, "take these gauntlets. I found them on the field. They are a Rebel officer's and will make a good trophy." Higgins took the prize from Johnston and tucked them into his tunic. "I'll keep them safe for you."

Johnston spat blood, choking out, "I'll be seeing you, boys!" as a pair of men carried him to the rear.

Another shell soared in, showering dirt on the ranks.

"Blast this!" growled Higgins at their predicament. No one liked standing under fire. Veterans could take it for a time, but green men were likely to break at any minute. Even now, Higgins could feel the fear inside of them. Their eyes followed him everywhere, urging him to do something, to go somewhere; anywhere other than to remain on this terrible field for Rebel target practice!

Climbing back onto his horse, Higgins glared at his troops, willing the men to hold their line through the sheer force of his personality. They had marched and counter-marched under fire all morning and no one in command seemed to know where they should be. At one point, the entire One Hundred and Twenty Eighth Pennsylvania had even marched through their ranks en route to the right. Those men had then met an unfortunate fate within sight of Higgins's own boys. After entering the larger cornfield, they came tumbling back when a sequence of devastating volleys from veteran enemy troops shattered their line.

Here was the scenario that Higgins feared most, the one about which he had warned Szink in Frederick. Green troops fought poorly under most circumstances. In a stand-up slugging match against an experienced enemy, they stood no chance at all.

Higgins scanned the faces of his men and felt he must say something to strengthen them. "Come with me, Szink," he called out, wheeling his horse along the front of the line. "Boys! the moment of your baptism as soldiers is upon you!"

His mount stepped sideways and Higgins tightened the reins. "Remember what you learned in drill! Every one of you depends on the man beside him. Be firm! Do your duty and remember why we are here—for the love of our country and Constitution! Rebellion threatens both these precious things and only men of conviction such as yourselves can put a stop to it." Higgins pointed at the rumbling, smoking forest to their front. "The enemy in those trees believes his cause is just! He is willing to do his duty unto death. You must meet his courage with your own. Stand fast, remain brave, and victory will be yours!"

The men raised a cheer, waving their caps.

"That seems to have done the trick," nodded Szink.

"Let's hope so," said Higgins, distracted by a rider coming from the front. An officer he did not know reined in, his face slick with perspiration. "Colonel! My troops are falling back for want of ammunition. Will you advance your regiment to my support?"

Higgins tugged at his beard. "I don't have orders to advance, but I'll go to General Crawford immediately and ask."

"I'd be grateful! My men's lives depend upon it. Rebels are thicker than flies in those trees."

"Szink, wait here," commanded Higgins before spurring off to find Crawford. Searching the line to the rear, Higgins spotted the general atop his horse in the shade of a walnut tree, an aide by his side. Higgins urged his mount into a sprint and pulled up hard before Crawford, hooves throwing dust.

"Sir, the colonel commanding a regiment ahead of me has reported that his men need to fall back for want of ammunition. He asked if my regiment will advance to his support."

"By all means, Colonel Higgins!" replied Crawford. "General Hooker says those woods must be held at all hazards. If we lose them, the entire right flank of the army is imperiled. Go in, man! Go in!"

"Sir!" Higgins swung his horse back to his regiment. "Szink," he cried, "we're going in! Shake out Company G as skirmishers."

The lieutenant colonel snapped a salute and guided his horse to the front. "Captain McKeage! Send out your company as our skirmish line and advance immediately!"

The captain saluted, bawling for his men to fall out. The Pennsylvanians spread into a widely spaced line and moved ahead into the trees. Observing from behind the second rank, Higgins pulled out his saber and hollered, "regiment, shoulder arms!"

Nine-hundred bayonet-tipped Springfields shifted onto the right shoulders of the men and a thin captain stepped out from near the center of the line. Raising his saber above his head, he cried, "boys, remember our battle-cry! In God we trust!" over the din of gunfire.

The men chanted the cry, their voices growing louder as it echoed down the line. "*IN GOD WE TRUST!*"

Pride shivered down Higgins's spine. His greenhorns might fight after all, and so taking a deep breath he gave the order. "Regiment, forwarrrrrd march!"

Raising a shout, the sons of central Pennsylvania stepped off. Pushing first through a small field of corn, they shifted left to the edge of the wood lot. Troops from the withdrawing regiment ahead of them filtered back through their lines, calling, "go get 'em, boys!" as they passed.

The Keystone Staters plunged into the shadow of the trees, where the rattle of musket fire became muffled. Then the Federals still in the woods ahead of them loosed a volley. File closers trailing Higgins's men urged them to hold their line. Firing erupted on the right now, too, as combat convulsed along the front.

"Keep moving!" growled Higgins, his eyes scanning for signs of the enemy.

Onward the men strode through the trees, their formation shorn into tatters by obstacles in their path. Then the gunfire slackened ahead of them and cheers broke out. Higgins kept his line going until he could see light at the southern perimeter of the woods.

"You men stop and throw down your weapons!" cried the thin captain that had encouraged the regiment before entering the forest. Higgins turned his horse toward the man's voice, being as careful as he could to avoid trampling the wounded lying around him. Out from behind a tree strode three Southerners, their hands raised above their heads. A man from the One Twenty-Fifth trailed behind them, his bayonet leveled. Higgins scrutinized the prisoners. Clad in uniforms of homespun cloth, the Rebels wore trousers and jackets covered with patches. Two of the three men walked without shoes, their bare feet black with dirt.

"You men, stop!" he commanded. "What unit are you boys with?"

"The Twenty-First Georgia," drawled the oldest of the three.

"Georgia, you say?"

"Yassir, that's right. Gen'rl Colquitt's brigade.

"I see," nodded Higgins. "You boys are a long way from home. You probably haven't eaten in a while either, have you?"

"No, sir," replied a younger man with dark eyes. "We ain't had nare but green apples and roasting cawn for days on end."

"Is that so? Well, we can help you with that, I'm sure. Private, make sure these boys get something to eat when you get to the rear."

"Yes, sir," nodded the musket-wielding guard. "Alright, now, you boys walk on."

Higgins watched them until the prisoners disappeared among the trees. Then he steered his horse back toward the southern edge of the woods, where Lieutenant Colonel Szink walked his mount from the right.

"Szink, what happened here?" asked Higgins. "Where did the Rebels go?"

"Their line appears to have collapsed, colonel. If you look out of these trees, you can still see them running."

Higgins followed Szink's gesture, spotting the mob of broken Butternuts loping toward a large stand of woods in the distance. A dark blue line of Union troops pursued them amidst a maelstrom of artillery fire.

"Are those Tyndale's men?"

"I believe so, colonel, and Colonel Stainrook's men beyond them."

A battery of smoothbore guns came clattering loudly down the road to their left. The drivers lashed their teams into the field in front of Higgins and quickly loaded their pieces. Shells screamed in from Confederate batteries atop a limestone shelf several hundred yards to the south. A round of case shot soared past the Napoleons, exploding in the air above Higgins's gathering regiment. Men shrieked as the iron shards tore into their flesh.

"Everyone on the ground!" cried the colonel. Another round burst loudly in the trees, sending leaves and branches crashing down. Yanking out his field glasses, Higgins surveyed the field. Smoke drifted across his view from the smoldering ruins of a house on his left, but no organized Rebel unit stood between his men and the large forest that loomed in the distance. A small building sat at the edge of the trees, its whitewashed exterior pockmarked by shellfire. Shifting his glasses to the left, beyond the roaring guns of the battery just ahead of his regiment, Higgins spied the line of Rebel guns that had taken his men under fire. Tyndale's regiments were nearly upon them, and Higgins could see the artillerists scrambling to limber up. Within seconds, they had dragged the battery from the field, leaving a jumble of wrecked caissons, dead horses, and slain men.

Ordering his troops to their feet, Higgins called for his company commanders to realign their men; A on the left through G on the right. "Proper formation, now, boys, hop to it!"

The captains shouted and cussed their companies into position. Then Higgins called them to attention. "Close up and dress on the colors!" The ranks tightened, their muskets at right shoulder rest. The sight of them moving properly swelled Higgins's chest with pride.

A lieutenant rode up from the rear. "Colonel, sir, General Crawford sent me with orders for you to push on. You are to take your regiment into that wood lot ahead of us."

Higgins scanned the open field. "My men will be terribly exposed there, lieutenant. Has the general promised us any support?"

"He hasn't, sir, but General Sedgwick's division is coming up now and will be here soon. The general desires that you support General Greene's men over there." The lieutenant pointed to a Federal line under fire to their south.

"Ah, well, tell the general we will advance directly," Higgins sighed.

"Very good, sir," saluted the man, spurring his horse back through the trees.

Tightening his reins, Higgins steered his mount to the front of his line. "Colonel Szink, sound the advance!"

Szink bellowed the order and his bugler blasted the notes. The regiment's front rank stepped off, unevenly at first, but with growing precision as they moved. Passing through the guns in front of them, which had by now fallen silent, the men maneuvered toward the road on their left. Onward through the clover they marched, stepping over the dead and wounded as shells hissed overhead and miniés pattered in the dirt.

The road embankment on the left shielded the regiment from direct enemy fire in that direction and Higgins made for it until a battery of smoothbore cannons rumbled past. The guns pulled off the road up ahead and onto the limestone shelf previously occupied by the enemy. The two guns on the left pointed their muzzles southeast toward an unseen foe. Higgins watched the Napoleons buck rearward with each fiery round they shot, only to be rolled back into place and re-loaded. The other four guns unlimbered to this section's right and began pouring a rapid fire at the woods.

Onward strode his brave men.

BOOM!

A case shot detonated above the right flank of the line, sending iron fragments showering groundward. A man in the rear cried out, his hands grasping at his face and musket dropping to the ground. Pitching back, he fell writhing in the clover, blood streaming through his fingers.

One hundred yards from the bucking guns.

Miniés flew thicker now, zipping like angry wasps past Higgins and his men. The colonel shot a glance to the left-rear where Szink walked his horse. The lieutenant colonel nodded back at him, his face trying to mask the fear that Higgins saw in his eyes.

"Ahhh!" screamed another one of the men, pitching face-first to the ground.

An orderly appeared from the rear. "Colonel, General Williams orders you to support that battery on your front!" he cried. Higgins nodded he understood and went on. "Steady, boys! Steady now!" he called out.

Fifty yards from the guns and the small white building.

Was it a schoolhouse? A church? Higgins could not tell. Company A began to drift leftward, opening a gap in the line. "Dress on the colors! Captains, do not lose your line!" bellowed Higgins. Captain Bell steered his men back into place with a few decidedly un-Christian words.

Twenty yards from the roaring battery, which was now enveloped in smoke and under heavy enemy fire.

Higgins called for his men to halt. Riding to the left, he trotted to high ground beside the last gun. Musketry spattered below him where General Greene's men exchanged fire with Rebels assembling in a farm lane. Peering to the right, Higgins spied Rebel artillery on a far rise and formations of Grayback troops gathering in the swale between the ridge and the southern extremity of the forest. Shells and canister from the battery beside him sent the Butternuts scurrying for cover. A Rebel shell shrieked past Higgins as he steered back to his command.

"Szink, order the men to lie down!" he cried. "The fire here is too hot to stand out in the open."

"Right away, sir!" Spinning his horse, Szink rode along the line, calling out, "on the ground, boys! Lie down!" The men needed no further encouragement. Dropping quickly into the partially plowed field, musket fire peppered them from the woods ahead.

Szink rode back to Higgins, the alarm obvious on his sweat-slick face. "Colonel, we need to dismount!" he shouted as a case shot burst above them. A second shell sailed in, blasting dirt and rocks skyward.

"You're right, Szink! Get down, now!"

Szink threw a leg over his saddle and still had his foot in the stirrup when another projectile hissed in. Snapping the leather strap before it burst in a thunderclap, the explosion threw Szink hard to the ground and terrified his horse, which promptly sprinted away. Higgins's mount reared at the same time, knocking the colonel from his feet.

Szink lay motionless as Higgins reached for his hat. His vision blurred. He shook his head to clear it. Behind him, the orderly who had brought the command from General Williams struggled to disengage himself from the reins of his horse. He had dismounted just before a solid shot blew through his horse in a fountain of blood, bones, and ropy entrails.

As his vision cleared Higgins saw Szink lying still several yards away. "Colonel Szink!" shouted Higgins as he scrambled on his hands and knees to the man's side and cradled Szink's head. There was not a mark on him. When Higgins changed position, his hand came away drenched with blood. He slapped Szink's cheek, but could not rouse him. Higgins yelled for help and ordered several men to carry the stricken officer from the field. He climbed to his feet and propped his cap on his head. He was straightening his saber and sash when General Hooker rode up from the rear.

Higgins stared at Hooker in disbelief. Balls hissed through the air all around them and yet there sat the general upright in the saddle. "Sir, you should dismount at once! The fire is too heavy here!" he cried.

"Sound advice, colonel," replied Hooker, swinging down to the ground. "Are any of our troops in those woods?" he asked, pointing to the forest on their front.

"None but Rebels, sir. My command is in front of our line."

"That it is," replied Hooker. "I—"

The general's horse let out a piercing scream. "Sir, your mount has been shot!" yelled Higgins.

"So, I see, colonel," replied Hooker as if in a daze. "Please, excuse me." Striding away, Hooker left Higgins gawping at him in disbelief. The colonel turned back to his men and sank to one knee. "We must get away from this place," he muttered, focusing his gaze on the woods some fifty yards to their front. Cover could be found there, but puffs of smoke betrayed Rebels lurking among the trees.

Higgins peered back the way they had come. A brigade was deploying at the southern edge of the trees. It might be his salvation if only his men, desperate for relief and more of them dying by the second, could just hold on.

30

Wednesday, September 17, 1862
8:30 to 10:30 a.m.
Ninth Corps, Left Flank of the Army of the Potomac
Rohrbach Bridge, south of Sharpsburg, Maryland

Burnside put the field glasses to his eyes. Sitting atop his dappled gray on the crest of a knoll, he peered at the countryside east of Antietam Creek. Beside him on the right thundered the Parrott rifles of Lieutenant Benjamin's battery, adding their clamor to the artillery fire echoing across the valley from the north. Other guns to Burnside's left roared as well, returning the fire of Rebel artillery on the heights east of Sharpsburg. Burnside paid little attention to the guns. An aide from General McClellan had arrived soon after eight o'clock with orders to prepare an attack on the triple-arched bridge in front of the Ninth Corps. Now the general scrutinized the approaches to the bridge, seeking one that would bring his men as close to it as possible before they exposed themselves to the murderous fire of enemy riflemen perched high on the heights above.

Burnside frowned at what he saw. The field of grass before him sloped downward to a double line of snake-rail fences bordering a farm lane that ran through a wooded hollow. On the left of the stubbled field stood acres of mature corn, their tassels gold in the morning sun. Still farther to the left flowed Antietam Creek, its dark green current rolling sluggishly southward. The approaches to the bridge offered no cover past the wooded hollow.

A plowed field in front of the bridge led up to a grassy hillside with an orchard on its right-rear. Beyond that lay nothing but a broken line of trees running parallel to the creek some seventy yards away from the eastern bank. A dirt road also ran alongside the creek, its left shoulder partially faced by a tall post and rail fence that might offer attacking troops some protection. Getting men there safely would be the trick and Burnside seriously doubted they could do it.

Shifting his glasses to the left, the general scrutinized the one-hundred-foot-high ridge on the opposite side of the creek that dominated every approach. Hundreds of Grayback gunmen huddled there in makeshift field works, waiting to rain hell upon any Federal who dared to show himself. He could see the Rebels clearly, their musket barrels glinting in the sunlight and crimson battle flags poised above their heads.

Hoofbeats stirred Burnside from his thoughts, and he brought down the binoculars to find Jacob Cox at his side. "Good morning, general," he greeted the Ninth Corps' new commander. "It will be hot today, I think."

Cox nodded a greeting and peered up at the milky blue sky. "I reckon you're right, sir. I've ordered the men to fill their canteens before we step off."

"That's good, Cox. How are the men faring this morning?" asked Old Burn.

"As well as can be expected, I guess. We've had some casualties already from Rebel artillery fire. Colonel Fairchild reports thirty-six men hit in his brigade alone."

"So many?"

"Unfortunately, sir, yes. The placement of my command in the dark last night failed to consider exposure to enemy cannon fire. When the Johnnies opened on us at first light, they had clear lines of sight to our boys. It took me the better part of an hour to get them under cover."

"That is unfortunate, General Cox, but there is nothing we could have done about it. I never received new orders from General McClellan to reposition your men, even though he told me to expect them. How are the preparations coming for our attack?"

"Sir, I've directed General Rodman to scout the ford on his front to determine its usability." Cox pointed past Burnside's nine o'clock at a hard westerly bend in Antietam Creek.

"Rodman informs me that the water looks awfully deep. I've told him to investigate it anyway and keep me informed. As for General Sturgis's division, over in that direction—" Cox shifted his hand to three o'clock, past Benjamin's battery, on the right. "I've ordered him to scout approaches to the creek so he can move up quickly. Crook's brigade lies ahead of us over the slope of that hill, while the rest of the Kanawha Division, and the division of General Willcox, is to our rear. All we are waiting on now are your orders."

"Excellent, general," nodded Burnside. "I am pleased to see your command well handled. I have delayed giving you orders, because I am seeking the best route for attacking the enemy's position. To that end, look there, Cox." Burnside pointed his binoculars at the fortified ridge beyond Antietam Creek. "That is the strongest defensive position I have ever laid eyes on. The Rebels have dug in along the entire length of it, as far as I can see. Our losses will be heavy taking the bridge."

"Yes, sir, I can see that. What are you thinking?"

"My inclination is to have Rodman use the ford on our left—if it proves practicable—to turn the enemy out of his works. A frontal assault on the bridge itself would be suicide."

"I understand, general, but wouldn't a frontal attack in mass yield the fastest results?"

Burnside scowled at the open area leading up to the bridge to which Cox had gestured. "It might, general, but look at how exposed the ground is there. Our men will suffer greatly and with no guarantee of success."

"Respectfully, sir, this is war. I've made a study of it, and from what I can tell, there is never a guarantee of success."

Burnside sighed at the truth in this and fell silent. Meanwhile, the heavy fighting they heard to the north made its way closer.

"Whatever you choose, general, I propose we do it quickly," Cox offered. "From the looks of it the rest of the army is heavily engaged. General McClellan expects us to attack on this flank."

"I understand that, Cox! I would simply like to avoid a needless expenditure of blood, if it is at all possible. Send to General Rodman again and ask what his reconnaissance of the ford has yielded. Ask him if he thinks he can force his way across."

"As you wish, sir. I'll send a courier to him forthwith."

At that moment, a rider came up from the right. Proffering a salute, the man handed Burnside a note from General McClellan. Taking the note, Burnside read its contents:

General Franklin's command is within one mile and a half of here. General McClellan desires you to open your attack. As soon as you shall have uncovered the upper stone bridge, you will be supported, and, if necessary, on your own line of attack. So far, all is going well.

"General McClellan wishes us to open our attack," said Burnside, looking up. "There will be no additional time for General Rodman to reconnoiter the ford. Order him to cross the creek where he is, and proceed directly north along the ridge line. I will ride to Colonel Kingsbury of the Eleventh Connecticut—I know him from prior service, he is a good man—and have his regiment act as skirmishers for General Crook while you detail Crook to make the assault with his brigade. Kingsbury will advance to the bridge and hold position until Crook's men can move up and get across. Is that understood?"

"Perfectly, sir," saluted Cox. Cinching his reins, the Buckeye general rode off, leaving Burnside on the knoll with a handful of staff. The Rhode Islander shouted orders that the batteries firing at distant targets should concentrate on suppressing Rebel artillery supporting the defenders of the bridge. Then he looked down at his watch to find the hands at nine thirty-five.

*   *   *

Half an hour later, Burnside looked on as his batteries pummeled the enemy positions above the creek. Clouds of dust enveloped the heights, obscuring them from view, yet the cannon fire continued, sending dirt, rocks, and even small trees spouting skyward in blasts of fire-laced smoke.

Meanwhile, on the open ground approaching the bridge, the Eleventh Regiment of Connecticut Volunteers struggled to advance. Upon entering the field of tall corn at the base of the hill where Burnside stood, the Nutmeggers came under a withering fire from sharpshooters, howling their unnerving yell. The Ninth Corps' artillery had suppressed some, but clearly not enough, of the enemy's fire.

Men dropped in the corn, muskets flying from their hands. Kingsbury's boys went on regardless, stacking up at a tall rail fence blocking their path. Dozens of men scaled the fence while their comrades sought to tear it apart. The exposed Nutmeggers made excellent targets, and the Rebels gunned them down as quickly as they were able. Men fell, but their comrades went forward into the plowed field and formed into two battle lines positioned end to end.

The line on the left stepped off first, surging toward the bridge in a hail of gunfire. Rebel musketry rose in volume with every step the Nutmeggers took. Then shells began dropping in from long range Rebel guns. Columns of dirt and smoke erupted in and around the screaming men, yet they kept moving toward their objective.

"Go on, boys! You can do it!" Burnside found himself crying, his voice joined by those of the cheering staff and orderlies around him.

The line on the left reached the creek side, the desperate men there taking shelter behind the rail fence. From that position, they returned the enemy's fire, but every passing second brought death raining down from the heights above. An officer leaped up to charge the creek and Burnside held his breath. Plunging into the water, the courageous, saber-waving man sank to his chest, beginning a long, laborious trek to the other side.

Miniés struck the water around him. The few men who had followed fell along the bank, their bullet-riddled bodies splashing into the creek. More made the attempt, but they floundered in the water and miniés cut them down as well. One man's hands went to his throat, his musket sinking into the depths. Then his grip relaxed, and he floated listlessly downstream amidst a spreading crimson stain.

Fortune appeared to smile on the officer in the lead and he slogged ahead, every achingly slow step carrying him closer to the opposite bank. Then he staggered as a ball struck him in the breast. Still, he kept going until he reached the far bank and collapsed in the grass. Behind him, the bodies of those who had tried to follow drifted silently with the current.

Disgusted by the awful sight of these things, Burnside shifted his glasses in search of Kingsbury. Through the smoke, he caught sight of the man along the rail fence lining the road. Relief swept over him that the colonel still lived, but at that moment Kingsbury dropped to one knee, grasping at his foot. The saber fell from his hand, and he toppled over, now reaching for his leg. Two men ran to aid him, and taking the colonel under the arms, they dragged him toward the rear.

Peering still farther north, Burnside focused on the Eleventh's second line. This portion of men had halted in the field beyond the bridge. A volley ripped out from their muskets with no visible effect on the enemy, who cut down the New Englanders with a withering return fire. A pair of guns arrived on the hill above them, opening a brisk fire of their own. All to no avail. Burnside watched through his field glasses as his men dropped in the grass. The Eleventh's line thinned, but held its ground. Then, suddenly, a handful of companies emerged from the tree line, driving toward the creek.

Pulling down his glasses, Burnside yelled, "whose men are those?" over the roar of the guns.

"I think they are General Crook's, sir!" cried General Parke. "His command ought to be moving up now." Parke took a longer look through his field glasses. "It is Crook's men!" he shouted. "I see the blue regimental flag of the Eleventh Ohio."

Burnside followed Parke's outstretched finger to see a firing line behind Kingsbury's men blasting away at the enemy. Moving his glasses to the left, he watched the small formation of men that had appeared on Kingsbury's right push ahead. Concentrated musket fire stopped them dead in their tracks, however, and they fell back in disarray. The remaining men of the Eleventh Connecticut now gave way as well, realizing that to hold their position without support meant certain death. The big guns on the heights continued blasting away, but the musketry fell silent as the Northerners withdrew, leaving a misty powder smoke settling in the hollows.

A howling cheer went up from the Rebel line, sending Burnside into despair. Lowering his glasses, he stared at the grim slaughter, his stomach souring. His face grew red, and he began to pace. "What in God's name happened there?" he asked Parke, his finger pointing rigidly at the field of dead and wounded men.

"I—I do not know, sir," stammered the chief of staff. "General Crook was supposed to support Colonel Kingsbury's attack with his whole brigade, not two guns and a regiment."

"It's flat incompetence, that's what it is!" growled Burnside, pacing angrily. "Good men's lives have been wasted, and all for nothing. I can only hope my friend Kingsbury is not too badly hurt." Stopping in the grass, Burnside turned to Parke. "Send word to General Cox," he demanded. "Tell him to initiate General Sturgis's attack."

"Yes, sir, right away," saluted Parke before moving away.

Burnside irately resumed his pacing until the sound of beating hooves drew his attention. Looking up, he saw a bulky officer with a sharply pointed salt and pepper beard rein in. "Good morning, General Burnside," saluted the man. "General McClellan has sent me. He directs that you move your troops across the bridge or stream in your front at once, and then push forward vigorously, without a moment's delay, to secure the heights beyond."

"That is easier said than done, colonel—?"

"Sackett, sir, Delos Sackett."

"Colonel Sackett. Do you see those men down there?" Burnside pointed at the corpse-littered field below them. "They have just died trying to accomplish precisely what the commanding general ordered you to come here and say. McClellan seems to think I am not trying my best to carry this bridge. You are, in fact, the second man, sir, who has been to me this morning with similar orders!"

Sackett's cheeks flushed red. "I am sorry, general," he pleaded. "The commanding general is exceedingly anxious that you get your command across the creek at once. He believes it is of vital importance to our success."

Burnside turned toward the grim field. "So do I, colonel. You have fulfilled your orders. Now, you may go."

Sackett climbed down from his horse. "I'm afraid I cannot, sir. General McClellan ordered me to stay here with you until the bridge has been carried."

His own cheeks flushing crimson, Burnside wheeled on Sackett in a rage. "What! Am to be kept under observation like … like an errant child?"

"I'm sorry, sir, but those are my orders. There is nothing I can do about it."

"No, colonel, indeed, there is not," Burnside sputtered. "Remain here if you must, but stay out of my way. I'll not have you interfering with my operations."

"As you wish, sir. I shall remain … inconspicuous."

Burnside turned as a rider came up from the southern part of the field. "Message from General Rodman, sir!" said the man, drawing out a note.

Taking the paper, Burnside read it with a sigh.

"Is something wrong, general?" asked Colonel Getty, the Ninth Corps' artillery chief.

Burnside waved the paper in his hand. "From General Rodman. The ford across the creek assigned to him yesterday by McClellan's aide is too deep to use under fire. Secesh has the crossing well protected by infantry and the water is chest-high. His men would be shot down before they ever made it to the other side."

"Does the general have an alternate plan, sir?" inquired Getty.

"He does, but it will take time—and that is something General McClellan says we do not have."

Burnside fell silent for a few moments before shooting an acid glance at the hapless Colonel Sackett. "General Rodman says a local farmer has offered to show him a better ford downstream at a place called Snavely's farm. We must continue the attack on the bridge here until Rodman can get around the enemy's works."

"General Sturgis can do it, sir, I'm sure of it," insisted Getty in an effort to encourage his chief.

"Let's hope so, colonel. I've tried to limit our losses and still accomplish our objective in so far as I've thought practical."

"Yes, general."

"Many good men will lose their lives in the attempt and when they do, it will be through no fault of my own," announced Burnside. "May God almighty have mercy on General McClellan's soul."

31

Wednesday, September 17, 1862
9:00 to 10:00 a.m.
One Hundred and Twenty-Fifth Pennsylvania Volunteer Infantry Regiment
West Woods, north of Sharpsburg, Maryland

Higgins rose to his feet amidst the clattering of musket fire on his left. The bucking guns of Captain Monroe's battery had by now driven off the enemy guns targeting Higgins's regiment, but ahead of them Higgins could see shadows flitting among the trees. He took a quick count of them, coming rapidly to the conclusion that they were men detached from their regiments and not full-sized Rebel units.

Whinnying loudly, his horse pulled at its reins. "Shh, shhh!" murmured the colonel in his animal's ear. The irony of him trying to calm his horse's jangled nerves struck Higgins, for in truth he felt just as edgy. His regiment occupied a perilous position. No friendly infantry stood within several hundred yards in any direction. The One-Hundred Twenty-Fifth, its ranks utterly green, lay alone on the field, except for Captain Monroe's battery.

Between him and the one friendly regiment on the right that he could see loomed the dark green wall of the western woods. Who knew how many Rebels lurked there just out of sight. The best he could do was hang on and wait for reinforcements. These appeared to be coming up, too, as behind him Higgins spied heavy formations of blue-clad troops. One line marched due west from the woods his men had passed through earlier that morning. Behind them trudged two additional lines of battle in brigade strength, their banners bobbing in the sun.

Sweat trickled past Higgins's already soaked collar. Looking over his boys lying on the ground, he saw apprehensive faces peering back at him. They waited for him to bawl out their next orders. Would those instructions take them back to safety or push them into the terrifying unknown? Even Higgins himself did not know at that moment.

The beating of hooves caught the bewildered colonel's attention, and he looked over his left shoulder to see a brigadier he did not know riding up from the rear.

"General?" saluted Higgins as the man reined in.

"Colonel, your regiment must advance," said the newcomer.

Higgins's brow furrowed. "Advance, sir? To where?"

The general pointed straight ahead of them. "Into those woods, colonel, and once you are there, you are to stay and hold them."

Incredulous, Higgins gawped open-mouthed at the trees and then back at the insistent officer. "Sir, my regiment is alone here," he replied. "Will we have any support?"

"You shall soon enough. You see those men approaching in the distance?"

"I do."

"Very well, then. They will follow you as they come up."

"Alright, sir, I understand," replied Higgins with visible relief. "We will advance immediately."

Wheeling his horse to the rear, the brigadier rode off as Higgins cried out the order.

"To your feet!"

The men rose and formed into tightly packed lines while Higgins climbed back atop his horse. He drew out his saber and called for his bugler to sound the advance. "Alright, men! We're going forward!" he bellowed. The bugle blared out as the Pennsylvanians stepped off under their flags.

Shots popped out from the trees, and a man in the first line pitched onto his face. His comrades in the second line stepped over him and kept moving, the ranks shifting to close the hole his loss had created. Rebel artillery on a distant ridge noted the advance, too, and took the Keystone Staters under fire. Loud flashes above the line sent hot shards into the men, evoking cries of agony as the metal struck home. Dread rose in Higgins's heart and a profuse sweat broke out on his brow. He scrutinized his men, looking for them to falter, but they remained stalwart and continued moving forward in good order.

Forty paces to the forest and the small white building on their front-left.

A soldier on the right of the line suddenly broke out in Scripture, his voice ringing clearly over the field. "The Lord Jehovah is my shepherd and I shall not want!" Comrades around him quickly took up the psalm, their voices rising into a powerful chorus. "He maketh me to lie down in green pastures. He leadeth me beside still waters. He restoreth my soul. He guideth me in the paths of righteousness for His name's sake."

Thirty paces to the trees, past wrecked caissons and Rebel artillerists lying dead in the grass. The empty hands of one man grasped toward heaven, but Higgins's men, still in prayer, stepped over him and kept going.

"Yea, though I walk through the valley of the shadow of death, I will fear no evil, for Thou art with me. Thy rod and thy staff, they comfort me!"

Twenty paces.

Two more men fell at the front, gunned down by unseen marksmen. Then the few remaining Secesh ahead of them melted back into the woods. The prayer went on, growing in volume as men cried out to God.

"Thou preparest a table before me in the presence of mine enemies! Thou hast anointed my head with oil! My cup runneth over! Surely goodness and loving kindness shall follow me all the days of my life and I shall dwell in the house of the Lord forever!"

"Regiment, halt!" bawled Higgins as the ranks fell silent. "Tear down that fence!" Squads from the front rank ran out to pull apart the rails that lined the Hagerstown Road.

"Colonel, we've found a Rebel officer!" shouted a company captain. Higgins steered his horse around the ranks and dismounted. The stricken lieutenant colonel lay propped on one elbow with several Pennsylvanians huddled around him. Kneeling by the man's side, Higgins asked his name.

"Newton. Colonel—ah!" he gasped. "Colonel James Newton, Sixth Georgia Volunteers. Sir, do you have any laudanum … or chloroform, perhaps?"

Higgins shook his head. "I'm afraid not. We're too far from our lines for any of that."

Newton winced in agony, his eyes tearing up. "Oh, I am shot through!" he sobbed. "Oh, my God, I must die." Then he sank down onto his belly and breathed his last in a long, soft hiss. Higgins shook his head as some men around him crossed themselves. One, however, turned his face and spat. "I'll not trouble myself over a damned dead Johnny, 'specially when they're shooting at us!"

Rising slowly to his feet, Higgins glared at the man. "Captain McKeage, to me, if you please!" McKeage rushed up, snapping a salute. "Captain, your company will form a skirmish line and push into the woods. Get to it!"

"Yes, sir! Company G, fall out for skirmish duty and look smart about it!" The men stepped out ahead of the regiment, dispersing into a widely separated line, before melting into the trees. Higgins called for Captain Ulysses Huyett, the commander of Company B to approach. "Captain, take your company and reconnoiter that place," he said, pointing at the whitewashed building some twenty yards from where they stood. "Make sure there aren't any Rebels hiding in or around it that can take us in the flank. Report to me what you find."

"Yes, colonel!" saluted Huyett, turning to call for his men.

Higgins faced the rest of his command. "You remaining companies close up and prepare to advance!" The men shifted about, filling in the hole where Company B had once stood. A minute later, Higgins called for them to move, and the ranks lurched toward the shadowy woods.

The colonel followed them on foot over slightly rising ground. Among the trees, the roar of battle off to the left became muted, and the men fell silent. Their anxious faces looked this way and that as they stepped over the corpses scattered about. Twigs cracked and dry leaves crunched underfoot. Men cursed at the uneven footing, their weapons and uniforms becoming tangled in low branches. The color bearer hauled down the flag to keep it from becoming snagged.

Sniffing the musty scent of timber, Higgins searched for McKeage's skirmish line. It lay some yards ahead of the main force where McKeage had halted it to wait. The captain peered back at them through the trees before ordering his men to resume their advance. Disappearing among the trunks, they proceeded down slope into a shallow ravine on the right. The main line, meanwhile, attained a plateau some seventy yards northwest of the small white building, which now lay on their left rear. Here, the colonel called for them to halt.

"Company captains, report what is on your front!" he bellowed before ordering a man near him to "go to the right and find out what's on our flank." Nodding, the corporal stalked off through the trees.

Shots popped out, prompting nervous glances in every direction. The men tightened the grip on their Springfields and Higgins waited quietly, listening for something to indicate where the enemy might be. The rattle of musketry intensified. His skirmishers must be engaged. Then the scout Higgins had sent came back.

"Colonel, there's nothing on our right," he said, almost in a whisper.

"No Rebels?"

The man shook his head. "No, sir, no Rebels, but none of our boys, either. There's no one at all over there."

"Colonel, we're in a dangerous position here," growled an aide.

"We are, indeed, lieutenant. What has Captain McKeage reported?"

"Nothing yet, sir."

"We'll give him more time, but pass the order to load. I want our boys ready if the Secesh come."

"Right away, colonel."

The lieutenant strode off to give the orders while Higgins waited. After a few minutes, a man ran up from the front. Higgins waved him over just as the lieutenant returned, too.

"Sir, Captain McKeage sent me," he said. "The captain reports his command has reached the western edge of the trees. A field is there, and Rebel troops are gathering in it. They've taken McKeage's men under fire."

"I see," nodded Higgins. "Are any friendly troops on our right?"

"I can't say for sure, sir, but I haven't seen any," replied the man with a shake of his head.

"Alright, lieutenant, we had better send back to General Crawford." Higgins turned to a young man on his left. "Take my horse—it's the only one we have—and ride to him. Tell him our situation here and ask him to send us support immediately. We're in advance of the entire corps and shall be flanked if we don't receive help."

"As you wish, sir."

"Good, and Joseph, for God's sake, be careful," said Higgins, pulling the man close. "Mother's heart would break if she were to lose one of us."

"I'll do my best, Jacob, er, colonel!" nodded the lieutenant to his older brother.

"Godspeed to you, then," said Higgins, handing over the reins of his horse. Joseph Higgins climbed into the saddle, and touching the brim of his cap, he steered off through the trees just as a torrent of gunfire opened on the right. A breathless man came pelting back through the trees. "It's the Johnnies!" he cried. "They're coming, and in number, too."

Higgins grabbed the man beside him. "Corporal, go ahead to Captain McKeage and tell him to withdraw his company. Hurry!"

The corporal ran off as Higgins sent a second messenger to recall Company B. Then he stalked down the line with his saber drawn. "Close up that hole there, boys!" he called, pointing out a ragged place in the formation. "All you men stand firm! Remember your drill and follow your company commanders. When you hear the order to fire, do so as one and reload. We'll come through this alright as long as we work as a unit."

Company G streamed back at a run, with Captain McKeage passing quickly through the line. "Colonel, a heavy line of Johnnies is behind us," he panted as he came up. "They're coming up the ravine on the right."

"I understand, captain," nodded Higgins before peering in the direction McKeage had come. "Put your company on the right of our line and hang on for my orders. We're going to meet them here."

McKeage scurried off to rejoin his command as Captain Huyett approached with Company B.

"Huyett, you look rattled. How are things on the left?"

The captain shook his head. "Sir, the small building you sent us to is a wilderness church. I thought it was a schoolhouse, but it turned out not to be. The place is crowded with Reb wounded. Many are hurt quite badly. It's a pitiful sight."

"And the enemy line, captain, did you see it?"

"Yes, colonel. There are at least two regiments coming at us from beyond the church."

"Two? My God, man, we must refuse our left flank!"

"I agree, sir. That would be wise."

"Alright, Huyett, position your company on our left with your line facing due south. Tell Captain Bell of Company A to face his men that direction as well and link up with your company. If you see any Secesh coming, you let them have it, understood?"

Huyett hurried off with a nod, leaving Higgins by himself. Amidst the rumbling cannon fire on his left, the colonel strode rightward down his line, shoving men closer together and closing holes.

Then a cry went up.

"They're coming!"

"I don't see them. Where the devil are they?" demanded Higgins, craning his neck to see through the trees. Soon, he spotted a dark mass pushing through the forest.

"Steady, boys, and prime your weapons!" he cried. "Sergeant Simpson, unfurl those colors!"

Simpson released his grip on the regiment's flag, allowing it to fold outward. Onward the Johnnies pressed, a raucous howl spilling from their line. Seventy-five paces away, then sixty.

"Regiment, prepare to fire!" Higgins bawled, hoping his men would remember their drill.

Hundreds of Springfield muskets lowered at the approaching enemy.

"AIM!"

Hammers clicked back.

"FIRE!"

A sheet of flame lashed out from the Pennsylvanians, blowing chunks of bark into the air. Southerners struck by the balls shrieked and yelled, their bodies crumpling to the ground.

"LOAD! LOAD!" roared Higgins as the Butternuts lowered their muskets and pulled their triggers.

The wave of lead crashed into Higgins's men, dropping his boys into the leaves. A fellow on the left flew backward, his musket crashing to the forest floor. The Keystone Staters answered the Rebel yips with a cheer and leveled their muskets for another round. Again, Higgins bellowed the order and flame-laced smoke exploded from the line, filling the forest with the tang of burnt gunpowder.

"Load and fire at will!" shouted the colonel now, stalking behind his line to the left.

"Here's your *Baltimore Clipper*, you bastards!" cried a man near him as he aimed his musket and pulled the trigger. Higgins grinned at the name of a newspaper being used as a pun. Then he heard a volley roar out on the left. Hurrying around a tree, he found Company B engaged with a second howling wave of enemy troops.

Musketry roared along the entire line now, drowning out the thoughts in Higgins's head. Rammers rose and fell as smoke fouled the air. A devout man, one of the regiment's many true believers, screamed hysterically for God's help, his sanity shattered by terror. Wounded men stumbled back from the line, a few collapsing motionless onto the ground. Higgins returned to the middle of his position to find his flag in the hands of a new bearer. Two bodies lay at the man's feet, one staring lifelessly back at Higgins, a crimson hole in his forehead.

"Uh!" grunted a soldier to Higgins's left, a gout of blood bursting from his mouth. Staggering back a step, the youth half turned before dropping onto his knees. Then the color-bearer went down in a heap, his blood spraying onto Higgins's uniform as a ball passed out of his back. Higgins's hand went to his cheek, smearing the red droplets. A fourth man with a crazed look on his face took up the flag and poured a torrent of profanity as he waved it back and forth.

"Kill my friends, will you? God damn all you Rebel sons-a-bitches to hell!

"Boy, I tell you, you're going straight to the devil just for saying that!" shouted a man on his left.

A ball whizzed past Higgins's ear, striking the tree behind him. Bark blown from the trunk peppered his uniform. Stepping back from the line, the colonel looked to the right and then to the left, trying to determine the state of his command. A hand clasped his shoulder, and he turned to find a handsome, mustached face peering at him.

"Colonel! I'm General Gorman," shouted the brigadier. "My brigade is some distance back, but I have a regiment coming up on your left. Can you hold this position?"

"I don't know, sir! The enemy's strength is growing."

Nodding, the general leaned in close. "Do what you can, colonel. We'll be here soon!" Higgins saluted as Gorman went back.

Captain Huyett ran up, his face streaked black with powder and eyes wide with fear. "Colonel, the enemy is past my left flank. We can't stop them!"

"Blast!" cried Higgins. "Show me!"

They hurried to the left side of the line where a yipping horde of Butternuts poured a deadly stream of lead into Huyett's boys. Peering through the smoke, Higgins spied a line of Rebels swinging toward their left rear. Behind them advanced an even heavier enemy formation. Turning to his right, Higgins rushed to the elbow of his command, where the right side of Company A met the left end of Company C. Dark masses of Rebels shifted in the trees ahead, their fearsome yell growing into a deafening clamor.

"We can't hold against this!" muttered Higgins in alarm and turning to his men, he bellowed "RETREAT!" at the top of his lungs.

Not a man moved. Not even a head turned in Higgins's direction.

"What the devil? I said RETREAT!"

Again, the Keystone Staters failed to hear him. Higgins grabbed an officer on the line and pulled him by the collar. "Lieutenant, what are you doing with a rifle in your hands?"

"Sir, the boys need help!"

"Damn it, man, look around you! We must withdraw or we'll all be killed! Run down the line and direct the men to fall back. NOW!"

Higgins shoved the man to his right. He took two steps before a Rebel ball struck him in the side, tumbling him into a tree.

"Blast!"

Higgins set off down the line himself to grab men by the collar and scream "retreat!" into their faces.

The Butternuts pressed in close now, their three deep ranks only twenty paces away.

"Come on yanks! Give it up!" called one of the Johnnies.

"Yeah, you boys surrender!" added another.

Down the line Higgins strode, bawling, "run! Save yourselves! Retreat!" as he shoved men to the rear. Their filthy faces gawped at him uncomprehendingly.

"Run, blast you! RUN!" he roared.

At last, his regiment gave way before the Rebel avalanche, its fleeing men nearly jostling Higgins off his feet. The colonel staggered backward in the stampede as the cheering enemy came on. They ran up so quickly that Higgins could see triumphant expressions of victory on their lean, sunburnt faces. He took a step backward, peering around him to make sure that none of his men remained. Then he turned on his heels and fled from the trees as fast as he was able.

32

Wednesday, September 17, 1862
9:00 to 11:00 a.m.
Advance and Repulse of the Second Corps
West Woods, north of Sharpsburg, Maryland

situation felt entirely wrong to George Custer. With the men of Edwin Sumner's Second Corps loitering all around him, he ought to feel safe. Instead, Custer felt jumpy, as if lightning was about to strike.

Custer loosened his pistol in its holster and peered into the trees enclosing them on two sides. The darkness there spooked him. General Hooker had selected this same stretch of timber as his objective earlier that day, only to have his corps and that of General Mansfield wrecked when they approached. Now Sumner had pushed his lead division under John Sedgwick into the edge of the trees where untold numbers of Rebel troops might be lying in wait for them.

Some of the enemy Custer could see. About fifty yards ahead of him, a portion of Sedgwick's boys had entered a wooded hollow and were exchanging fire with an enemy line to their front. Two more Federal lines of battle stretched north across the length of the "L" shaped field in which Custer sat atop his horse.

General McClellan had warned repeatedly about the fearsome size of Lee's army, and his words echoed in Custer's mind. What if Little Mac had been correct after all and Lee's men outnumbered the Army of the Potomac's by a wide margin? The Gray Fox could have set a trap in these woods for an impetuous man like Sumner to stumble into. Old Bull never shied from a fight, which Custer found admirable, but the crafty Lee, with his legions of tatterdemalions hidden among the leaves, might crush the Second Corps before Sumner knew what hit him.

Custer eyed the old general warily, wondering if a man his age could rescue things on the army's right flank. Events had changed quickly. When the Rebel battle line broke for a final time that morning, the fight appeared won. For one fateful moment, they held victory in their grasp, like a ripe peach waiting to be plucked.

Then Hooker fell.

Of all the rotten luck, Custer snorted. Hooker went down at the worst possible time. If only McClellan had been on the field, he could have taken control of the situation. But Little Mac was not there. Bull Sumner was, sent by McClellan to reinforce Hooker's line. McClellan's judgment had undoubtedly been correct in moving up the Second Corps, but Sumner did not inspire confidence. Custer himself had heard

McClellan call the ancient officer a fool more than once. That same old fool now held the fate of the army in his hands. To Custer, it made no sense.

When he had brought Sumner up from Antietam Creek, they encountered Hooker's ambulance making its way to the rear. Stopping alongside the wagon, Custer noted the drained pallor of Hooker's ordinarily ruddy cheeks. He lay on a stretcher in the back, one boot off and a blood-soaked rag wrapped around his foot.

Climbing down from his horse, Sumner removed his hat, asking, "my dear General Hooker, what has happened?"

Hooker turned to Sumner as if he meant to speak, but all he could do was groan.

"Sir, he's lost a lot of blood," offered an aide on Hooker's staff. "The general's delirious."

"He must wake up!" Sumner snapped. "I need to know where to put my troops. He is the only man on the field who can tell me."

Returning to the stricken general, Sumner tapped lightly on Hooker's cheek. Hooker stirred some, his eyes cracking open. "General Sumner," he said weakly, "I am shot, and my corps is used up."

"Used up? Good God, general, what do you mean? Are there no men left on the field?"

Hooker shook his head. "Used up. My men fought bravely. Too many Rebels. Too many."

Scowling, Sumner asked, "well, what of General Mansfield's men? Where are they?"

"Mansfield … shot," mumbled Hooker. Then he passed out cold.

"Hooker? General Hooker! Blast it all! He's gone."

The ambulance rolled off and Sumner, turning to his staff, ordered them to fan out and locate the senior officer on the field. The assorted aides rode away, leaving a few orderlies and Custer by Sumner's side. "You, Captain Custer, will come with me," he said. "You've been on the field all morning, have you not?"

"I have, sir, but much has happened since I left to guide your command across the creek. I don't know what the situation is now."

Sumner swung back into the saddle. "That's not important. What is important is that I locate the front line and put my corps in the proper place. I hear firing to the west and to the south. Has the enemy's left flank been driven in as General McClellan ordered?"

"Last I knew, Mansfield's men had pushed it back to a line of trees on the western side of the field. Even by that time, though, the First Corps had incurred heavy losses and General Mansfield himself was carried off. I don't know what became of his command."

"I see. Well, then, we must find out," said Sumner, tightening his reins. A rider came up from the creek. "Sir, I have a message from General McClellan. There is a note for General Hooker as well. Do you know where he may be found?"

"General Hooker has been wounded," Sumner replied. "You passed his ambulance on your way here. Give both notes to me."

The courier held out the papers. "I understand, sir. Is there anything you'd like me to tell the commanding general?"

"Yes. Tell him that Hooker has been knocked out of the fight and that General Mansfield is wounded, perhaps badly. Inform General McClellan that I have assumed command on the field."

"Very good, sir," saluted the courier, who then turned and spurred away.

Sumner peered down at the note, his lips twisting as he read.

"Sir, may I ask what the general writes?" inquired Custer.

"You may, captain. He writes that General Hooker has driven the enemy, and that if he does not require our assistance on his right, I am to push forward on Hooker's left, and take possession of the woods on his front as soon as possible. Clearly, the commanding general wrote this in ignorance of Hooker's injury."

Handing the paper to a member of his staff, Sumner opened McClellan's note to Hooker. "This one says basically the same thing."

Sumner peered at the wood lot ahead of them. "Are those the woods to which General McClellan refers?"

"I don't think so," replied Custer. "General Mansfield's men took them earlier this morning. There is a larger set of trees farther to the west. They must be the woods the commanding general means."

"I see. So that is where the firing I hear must be. The enemy's left must not be broken. It has only been driven back."

"I can't say for sure."

"Alright, captain. Since you know as little as I do, I'll scout the field myself." Turning to an aide, Sumner ordered him to go to General Sedgwick and push on as quickly as possible. "Tell him he is to deploy his command in three lines of battle," added Old Bull, "and advance to that wood lot."

Sumner pointed to the western tree line in the distance. Then he spurred his horse into the closer stand of woods where Twelfth Corps men had broken through earlier that day. Finding it still firmly in Federal hands, Sumner placed artillery along the western edge of the trees to command the open area between the two forests. Thereafter, he proceeded south toward the small, white building on the Hagerstown Road. A regiment of Union troops waited near it behind a battery of cannon, taking fire from Rebel guns atop a far ridge.

Crossing the dirt road to Smoketown, Sumner crested the embankment and stopped there after spying a large formation of Bluecoats lying on the rear of a hillside that rolled down to a sunken farm lane packed with Rebel troops. At last! Here was the enemy's line.

A bugle blared while Sumner studied the enemy position and the regiment by the white structure stepped off, melting into the forest. Sumner dropped his field glasses and rode up in the regiment's wake.

"Sir, this building was General Hooker's objective this morning," Custer told him as they stopped on the Hagerstown Road.

Sumner waved at the structure. "The general had more success than you supposed, captain. This place is now in our hands. Hooker drove at least a portion of the Rebel left into the trees."

Thumping hooves caught Sumner's attention, and he turned to find George Meade riding up.

"Ah, General Meade," he nodded. "At last, here is someone who can tell me what is happening."

"I'll do my best, sir," frowned the Pennsylvanian. "General Hooker named me to command of the First Corps after he was shot ... well, what's left of it, at least."

"I saw Hooker on my way here. He said his corps is used up. Is that true?"

Meade scratched his chin. "It is, general. We drove them at first light all the way to this small house." Meade gestured to the white building. "But the Rebels counterattacked and forced us back to where the fight began. That is where what remains of my men are presently."

Sumner peered northward. "I do not see them, general."

"They are there, sir, just beyond the lip of that small rise," replied Meade, jerking his thumb over his shoulder. "Where would you have me put them?"

"I'd like them right here, general! There's a line of our men just over this ridge to the south. Bring up your men to support them."

"My command is a mile north of this position, sir. Then there is the right flank to think about. We have very few men on the line there."

Sumner went to speak when another officer rode up, this time from the Twelfth Corps. "Sir, General Williams sent me," he said. "The general sends his compliments and wishes me to report that he is once again in command of the Twelfth after General Mansfield's unfortunate wounding."

"Yes, I've heard that poor Mansfield is injured," Sumner nodded. "Where are General Williams's men now?"

The officer pointed at the hillside where Sumner had seen the lines of Federal troops lying in the grass. "General Greene's division is over there, sir." Then he directed Sumner's attention back to the eastern woods. "General Gordon's brigade is forming up yonder."

Sumner spied a body of men collecting on the southern edge of the eastern woods near the troops of Sedgwick's Second Division.

"And the rest of the Twelfth Corps, where is it?" Sumner asked.

"Withdrawn to the rear, sir. General Williams asked me to tell you that the men are well-nigh worn out from the fight this morning and are nearly out of ammunition."

Sighing, Sumner leaned forward on his saddle, the leather creaking under his hands. "What you're telling me is that my command is the only one on the field in any real condition to give battle."

"My men will hold a defensive line," offered Meade, "but getting them to attack again after all they've been through is probably not possible." He fell silent, adding after a moment, "we gave them hell this morning, general, but we took a took an almighty whipping ourselves in the process."

Sumner's shoulders slumped. "Alright, gentlemen, I've heard enough. Despite the depleted state of your commands, General McClellan has ordered me to secure these woods. Your commands appear to have been successful in driving the Rebels back through these trees. I will send General Sedgwick's division ahead to occupy a position between our line here and the northern edge of these woods. If we can punch through what remains of the Rebel left, the day will be ours. Return to your commands and wait to hear from me. If I need support, I'll depend on you to answer as best you can."

The assembled officers raised a salute before Sumner sent them away. An aide came up to report the remaining batteries of Second Corps artillery were moving into position west of the eastern woods. Sumner nodded his thanks and spurred off toward Sedgwick's lines south of those same woods.

Meeting William French, the mustached commander of the Second Corps' Third Division, on his way, Sumner ordered French to support General Greene's two brigades against the enemy in the sunken farm lane. Then he pushed Sedgwick's men toward the western woods in a dense formation of three battle lines merely fifty yards apart. Custer, trailing Sumner across the field, advanced with them, remarking on the magnificent sight of so many men moving in tight formation, their bayonets glittering in the sun.

It had seemed at first as if nothing could stop them. They crossed the Hagerstown Road and entered the western woods, encountering a smaller Rebel force on the right. Sedgwick's boys drove the enemy back after a stubborn fight. Then his second line came up, halting in the L-shaped field with its left pushed into the woods. Custer had reined in not far from the corner of the L where the tree line made a hard northerly turn. A New York regiment stood nearby, its line partially in the woods and partially in the open field. The men rested there with the butts of their muskets in the grass. Behind Custer stood the massed ranks of General Howard's Second Brigade stretching north. Line officers around him shouted orders, expecting to see action at any time.

Swigging water from his canteen, Custer tried to tell himself that all was well, but a nagging sense of dread would not give him peace. Then he heard it—a storm of gunfire that exploded deep in the forest beyond Sedgwick's left flank. The heads of every man in the area turned in that direction and Custer walked Wellington toward the growing racket. The horse caught a scent of the fear, too, shifting nervously under Custer as he squinted to see what might be taking place among the trees.

Crashing gunfire grew louder, accompanied by a familiar wolfish howl. The left flank of Sedgwick's command had clearly become engaged, but where was the deep cheering of Northern voices? Typically, when the lines clashed, McClellan's boys would answer the Rebel yell with a manly cry of their own.

A blue-clad soldier emerged in a panic from the trees. Wild-eyed, he looked around him in a panic before sprinting northward. The troops in formation watched him run by, muttering to each other as the gunfire rose in volume on their left.

"A lone coward," sniffed Custer, but Wellington continued to stamp nervously under him. Custer jerked the reins to keep him steady.

A second man emerged from the foliage, his hands empty. Then a third man burst out, his face clouded with fear. "The Rebels are coming! Run for your lives!" he bawled, rushing past. The torrent of musketry rose into a roar on the left of the New Yorkers and the men there suddenly gave way, their ranks blasted apart by a tide of onrushing Graybacks. Wellington stamped in a circle, unnerved by the howling yips and barks that filled his ears.

General Sumner sped past, his hat flying from his head. "Get back, boys! For God's sake, move back! You are in a bad fix!" he cried, waving to the men behind Custer. The nearest regiment, veteran Zouaves from Pennsylvania, clothed in short jackets, light blue trousers, and white gaiters, broke in a flood, as the men hurried to save themselves. Where once a solid wall of troops had presented itself, only a few confused souls remained standing. They looked around them in the chaos before also turning tail and running for all they were worth.

Custer soon spotted the enemy, a surging mass butternut and gray closing rapidly on him. Miniés whizzed past, sending Wellington into a rear, and Custer leaned forward, pulling on the reins so as to not lose his grip. He yanked his pistol from his holster just as the Morgan's front hooves returned to the earth. A Rebel voice called to him.

"You there on the horse, give it up!"

Custer spun in the saddle and pulled the trigger, putting a bullet in the man's chest. He pulled Wellington hard to the right and crammed his heels into his sides. The Morgan surged into a sprint as a minié grazed Custer's boot, shearing off a sliver of leather. A mob of Rebel infantry surged from the trees behind Custer, and he shot a glance back over his shoulder to see an even larger horde of Butternuts coming up than had confronted General Hooker that morning. Sumner truly had stumbled into a trap!

Speeding north to the bloody cornfield, Custer pulled Wellington to a stop. Running soldiers passed him to join regiments rallying in the distance. The Graybacks came on, seeking to break their enemy once and for all. Fleeing Federals cleared the field, however, uncovering the long line of guns that Sumner had called up. The batteries unleashed a murderous salvo of canister and case shot on the exposed enemy from only three hundred yards away.

The Rebel horde murmured with a mournful cry, guiding first to the north and then to the west, as the canister tore through their ranks. A man clutched at his face, writhing in pain as he fell. Solid shot bounded through the enemy, taking legs and arms as it passed until Custer finally averted his eyes, unable any longer to witness the butchery. At last, the Rebel mass reeled back into the trees and the reverberation of Federal cannon fire drifted away across the valley.

Custer walked Wellington into the eastern woods. Groups of broken men huddled there among the trees, the few officers among them calling out for their regiments. As he passed, Sumner's men gazed at Custer with hollow eyes, their faces fraught with despair. The sour stench of defeat and fear filled the air around them.

"They're whipped," muttered Custer to himself. "Beaten like curs at the hand of a heartless master."

The last Rebel attack had utterly shattered this portion of Sumner's command and General McClellan must know it before any further disaster could be allowed to pass. Custer spurred Wellington back toward Antietam Creek to report on all that he had seen and to warn Little Mac how desperate the situation on this part of the field had become.

33

Wednesday, September 17, 1862

11:00 a.m. to 1:00 p.m.

Ninth Corps, Left Flank of the Army of the Potomac

Rohrbach Bridge, Sharpsburg, Maryland

Duryée, you will proceed as ordered!" barked Brigadier General James Nagle as Generals Jacob Cox and Sam Sturgis looked on. Colonel Jacob Eugene Duryée, commander of the Second Maryland Infantry, continued, however, to plead his case.

"Sir, I must protest!" he yelped, his cheeks flushing red above his bushy mustache and hands held out helplessly in front of him. "My boys suffered terribly assaulting an entrenched Rebel position at Bull Run a few weeks back. Now you want them to do the same here? Look at the enemy there, sir. My men cannot take that bridge alone."

"Colonel, they will not be alone," replied the goatee-toting Sturgis, commander of the Ninth Corps' Second Division. "I have ordered the Sixth and the Ninth New Hampshire to support the attack. You will also have the Forty-Eighth Pennsylvania on your flank, and anyone else I need to bring up until we attain our objective."

Surrendering to his superiors, Duryée cinched up the belt from which his long saber dangled. "I see, general. Well, my boys will, of course, give it a go. That's not my complaint. It is only that I cannot vouch for the spirit with which they'll try. They fought hard at Bull Run, but ended up surrounded on three sides and had to shoot their way out of the trap. You can understand, I hope, if they are a bit gun-shy."

"Gun-shy or not, colonel, that bridge must be taken as promptly as possible," responded Cox. "Do you hear those guns to the north? Those are our comrades engaged with the enemy. General McClellan has made it clear that our attack here is critical to the outcome of the battle. It may even result in an end to the war itself. Your men have the opportunity to win glory by taking that bridge. Imagine it, colonel, the Second Maryland will go down in history! Would you deny your men a chance at immortality? A chance to be the victors in this war?"

"Certainly not, general!" cried Duryée, his chin jutting proudly forward. "I am sorry for causing any delay. My men will step off immediately."

"Bully for you, colonel!" said General Nagle this time. "Taking that bridge will not be an easy task, but by thunder it must be done! Go now and may God bless you and your men."

"Thank you, sir." The lieutenant colonel saluted and rushed to his regiment of loyal Union men from Baltimore who had joined after the president's first call for volunteers in the spring of 1861. Arriving where they stood along a dirt road at the edge of a cornfield, Duryée barked orders for them to fix bayonets and move by the left flank over the furrows of a plowed field that stretched nearly to Antietam Creek.

The assembled artillery on the heights opened on the Rebel positions west of the creek as Duryée finalized his formation. Gun crews rammed powder charges and rounds of ammunition down their tubes before pulling their lanyards tight and loosing hell on the enemy. Thunderous concussions of smoke and fire leaped out on hills opposite the creek as the vicious close-range salvo sent geysers of dirt and smoke skyward. Trees blasted by the barrage, dropped down the slope in clouds of dust and leaves. A black walnut rolled creekward, its branches splayed at the bottom and exposed roots open to the sun. Haze and smoke enveloped the ridge line, hiding the enemy's rifle pits.

"If you are going to go, colonel, let it be now!" shouted Cox melodramatically, knowing full well that Duryée could not hear him from where he stood. At that moment, the regiment's bugle blared and Baltimore's loyal sons rushed forward with a cheer. Several men sprinted ahead of the charging column toward a tall post and rail fence on the far side of the plowed field. Shots cracked out from the Johnnies posted across the creek, dropping Marylanders into the dirt. The men in the fore reached the fence and struggled to pull down the rails. A red mist burst from the side of one man's head, crumpling him to the ground.

A rail came off as the front of the charging column ground to a halt. Then a second length of chestnut dropped, and finally a third, opening a gap wide enough for three men to squeeze through. A spirited cry rose again from the ranks, and they rushed the fence as the enemy let loose at the head of the column.

Bellowing men poured through the hole in the fence to meet a wall of lead. A Marylander sprinted ahead, going five paces before a ball passed through his heart. The bodies of the fallen blocked the gap through which the struggling mass tried to push. A few made it and kept going across the pasture and toward the dirt road that led up to the bridge. Then a man at the rear ran away with a mounted officer waving his saber hard on his heels. More men wavered at the slaughter in front of them and they, too, lit out as fast as their legs could take them.

Regimental commanders leveled their sabers, too, and pushed the rear ranks into the backs of their comrades. A few made it through the gap, then a few more, but a good number lay sprawled in a gory pile by the opening. The few who made it through huddled along the same fence by the creek where the boys from Connecticut had earlier sought shelter.

When the final Marylander stumbled past the fence over the bodies of his countrymen, General Nagle bellowed orders for the Sixth New Hampshire to make its advance. Lurching forward with a shout, the Granite Staters rushed across the plowed field toward the same hellish gap through which the Maryland boys had plunged. The head of the column slowed as the front ranks bunched up and the rear of the regiment compacted like an accordion.

Rebel marksmen opened on them, dropping the helpless New Hampshire men onto the corpses of the Marylanders who had passed before them. Pairs of struggling New Englanders pushed through, only to be gunned down after taking a step. The bodies around the opening in the fence piled up, forcing the Granite Staters to scale them. A good number of men made it past, however, joining their Maryland compatriots along the fence at the creek. There they remained, pinned down by enemy musketry.

Rebel artillery on the heights east of Sharpsburg joined in the fight and spouts of fire and smoke erupted along the fence where the Maryland and New Hampshire troops lay trapped. An agonized cry went up and men ran back from the creek side, seeking to escape with their lives and limbs intact. Blasts of iron case shot burst in the air above them, raining down a hail of deadly shards. The attacking men faltered, failed, and, finally, fell back in a mass, leaving the field covered with the bodies of their dead and wounded comrades.

Observing the grim, fruitless sacrifice, Cox heaved a sigh and turned to Sam Sturgis, seated on a chestnut horse beside him. "Blast it, Sam. General Burnside may think it best to attack from the flank, but I have seen enough killing to know that he is dead wrong! We should assault the bridge from the front. The faster the men cross that open ground and get over the creek, the faster our boys will stop being uselessly slaughtered."

"That's sound reasoning," nodded Sturgis. "What should I do?"

At that moment a rider appeared with orders from General Burnside. "General Sturgis, sir, the general directs that you carry the bridge at all hazards. Let nothing deter you."

Cox turned to Sturgis. "Well, general, there is your answer."

"Yes," nodded Sturgis," but General Burnside did not say how I should accomplish the task. With your permission, sir, I'd like to try the approach you suggest." He pointed at the sharply sloped hillside directly opposite the bridge. "I'll send two regiments down the center of that grade. Moving at the double-quick they can get over the creek before the Johnnies have a chance to fire too many rounds."

"I agree, General Sturgis. Let it be done, and quickly, too. I'm going to inform General Burnside of the change in your approach. Good luck to you and your men."

"Thank you, sir. We'll need it," replied Sturgis, who saluted as Cox spurred his horse back to Burnside.

Finding the general atop the knoll beside Lieutenant Benjamin's battery of rifled guns, Cox reined in and slipped to the ground. A colonel Cox did not know stood near Burnside, the reins of his horse held loosely in his hands. This man also walked up as Burnside turned to face the Ninth Corps' commander.

"General Cox, what in damnation is going on down there?" asked the restless Rhode Islander, his shaking finger pointed at the corpse-strewn field.

"Sir, General Nagle's men made a go of it and failed. General Sturgis will make another attempt soon, but this time it is going to be a direct assault. We've tried approaching the bridge from the flank, but the Rebels are posted too strongly there. They have the chance to pour fire into our boys for two hundred yards before they can even get close."

"Does Sturgis think a frontal assault will work, Cox? That bridge is awfully narrow," frowned Burnside.

"He does, sir, and so do I. We must at least give it a try. General McClellan expects us to make the attempt at all hazards." Cox shot a glance at the unfamiliar colonel behind Burnside, who nodded silently in agreement.

Returning his gaze to Burnside, Cox asked if word had been received from General Rodman.

"No, Cox. Not since he reported that the ford General McClellan's aide selected for him to use is too deep. Oh, how I wish we had sought out a different crossing ourselves rather than relying on a headquarters man! Now we are forced to attack that bridge frontally instead of turning the enemy's flank, as I would have liked."

"Does General Rodman have a plan?" asked Cox.

"He does. He's enlisted the help of a local to identify a new crossing farther downstream."

Cox frowned at this. "A new crossing? That is going to take time, sir."

Burnside looked out over the dismal field. "I know that, general. In the meantime, we will do our best and hope that General Sturgis is able to achieve some success."

Cox swallowed hard. "Yes, sir. May God smile on his effort."

* * *

George McClellan stared down at the message in his hand, received by signal flag a short time earlier.

General Hooker is wounded. General Sumner is in command.

McClellan heaved a long sigh. "Sumner is in command?"

Crushing the note, he returned to the place beside a fence post he had occupied for the last half-hour. The post, and a part of the rail fence that remained standing, ran along the knoll behind the large brick house that Hooker had used as his headquarters. Atop the post lay a pair of field glasses strapped down with a leather tie. Where the spyglass had gone, McClellan could not say. Removed by one of his aides for service elsewhere, he surmised.

Stooping to peer through the binoculars, he spied clouds of smoke on the right where Sumner's command grappled with the seemingly impervious left flank of the Confederate army. His field commanders had launched three successive attacks against the enemy in the western woods, and yet no victory had come. In fact, just the opposite had occurred. The remnants of Hooker's command lay torn to pieces where they had stepped off earlier that morning, and the news from Mansfield's Twelfth Corps was no different. Both corps might be able to hold their ground against an enemy attack, but renewing offensive operations with either of them was out of the question.

Sumner's corps remains our only hope on the right, mused McClellan bitterly to himself. Bull Sumner, headstrong and impetuous. Oh, that General Hooker had not been hurt. I would much rather that he remained in command.

Alas, it could not be. Sumner must carry on without the stricken Hooker. By all reports, the old man had done well so far, but this did little to soothe McClellan's jangled nerves in light of the situation. An hour earlier events had appeared to be going his way. Hooker reported driving the enemy with the help of Mansfield's men. Then a kind of muted inactivity settled over the field after yet another Rebel counterattack. Now, Sumner pushed Sedgwick's Second Division toward the western woods in three heavy lines of battle while his Third Division under General French moved south toward an enemy position in the center of the field.

It is a good thing I sent General Richardson to support Sumner, reflected McClellan silently on the orders he had given for the First Division to enter the fray.

Rising from the glasses, McClellan began to pace. The members of his staff watched him from afar while they observed the fighting. Friendly faces surrounded McClellan and yet at that moment he felt utterly alone. In his heart, he knew this day's fight was the battle of the war. The fortunes of the Republic would be decided here based on the decisions he made. Win this battle and the nation would hail him as a victor. Lose it and his name would recede into dishonor forever.

"I must not lose this fight!" he hissed through gritted teeth.

"General, did you say something?" asked General Marcy, standing nearby.

McClellan shot a glance at his chief of staff. "No, Marcy, not intentionally. I am thinking out loud. The army's right concerns me greatly. General Sumner appears to have the upper hand at the moment, but Lee has answered each of our attacks with equal force." McClellan threw a restive wave toward the western woods. "Who knows what lies in those trees? Lee could be waiting for us to shoot our bolt before he counters with an overwhelming attack on our flank!"

"Has information come in that such an attack might be pending, sir?"

McClellan stopped pacing to glower at Marcy. "No, general, but our observers cannot see the whole field, even from their elevation. The center of our lines remains a point of concern as well. I cannot move General Porter's troops from there in case of an enemy attack. We cannot see what lies behind those hills."

"I understand, general. Perhaps General Franklin's command can be thrown in when he arrives. He is due soon, I think."

McClellan peered at the battlefield. "He is indeed, Marcy. Franklin will be here within the hour. What to do with his command is the question. Do I use it to reinforce our center or do I send him across the creek to support Sumner? Then there is Burnside's front to consider. Have we heard anything from Colonel Sackett? He has been gone a long while."

"No, sir, I have not seen any message come in. There are reports of heavy fighting at the lower bridge, however. It appears General Burnside is making a go of it."

"He must do a sight better than that!" barked McClellan, displaying his fraying nerves. "He must take that bridge and soon! I have read reports all morning of Rebel troops moving north from their right. My plan is working! General Lee is weakening his lines in front of Burnside's command. He must apply pressure there as soon as possible. It is critical to our success. If Lee counterattacks on our right because Burnside has been too slow in coming up, it could be disastrous!"

Aggrieved by the general's tone Marcy fell silent, allowing McClellan to ruminate on his own. A clamor of musket fire rose suddenly in the west. Escalating into a roar, McClellan stared breathlessly through the binoculars at masses of men in blue were spotted skedaddling from the western woods. Prodigious clouds of smoke rising from the trees spread from south to north as the fighting spread.

McClellan shifted the glasses farther right and gasped. Even larger bodies of men—his men—were fleeing from what appeared to be a powerful enemy onslaught. Heavy cannon fire kept the Rebel assault from gaining more ground, but Little Mac's hopes sank at the sight of his fears coming to pass. Lee had launched his counterattack and crushed Sumner's command. What now remained of his army's right flank?

The fight closer to the center continued, meanwhile, with wave after wave of Federal troops advancing against a formidable enemy position in a sunken road. Despite launching three attacks already, General French's command had fallen back toward Antietam Creek, with each assault repulsed. General Richardson's troops could now be seen approaching the field. They gathered in lines just in McClellan's sight and opposite the Rebel position. Uncasing their flags, Richardson's regiments moved into alignment and stepped off toward the enemy. They advanced smartly to the lip of the hill before stopping to unleash a storm of musketry at their foes on the far side of the hill.

Turning from the field glasses, McClellan peered at Marcy through weary eyes. "General, get me Colonel Key," he commanded. "I wish to speak with him immediately."

With a nod, Marcy hurried off to fetch the colonel. Some minutes later, the army's slim Judge Advocate General appeared at McClellan's side, his glasses propped upon his nose.

"Sir, you sent for me?" he asked.

"Yes, Key, I did!" snapped McClellan tensely. "I want you to go to General Burnside with a message."

"Me, sir? But I am not a messenger."

"You are now, colonel. I am sending you because I trust you and because you are close to General Cox."

"I see, sir. Very well. What would you have me say?"

"You are to tell Burnside that I have ordered him to push his troops forward with the utmost vigor and carry the enemy's position on the heights opposite Antietam Creek! Say to him the movement is absolutely vital to our success and he must not stop for loss of life if a great victory can be secured. Add that if, in his judgment, his attack will fail, he is to inform me at once so that that his troops might be withdrawn and used elsewhere on the field. We are in desperate need of reserves."

"As you wish, general. Is there anything else?"

"No, colonel, that is all. Just go quickly, now, please."

Key hurried off to his horse, leaving McClellan with Marcy. "Perhaps sending someone Cox knows will urge General Burnside along," he said.

"I hope so, sir," nodded the older man.

Folding his hands behind his back, McClellan stared down at the grass beneath his feet. Then he peered at the fighting on the far hills. "Marcy, I've made a decision," he announced. "I want you to send an order to General Pleasonton. Earlier this morning, I had him push several regiments and some of his horse artillery across the middle bridge to bring pressure on the center of the enemy's line. Tell him now that I wish him to add to those forces. He is to bring all the guns he can to bear on the hills east of Sharpsburg. That way, he will be able to protect our center from an enemy advance."

Marcy scribbled in his dispatch pad. "Very good, general. Is there anything else?"

"Yes, Marcy, there is. Have a message sent to General Franklin as well. Tell the general that he is to hold his two divisions in readiness by the bridge that General Hooker used to cross Antietam Creek yesterday afternoon. If Franklin receives word from Sumner that he is in need of support, Franklin is to come to Sumner's aid forthwith. Is that understood?"

"Forth ... with. Yes, sir, I have it."

"Good," nodded McClellan. "Now, general, take one more note. This one is to be communicated to Sumner by signal. Inform Sumner of Franklin's approach and let him know that he is free to call upon General Franklin's troops if he finds himself in need of them."

"I understand, sir. You remain concerned about the army's right."

"I do, general. I've received no word of an enemy movement on the left. Lee, however, continues to challenge Sumner and there is space for maneuver on that flank. If Lee strikes, it will be on our right. I am certain of it."

Marcy hurried off as McClellan resumed gazing through his field glasses. Immense clouds of smoke and rattling musket fire rose from the center of the field where General Richardson's division was engaged. A Federal regiment fell back from the front, its ranks in disarray. Tapping nervously on his thigh, McClellan stepped back from the glass to stare down at his right hand. The fingers quaked, and he shook it in irritation. "Get a hold of yourself, George," he muttered, and tugging out his watch, he looked at the time. It read eleven-thirty.

*   *   *

Ambrose Burnside fidgeted nervously in anticipation of a new assault by General Sturgis's men. A note from Sturgis received only a short time earlier revealed the general's intent to take the bridge via a direct attack with two regiments, the Fifty-First New York and the Fifty-First Pennsylvania. The New Yorkers and Keystone State boys would attack straight down the barrels of the defenders' guns, taking precisely the dangerous approach that Burnside had attempted to avoid all morning.

The constant badgering from McClellan, however, as well as the costly failure of attempts to storm the bridge from the flank, had finally convinced Burnside that no other option remained. The fields in front of him lay covered with the bodies of men who had given their lives to capture the objective. Their sacrifice must be made good.

Burnside stood atop his hill, anxiously gnawing his fingernails in anticipation of Sturgis's advance. Two guns posted on a hilltop some three-hundred yards opposite the eastern end of the bridge burst into action, followed by those of another six-gun battery nearby. Benjamin's guns close to the general joined in the salvo, throwing shells at the Rebel rifle-pits atop the heights west of Antietam Creek.

Burnside heard a bugle and shifted his glasses to the right. A pair of flags flapping at the head of two regiments running at the double-quick emerged over the crest of the hill. Cries went up as men watching the attack added their voices to the cheers of advancing troops. The northern boys, their ranks bristling with bayonets, surged down the grade toward the bridge, presenting the enemy with a narrow front.

"Go, boys! Get at them!" cried Burnside, his eyes alive with hope. "Look at them, General Cox. Just look at how magnificent they are!"

Jacob Cox, standing beside the general, lowered his field glasses. "Indeed, sir, they look brilliant!" he shouted over the din.

Enemy riflemen took aim at the onrushing Yankees and pulled their triggers. As they had when previous regiments attacked, the leading ranks suffered most. Men struck by the musket fire collapsed into the grass, their comrades behind them tripping over the bodies. For a moment, the charge faltered. Then the attack recovered, and with their heads down, Sturgis's troops advanced through the storm of iron and lead until they had reached the eastern bank of the creek.

On the right, the boys from Pennsylvania sought shelter along the stone wall that ran north from the mouth of the bridge.

"No, keep going!" shouted Burnside, afraid that they, too, would suffer the miserable fate of their comrades. The stone wall, however, provided better cover, and the Pennsylvanians began to return the enemy's fire. The blazing musketry escalated into a roar as the New Yorkers on the left reached a rail fence that enclosed the right side of the road leading to the bridge. Small figures in blue scaled the rails, only to be shot down. A man hit in mid-stride, slumped over the top rail, his musket falling into the road. Too many men scrambled forward for the Southerners to shoot, however, and a large number collected along the corpse-lined fence beside the creek. These men joined their comrades in firing at the smoky heights.

Bugle notes pierced the thunderous gunfire, and Burnside shifted his glasses to the foreground to see another regiment barreling toward the bridge along the route that the heroic men from Maryland and New Hampshire had taken. This time the boys rushing ahead were from Massachusetts, as revealed by the large blue flag in front of their regiment. They quickly reached the left flank of the New Yorkers huddled against the chestnut fence and they too opened a brisk fire. Yankee rifles now blazed away at close range for several hundred yards along the eastern bank of the creek.

Burnside shifted his glasses to the Rebel positions on the left. Small figures in the smoke and dust lit out suddenly for the rear. First, two men ran, then more, and the enemy's fire began to slacken.

"Cox, they must hurry! The rebel defenses are collapsing!" he cried.

Then, as if they had heard Burnside's comment, up rose the New Yorkers. Dashing along the fence with their regiment's flag at the column's head, they surged toward the bridge. A cheer went up along the lines as the taste of victory grew palpable on the tongues of those watching.

Not to be outdone, the color-guard of the Pennsylvania regiment leaped to its feet and charged the bridge from the right, meeting the New York boys in the road. Together, the two color-bearers stepped onto the gravel surface of the bridge, followed by a surge of men who crossed the creek to fan out along the base of the Rebel-defended heights.

Burnside let out a yelp of triumph! At last, after five hundred men had fallen in the three-hour assault, he had taken the bridge over Antietam Creek. The weakened right flank of Lee's army now lay wide open.

34

Wednesday, September 17, 1862
1:00 p.m. to 2:30 p.m.
Field Headquarters, Army of the Potomac
Philip Pry House, Keedysville, Maryland

reverberation of a lone gun echoed in the distance, leaving a sudden stillness on the field. Startled by the silence, General McClellan looked up from the dispatch in his hand. The cannons had been roaring for so long that he could still hear them in his head.

Turning to his field glasses, still strapped atop a fence post, McClellan worked them to the left where Burnside struggled to take the lower bridge across Antietam Creek. Smoke hung in a dense cloud over the landscape, but no gunfire emanated from the hills, not even from the Rebel guns on the heights east of Sharpsburg. Like two exhausted boxers, the Army of Northern Virginia and the Army of the Potomac stood panting in their corners, anticipating the final round of fighting to come.

Little Mac peered now at the center-right of his lines, where a final furious clash had erupted in the vicinity of the small, whitewashed building a short time ago. For the third time that day, a Rebel force had emerged from the forest to drive back Union troops to that part of the line. A murderous barrage of cannon fire from Sumner's batteries assembled on the northern and eastern parts of the field blunted their assault, but the very fact that Lee had seen fit to launch yet another attack made McClellan very uneasy. He gazed at the long line of trees, wishing he could see into their depths. Tens of thousands of Rebels could be hiding there just out of sight.

McClellan looked back at the note in his hand. Israel Richardson, the hard fighting commander of the attack against the sunken road, had been mortally wounded. How many lost senior officers did that make? Joe Hooker, commander of the First Corps, shot in the foot. Joe Mansfield, the commander of the Twelfth Corps, mortally wounded. John Sedgwick, commander of the Second Division, Second Corps, shot multiple times and out of action. Brigadier General Napoleon Dana, a commander in Sedgwick's division, carried off the field. Now "Fighting Dick" Richardson, a major general, had been felled by a shell fragment.

McClellan paced the stretch of dirt he had worn in the grass. The loss of Hooker and Sedgwick hurt, but with Richardson's fall, the action in the center of the field deteriorated into a muddle. Deep-throated cheers carried from the hills suggested that the general's command had won a victory there, but as yet, no word had arrived to confirm it.

The silence on the left puzzled Little Mac, however, and he turned to gaze in that direction. General Marcy, noticing the general's furrowed brow, ventured to speak. "Burnside's attack is slow in developing," he observed.

"It is indeed," sighed McClellan. "Even Colonel Sackett hasn't returned with news of its progress. That bodes ill. Perhaps I should not have sent that reprimand of General Burnside last night for bringing up his command too slowly from South Mountain, and for dawdling when carrying out my orders yesterday afternoon."

"Those are serious missteps, sir. Do you suspect Burnside is frustrating your plans on purpose?"

"I don't know, Marcy. It would be difficult to believe. Burnside is a patriot and a loyal man. He wants to end to the rebellion as much as I. It's just—it's just I wonder if I ought to have waited to call him onto the carpet. It may have led him to be distracted, or to not give me his maximum effort. He is emotional, Marcy; irritatingly so, sometimes."

McClellan peered past the old general to see Thomas Key coming up the lawn. "Ah, here is Colonel Key back from Burnside! Let us hear what he has to say."

Key returned McClellan's wave and tossed a brisk salute. "Sir, General Burnside has taken the bridge."

"A-ha! I suspected it from the lull in the shooting! What happened there, colonel? Don't leave out a single detail."

Removing his eyeglasses, Key polished them with a handkerchief. "I arrived just as Burnside ordered a third assault, and found him on a bluff overlooking the bridge and the creek. He expressed some surprise, and even a touch of consternation, that you had sent me. I conveyed your orders that he push across the bridge and move rapidly up the heights, even at the point of the bayonet if necessary, and not to stop for loss of life. His face grew red, and he directed my attention to the field in front of the bridge, asking me if the dead men lying there looked to me like a sufficient sacrifice."

"He did not!" exclaimed Marcy.

"He did, general."

"As I just observed, Marcy, the man is emotional," sniffed McClellan. "Colonel, what did Burnside say then?"

"He said that a new assault was already underway and directed my attention to two regiments rushing over a hill. Those regiments, after some hesitation, charged over the creek and captured the bluffs from the Secesh. The bridge is now in our hands."

"And is he pushing his corps across?" inquired Little Mac, now visibly excited.

Key placed his spectacles back on his nose. "Slowly, sir. He said that General Cox had complained of his men lacking ammunition, so he planned to bring some up before he resumed his attack. There is also the matter of an enemy battery on his left that is resisting his advance. The general said he would go as far as the enemy would permit."

"As far as the enemy—? That is UNACCEPTABLE!" boomed McClellan, drawing the glances of every man within earshot.

"Colonel, you will return to General Burnside straightaway and tell him he is to push forward his troops with the utmost vigor and proceed to Sharpsburg. He is to storm the battery in his way, or somehow get around its flank. This movement is vital to our success, and he must not delay! Add that if he judges his attack will fail, he is to inform me at once."

McClellan pointed to the northwest. "If General Burnside will not advance, then General Sumner can use the Ninth Corps' men on his part of the field." His hand shifted to the center. "So can General Porter. We must press the enemy while we can and without delay!" McClellan smacked his fist into the open palm of his other hand.

"As you wish, sir," bowed Key, who turned down the hill to retrieve his horse.

McClellan watched the colonel go until an aide appeared with a message from Sumner. The lieutenant handed over the paper, which McClellan scanned, his eyes shifting rapidly from side-to-side.

"This makes no sense," he said. "Lieutenant Wilson, you tell General Sumner that I have given no orders for a new attack. He is to risk nothing! I expect him to hold his present position at all costs."

"I will, sir," replied Wilson, "but to clarify, I believe General Sumner desires to hold his position. He does not want to attack. It is General Franklin who wishes to attack."

McClellan's brows knitted together. "Franklin wishes to attack? With what force?"

"With the two brigades of his corps that are on the field."

McClellan opened his lips to speak when another of his aides returned from the front. Little Mac pushed past Wilson to greet the man. "Major Hammerstein, I'm glad to see you. What word is there?"

Puffing loudly from his climb up the hill, Hammerstein proffered a salute. "Thank … you … general. I've come from General Franklin. He sent me to tell you that he wishes to make an attack on the western woods in the vicinity of the small church."

"So Lieutenant Wilson informs me," waved McClellan. "What church is Franklin talking about? Does he mean the white building there? Is that a church?"

"It is, sir," nodded the major. "The general has two brigades of General Slocum's division in position for the assault. He believes he can break the Rebel line in the forest and drive back their left."

"Pshaw! With only two brigades?" Marcy huffed. "General Sedgwick lost an entire division in those woods."

"Yes, sir. General Sumner directed General Franklin not to make the assault. He is convinced that if the attack fails, he will have no troops on the right to defend his line."

"And so General Franklin sent you to me for a decision instead," stated McClellan.

"He did, sir. The general thinks the attack ought to be made as soon as possible, while the Rebels are in disarray."

McClellan fell silent. Rubbing his forehead under his cap, he turned back to Wilson. "Lieutenant, I have changed my mind. Return to General Sumner and tell him to crowd every man and gun he has into his line. If he thinks it practicable, he may advance Franklin to carry the woods in his front while holding the rest of the line with his own command, along with the remnants of Mansfield's and Hooker's commands. Do you understand?"

"Yes, general," saluted Wilson. "I'll go right away."

McClellan nodded the man off and faced Marcy. "Well, general, it appears I must go to the right and see to matters there myself. Sumner rarely expresses doubt about going on the attack, so if he is voicing concern, it is worth taking seriously."

"I agree, sir. Your presence on the field will undoubtedly be helpful."

Little Mac thanked the older general and peered over at George Custer, reclining in the grass with a stem of grass protruding from his lips. "Captain, come here, if you please," he called out.

Custer climbed to his feet and approached the general. "You saw the situation on Sumner's line when the Rebels attacked. Can his command be as weak as he claims?" asked McClellan.

"I believe it can be," Custer nodded. "When General Sedgwick's division fell apart, his men skedaddled all over the field. They must have become mixed up with those of General Hooker and General Mansfield, too. It was unavoidable given the strength of the Rebel attack. They hit us like a thunderbolt. The forest behind General Sumner's guns was filled with men from different regiments calling out for one another. Honestly, sir, if you'll forgive the language, it looked like a damned mess."

"I see," sighed Little Mac, who fell silent for a moment. Eventually, he threw up his hands. "Well, there is nothing for it. I must go to the right and see for myself the state of Sumner's command. Colonel Key will, I trust, get General Burnside moving on the left. Let us see if Sumner's fears are justified, or if General Franklin's attack can be made without inordinate risk. In the meantime, perhaps I can rally the men myself if they see me on the field. Captain Custer, you come with me."

Returning to his mount, McClellan called for two more of his aides, including Henry Hunt, his chief of artillery, to come along, then he climbed into the saddle and pulled Dan's reins tight. The group trotted toward the stone bridge across the Antietam, greeting cheering troops along the way. McClellan tipped his cap to them as he passed by and guided Dan around a train of ammunition wagons creaking toward the field. Crossing over the bridge, he steered to the left, asking Custer which way they should go. Custer pointed to the thickest part of the forest on the ridge, stating that the last time he saw Sumner was among those trees.

"Very good, captain," McClellan nodded. "I'll conduct the attack on the right myself, if one is to be made."

Approaching the eastern woods, McClellan spotted an officer on foot and called out to him, "General Gordon, it's good to see you. How are your troops?"

George Gordon turned to McClellan and proffered a salute. "Ah, sir, it is good to see you on the field. It will do the men some good. My men have done well, but they have suffered severely and are somewhat scattered. I'm attempting to find them now."

"Very well, general, collect them at once and tell them that 15,000 fresh troops have just come up. Still more will arrive during the night. We must all fight tonight and tomorrow! If we cannot whip the enemy now, we may as well die upon the field. If we succeed, we end the war."

Gordon's face brightened. "This is good news, sir! The men will be glad to hear it. I'll spread the word."

McClellan tipped his hat and steered Dan to the right in search of Sumner. Behind him, Custer shot a puzzled glance at Henry Hunt, mouthing the words, "fifteen thousand?" Hunt shrugged in response, muttering, "militia from Pennsylvania."

The small entourage traversed the eastern outskirts of the woods to the cheers and huzzahs of the men they encountered. Some regiments appeared to be in good order. Others lay about in disorganized clusters. Coming up to a man slumped on the side of the road to Smoketown, Little Mac pulled Dan to a stop. The soldier sat there with his face down and his arms folded on his upraised knees. "You there, are you injured?" inquired the general.

The man raised his gaze to see McClellan peering down at him. "No, sir, I ain't hurt."

"Impudent wretch! Do you not rise and salute your commanding officer?" growled Hunt.

The filthy-faced man looked at Hunt as if in a daze. Then he peered back at McClellan and climbed slowly to his feet. Once erect, he offered a weak salute. "I'm sorry, general."

Pointing down at the man, McClellan shot a glance at Hunt. "What's wrong with this soldier?"

"I-I don't know, sir."

"General, I believe he's in shock," volunteered Custer. "Private, do you know your unit?"

The man turned to Custer, staring blankly at him. "Sure, the Seventh Michigan Infantry. Colonel Hall's command."

"And where are your comrades?" inquired McClellan.

"Killed, sir."

"Killed? All of them?"

"I reckon so, general. Last I saw, 'most half my company had fallen in the woods. I got the button of my blouse shot off. The fire was so hot."

"And where are the rest of your comrades now?"

"Don't know. Here. There. Everywhere, I reckon." The man gazed around him emptily.

Flustered by the unnerving encounter, McClellan cleared his throat. "Ahem! That's enough of this. Private, carry on," he commanded, and waving to his staff, they rode on past other men looking as dazed as the first.

Some distance on, Little Mac pulled Dan to a stop under a towering oak tree. "Captain Custer," he said, "I don't like what I'm seeing here. These men are utterly disorganized. I've seen only a handful of regiments prepared to go back into the fight. You go back across the creek to General Porter and tell him to send up two brigades from his corps. They are the only available men and must reinforce our right."

Custer wheeled Wellington back the way they had come as McClellan gave the order to continue on. At last he found Edwin Sumner in the shade of some trees, with couriers coming and going around him. Beside Sumner stood William Franklin and a number of other officers, a few with cigars in their hands. Sumner glanced up as Little Mac reined in.

"Ah, here is General McClellan, come to join us," he called out. "Greetings, sir."

"General Sumner, gentlemen," nodded Little Mac.

Sliding to the ground, he approached the group, shaking the hands of several officers. "You've done well today. The Rebels have been driven back on all parts of the field and we hold the advantage. From your note, General Sumner, I gather you would prefer that we hold our current position rather than renew the attack. Is this an accurate assessment?"

"It is, sir. I am of the opinion that we have sufficient men and guns to defend the army's right flank against any attack the Rebels might launch. I do not believe, however, that we can remain in a strong defensive position if we go on the attack and are thrown back. We cannot both attack and defend. It must be one or the other."

General Franklin sucked his teeth loudly at this. "Sir, General Sumner is gun-shy. My boys are ready to go in. We can drive the Rebels from the area around the church in the woods. It's the key to their position. If we capture that high ground, they'll be forced to fall back north of Sharpsburg. Then we can pursue and destroy them." The stout general shook his fist for emphasis.

"Excuse me, sir," said Sumner, casting an acid glance at Franklin, "the general here was not in the western woods like I was when the Secesh counterattacked. I was fortunate to escape with my life, much less my command. Now my corps is all cut up. In fact, it is still in disarray."

"I observed the disorder behind your lines on my ride here," noted McClellan. "Every man we spoke to had the same tale—he didn't know where his regiment was or how to find it. I think your concern about the coherence of our defensive line on this flank is well founded."

Franklin grimaced, but Sumner took heart, going on to plead his case. "I am adamant, General McClellan, that we should not go on the attack in our present state. General Hooker's men and those of poor Mansfield are equally worn out. Besides, General Franklin does not seem to appreciate the ability of the Rebels to strike back. No more than an hour ago they launched yet another attack from the woods that nearly split my corps in two. No, general, we would do well to sit back and let things on General Burnside's flank carry us to victory."

McClellan studied the faces of the men around him. "Are all of you in agreement about this?"

Every man nodded but Franklin.

"Very well, then. General Sumner, you will hold your present line and have the fresh brigades from General Slocum's command replace those of yours on the line that are fatigued. Also, mass your guns to deter the enemy from making any advance."

"Already done, sir," nodded Sumner.

"Good, good. Do take special care to look to your right and continue to collect your regiments. In the meantime, I will rescind the order for General Porter to send two brigades here, as you will not be needing them."

"Sir, how are things on the left with General Burnside?" asked Franklin.

"According to the last report, they are going well. Burnside is across the creek and General Pleasonton has established a cavalry bridgehead on the hills near Sharpsburg. In fact, things have gone so well for us all over the field that I do not wish to risk the day by chancing another attack here. If Bobby Lee finds our position weak, it could be the end of this army. No, gentlemen, we will hold here and give Burnside an opportunity to see if he can accomplish something more on his part of the field."

The assembled officers nodded their assent.

"There is one other matter I must attend to," added McClellan. "I would put General Hancock in command of Richardson's division. Are either of you opposed to that?"

Sumner and Franklin looked at one another. "No, sir," they replied, practically in unison.

"Good, then let it be done," said McClellan. "Richardson believed his division too used up to advance further, especially without artillery support. Have Hancock assess the situation with fresh eyes and report to me what he finds."

Pausing, McClellan dug out his watch. "It is now two-thirty. I'm returning to headquarters to await word from General Burnside. With a little luck, and help from the Good Lord above, we will win eternal glory this day and save our nation!"

"Hear, hear! Bully!" shouted the assembled army brass. Little Mac returned their salutes and swung back onto Dan Webster, conscious of the irony that of all his subordinates, it would need to be Ambrose Burnside who won the day for them. He hoped only that the man could be counted on to accomplish the task.

35

Wednesday, September 17, 1862
2:00 p.m. to 5:30 p.m.
Ninth Corps, Left Flank of the Army of the Potomac
Rohrbach Bridge, Sharpsburg, Maryland

A long line of ammunition wagons creaked over the Rohrbach Bridge under the scowling eye of Ambrose Burnside. Upon attaining the far side of the creek, they rolled sharply to the right and began crawling up the hillside to Cox's Ninth Corps men assembling on the crest. Cox himself had ridden across the bridge soon after its capture while Burnside, urged on relentlessly by General McClellan, ordered a new attack as quickly as Cox could deploy.

Upon consulting with General Sturgis, however, Cox learned that many of his men had exhausted their ammunition. If they were to make a final push against the enemy's right flank, their supplies must be replenished. He therefore sent a request to Burnside, this one doubly frustrating to the Rhode Island general, that Orlando Willcox's division be permitted to lead the attack. With Rodman's troops on the left and Willcox's on the right, Sturgis's ammunition-depleted command could be put in reserve. The request made sense, but Burnside complained it would delay Cox's attack by at least another hour.

"Alas," he had sighed to the Ninth Corps' commander, "I want your assault to have the best chance of success, so I'll accede to your request, but be quick about it! General McClellan won't be pleased with the delay, and he's already ridden me today like a damned army mule."

"I'll see to it, general," saluted Cox, riding off to give the orders.

An hour later, Burnside sat on his horse along the road that led to the bridge. Teams of men collected the bodies of fallen comrades lying around him and carted them off to the rear. A shell crashed into the Antietam, blasting water loudly into the air and showering a mule team pulling an ordnance wagon. The braying beasts reared in fright, dragging their burden askew on the road.

"Blast it!" growled Burnside, who cinched up his reins and spurred his bob-tailed gray toward the chaos. "Driver, get those animals under control at once!"

The rattled man yanked hard on his reins. "Yessir! I'm doing the best I can. They won't move."

Burnside tugged out his pistol. Walking Major to a spot behind the mule team, he pointed the barrel at the ground and pulled the trigger. The gunshot flattened the mules' ears on their heads and with a loud screech, they lurched forward, dragging the wagon with them. Slipping his revolver back into its holster, Burnside edged out of the way.

"That's an effective method you have there, general," said a voice behind him. Burnside spun in the saddle to find an unwelcome visitor. "Colonel Key. Why are you here? Didn't you report to General McClellan that we have taken the bridge?"

"I did," leered Key, bringing to Burnside's mind the image of a snake. "He sent me back."

"He did, eh? Pray tell me, colonel, what our esteemed commander desires this time?"

"Tsk, tsk, General Burnside. Sarcasm does not flatter you. Our commanding general sent me back to urge that you advance with vigor against the enemy on the heights. He said you are to storm the battery that is harassing your men and carry on to Sharpsburg as quickly as you are able."

"Of course, colonel. As you can see, I am pushing supplies, and soon another division, across the creek for just such an attack." Burnside gestured to a column of men marching toward them behind the last covered wagon. "When we are ready, I will order General Cox to advance and we will crush the enemy's flank."

Key stared at the marching column. "So I see, general. You are active, indeed."

Annoyed by Key's glib response, Burnside changed the subject. "How are things going elsewhere, colonel?"

"They are going splendidly, but our losses have been heavy. General Hooker has been wounded. Shot in the foot, I recall, but he will live. General Mansfield, however, seems to have received a very serious wound earlier in the day. I do not know if he will recover. General Richardson and General Sedgwick have been injured as well, the former grievously."

"Those are grave losses," frowned Burnside, carefully masking his pleasure at hearing of Hooker's fate. "I don't hear much firing to the north. Is the fighting there finished?"

"I don't know, general. Perhaps it has taken a pause. The last I heard, General Sumner is considering a new attack on the right."

"So, the enemy's left flank remains intact? Now I understand why General McClellan has been so keen to press our attack here."

Burnside paused for a moment, a thoughtful expression on his face. Then he looked back at Key.

"Colonel, I assure you we are doing the best we can. It is difficult to get Cox's command into place with so narrow a bridge to cross, but I will not make excuses. Return to General McClellan and inform him that we will attack as soon as General Willcox's division is up."

"Thank you, sir, but I will not be leaving. The commanding general wishes me to stay until your attack is underway."

Burnside shook his head. "Again, General McClellan demands that an overseer watch me and my men."

The enigmatic grin returned to Key's lips, and he bowed gently in the saddle. "Not an overseer, my dear general. Merely an observer."

"Very well, then, Colonel Key. If you are to observe, I recommend the hilltop behind us by Lieutenant Benjamin's guns. His battery commands a broad view of the field. Now, you must excuse me. I am needed on the far side of the creek."

"Very good, sir," saluted the colonel. "Godspeed to you and good luck."

Returning Key's salute, Burnside called for his staff to follow him, and he kicked Major toward the bridge.

*   *   *

A legion of gnats circled the heads of Tom Kelly and his comrades in Company C. Kelly swatted ineffectually at them, first with his hand and then with his cap. Davey Parker, standing beside Kelly with the butt of his musket resting in the grass, choked suddenly, and doubled over coughing.

"One of them midges get you?" winked Kelly with a slap on his old friend's back.

"Agh! The damned thing flew down my throat!" Parker spit into the grass as a Rebel shell shrieked overhead.

"That's poor shooting, ye bastards!" jeered Kelly at the battery that had sent the round their way.

The cannons sat atop the ridge ahead of them with a clear view of the Antietam Valley. After wading across the creek on the right of the enemy's position above the bridge, Kelly and his companions had scaled the bluff overlooking the creek. There they caught sight of the Rebels who had held back the Ninth Corps for so long that morning. The retreating Graybacks scampered across a plowed field and into an enormous stand of corn, disappearing among the tall stalks before anyone could draw a bead on them.

Now, the hungry boys of the Twenty-Third Ohio stood in double ranks on the left side of a growing body of Union troops massing in the fields above the former Rebel position. To the left of Kelly and his friends stood the Thirtieth Ohio, their double lines stretching down the gentle slope in mirror image to those of the Twenty-Third. To the right, rank upon rank of Northern troops fell into position in an uneven line that undulated out of sight into a ravine.

A heavy first line of troops waited ahead of them behind two batteries of guns, exchanging shots with the enemy's batteries off to the right. A third battery of smoothbore Napoleons, its brass barrels glinting in the sun, occupied the edge of the plowed field some seventy-five yards directly ahead of Kelly and his comrades. Beyond this battery stood an expanse of corn and patches of meadow that rolled upward to the Rebel-capped ridge line.

Teams of pioneers from the two Buckeye regiments fanned out ahead of the line to hack down post and rail fences that criss-crossed the landscape. No barrier would be allowed to break up their formation when the call came to advance. Enemy gunshots cracked at the pioneers from the cornfield.

"Look at them cowardly Johnnies shooting at unarmed men," Kelly carped. "They ought to be ashamed of themselves."

"You'd do the same, I reckon," said Sam Carey, on Kelly's right. "The pioneers are preparing the way for us."

Kelly sucked his teeth skeptically. "Maybe, Sam. I'd rather meet a man in an honest fight, you know?"

Carey shook his head violently as a gnat buzzed into his right ear.

"When're we stepping off, is what I want to know," grumbled Parker on Kelly's left. "We've been standing here for near an hour making a meal for these goddamned flies. Let's get this over with already and get something to eat." Heads nodded around him. No man in his right mind liked standing idle for a stray minié ball or artillery shell to send him off to his Maker. The sooner the attack got off, the better.

Kelly rubbed a sweating palm against his thigh and reflected on what had happened to them that morning. After waking in a chilly mist, they got orders to break camp and fall in. Long-range Rebel artillery shells rained down among them, so General Rodman ordered everyone under his command to shelter behind the crest of a slope. There, Kelly devoured the last crust of bread he had received from Lucy Settle. Then, after a space of time listening to the thunderous battle raging to the north, orders arrived for the regiment to fall in. Major Comly got them into column, and they joined the other regiments marching down a steep hill to the creek. Upon reaching the creek they waited … and waited … and waited until orders arrived, sending them to a new ford some six hundred yards to the west, across the steep, broken face of a hillside.

When his turn came to cross, Kelly dropped into the water with his musket and cartridge box held high above his head. He sank to the bottom of his ribcage and grumbled that if this was really a ford, he would turn in his Catholic rosary beads for a Quaker's frock. His comrades, accustomed to Kelly's relentless banter, ignored him and tried to wade across as quickly as possible. Once on the other side, they climbed to the top of the bluff and moved into position on the left of General Cox's line. Now, they stood under sporadic artillery fire and the cloud of incessantly buzzing flies.

"I sure wish I had me pipe about now," Kelly sighed. "Here now, Davey, why didn't ye take care of me things back on the mountain?"

"Your things?" scowled Parker. "We thought you were dead. Then you show up two days later with a sack of food and some wild story about a crazy woman nursing you in Middletown? How was I supposed to know you'd be back for your things?"

"Ah, Davey, you'll never learn. The Johnnies can't kill me. I'm what they call impregnable."

The men around him let out a whoop.

"What are youse laughing at?" glared the Irishman.

"Impregnable! That's right funny," chuckled Carey. "Invincible, is what you mean. Works are impregnable, not men. And you ain't invincible neither."

Kelly blushed in the afternoon heat. "Oi, that there's a gaffe, eh, Sammy?"

"It surely was, but a good one anyway. A body would think English is your second language if he didn't know better."

"Well, it is! Me first language is Irish, taught to me in secret by me poor mother. God rest her soul."

"In secret? What are you talking about? You didn't learn your own language in school?" asked George Love from the second rank.

Kelly peered back over his shoulder. "School? No, George, I didn't. None of us did. Learning Irish is against the law in Ireland. The bastard English see to that."

"Can't learn your own language in your own country? Why, I never heard of such a thing," said Love with a shake of his head.

"I told ye things in me homeland were bad, didn't I?"

Love nodded. So Kelly had.

"Oh, how I could use a puff o' smoke," Kelly groaned again and still to no avail.

Bored stiff, he let his thoughts drift and soon found himself daydreaming about Lucy Settle. He recalled her shining gray eyes and her smile, which she flashed at him when he had not made her cross. One time, she caught him staring at her when he thought she was not looking. The ends of her lips had turned up pleasingly then, her cheeks blushing the color of pink roses. Kelly thought Lucy a thing of beauty at that moment; a soft, vulnerable, living manifestation of God's goodness.

If only so many strange ideas did not fill her pretty noggin, he chuckled to himself. Voting! For women? He could not fathom it. But, strange notions or not, he felt a small tug in his heart when he thought of her; a tiny sensation that spoke wistfully of love. And so he made a quiet vow to himself. He would fight for the causes she held dear and make himself worthy of her affection when this war was over.

Booming guns brought the dreaming Irishman back to his senses. The cannons ahead of him bucked and roared, sending fiery rounds screeching toward the enemy on the ridge above. The Rebels, though, gave better than they got, as marksmen hidden among the mature corn kept up a relentless fire on the crews manning the guns. Shells soared in from two directions, too, exploding among the hapless Napoleons. The rate of enemy fire had picked up along the entire line, in fact, and blazing pillars of smoke erupted close to the packed troops of Jacob Cox's command. Men cried out for help with their wounds as Federal batteries bellowed violently in response.

"Can you hear it, Tom? Something's about to give!" shouted Parker above the din.

"I hear it alright," Kelly nodded.

Every veteran on the field knew that a rising rate of fire signaled an attack about to begin and, sure enough, orders came down the line for them to load.

"No primers!" bawled Captain Skiles as he stalked past.

Kelly tore the end of a cartridge with his teeth, tasting the bitter tang of gunpowder as he poured the contents down his barrel. The ball rattled home at the base of his Springfield and Kelly packed it tight with his rammer. Then they waited as bugles blared and the regiments to the right of them stepped off with a loud cheer.

Long lines of men in blue advanced toward the high ground, their bayonets glittering in the late day sun. Rebel batteries took them under fire, sending rounds of case shot and balls of solid iron careening through their ranks. The explosions blew holes in the lines and shouts of anguish went up. Officers in the rear closed the files, guiding replacements into the gaps as the attack rolled onward.

"Will ye just look at 'em, Davey! They look superb!" cried Kelly, waving his cap.

Other men in the regiment did the same, cheering on the assault of their comrades intended to break Robert E. Lee's army once and for all. Yet, as they approached the crest, the blue lines ground to a halt. Rebel infantry met them there with musket and cannon fire and a pitched fight broke out. The gunfire exploded into a roar and heavy clouds of smoke enveloped the field. Tiny figures in blue could be seen limping back from the front, carrying wounded comrades.

Three regiments on the Twenty-Third's left advanced now into the vast field of corn under the flags of Connecticut and Rhode Island. Meeting no resistance, they pushed on until only the ornamental gold pieces at the tips of their flagpoles could be seen moving through the stalks. Then, without warning, a terrible volley of musket fire erupted on the advancing New Englanders. They had run headlong into regiments of Southerners hiding among the crops. The lines engaged and smoke enveloped the corn there, too.

Kelly, Parker, and the others watched this fight closely, alternately cheering or groaning as the struggle twisted and turned. A battery moved into place ahead of them and to the right, the guns opening fire on the Rebel batteries shooting down slope.

"Twenty-Third, shoulder arms!" came the order. Kelly hefted his rifle onto his right shoulder and looked around. Major Comly strode in front of them, a saber in his hand.

"Right face!" Kelly pivoted on his right foot to face the sweat-stained back of Sam Carey. "Forward, march!"

Stepping off left foot first, the Buckeye soldiers moved ahead, and then leftward, to a position some forty yards behind the new battery. There, they received orders to halt as the fight in front of them carried on. But whereas the afternoon's attack had started with promise, it now appeared to waver. A large body of Federal troops withdrew on their right, followed in short order by other regiments still farther to their right.

"Oh, that damned Secesh caterwauling!" growled Parker. "What do you suppose is happening up there?"

"Can't say!" yelled Kelly above the tumult. "Maybe the Johnnies got the best of them."

The battle on the left now also shifted in favor of the enemy as New England boys came reeling out of the cornfield.

"Hey, here comes the colonel!" pointed Carey to the thickly bearded Hugh Ewing.

The brigade's new commander, Ewing, rode to Major Comly, standing some fifteen feet ahead of the Twenty-Third. "Major, our attack is faltering!" bawled Ewing within earshot of Kelly and his friends. "Colonel Scammon has ordered me to advance. Get your men to that wall up the hillside on the double-quick!"

"Yes, sir," shouted Comly. Throwing the colonel a salute, he turned and began barking orders.

"Twenty-Third, fix bayonets and prepare to advance! Make it quick, boys!"

Steel blades clattered onto their rifles. Kelly fastened on his bayonet and drew out his rosary. Clutching the crucifix tightly in his palm, he shut his eyes and prayed for God's mercy with all of his might.

Comly cried out the order. "Regiment, at the double-quick! FORWARD!"

Bellowing a deep yell, Kelly and his comrades launched themselves over the grassy turf. They ran through the line of guns, which had fallen silent to let the Buckeyes pass. Descending into a swale, they scaled a snake rail fence that enclosed one side of a farm lane, and then a second one, before entering a plowed field. The tilled earth there gave way under Kelly's flat-bottomed boots, and he slipped and stumbled, his chest heaving. Blood pounded in his ears as shells screamed in from the heights, their impacts shaking the ground under his feet. He cried out in terror when a blast of black smoke and dirt lifted him backward off of his feet. Crashing hard to the ground, he lay stunned for a moment, spitting soil from his mouth. Then he sat up and ran his hands over his body, looking for a wound.

"Am I hurt? I'm not hurt. I'm not hurt! Thank you, Lord Jesus!" he shouted before scrambling to retrieve his dropped musket.

"To the wall!" cried Comly, pointing his saber at the stone structure rolling unevenly across the ground from left to right. The Buckeyes surged up the slope before collapsing against the rocks. Kelly wiped sweat from his brow and shot a glance at the Thirtieth Ohio stacked up against the wall on their left. The left flank of the Thirtieth had halted deep within the enormous and foreboding cornfield.

"Get ready, boys, they're coming!" shouted Comly. Kelly pocketed his rosary and plucked a priming cap from his belt pouch. Seating the cap on his Springfield, he clicked back the hammer and rested it against the stones.

"Davey, do you—do you see them?" he panted.

Parker scanned the field ahead. "Not yet. Hold on! There they are."

Pointing to the far side of the plowed field to their front, Parker directed Kelly's gaze to a crimson battle flag bobbing out of the corn. After a few steps, Rebel soldiers hove into view in a line that stretched off well to the Federals' left.

"Oi, here they come!" exclaimed Kelly.

"It's a good thing we filled up on cartridges!" shouted Parker. "I sure don't mind fighting behind a wall, either. Those fellows are out in the open."

Major Comly stalked behind the line. "Hold your fire until they get close. I'll tell you when to let them have it."

Kelly and his comrades laid their rifles across the wall and waited. The enemy line drew nearer, and Kelly took aim at a fellow in a red-checked shirt.

"FIRE!" bawled Comly.

Kelly pulled the trigger, watching his target pitch backward into the dirt. A second man took his place as the Butternuts howled their eerie yell.

Peering to the left, Parker yelled, "Tom, get down!" Kelly flopped onto the ground beside Davey as a volley exploded from a second Rebel line approaching them at an angle. Miniés whistled overhead, chipping bits of stone from the wall that pattered onto Kelly's jacket. A man several yards away cried out and fell backward, his hands grabbing at his face. Wiping away the dust, Kelly rolled onto his elbow and tore open a new cartridge. Then he rammed home the round and rose to his knees.

"Where in God's name did that come from?"

Parker, still lying on his back, jerked his thumb toward the second Rebel line. "That way!"

A geyser of fire and smoke exploded in front of them, sending Kelly once more into the dirt.

"Christ and the twelve apostles, what are we doing here?" he bellowed.

Rising tentatively, he looked in the direction that Parker had pointed. A battle line of troops, clad in a mixture of Union blue and Southern homespun jackets converged on the Thirtieth Ohio from the left at the same time as the Butternut line ahead of them closed in from across the plowed field.

"Davey, are those our boys?" cried Kelly as a ball thwacked into the wall near his head.

Parker shot an angry glance at them. "I don't think so. Why in the hell would they be shooting at us?"

Major Comly's sword sliced downward through the air behind them. "Regiment, FIRE! Let them have it, boys!"

Kelly and Parker rose to their knees and blasted the Johnnies in the open field. Men fell screaming, opening gaps in their line. Still, the Rebels held their ground, shots cracking out from their muskets. Again, Kelly and Parker ducked behind the stone wall. Muskets roared and a shrieking fellow pitched lifelessly across Parker's legs.

"Ah, get offa me! Get off, dammit!" Parker hollered, kicking away the corpse.

"Fire at will, gentlemen!" shouted Comly.

Parker turned to Kelly as he rammed home another round. His eyes filled with a wild light that the Irishman saw only when his friend went into battle; a kind of bloodlust that Kelly himself could not understand. It made Parker a terrible opponent in a fight, but a good man to have by your side. Nodding to his battle-mad friend, Kelly rose again from behind the wall and took aim. His rifle bucked hard against his shoulder, blowing out the brains of a Butternut soldier only thirty yards opposite him. Kelly knew he had hit the man directly from the red mist spraying into the air before he pitched backward into the dirt.

The Rebel line, now thinner than it had been, wavered for a moment as the roar of muskets on the Thirtieth Ohio's left grew louder. Kelly slumped against the wall and took a swig from his canteen as Parker sent another round flying at the enemy. Then a cry of panic went up from the corn. Peering in that direction, Kelly watched a wild-eyed man scramble by.

"The Rebels are flanking us! They're past our left!"

Crazed with battle-fever, Parker half raised his musket in the man's direction. "Come back, you damned coward! I should put a ball in you!"

Colonel Ewing hurried by, shouting for them to rise and march to the left. Climbing to his feet, Kelly saw men in blue coats advancing toward their flank. "Are those our boys, Davey? Why are they coming at us?" he yelped.

Both men reeled into the confused ranks of Buckeye troops. Major Comly pushed them into line as a minié thudded into the chest of the regiment's color bearer. The man beside him caught the falling flag when it dropped toward the earth. By now, the Rebels had come so close to the Thirtieth that their wolf-like yelps became deafening amid the crack of rifles and booming cannons. Smoke fouled Kelly's nostrils and burned his eyes. Then Major Comly bellowed the order to advance, and they stepped off by the right flank.

Wheeling the regiment straight for the dreaded cornfield from which they had watched the New Englanders flee only a short time earlier, the men of the Twenty-Third joined with the Thirtieth Ohio on their right, forming a thin line against the oncoming enemy, many of whom appeared to be wearing Union uniforms.

The Rebels advanced with precision to the edge of the corn, coolly leveled their muskets, and pulled their triggers.

Parker dropped his musket with a grunt. Kelly looked up from seating a cap to see his friend's powder-streaked face turn toward him. Parker's blue eyes opened wide, and his hands clutched at his chest, folding over a wound from which blood gushed in spurts. The stream burst through Parker's fingers, splashing onto Kelly's blouse, and dripping into the dirt. Parker's mouth fell open, dark and voiceless.

"Davey!" screamed Kelly as his friend collapsed.

A minié whistled past Kelly's face, close enough for him to feel it move the air. His head snapped back toward the enemy, and the roar of gunfire around him exploded once again into his senses. With tears streaming down his face, Kelly leveled his musket and let fly. If he hit his target, he could not tell amidst the smoke and screaming, cursing men. Sam Carey stood on his left now, and Kelly shot him a terrified glance. Stalwart Sam, as calm as ever, nodded silently at Kelly before lifting his rifle to fire.

Kelly slammed home another round and seated a cap when a cry of panic erupted on the right. He gazed up to see what remained of the Thirtieth Ohio peel away from the stone wall it had been defending. Bluecoat bodies lay along and slumped over the wall, bearing silent witnesses to the execution done there by Rebel gunfire.

A howl of triumph went up from the Butternuts, and they pushed forward to drive in the Buckeyes' flank. The remaining men in the Thirtieth's line blew away like chaff in a strong wind. Peering back at the Rebels in front of him, Kelly lifted his Springfield and pulled his trigger. Then something punched him hard in the gut and he stumbled backward.

Carey grabbed Kelly by the shoulder. "Tom, we've got to get out of here! The whole line's giving way!"

Kelly stared blankly at him. "Sammy boy, I—I've been shot."

Carey looked down at the dark stain spreading on Kelly's abdomen. The Irishman sank onto his knees, his musket falling from his hands.

"Tom!" cried Carey, shooting a glance from his friend to the oncoming enemy. Now, the Butternuts edged forward to drive off what remained of the Twenty-Third. Out of time, and lost in a moment of terror, Carey fled for his life.

Kelly crumpled into the dirt beside Parker, the whirl of battle gone quiet around him. Lifting his shaking hand to look at it, he found his palm slick with blood. Somehow, though, he felt no pain. A sweat-soaked man with a grimy face and bad teeth stepped near him to rifle through Parker's pockets. Finding nothing of value, he turned to Kelly as a tear fell from the Irishman's eye. Kelly's fingers closed around his rosary. The Southerner regarded him coldly, grabbing at Kelly's clutched hand to see what treasure it might hold. Kelly, though, held on tightly, and shaking his head, his lips formed the word, "no." The Rebel insisted, threatening Kelly with a wicked-looking blade tucked in the rope belt that held up his trousers. Kelly opened his palm to reveal his bloody crucifix. Then the man understood, and with a nod he closed the Irishman's hand to let Kelly to die in peace.

36

Wednesday, September 17, 1862
5:30 p.m. to Nightfall
Field Headquarters, Army of the Potomac
Philip Pry House, Keedysville, Maryland

general looked up from his binoculars, frustration clear on his face. Glancing back at Fitz John Porter, George McClellan waved a quivering hand toward Burnside's attack. "Did you see it, general? Did you see how Burnside has been checked?"

"I see it, sir," nodded Porter grimly, the smoldering stub of a cigar clenched between his lips. "Lee brought up more men. How many can he possibly have at his disposal?"

"More than I have, I'll wager!" barked Little Mac, his hands flying into the air. "I can't tell you the number of times I have sent to that fool, Halleck, for reinforcements. We must not leave the capital vulnerable to the possibility of a Rebel strike, he says."

McClellan thrust his finger at the fighting across the creek. "The Rebel army is here, sir! Here before us! There is no threat to Washington!"

Fuming, the general stared down at the idle troops behind the ridge along Antietam Creek; some four-thousand men at most. "What about your command, General Porter? Can we not throw it into the fight?"

Porter blew out a stream of smoke. "You could, sir, but my troops are the only men defending our center. We cannot spare them now, particularly with the threat on our right."

McClellan scrutinized the cannon fire thundering on General Sumner's front. Signalmen behind Federal lines reported Rebel troops moving north, threatening for the second time that afternoon to launch the attack on his right flank that McClellan feared most. How could he commit troops to the left with Sumner facing a potential enemy assault?

Little Mac folded his hands tightly behind him. "The opportunity to crush Lee's army is slipping from my grasp," he muttered quietly. "How could Burnside have moved so slowly?"

"The day is also long gone, sir," added Porter, overhearing the general. "Do you wish to pursue the fight in darkness?"

McClellan stared at the sliver of orange sun on the horizon. "No," he replied with a shake of his head. "I would, however, speak with General Sykes about the possibility of pushing forward in the center, if it can be done quickly. Will you come along?"

"Of course, general," nodded Porter, dropping the stub of his stogie into the dirt.

McClellan turned from the fence and called for his staff to follow. Custer fell in at the rear of the group as Little Mac strode to his mount. After climbing into their saddles, McClellan led them down the road and over a rolling field. The troops there climbed to their feet as McClellan passed by, raising their voices for him, and waving their caps. Little Mac doffed his kepi and cantered on to General Sykes. The tall West Pointer saluted when McClellan rode up.

"Good evening, sir. It is good to see you." he said.

"Hello, Sykes," nodded McClellan. "I've come to ask your advice."

"I'm honored, general. What can I do to help?"

"You can tell me your thoughts on the state of things. Should I order your division to cross the creek and press the enemy's center?"

Sykes gnawed his bottom lip. "I'm afraid I can't answer that without taking another look at the situation. Will you accompany me to the top of this ridge?" he gestured to the long slope beside them.

"Certainly. You men stay back," McClellan commanded his staff. "We don't want to present a target for Secesh gunners. Lead on, general."

Sykes climbed into the saddle and turned his mount toward the summit as a rider came pelting toward them from the direction of Burnside's command. Spotting McClellan, the man reined in hard, his horse's hooves throwing up clouds of dust.

"General McClellan, thank goodness I've found you! General Burnside sends me to request reinforcements and guns. He says that if he does not get them, he cannot hold his position for half an hour."

Sykes and Porter stared at Little Mac, whose lips tightened into a thin line. "Can things on the left be so tenuous?" asked Porter.

McClellan stared at the darkening sky, leaving Porter's question hanging unanswered in the air. "Tell General Burnside this is the battle of the war," he said finally. "He must hold his ground at all costs. I'll send him Miller's battery, but I can do nothing more at this point. I have no infantry to spare."

"Yes, sir!" saluted the courier, who wheeled his horse back in the direction he had come.

"And corporal!" called McClellan as the man spurred away, bringing him bounding to a stop. "Also tell General Burnside that if he cannot hold his ground, he must hold the bridge to the last man! Always the bridge! If the bridge is lost, all is lost. Do you understand?"

"Yes, sir! Hold the bridge at all costs," nodded the soldier. Then he rode away.

Turning back to Sykes, McClellan told him to have Miller's battery of the Fourth U.S. Artillery sent to Burnside. The three officers then steered their horses up the hillside to the broad summit, where two batteries of rifled guns sent rounds flying at the enemy on the far hills. The exhausted gunners, jaded after a full day's work, stared dully at Little Mac as he rode to a spot just behind them.

"So, general," said Sykes, gesturing to the rising ground across Antietam Creek, "per earlier orders, I sent four battalions of infantry to the other side, along with two batteries of artillery, Robertson's and Hains's, there and there." Sykes pointed to the three-inch ordnance rifles in the near distance. "Those are General Pleasonton's men directly below us. His guns are active on the hillside to the right."

McClellan peered down at the ranks of dismounted horsemen waiting behind the slope of a hill on the far side of the creek. Taking out his field glasses, he put them to his eyes, scanning the far ridge for Rebels.

"I see only a few guns on those heights!" he bawled above the banging gun fire. "The enemy's center looks vulnerable."

"I—just a moment, sir." Sykes turned to meet a courier. Reading the note, he extended it to Little Mac. "This agrees with your assessment, general."

McClellan let his binoculars hang on their strap. "Who is this, Captain Dryer? Is his judgment sound?" he asked, looking up from the paper.

"Very sound," nodded Sykes. "Captain Dryer commands the Fourth Regiment of U.S. Infantry. Earlier this afternoon, I sent him across the creek with the others. You can see them there on the far ridge." Sykes pointed at the thin line of men in blue.

McClellan followed the gesture, his eyes narrowing. He turned back to Sykes. "General, this report is remarkable. Captain Dryer says he has looked personally into the enemy's lines and found only two regiments and one battery before him. If this is true, then the Rebel army's center is much weaker than I thought."

"Indeed, sir. We should have a go at them."

"Maybe," replied Little Mac, his eyes lighting up at the possibility of splitting Lee's army in two.

Three more riders approached, and McClellan looked back to see General Marcy coming up with an orderly and Captain Custer. The older officer reined in, offering McClellan a note. "Sir, this just arrived by signal," he said. "It's urgent."

McClellan glanced down at the paper, his eyes growing wide.

"What is it, sir?" asked Porter.

Grinning, McClellan looked up. "It could be good news. The signal station behind us reports that the enemy is withdrawing toward Shepherdstown. Marcy, send this message to General Burnside immediately and ask him to determine if there is any truth in it. If there is, he is to push forward vigorously and let me know if the enemy is indeed retreating. If he is, I'll advance in the center straightaway. By all means, hurry, man!"

"Orderly!" barked Marcy, yanking out his dispatch book. Scribbling out the message, he wrapped the signal officer's dispatch in his own and sent the man racing toward Burnside's position.

"General Porter, how quickly can your men move up?" asked McClellan, an edge of impatience in his voice.

"Within the hour, sir, but do you believe an attack is wise? We have no reserves."

"I'm well aware of that, general, but we have a chance to whip Lee's army and end this war. I'll throw in every man if I must!"

"Very well, sir. In that case, General Sykes's command can move immediately."

"That's true. My division can be ready forthwith," nodded Sykes. "The problem, sir, is daylight. It will be dark soon."

McClellan stared up at the sky, noting the purple and orange hues of dusk. "What is the time now?"

"Six-twenty, sir," replied Marcy.

"General, there's no way my whole command can be ready to move before dark," said Porter. "Sykes can move, and I have another brigade from Morrell's division that can follow him, but the two brigades you ordered to Sumner haven't returned yet. They'll never make it here in time."

"Blast!" thundered McClellan in frustration.

Staring at the sparsely defended hills beyond Antietam Creek, he watched as nightfall descended over the countryside. It's arrival quieted the gunfire on the left first. Then the guns on the far right fell silent, leaving Little Mac waiting in vain for Burnside's reply. Sitting exasperated atop Dan Webster, the general shook his head with dismay.

"Gentlemen, we can do nothing more today," he said at last. "Our army holds the field on the right. We have a bridgehead in the center and Burnside possesses the heights above the lower bridge. Although we have not destroyed the enemy, we have thrown him back everywhere we have met him."

Yet we cannot declare victory, thought George Custer, reflecting bitterly on the slaughter he had witnessed that day.

Porter, however, fawned over their commander. "Sir, I must say you fought the battle splendidly. I have never seen better. It was a masterpiece in the art of war."

McClellan took some solace from Porter's praise. "Thank you, general, you are too kind, but tomorrow is a new day. We will renew the contest then, if Lee is still there in the morning."

"What do you plan to do, sir?" asked Sykes. "I would have my men ready, if they are to be needed."

"They shall be, General Sykes. I can assure you of that," nodded Little Mac. "I have called up reinforcements. General Humphreys of General Porter's corps is on his way here now with his division from Frederick City. I have urged him to force his march if he must. I will also call General Couch's division to us from Harpers Ferry and have General Reynolds meet us with his militia from Pennsylvania.

Governor Curtin informed me some time ago that Reynolds has 15,000 men ready to march on Hagerstown. Imagine what we will do with them, and the rest of our army collected in one place! General Franklin also told me of a plan to renew the attack on our right. A strategic hill there is his objective. When he attains it, he will turn the Rebel army's left. That is when you, General Sykes, along with the rest of your corps, General Porter, will strike the enemy's center. Together with General Burnside advancing on the left, we will crush the Rebels once and for all!"

McClellan shook his fist in the air for emphasis.

Custer listened quietly to this, thinking he had heard all of it before. The plan of attack that morning had called for almost the same steps—for Hooker to assault the Rebel left before Porter struck their center and Burnside their right. Those designs had wrought little more than a stalemate. Leading the army from the front ought to have been McClellan's job, ruminated Custer. Why had he not taken to the field with his men instead of remaining behind the lines to steer things from afar? General Hooker had done it, which Custer respected, even though the man could be an infuriating braggart.

For the first time since he had known McClellan, doubts about the general crept into Custer's mind. He had watched Little Mac grow erratic that afternoon, his mood changing more often than the weather on a November day. Good news sent McClellan soaring. Ill tidings threw him into despair. The extremes of temperament struck Custer as unnerving in a man who held the lives of so many in his hands.

How could a man he admired be so unwilling to risk everything by fighting not to lose as much as he had fought to win?

Had McClellan committed all three of his corps on the right that morning, they might be celebrating with a glass of brandy in Sharpsburg. As it was, the fight would continue tomorrow, or so the general said. Could Custer take him at his word? Doubt gnawed in his gut. If Little Mac resumed the attack in the morning, so much the better. If not, history would remember him for what he might have accomplished rather than what he had done. At that moment, Custer made a silent vow to himself. If he ever had the opportunity to command men, he would not shrink from pitching into the enemy with all the force he could muster. He would do what needed to be done.

God willing, it would come out alright.

37

Thursday, September 18, 1862
Late afternoon
Behind Ninth Corps Lines, Left Flank of the Army of the Potomac
Near Sharpsburg, Maryland

The wagon carrying Simon and Lucy rattled over the pitted turnpike between Keedysville and Sharpsburg, passing meadows packed with wagons, horses, and artillery. The pair scanned the countryside for signs of army field hospitals— grim places filled with suffering and, in many cases, slowly dying men.

"I dunno about finding Mister Tom in all this mess, Miss Lucy," said Simon with a shake of his head. "We been all over this place and ain't seen a body who knows him."

"I know, Simon, but we must keep trying," replied Lucy calmly. "Something inside of me says that Tom is in need. The fighting yesterday sounded terrible, even in Middletown. I'm worried he's been hurt."

"You sure gone sweet on Mister Tom, ain't you, Miss Lucy?" grinned Simon.

Embarrassed, she lowered her gaze. "I admit I have, Simon. He can be infuriating, but he has a sweetness about him that my heart can't ignore."

"You been thinking on him since he left, I reckon?"

"I have. He's been in my thoughts since you took him away. I don't know what draws people to each other, Simon. Whatever it is, Tom and I feel it, I think. We must find him."

A musket-bearing sentry hailed them, and Simon pulled his team to a stop.

"Ma'am," nodded the man with a touch of his cap. "Civilians aren't allowed to pass this way. You'll need to have your boy here turn around."

"Simon is not my boy," bristled Lucy. "He's a man helping me find a soldier I fear has been wounded."

The sentry glanced from Miss Settle to Simon, who kept his gaze focused straight ahead of him, and then back to her. "That may be, ma'am, but I still can't allow you to pass. There are shells falling in the area. It's too dangerous."

"Shells?"

"Yes, ma'am. Those explosions you hear every so often. Those are shells."

"I see. Forgive me, sir, I'm not familiar with the vocabulary of war. Is there still fighting going on?"

"No, ma'am. Talk is we're waiting on reinforcements. I reckon we'll take another crack at them tomorrow."

Lucy considered this for a moment. Then she softened her expression and batted her eyelashes at the sentry. "It sounds dangerous, sir, but are you sure we cannot pass? I'd be ever so grateful if you'd let me search for my husband. He is here among you somewhere."

Simon shot a sidelong glance at Lucy, who kicked his ankle from under her skirt.

"Oh, you say the man's your husband?"

"Indeed, he is. We've come a long way to find him, too. I have a basket of things for him. They'll go to waste if I don't give them over." She reached into the back of the wagon to lift the cloth that covered a basket of fruit, bread, and other edibles.

The sentry scrutinized the basket, nodding to his comrade in the process. "What do you think, Charlie? Should we wave them through?"

"Don't see why not," shrugged the second sentry. "I'd want to see my missus if she was here. What harm can it do?"

"I guess you're right. Alright, ma'am, we'll let you pass, seeing as how you're here to visit your man." He shot a furtive glance around and lowered his voice. "Say, can you spare anything from those vittles that Charlie and I might like?"

Lucy feigned a cunning look, as if she had just been let in on a joke. "Why, of course, sir," she chirped. "Would you and Charlie like a jug of apple cider? I have one right here I can give you."

The man's face lit up. "Oh, yes, ma'am, we'd appreciate that very much!"

Reaching into the wagon, she hefted a small ceramic jug and handed it down to the guard. He took it with a grin and stepped back from the wagon, waving for Simon to drive on. Lucy, though, laid a hand on Simon's arm, commanding him to stop.

"Before we go, sir, perhaps you can tell me something," she said.

"I'll try, ma'am."

"I'd be grateful. I'm hoping you can direct me to the men of the Twenty-Third Ohio. Do you know where they might be camped?"

The man looked down at his boots, a hand rubbing his chin.

"Who's she looking for?" called Charlie from the far side of the wagon.

"The Twenty-Third Ohio. You heard of them?"

Charlie ruminated for a moment before speaking. "They're part of that new outfit from out west, ain't they? The Kanaw division, or something like that?"

"I believe you're right. Are they new to this army, ma'am?"

"That's correct, sir," nodded Lucy, batting her eyes a second time for good measure.

"Well, then, that would put them on the left with General Burnside, I reckon. Rough time those boys had yesterday. I hope your man is alright."

Lucy's expression darkened. "They saw fighting, then?"

"They did, ma'am. Hard fighting, too." The soldier pointed straight ahead. "Follow this road to those hills in front of us and then turn off to the left when the ground slopes down. Keep going in that direction and ask for the Ninth Corps, General Burnside's men. Someone'll steer you right."

"Did you hear that, Simon?" Lucy asked.

"Yes, Miss Lucy, I heard him."

"Very well, then, let's drive on. Thank you for the kindness, sir, and for yours, too, Mister Charlie."

"Our pleasure, ma'am," saluted the sentry. Both men stood back as Simon flicked his reins.

Their path took them past more wounded troops making their way to the rear. Wagons filled with the suffering bumped east down the turnpike, the men inside groaning with agony at every jolt. Lucy scrutinized the stricken figures as they passed; boys with hollow eyes who stared at her as if she was an unearthly vision. Those with caps doffed them to her while those without bowed gently at the waist if they were able. To all this, Lucy waved and nodded, her lips parted in a gentle smile even though her inner being reviled the things she saw.

"Simon, I don't know how they do it," she whispered. "How do they carry on in the face of such horror?"

"I dunno, Miss Lucy. Maybe some of 'em believes like you 'bout the war. You say a man needs more than an earthly desire to make him go. Maybe the Lord done gave these boys that spirit."

She thought over the wisdom in this as Simon steered the wagon off the road to the left. They entered a pasture and rolled onward, asking along the way where to find the Ninth Corps of General Burnside. Eventually, they crossed a low hill to a field near an orchard covered with small canvas shelters. Dozens of men lay under them in various states of health. The slightly wounded chatted quietly while the more seriously injured lay moaning in bandages stained red with blood. Several of the more alert turned with curiosity to regard the oncoming wagon.

Orderlies, civilian aides, and physicians moved among the injured, ministering to wounds and providing water. Simon drove up to the outer edge of the encampment and pulled his team to a stop, allowing Lucy to climb down from the bench.

"Pardon me, sir," she said, walking up to one of the attendants, "are these poor boys from the Ninth Corps, General Burnside's men?"

"Yes, ma'am, all of them are," he nodded. Lucy glanced anxiously at the injured, her heart aching with sorrow. God forbid Tom lay among them.

"We've made progress, then," she said at last. "Perhaps you can help me. I'm searching for a man named Kelly—Thomas Kelly. His Irish brogue is so pronounced you'd be able to identify him the moment he opened his mouth, and he never has trouble doing that. Tell me, please, have you met any Irish among the wounded?"

Pulling off his cap, the orderly scratched his head. "No, ma'am," he replied. "I haven't met any Irish today. You're welcome to look around, though."

"Very well. I'll see if I can find him. May we park our wagon here?"

"Yes, ma'am. That copse of trees is where the most gravely wounded have been collected. Horses and wagons are tied off on the far side."

He pointed to a stand of locust trees a short distance away. Lucy thanked him and climbed back onto the bench beside Simon, directing him to steer toward the copse. Simon walked the team to the place indicated and set the handbrake as she climbed down.

"Do you want me to come with you, Miss Lucy?" he asked.

"Yes, Simon, of course. Four eyes are better than two. The faster we look, the faster we can find Tom ... if he's here."

Simon stepped to the ground. "You sure he's hurt? He could still be with the others out there." Simon waved in the direction of blue-coated troops visible atop the ridge beyond the creek.

"I don't know, Simon. Something tells me he is near. We must find him."

"Alright, then, Miss Lucy, I'll get looking."

Lucy strode into the shade. The sky had grown heavy with clouds threatening rain. Stricken figures lay stretched out on the ground under woolen blankets. Low moans came from some, but most held as silent as death itself. She stepped around them carefully, peering into the men's faces for Tom Kelly.

Glancing this way and that, she covered most of the copse before coming to a large locust tree on its far side. The long, leafy branches sheltered several injured men lying there. A young soldier holding his cap in his hands stood beside a comrade on the ground. Beside him knelt a minister clutching a Bible. Making the sign of the cross, the preacher muttered the end of a prayer and climbed to his feet. Lucy made for them, gasping out loud when she spied the man's ashen face.

"Tom? Oh, dear God, no!"

"Miss Lucy, wait!" cried Simon, reaching after the bolting woman.

Turning as Lucy rushed up, the young soldier standing nearby caught her in his arms. "Hold on a minute! Who in the blazes are you?"

"Let go of me! I know him!" barked Lucy as she struggled to escape.

Kelly's eyes cracked open at the commotion. "Lucy? Is it really you?" he whispered.

"Tom, do you know her?" asked Sam Carey.

Nodding, Kelly waved her on. She flew from Carey's grasp and threw herself across Kelly's chest.

"Oh, I was right!" she cried. "Something told me you'd been hurt, Tom, and now I see it's true. Are you badly injured?"

"He is dying, miss," intoned the minister. "I've done the best I can for him, but he's a Catholic and I'm of Protestant faith. We don't have the Last Rites they ask for when they're on death's doorstep."

Tears filling her eyes, Lucy stared at the man. Then she wiped her face and looked back at her stricken love. "Tom, you will come back to Middletown with me this instant. I'll have none of this talk about you dying. We have each other to live for now. I've nursed you back to health once already. I can do it again."

"Now I know who you are!" exclaimed Carey. "You cared for Tom after the fight on South Mountain. You're the one who gave him the food we all shared."

She looked up. "That I did. My name is Lucy Settle. Tom convalesced in my house. He has become ... special to me."

"And you to him," offered Carey. "Tom speaks fondly of you, Miss Settle. Not in detail mind you, but there's a light in his eye when he mentions your name. Only a man in love looks like that."

Lucy stared miserably at Carey, her bottom lip trembling. She wiped furiously at her tears, determined not to show Kelly any weakness at that moment.

"Come home with me, Tom," she whispered, leaning in close to him. "I love you, you Irish fool."

Kelly's hand closed around Lucy's. "No time, my dear. None at all. The Lord is calling me home, but me heart will always belong to you, Lucy. I promise."

Lucy sobbed openly now, her tears dropping onto Kelly's blanket. He mustered a smile and waved her close. "I did what you asked of me, Lucy. I kept me promise and fought with your cause in my, my—oh, sweet Jesus, the pain—your cause in my heart."

Sniffling, Lucy pulled back. "My cause? What are you saying, Tom? Tell me."

His teeth gritted, Kelly raised a quaking hand to Simon, weakly beckoning him to approach. The black man looked apprehensively at Lucy, who nodded for him to come forward. Simon pulled the hat from his head and stepped up, sinking onto one knee by Tom's side. Kelly reached out, offering to take Simon's hand. Simon once more glanced uneasily around him.

"Go ahead, Simon. Take it," urged Lucy quietly.

"Yes'm, Miss Lucy," Simon nodded and clasping Kelly's fingers, he squeezed them tightly. Kelly smiled at this and nodded before quietly breathing his last.

Afterword

McClellan ended the day on September 17, 1862, with every intention of renewing his attack on Robert E. Lee's army the next morning. He even had in place an operational plan that General Franklin, commander of the army's Sixth Corps, had suggested toward sundown. Franklin proposed moving his command to the far right of the Union line for an assault on Nicodemus Hill, the summit from which James Ewell Brown "Jeb" Stuart's Confederate artillery had pounded the Union right all day during the battle. Franklin correctly identified the hill as a key landmark on the field. Take it, he reasoned to McClellan, and it would turn the Rebel army's left, effectively completing the plan that McClellan himself had set in motion when he ordered Hooker's corps across Antietam Creek on September 16.

McClellan initially approved Franklin's idea, but by dawn on September 18, he had countermanded the order, telling the Sixth Corps' commander to stay put, until, as Franklin later explained, General John Reynolds could reach the field with 15,000 fresh men from Pennsylvania. These troops, untrained militia raised in a last-minute panic by Governor Andrew Curtin to meet the Confederate army's approach, never arrived. After marching to Hagerstown, they balked, refusing to move another inch farther from the Pennsylvania State Line. They had, after all, taken up arms to defend Pennsylvania, not to intervene in events in Maryland. McClellan waited in vain for these reinforcements, therefore, allowing September 18 to pass without renewing his offensive.

General Lee kept his troops in position all day after the battle. When no enemy attack developed, he began pulling back across the Potomac and by early September 19, he had once again reached the safety of Virginia. Lee might have stayed in Maryland to resume the fight on September 19, if a driving rain late in the afternoon on September 18, had not threatened to make the river behind him impassable. He had also received few replacements for the men he had lost while McClellan steadily added the previously detached parts of his command, including the infantry division of Darius Couch, which arrived from Pleasant Valley, and that of Andrew Humphreys, which made a forced march from Frederick to arrive late in the day on September 18.

By that point, Lee had begun his retreat, and on the morning of September 19, McClellan sent Alfred Pleasonton's cavalry and the two divisions of Fitz John Porter's Fifth Corps in pursuit. These forces arrived too late to intercept Lee's troops before they crossed back into Virginia at Boteler's Ford. McClellan then authorized Porter to attack the rear elements of the Rebel army on the Virginia side of the river, resulting in a clash outside of Shepherdstown on September 20, that ended in a Union defeat when Ambrose Powell Hill threw back Porter's attack with heavy losses. This final action brought the Maryland Campaign to an end, although the armies would continue watching each other for the next five weeks, and Stuart would lead a cavalry raid into Pennsylvania in early October.

McClellan concluded the campaign believing that he had decisively defeated Robert E. Lee at Antietam, thereby saving the nation and delivering Maryland and Pennsylvania from the threat of Rebel invasion. President Lincoln, McClellan's numerous enemies in Washington, and even some men on his staff, such as topographer Lieutenant Colonel David H. Strother, remained less sure. Criticism that Little Mac had not bagged the entire Rebel army at Antietam surfaced almost immediately, putting the general on the defensive. He expressed this frustration in a letter to his wife on September 21, complaining,

> *Do you know that I have not heard one word from Halleck, the President, nor the Secretary of War! ... All, except fault-finding, that I have had since leaving Washington was one [message] from the President about the Sunday battle (i.e., South Mountain), in which he says, 'God bless you and all with you!' That is all I have; but plenty from Halleck couched in almost insulting language and prophesying disaster! I telegraphed him last night that I regretted the uniformly fault-finding tone of his despatches, and that he had not as yet found leisure to notice the recent achievements of my army.*

Did George McClellan win the glorious victory at Antietam that he believed he had? Historians have been content to declare the fighting on September 17 a tactical draw, but the overall result of the campaign was a strategic victory, because it ended Lee's operation in Maryland. A decent case could be made, however, for McClellan's army having won both strategic and tactical victories at Antietam. As the late historian, Joseph Harsh has noted, Lee's lines collapsed five times during the fighting that day. It was only after the fortuitous arrival of A. P. Hill's Light Division late in the afternoon that Lee avoided a total catastrophe.

Sunset found McClellan's men in possession of every position the Confederates had occupied at the start of the battle, and while the Army of Northern Virginia had not been destroyed, it had been driven back at all points and battered severely by McClellan's troops. Lee's reluctance to retreat on the night of September 17 amounted to little more than posturing that gave the appearance of a tactical draw, but in reality, McClellan's men had mauled the Army of Northern Virginia, making its withdrawal all but inevitable. This is roughly the same result achieved by George Meade at Gettysburg in July 1863, and yet that battle is declared a clear Union victory, while Antietam is not.

The Army of the Potomac nevertheless suffered terribly while giving McClellan his triumph. Lee's troops inflicted 12,401 casualties, including 2,108 killed, 9,540 wounded, and 753 missing. The Army of Northern Virginia, by comparison, lost 1,546 killed, 7,752 wounded, and 1,018 missing, for a total of 10,316 casualties. The combined total casualties for both armies came to 22,717, making Antietam the bloodiest single day of combat in the American Civil War, although higher numbers of men would be killed in battles yet to come.

McClellan would later cite this punishment of his army as a reason why he did not resume his attack on Lee the following morning. Losses in general officers also figured largely in his thinking. Multiple experienced commanders from the corps to the brigade level were either killed or wounded at South Mountain (Reno) and at Antietam (Mansfield, Hooker, Sedgwick, Rodman, Dana, Hartsuff, Richardson, etc.). Other officers took their places, but many of them were unproven in their new capacity, a reality that made McClellan concerned about the operational efficiency of his force. On September 18, therefore, he chose to wait until reinforcements could be brought up, ammunition could be replenished (many front-line regiments started the morning with empty cartridge boxes), and the men rested. Had Lee stood his ground on September 19, it is likely that McClellan would have resumed his attack, adding further to Antietam's grim toll of dead and wounded.

Some historians discount McClellan's concerns about reinforcements and ammunition given that portions of his army, particularly Porter's Fifth Corps and Franklin's Sixth Corps, did not see combat on September 17. Recent research by historian and licensed battlefield guide, Steven R. Stotelmyer, suggests that the number of fresh troops McClellan had at his disposal was far smaller than earlier generations of historians have believed.

The point is not to quibble over numbers, but to recognize that McClellan's decisions on September 18 were informed by his concern about the condition of his men. He remained keenly aware of his responsibilities to the army and the nation, responsibilities that entailed keeping his force in fighting shape, and ensuring that the Army of Northern Virginia could not launch a new expedition north of the Potomac. To recount McClellan's own words, written in his lengthy report of August 1863:

After a night of anxious deliberation, and a full and careful survey of the situation and condition of our army, the strength and position of the enemy, I concluded that the success of an attack on the 18th was not certain (emphasis added). I am aware of the fact that under ordinary circumstances a general is expected to risk a battle if he has a reasonable prospect of success; but at this critical juncture I should have had a narrow view of the condition of the country had I been willing to hazard another battle with less than an absolute assurance of success. At that moment—Virginia lost, Washington menaced, Maryland invaded—the national cause could afford no risks of defeat. One battle lost and almost all would have been lost. Lee's army might then have marched, as it pleased, on Washington, Baltimore, Philadelphia, or New York.

These were not unreasonable fears on McClellan's part, particularly since he irrationally continued to believe in Lee's numerical superiority. Again, a similar situation can be said to have prevailed on July 4, 1863, when George Meade also decided not to attack the bloodied Rebel army at Gettysburg. Meade had more fresh troops he could have thrown in than McClellan, but has received little of the criticism McClellan had endured.

There is another factor to consider when weighing the success of McClellan's effort in 1862. Congressional elections loomed in November. If McClellan had decided to continue fighting on September 18, and wrecked his army in the process, it might have resulted in a decisive defeat for the Republicans that could have changed the course of the war. Ironically, then, by keeping his army intact and by holding Lee at bay, George McClellan may have saved both the Union war effort and Abraham Lincoln's presidency.

It is easy to overlook the potential for a Union disaster at Antietam rather than the success that McClellan actually achieved. This is almost certainly the case because the general's political enemies, Lincoln's criticism, and the heavily biased judgments of later writers such as William Swinton and Francis Winthrop Palfrey skewed public understanding of the events. Their criticism set the tone for an unfavorable view of McClellan that holds sway to the present day.

There is plenty in McClellan's performance to be critical of—his tardiness moving Hooker across the Antietam on September 16, his confusing interruption of Burnside's deployment that afternoon, and his detached approach to the fighting on the morning of September 17, are but a few examples. There is, by contrast, much to praise in his handling of the situation, and in the favorable result he achieved. Under similar conditions, few generals on either side in the Civil War might have done better.

The one thing McClellan did not do well was adjust to the political climate, and for this his reputation has justifiably suffered. Talk of turning the army against the Republican administration continued to simmer among his officer corps after Antietam, particularly when President Lincoln announced his preliminary Proclamation of Emancipation on September 22, 1862. As Ethan Rafuse cogently explains, the political winds shifted toward a hard war policy in 1862 that targeted slavery as a means of undermining the South's ability to fight. Rebel soldiers employed at home planting crops instead of slave labor could not wield muskets at the front.

McClellan, and many of his senior officers, vehemently opposed Lincoln's policy, arguing they fought to save the Union, not to end slavery, opinions I have sought to make clear in conversations between Colonel Key and others, as well as in the ranks of the common soldier. The reality is that Lincoln's emancipation announcement caused a great deal of bitterness among Northern troops in McClellan's army and elsewhere. This fact that has been lost over time as public memory conflates the Battle of Antietam with abolition. Lincoln may have used McClellan's victory to advance his agenda, but for many in the Army of the Potomac, slavery's abolition and the Union war effort bore at best a tenuous relationship.

Talk against the administration grew so common, in fact, that McClellan felt compelled in early October to issue a public reminder to his men of their responsibility to carry out the policies of the civilian government. His orders counseled respect for civilian authorities when discussing political matters, and he admonished the men that elections were the proper means of voicing political dissent. That McClellan thought it necessary to issue such orders reflects both an attempt to reassure Washington of his personal loyalty, and the high level of discontent in his army over the policies being pursued by the administration. The unvarnished reality is that as much as one might wish it to have been, in 1862, the Army of the Potomac was not the virtuous army of liberation it has been made out to be.

McClellan continued to wrestle personally with this issue as well. Concerned about abolition's radicalizing effect on the war, the general became alarmed by Lincoln's suspension of the writ of habeas corpus for criticism of the conflict. McClellan resolved publicly to continue doing his duty, but privately he loathed the administration's policies, calling them an "accursed doctrine [of] servile insurrection" and a twisting of republican institutions toward despotism; language quite similar to what one might have read in the *Charleston Mercury* or any other of the other fire-eater newspapers in the South.

Unsure how to approach these policies, McClellan wrote to political allies for advice, and at the end of September he even hosted a dinner at his headquarters during which he asked Jacob Cox, Ambrose Burnside, and others what he should do in response. Cox and the others advised McClellan to refrain from the "fatal error" of opposing the administration, even though some prominent Democrats urged him to do so. McClellan remarked that slavery would wither away with a Northern victory, noting correctly that it disappeared wherever the army went in western Virginia, on the James River Peninsula, and during Burnside's early operations in North Carolina.

What McClellan opposed was the use of a presidential order to implement a radical political policy that would give the South no reason to negotiate. The war, McClellan believed, would proceed until its bitter end with one combatant or the other utterly destroyed. Better to pursue a conservative policy of reconciling with the South to bring the seceded states back into the Union and then work toward ending slavery. Cox and Burnside disagreed with this, advising McClellan to make a public announcement that would, as Rafuse has written, "quell agitation in the army over the proclamation." McClellan's October decree was the result.

President Lincoln, meanwhile, harbored no illusions about McClellan, or about the dissent seething in the ranks of the nation's largest army. In late September, a comment came to light, uttered by Major John Key, the brother of Colonel Thomas Key, McClellan's closest personal advisor, that alluded to a conspiracy. Claiming to a colleague that McClellan had deliberately not "bagged" Lee's army at Antietam, Major

Key stated, "that is not the game. The object is that neither army shall get much advantage of the other, [and] that both shall be kept in the field till they are exhausted, when we will make a compromise and save slavery." Lincoln caught wind of this and called the younger Key to account for it in the White House. When Key did not deny the sense of what he had said, Lincoln said his goal was to break up "the game" and he promptly had Key expelled from military service.

There is no proof that McClellan agreed with such a policy. Major Key may have been speaking out of turn, or simply parroting things he had heard said by his older brother. The available historical evidence shows that McClellan had legitimate concerns about the state of his army after Antietam, and that these account for much of his inactivity. Evidence from regiments on the front line shows nevertheless that as of dawn on September 19, they had orders to push forward and renew their attack upon the Rebels. When they did this, they found Lee's men gone.

Conceivably, McClellan could be forgiven for showing less energy on September 18-19 because by that time he was suffering from a full-blown flare up of malaria—his old "Mexican disease" as he referred to it. The malady, alluded to several times in *The Guns of September* as symptoms of diarrhea, cold sweats, and aching muscles, incapacitated him for several days after the battle. Lincoln could not have known this when he set out with Major Key to see the army himself and to prod McClellan to advance. That visit produced several remarkable photographs of the president and the general taken by Alexander Gardner. It also convinced Lincoln to conclude on October 2 that the Army of the Potomac was not his to command. Rather, it was "General McClellan's bodyguard."

McClellan did at last move his refit and rested army at the end of October. Marching east of the Blue Ridge Mountains, he slipped into Virginia before Lincoln finally relieved him of command in early November, just after mid-term elections had passed. Following his removal, McClellan went on in 1863 to defend his record before the congressional Joint Committee on the Conduct of the War. He then made an unsuccessful run as the Democratic Party's candidate for president in 1864 before finally passing from the public scene.

Lincoln, in the meantime, elevated Ambrose Burnside to command of the army in November 1862. Burnside did not want this authority, but when confronted with the possibility that his nemesis, Joe Hooker, would be given it instead, he relented. Subsequent events would prove Burnside to be a realistic judge of his poor executive abilities when he shattered his army by launching repeated frontal assaults against the entrenched Confederate line at Fredericksburg, Virginia, in December 1862. These fruitless attacks cost more than 12,600 men, a needless waste of life that wrecked the army's morale until the following spring when Lincoln relieved Burnside of command and placed Hooker in charge.

Hooker achieved some success restoring the fighting spirit to his disheartened troops, and after developing an excellent plan to turn Lee out of his works near Fredericksburg, he moved his army across the Rapidan and Rappahannock Rivers in late

April-early May 1863. Lee met Hooker at Chancellorsville and decisively defeated him after Stonewall Jackson made a long march around the Federals and struck their right flank. This battle, considered by many to be Lee's masterpiece, cost both armies dearly in dead and wounded. Lee also permanently lost Jackson after troops from North Carolina mistakenly shot him while he scouted the front line in near darkness.

After Chancellorsville, Hooker remained in command of the Army of the Potomac until Lee began his trek north to invade Pennsylvania. Disagreement with General Halleck over reinforcing Harpers Ferry—an echo of events during the Maryland Campaign—led to Hooker's dismissal from command at the end of June 1863, three days before the Battle of Gettysburg; a fight that his successor, George Gordon Meade, won. Hooker served afterward in Tennessee under the scowling eye of William Tecumseh Sherman. The two men loathed each another, however, leading ultimately to Hooker's dismissal in the spring of 1864.

George Armstrong Custer went on to have an illustrious career after Antietam, becoming the youngest senior officer on either side in the Civil War when Alfred Pleasonton appointed him brevet Brigadier General of U.S. Volunteers in late June 1863. Custer served with distinction as a cavalry commander at Gettysburg, and throughout the rest of the war in the east, developing in the process a reputation for being a tough and aggressive fighter. He was present at the surrender of Lee's army in April 1865, and after the war he served in various capacities out west until he received command of the Seventh U.S. Cavalry regiment in the Dakota Territory. At the end of June 1876, Custer famously led his men into a Lakota Sioux ambush on the hills above the Little Bighorn River, resulting in his death and the massacre of his command.

After Antietam, Colonel Jacob Higgins of the One Hundred Twenty-Fifth Pennsylvania Volunteers participated with his regiment in the battles of Fredericksburg and Chancellorsville before he and his men mustered out in May 1863. Following a brief hiatus, Higgins rejoined the army during the Gettysburg campaign to command volunteer troops in the southwestern district of Pennsylvania. Many of his former troops also re-enlisted to defend their state against the incursions of Rebel cavalry raiders such as General John Imboden. Higgins recruited five companies of cavalry in 1863 and became colonel of the Twenty-Second Regiment, Pennsylvania Volunteer Cavalry. In 1864, he participated in the Valley Campaign under General Phil Sheridan and eventually rose to command the Second Brigade, Second Division, Department of West Virginia until he mustered out of the army for a final time in July 1865.

Lieutenant Colonel Jacob Szink, Higgins's second in command, left the army after the wound he received at Antietam. Returning eventually to his position as foreman of the blacksmith shop for the Pennsylvania Railroad Company, Szink did not remain out of the service for long. He re-enlisted in 1864, serving as the elected major of a volunteer battalion during Rebel general John McCausland's cavalry raid into Pennsylvania in July 1864. Szink was near Chambersburg when McCausland burned the town on July 30 of that year. After the war, he returned to working with the Pennsylvania Railroad until his death in 1872 at the early age of 48.

The inscrutable Colonel Thomas Key, McClellan's political adviser, remained by the general's side even after his removal from command of the Army of the Potomac. Key assisted with the writing of a 242-page report by McClellan that appeared in early 1864, just in time to inflate the general's military record for that year's presidential election. The report included letters and other documents that criticized Lincoln's handling of the war effort and proposed a return to the more conservative policy that McClellan had always favored. Key fell ill in the winter of 1863, just prior to publication of the report, with what doctors diagnosed at the time as "pulmonary consumption." Key's affliction was probably tuberculosis, but there is no way of knowing this for certain. His health recovered in 1864 during McClellan's failed campaign for president. Key ran twice for judge positions in Ohio after the war and lost both times. He married in July 1868, but again fell ill the following September before dying in January 1869.

Jacob Cox remained in the volunteer army (he never became a regular army officer), but his appointment to major general prior to Antietam lapsed in March 1863 and the Senate did not renew it. He served after the Maryland Campaign in several rear-area positions throughout 1863, until he was recalled to an active combat role for the Atlanta Campaign of 1864. Cox competently commanded the Third Division of the Twenty-Third Corps throughout the campaign and played a key role in defending the center of the Union line at the Battle of Franklin on November 30, 1864. After Franklin, the army recognized Cox's abilities by promoting him to major general. He nevertheless remained in the volunteer forces, and ended the war at that rank after occupying several other commands.

Mustering out in January 1866, Cox went on to be elected Governor of Ohio, and served in that office from 1866 to 1868, retiring afterward to Cincinnati. President U.S. Grant appointed Cox Secretary of the Interior in 1869, but Cox resigned from the office after less than two years, when he clashed with Grant over the issue of political patronage. Later years saw Cox elected to Congress as a representative from 1877 to 1879, and then serving as the president of the University of Cincinnati in the 1880s. Cox also wrote several books and essays on the war, helping to shape the later memory of those events. He died in August 1900 at 71 years of age.

Last, but not least, the men of the Twenty-Third Ohio returned to western Virginia following the Maryland Campaign. They participated in defending the emerging state of West Virginia through 1863 until orders brought them back east to serve in Phil Sheridan's 1864 Valley Campaign. The Twenty-Third has the distinction of spawning the largest number of leading political figures of any regiment in the Civil War. Colonel Rutherford B. Hayes, wounded at South Mountain, became president in 1877, followed by William McKinley in 1896. Another man named Thomas Stanley Matthews, who is not mentioned in this book, later served as a U.S. Senator, and Robert P. Kennedy, also not mentioned, was elected U.S. Congressman. Major James M. Comly, meanwhile, rose to the rank of brevet Brigadier General of Volunteers (not a regular army appointment) and served later as the U.S. Minister to Hawaii.

In the final analysis, South Mountain and Antietam would prove to be just another set of clashes during America's long and bloody civil war. Qualitatively, however, they differed from the others because of the political stakes involved. McClellan's blunting of Lee's offensive north of the Potomac denied the Confederacy what some believed was the victory it needed to bring Maryland into the war on the side of the South. McClellan's triumph also provided President Lincoln with the opportunity to announce his policy of emancipation, which effectively kept Great Britain and France out of the conflict.

Few participants in the Maryland Campaign knew that any of these things would transpire at the time, so we must remain vigilant not to judge both battles in the light of subsequent events. They were fights that challenged brave and idealistic soldiers on both sides to sacrifice everything for the causes they held dear, whether we agree with them or not. This is the best way to remember those men and the echoes of what they did during those fateful days in September 1862.

Acknowledgments

Authors tend to work alone, but no book is written in isolation. This historical novel benefited from input offered by several colleagues, including Professor James M. McPherson and Dr. Thomas G. Clemens, both of whom took valuable time out of their busy schedules to read the manuscript and provide feedback during its development. The late historian, Charles Theodore "Ted" Alexander, also offered meaningful comments before his unfortunate passing in 2020. Ted in particular offered high praise in 2019, when he wrote to me, "Your book of historical fiction reads like scholarly history." As an academically trained historian attempting to write fiction, this comment could not have pleased me more. My colleague and occasional co-author, Gene M. Thorp, provided the most important direct assistance. His extensive notes, emails, and comments concerning George McClellan's activities throughout the campaign cast the subject in a light I had never seen. I am blessed to have had Gene at my service.

No acknowledgments would be complete without thanking my wife, Melissa Dawn, for her never ending patience during the long hours I spent writing. Thank you, my love.

I would like to recognize the fine and dedicated staff at Savas Beatie for their support and assistance. This includes Veronica Kane, Sarah Closson, Sarah Keeney, Lisa Murphy, Donna Endacott, Angela Morrow, and Director Theodore P. Savas, for assistance with production, media, and book promotion. Ted enlisted the assistance of Rebecca Hill, and I am grateful for her sharp editorial eye. She suggested many changes that helped streamline the manuscript into the book you are reading. Ted and his team are the best in publishing. I'm truly fortunate to have had the opportunity to work with them.

About the Author

A resident of western Maryland, Dr. Alex Rossino is an independent historian and author. He earned Master's and Doctoral degrees in History at Syracuse University before working for nine years as a historian at the U.S. Holocaust Memorial Museum in Washington, D.C. Dr. Rossino turned his attention to the American Civil War in 2011. After several years of research, he produced *Six Days in September*, a novel of Lee's Army in Maryland, September 1862. The book proved to be popular among historians and enthusiasts alike.

Dr. Rossino is also the author of *Their Maryland: The Army of Northern Virginia from the Potomac Crossing to Sharpsburg in September 1862*, co-authored (with Gene Thorp) *The Tale Untwisted: General George B. McClellan, the Maryland Campaign, and the Discovery of Lee's Lost Orders*, and rounded out this trilogy of Maryland-related titles with *Calamity at Frederick: Robert E. Lee, Special Orders No. 191, and Confederate Misfortune on the Road to Antietam*. All three studies challenge long-held beliefs about the 1862 Maryland Campaign and offer new insights into one of the Civil War's most important periods.